DEATH AT THE AUCTION

The Stamford Mysteries

E. C. BATEMAN

One More Chapter
a division of HarperCollins*Publishers* Ltd
1 London Bridge Street
London SE1 9GF
www.harpercollins.co.uk

HarperCollins*Publishers*
1st Floor, Watermarque Building, Ringsend Road
Dublin 4, Ireland

This paperback edition 2022

1

First published in Great Britain in ebook format
by HarperCollins*Publishers* 2022

A catalogue record of this book is available from the British Library

ISBN: 978-0-00-856491-9

Printed and bound in the UK using 100% Renewable Electricity
by CPI Group (UK) Ltd

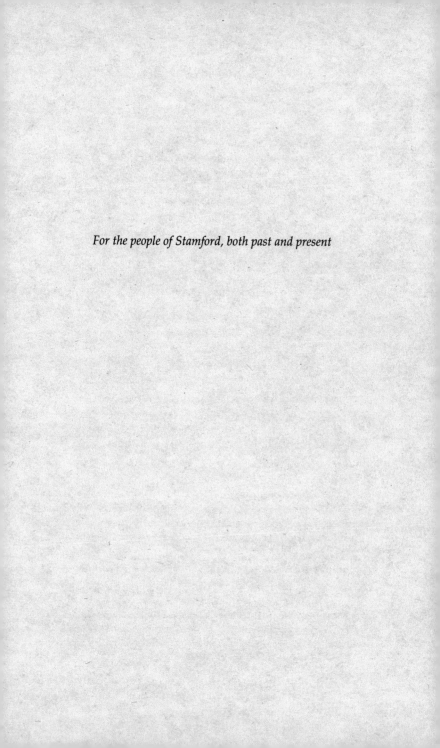

For the people of Stamford, both past and present

Prologue

Stamford had never looked better. It was a day of exquisite, languid beauty, of English spring sunshine on honey-coloured stone. And, yet, Colin Creaton didn't see any of it.

He was running faster than he ever had in his life.

He plunged down the narrow, twisting passageway between the houses, the sound of his shoes ringing off the ironstone walls that pressed in close on either side. The only thing louder was the rush of blood in his ears, singing, whistling like a boiling kettle as he gasped in ragged snatches of cool, shadowed air.

His heart bloomed in his chest, and he lurched to the side, one hand scraping down the rough-hewn wall, fingers finding purchase in the centuries' old chisel marks that still remained. He dared to allow himself to pause, just for a moment. Half a moment, even. Then he pushed away from the wall, staggering onwards. He burst out into the bright light of Broad Street, blinking in the sudden whirl of colour, movement and chatter. The wide thoroughfare thronged with people; Saturday morning shoppers clutching takeaway coffee cups, browsing the market stalls with their pinstriped awnings, locals with their dogs trotting alongside them, striding purposefully one minute, then bumping into someone they knew the next and falling into animated conversation, apparently any earlier impetus forgotten in the face of leisurely conviviality.

He weaved amongst them, limping now, his joints screaming with the unprecedented strain they'd been put under. Craning his neck, he tried desperately to peer through the crowd, but heads kept blocking his view, the sea of bodies seeming to crest and eddy like waves before his eyes.

He knocked into someone, an elderly lady with snowy white hair. Stuttering a panicked apology, he forced himself onwards, tripping slightly on the uneven cobblestones.

He was running out of time. Out of chances.

His eyes moved heavenwards, towards the crocketed spire of All Saints' Church, silhouetted against a clear, lupin-blue sky. The gilt hands of the clock glinted in the sunlight. His throat tightened in terror.

He veered up the wide stone steps to his right, ascending to the front door of a grand, three-storey townhouse. With the last of his strength, he flung himself across the threshold, groping for the edge of the reception desk.

"Too late…" he rasped. "Please. No time. Too… late."

The secretary looked down at him with a pleasantly puzzled expression.

"No, sir, you're not too late. The auction doesn't start for another ten minutes."

"Colin?" A strident voice echoed across the marble foyer. "What on earth are you *doing*? You were only meant to be parking the car."

Colin sagged against the desk, his whole body suffused with relief.

"Sorry, Margaret," he said meekly. "Market day traffic. Couldn't find a space anywhere."

"Well, you're about to miss it if you're not careful," she said shortly, slipping her plump, woollen-gloved hand into the crook of his arm and steering him away with an apologetic glance at the receptionist. The sort of glance he'd noticed her giving more and more lately. "And after you've made such a fuss about this wretched toy train, too. You know I didn't want to come into town today, but you insisted…" her chin wobbled faintly before settling into a resolute line. "In*si*sted! I haven't heard of anything else for weeks. And now to miss the thing… at least I had the foresight to get your bidding number for you." She waved a ping-pong bat-shaped paddle at him.

"Sorry, Margaret," he murmured again, but in truth, he scarcely knew what he was saying. For once, he wasn't even smarting over her description of his overarching passion as a mere plaything. His heart was blooming again, except this time not with fear and panic, but with elation.

He hadn't missed it. Thank *God*, he hadn't missed it.

The saleroom was already packed. Every chair was filled, and the latecomers had been forced to cram around the edges, squeezing into the spaces between the items of furniture that hulked at intervals around the room. Beside him, Margaret was pursing her lips in disapproval at not being able to get a seat. He'd hear about it all the way home in the car, he knew. Probably for the rest of the day. But it would be worth it.

He allowed himself to be established next to a formidable-looking wardrobe in pitch-dark wood. Leaving him with firm instructions *not to move under any circumstances*—"I mean *any* circumstances, Colin"—Margaret went off in search of tea. He stood obediently in position, resting his shoulder against the wardrobe as he studied his catalogue. Everyone else in the room appeared to be doing the same, the low drone of murmured conversation culminating to a dull roar as heads bent over booklets, fingers pointing out various lots.

Suddenly, he became aware of another sound, much quieter than the rest, and much closer at hand. A sort of long, slow scraping, like fingernails on wood. He eyed the wardrobe next to him warily. He sincerely hoped there wasn't a rat in there. Margaret would absolutely have a *fit* if she—

"What are you staring at that for?" She was standing in front of him, two polystyrene cups in hand. "You're not planning to put a bid on it, are you?"

She sounded horrified.

"Uh, no," he moved away from it quickly.

"Good," her relief was palpable. "'We'd never get it up the stairs. Why people want to buy old furniture is beyond me. Buy something nice and new which comes apart and hasn't had anyone else's underwear in, I say."

A proclamation like that didn't seem to warrant a response. Colin looked at the wardrobe again, finding himself edging further away from it, driven by a sensation he couldn't explain. Certainly not to Margaret, of all people. But there was something about that piece of furniture; something strange, foreboding. It made him uneasy, somehow.

"Colin?" She said sharply. "What is *wrong* with you today? It's like you've seen a ghost."

No, he thought. Not that. Not that way around, at least. If it didn't sound so ridiculous, he would almost have said that it was more like a ghost watching him. He could feel eyes on him, eyes he couldn't see. It gave him the shivers.

He would never know just how right he was in that moment. Behind him, illuminated by a thin seam of light creeping between the join in the heavy wooden door, an eye blinked, then melted back into the shadows as the hubbub died down, the bidders turning to the rostrum in tense expectancy.

The auction was about to begin.

Chapter One

Felicia Grant surveyed the devastation that surrounded her with a mounting sense of dismay.

There were things everywhere. Boxes of bric-a-brac balanced precariously on the edges of desks. Bin bags overflowing with newspaper and bubble wrap mounded on the floor. A huge teak bookcase occupied one wall, files apparently having been stuffed into it at random, then, later, papers not even making it into the files at all, but simply getting piled on the top. The Aubusson carpet underfoot was scarcely visible, and where it was, it was so thick with dust and general grime that the delicate pink rose pattern was impossible to distinguish from the faded beige background. Random objects were dotted about, some with old sale stickers on, apparently stuck in a purgatory of unknown owners, uncollected purchases, and—every auctioneer's worst nightmare—the bought then never paid for. A celestial globe sat on the highest shelf, golden constellations gleaming under the fluorescent strip light that was doing its best to illuminate the low-raftered room. On the small, cramped windowsill, a Qing period blue-and-white Chinese ginger jar perched next to the office tea-making paraphernalia. Stacks of gilt-framed paintings leant against the walls, waiting to trip the unwary.

It was even worse than she remembered.

Auctions weren't supposed to be glamorous; she knew that better than most. But they weren't supposed to be a death-trap and a bio-hazard rolled into one, either.

Why had no one *told* her it had got this bad?

"I expect it's a bit strange, being back here after all this time." Hugo Dappleton hovered behind her warily, fiddling with his tie. It had garden tools on it in a jaunty pattern; she wondered if he'd borrowed it from his dad. Everything Hugo wore looked like it had been borrowed from someone much older and larger than himself. Perhaps it was because he looked so young—he *was* so young, Felicia reminded herself—or perhaps it was because his cataloguer's wage didn't stretch to much better. He still lived with his family on one of the estates at the edge of town, in a crammed-to-the-rafters house that occasionally became roomier when his father flounced off on one of his well-known hiatuses. These could last for days, if not weeks, and she suspected that a lot of Hugo's earnings went into the family pot to support his four younger siblings during these lean periods.

She liked Hugo immensely. She'd been the one to hire him, in fact, eight years ago, just before it had all blown up between herself and her father and she'd stormed out of the auction house —and the career she'd built—never to return. Or at least, that's what she'd promised herself. And she'd stuck to it… thus far, at least, she amended, glancing around the room again. How many memories were trapped within the dusty air of this office. How many late nights and weekends had she spent finishing catalogues, uploading photographs, unboxing consignments? Too many to count, that was for certain.

Hugo had been a fresh-faced sixteen-year-old then. He'd turned up at the front desk with an unsurprisingly sparse CV but an eagerness in his eyes that had spoken as much to her business sense as her softer emotions. She'd taken him on as an assistant porter, but she'd always known that he would be more one day.

Now, here he was, having worked his way up to their main cataloguer, and he was training under her father to become a valuer. She was incredibly proud of him, and, more to the point, she knew that none of this was his fault. She dreaded to think how hard he'd been working, trying to hold it all together. So she spared him her true emotions; instead, she just smiled wryly.

"You could say that."

She'd been unceremoniously tugged from her sleep by the persistent buzzing of her phone on the nightstand next to her side of the bed.

With a groan, she prised open one eye. The room swam into focus, illuminated by the sunlight that crept around the edge of the curtains, casting everything in a sepia wash.

The ringing stopped. With a blissful sigh, Felicia rolled onto her side, taking the duvet with her.

It started again.

Biting back a curse, she stretched out an arm to retrieve it, slapping it to her ear with an exhaled, "yes?"

"Fliss? Are you awake?"

"Cassie?" At the sound of her best friend's voice, she struggled into a sitting position shielding her eyes from the low early morning sun. "No, of course I'm bloody not. What *time* is it?"

"Earlier than you're used to, I'll wager. If you had three kids under seven, you'd think the day was half over already."

"*I* was sensible. I stopped at one." Felicia groaned, flopping back against the plush pillows. "*Please* tell me you didn't wake me up at this ungodly hour just for a chat."

"No, I didn't." Cassie's voice had taken on a serious note, enough of an incongruity to make Felicia's eyes, which had just started to drift close, snap open again. "Listen, Fliss, can you come up to Stamford? Like, now?"

"Cass?" Felicia could hear the anxiety creeping into her voice. "What is it? What's happened?"

"Just… can you?"

"Well, yes, I suppose so." Felicia looked around her helplessly, as though the duck egg blue décor of her bedroom might somehow provide the answer. "We can be in the car in the next half an hour. But what…"

"It's your dad…"

Felicia felt herself go very still. Her fingers meshed into the edge of the duvet, bit down. She waited.

"He's fallen down the stairs," Cassie was beginning to sound breathless. Felicia wondered if she was on the move. It wouldn't surprise her; Cassie was constantly rushing about, often doing multiple things at once. "Tripped over the cat, apparently. But he's fine," she added hastily, at Felicia's sharp intake of breath. "Crotchety and a bit annoyed with himself, but fine. It's just a fracture, the hospital says. They're letting him out later."

Felicia felt her whole body relax with relief.

"Thank God you were there." She swung her legs over the edge of the bed, phone wedged between her neck and shoulder as she pulled on slippers. "I dread to think… what *were* you doing there so early, anyway?"

"Walking the baby," Cassie said shortly. "Bloody thing won't sleep. Alistair and I take it in turns to trawl the town at dawn. Your Dad's always at the window when we go past, making himself a cup of tea. It's become a bit of a thing, to wave at one another. When he wasn't there this morning, I was worried. Luckily I always carry that spare key you gave me."

Felicia bit her lip. She knew it wasn't all as casual and coincidental as Cassie made it sound. The morning route past her father's house would have been deliberately engineered; Cassie had taken it upon herself to watch out for Peter ever since Felicia had left. It was one of those tacit things, never asked for, never discussed.

"Thank you, Cass." *For everything, not just this.* She didn't need to add that last part, and Cassie wouldn't want her to. But she'd know it was there all the same. "We're on our way." She pictured the hospital, a Dickensian-looking building with turrets and gables in the distinctive golden stone that all of Stamford was built in. "Tell Dad I'll be with him in—"

"Actually, you're needed elsewhere first." Cassie suddenly sounded hesitant. Immediately, Felicia felt suspicious. That tone never boded well. "It's an auction day, Fliss. Had you forgotten?"

No, she hadn't. She still had the Grant's auction calendar memorised, even though she'd never admitted that to anyone. Not even to Cassie. It felt like a weakness, somehow, to admit that the place still mattered to her, even in a small, inexplicable sort of way.

Cassie didn't wait for her answer in any event. Typically, she plunged straight on to the crux of the matter.

"Can you take it? The auction, I mean."

Felicia nearly choked on air.

"Cass, I haven't auctioneered in *years*! I couldn't possibly—"

"Of *course,* you can," Cassie said coaxingly. It was the voice she used to get both fractious children *and* recalcitrant council members in line. "I'm sure it's like riding a bike."

"It's not," Felicia started to say defensively, then gave up. It didn't matter how many times you told people how complicated auctioneering actually was; they never really believed you. They thought it was just a lot of shouting out random numbers and crashing the hammer down for dramatic effect.

"Please, Fliss," Cassie wheedled. "We need you."

Felicia felt her eyes narrow.

"When you say *we*… did Dad ask me to do this?"

There was a pause.

"Well … not *exactly*."

"Don't hedge, Cass. It doesn't suit you."

"Look, you *know* how proud he is!" Cassie burst out. "But it's all I can do to stop him climbing out of the hospital bed and driving over there to take it himself. Believe me, Fliss, we *both* need you. Him to stop him from killing himself, me to stop *me* from killing *him*."

Cassie's desperation would almost be comical if it weren't for the sobering reality of her words. Felicia didn't doubt that her father would discharge himself from hospital if necessary and hobble across Stamford in his paper gown to avoid missing a sale. It wasn't just about pride; it was about money, too, and more importantly, about the staff who relied upon them every month. The auction finances just about stretched from one sale to the next; a single one missed meant that there wouldn't be enough cash to pay anyone's wages, let alone the plethora of other bills. She knew that despite his earthy exterior, her father felt deeply responsible for his staff. Worrying about them all kept him awake at night.

"Come on, Fliss. You know as well as I do that there's no one else who can do it. Not at this short notice."

Felicia wasn't conscious of making up her mind. She wasn't even sure, afterwards, that she *did* make it up, not as such. It was more a case that she knew that there was no other option, not one that she could live with, at least.

"All right," she pushed her hair away from her forehead. "I'm coming. Just... don't let him mount an escape, all right? Keep him there."

"I'll do my best. If I tell him you've got the auction covered... hopefully, that should get him to stay put." Through the phone, Felicia could hear her heels clicking on the tiled hospital floor; she was on the move again. "I've got to dash myself in a minute; the boys have got tennis club at eight-thirty. Then I've got to prepare for this tedious council meeting this afternoon." Her voice betrayed its exasperation. "On a Saturday in the Easter holidays, no less. You can tell that everyone else is retired, can't you? Weekly schedules seem to mean nothing to them."

"Poor you." Felicia smiled, fetching her silk kimono from the back of the door and slinging it around her shoulders. "Come up to the auction when you're free? I could do with the moral support."

"If you're *really* lucky," Cassie said archly. "I'll wear my mayoral robes."

Felicia rolled her eyes.

"Something to look forward to, then."

God knows, she thought, as she opened the curtains and gazed out across the jagged London skyline, tinted pink with the encroaching dawn. She was certainly going to need it.

Now, almost reflexively, she found herself around her father's desk, drawn to the low mullioned window that looked out over the town she'd once known like the back of her hand. A view that couldn't possibly be more different than the glass and chrome that had greeted her this morning.

Through the small, mottled panes, Stamford gleamed at her, illuminated in sloping lines by the pearlescent April sunshine. It turned the biscotti-coloured stone of the elegant Georgian townhouses into a warm, baked hue, and the panes of the sash windows into liquid gold. It skated down the spires of the five Medieval churches that clustered within the town centre, nestled in their respective cobbled squares.

She could imagine the rest, even though she couldn't see it. Beyond, hidden by the slate tiled rooftops, lay the meadows, straddled by the meandering path of the River Welland; the meeting point for many an illicit summer romance, the site of her first kiss, and home to some of the plumpest, most pampered ducks in England. Then there was The George, the famous inn that had been standing since the 10th century. She'd toasted many a success over a marmalade cocktail in its wood-panelled bar. Drowned many a failure, too, come to think of it.

And even further still, creating a boundary around one entire side of the town, the rolling green parklands of Burghley House. That was where she'd go when she needed to think. It was the last place she'd gone before she'd left Stamford for good. She'd stood by the lake, wondering if she was doing the right thing, yet simultaneously knowing that she didn't have any choice.

"Mum, Betsy says that I can help her with the phone bids." Algernon was at her side, gazing up at her beseechingly. "Can I? Please?"

She looked down into wide-set, dove-coloured eyes that mirrored her own and sighed internally.

The truth was, her son knew the auction better than she did these days. He probably knew Stamford better, too; unlike her, he'd been back many times in the interim, placed on a train that brought him into the town's tiny, gingerbread house-like station, from which his grandfather would pick him up on foot. They spent hours at the auction house together, with Peter showing him the ropes. And Algernon adored every minute of it, she could see that. He had an enthusiasm, a glow on his face when he spoke about it, which both tugged at her heartstrings and made her despair at the same time. Because she'd looked like that once; she'd *felt* like that once. The joy, the excitement of running her own business had filled her with so much energy. But it hadn't lasted.

There was no getting away from it; auctions just didn't make money. Not provincial ones, at any rate. They were a slowly declining breed; the dealers were getting older, retiring, some younger ones moving in but not enough to fill the void. The sad truth was that love just wasn't enough. Passion wasn't enough. The day she'd realised that, had been the day she'd grown up for good.

She'd done her best to protect Algernon from it, but it had found him anyway. And, somehow, she couldn't quite bear to tell him all of this. Even though it was probably the best thing for him, she couldn't be the one to trample on his dreams. Not that he'd listen, in any event, she had to acknowledge. *She* certainly wouldn't have done.

"Go on, then," she told him now. "So long as you're not in the way."

"He can score the bidding forms for me, can't you duck?" Betsy, the saleroom manager, appeared at the top of the stairs, wearing her green Grant's branded apron and her usual beaming smile. "It'll be a great help."

Felicia sent her a grateful glance over the top of Algernon's tousled head.

"We'd better go over." Hugo was balancing an overstuffed ring binder in one hand and a cup of tea in the other. "They'll be getting restless."

Algernon fairly charged off down the stairs. She heard the usual thudding sound as he jumped off the bottom two steps.

"Hang on. You'll be needing this." Wedging the ring binder under his arm, Hugo reached into the shelves and pulled out a polished mahogany gavel. *Her* gavel.

She took it, almost seeming to get an electric shock as she felt the familiar weight settle into her palm. Her fingers curved around the handle, moulding effortlessly to the well-worn grooves of the wood. The mallet head was battered at one end, the varnish having rubbed off with so many years of use.

"No one's used it since you left," Hugo said quietly, watching her.

She took a breath, trying to collect herself. Then her eyes met his.

"Come on, then. Let's get this thing over with."

Chapter Two

F elicia stood up on the rostrum, looking out over the crammed saleroom.

It was often remarked that a good auction was as entertaining and tension-filled as any stage show, and indeed, from her vantage point up on the platform, the scene was much akin to a theatre audience preparing for the curtain to raise. People were settling into their seats, wrestling their arms out of their coats whilst trying not to elbow their neighbour. A few were blowing on recently bought coffees from the van parked outside, or offering mints or biscuits to their companions. Some were still chatting away—a number of couples were having the inevitable heated last-minute discussion about how high they were willing to go on an item—whilst others sat still and silent, waiting with varying degrees of patience etched onto their faces.

Some people were even still trying to view, catalogues scrunched in hands as they desperately sought a path through the crowd to their chosen lot. There were always a few of those, people who left it until minutes before the sale started to decide whether they wanted to bid.

Then again, there were always a few of *everyone* in an auction room, Felicia acceded wryly. It never changed. If ever a place could be defined by its archetypes, an auction house was it. It seemed to draw in a mixture of people from all across society, people whose lives would never normally intersect. For a brief morning, reality was suspended, differences put aside. They were all thrown together in a cramped, stuffy room. They drank the same coffee, shared the same experience. Then, they were gone, off into their own habitats again. They probably wouldn't even recognise their fellow bidders in the street.

Her eyes scanned the audience, picking them out effortlessly. There were a good number of the traditional 'Lovejoy' style dealers, with their grubby overcoats, pockets overflowing with crumpled catalogues from other auctions, and flat caps pulled down low over their eyes. They clustered in small groups, murmuring to one another from the sides of their mouths, casting furtive eyes around the room to identify their other rivals.

However, there were other kinds of dealer here, too, far less obvious, far harder to spot to the uninitiated eye. A well-dressed man in the front row with a floral pocket handkerchief, one pinstriped leg crossed casually over the other. He looked like an off-duty aristocrat, here to pick up a new knick-knack for his stately home. In reality, Felicia knew he was anything but. That was Mr Clancy, the high-end furniture dealer. His face wasn't well known; he tended not to frequent the sales himself, preferring to maintain a mantle of anonymity. His presence was telling; Felicia frowned to herself, mentally flicking through the catalogue, trying to work out what it was they'd missed. Because *something* had been missed, that much was for certain; there was some good quality furniture in the sale today, certainly, but nothing that would normally enter Mr Clancy's orbit.

The escritoire, she thought dully. It had to be. her father had described it as Louis XV style, but she'd had her doubts even from looking at the grainy photo of the elegant little desk on the website. To her eye, it was too finely enamelled to be a reproduction. It was the sort of thing that, at one time, she would have pointed out to him, but not any more—it wasn't any of her business these days.

Her eyes continued their progress across the room. By the door, two young women in floaty floral dresses were talking quietly to one another. Their similarity in looks marked them out as sisters. Felicia didn't recognise them, but there was something about them that got her instincts prickling. They were trying to look inconspicuous, but they fairly screamed London start-up to her. Probably sold through Instagram. The old-school dealers weren't even glancing their way; Felicia couldn't help a small smile to herself. She had a feeling they were about to get a surprise when the bidding began. They didn't seem to have grasped that the landscape was changing, that new people were entering the game. People who didn't look like they did, and didn't play by their set of rules, either.

Finally, there were the casual onlookers. The regular locals, who liked to wander up to the auction for a coffee and to absorb the atmosphere, maybe buy one or two lots that took their fancy. It was a Saturday morning tradition, part of their routine. Her father liked to have them there; it was the reason he'd picked Saturday mornings for his sales in the first place, at a time when many auctions were only really interested in catering to the dealers and held them on a weekday. Peter Grant had always maintained that it made for a nice, convivial atmosphere; people could bring their children, their dogs, their grandparents. It cut through the professional tension, softened proceedings.

Not all of them were familiar to her these days, of course, but she still recognised a few faces. Evelina Fielding was sitting, as ever in the front row, graceful and gamine in a Schiaparelli pink gilet over a pale grey jumper. Her hair was the pure, creamy white of ermine, her eyes twinkling merrily from a lined yet still lively face. She must have been 90 if she was a day, but she looked as sprightly as Felicia remembered, although she noticed that she now had a walking stick with her, propped against the seat of her chair. When she caught Felicia's eye, she waved cheerfully, and Felicia smiled back, feeling her nerves abate a little. It was good to know there were some friendly faces out there. It had been a long time since she'd done this.

"Almost ready?" Hugo murmured from next to her, where he was seated at the computer monitor. "It's just coming up to ten now."

And then of course, there were all the bidders she couldn't even see, Felicia thought, with a glance at the screen, which was poised, a photograph of the first lot already showing, waiting for her to start. The countless people who were bidding in real time, live, from laptops and mobiles all around the world. Her gaze moved to the round mahogany table, where her staff were perched with phones and bidding sheets in front of them, awaiting the telephone bids that had been booked in earlier. She glanced down at her own sheets, which revealed the dizzying array of commission bids that had been left by people who couldn't be on the spot. It was her job to bid on their behalf.

She felt a sudden, jangling burst of nerves, which she sought to calm with deep breaths. It was better not to think about it all. Better just to do it.

She gave a sideways nod to Hugo, smoothing out her papers.

"Welcome to Grant's, everyone." She switched on the microphone, letting her voice ring out, reaching the back of the room. "Let's begin, shall we? Lot One: A pair of Delft vases…"

"Sold!"

The gavel crashed onto the rostrum, sending vibrations through the wooden frame. Felicia breathed a sigh of relief as she watched the screen flick onto the next lot. It was going well. Better, in fact, than she'd dared to imagine.

The first fifteen minutes had been slow, with her having to coax a lot of the bids, altering the tempo to draw out the on-the-fencers. But it had picked up markedly, and by the time they'd reached the end of the ceramics section, prices were solid. The sell-through rate was good, too, definitely higher than average. She was even starting to enjoy herself a little; she'd forgotten what a rush this could be. The challenge of reading the room, playing the mood, knowing when to risk an extra jump on the asking bid and when to have patience, to let the bidding build momentum on its own. It was an art form, subtle, little understood. She'd missed it, but God, it was tiring. She could feel the buzz of adrenaline already beginning to flag.

She took a moment to discreetly stretch her neck, running her eyes down the list. Not too far to go, now. Just through the collectables, then onto the home straight. Furniture. Her eyes flickered onto Mr Clancy. The dealer was sitting there patiently, not giving anything away, but she could tell that he was alert, waiting. A couple of seats along, Evelina was peering at her catalogue, clearly trying to work out what she'd just bought. She had a tendency to bid wildly, then realise that whatever it was either wouldn't fit in her house or wasn't what she'd intended to buy at all and ended up putting half of it back into the next auction.

The two sisters were at the back of the room now; they'd moved around a lot during the sale, seeming to be somewhere different each time she looked up. They'd popped out for coffees during the militaria, which hadn't surprised her. Spanish ceramics and weathered terracotta pots seemed to be more their thing. She'd been right about them, mind; they'd run amok over the old dealers, who were glaring at them balefully from beneath drooping tweed brims.

To their right, at the telephone table, Algernon was sitting next to Betsy, enthusiastically scoring through the used bidding forms, his legs swinging back and forth in that childlike habit he still had.

She glanced across at Hugo, who was rubbing his eyes wearily.

"You should swap with someone," she said quietly, covering her microphone with her hand. "I'll call a five-minute break."

He shook his head stubbornly.

"I'm fine. I can make it to the—" he broke off, sitting up straighter.

The silence stretched for several seconds. Felicia looked up to find her audience staring back at her impatiently, wondering what the delay was all about. She flushed, turning back to Hugo, who was still sitting in that frozen way.

"Hugo?" She prompted, in an urgent undertone.

He seemed to start slightly at the sound of her voice.

"Actually, you know what? Maybe you *are* right. I'll ask Amelia to take over."

And then he was gone, disappearing from his seat without even waiting for his replacement to arrive, leaving her completely on her own. For an awkward, stunned moment, she just stood there, before mercifully the promised Amelia, one of the saleroom staff who only came in for auction day, slipped into the vacant seat.

Felicia breathed an internal sigh of relief, collecting herself, wondering if she felt more annoyed or concerned. What was *that* all about? It was totally unlike Hugo to be so unprofessional. Automatically, her eyes followed where his gaze had been fixed, towards the shadowy corner at the back of the room, but there was nothing there. Just the same hulking dark wardrobe, filling the space. Despite herself, she felt a frisson of unease, one which she swiftly put down to exhaustion and stretched nerves. It was already proving a long day, and it wasn't even half over yet.

Amelia proved a competent, if slightly slower, sidekick, and for the next half an hour, Felicia's mind was otherwise engaged.

The sale wore on. It seemed to become a long, stretched-out blur, like a photograph of a waterfall taken with a slow shutter speed. Later, when she looked back, Felicia would say that the only points of reference that created any sense of time and space were the individual lots: when Evelina was at the back of the room, talking to a fellow elderly lady—that was the Cornish grandfather clock; when Betsy took her break from the phones—the group of enamelled vesta cases, she could swear to it. She noticed that Algernon had disappeared, too, during the mixed lot of copper and brass, but he was back by the time the fireside accessories came under the hammer.

There was only one person in the room who didn't seem to move around. A young man, with ruffled dark-blond hair and a tanned, lean face. For some reason, her gaze kept finding him again and again. He was always at the back, hands in his pockets, watching the action steadily.

"Who's that?" She murmured to Amelia, as they waited for the furore to die down after a particularly exciting lot.

"That's Jack Riding," Amelia looked at her as though she was half mad. "You know, the photographer? He works for us, sometimes. Didn't your dad tell you?"

"No, he didn't." Felicia said softly. The man looked up at that moment, and their eyes locked. Feeling embarrassed to have been caught staring, she glanced quickly away.

At that moment, the escritoire flashed up on the screen, and anything else she might have been thinking was swept away by a frisson of excitement. *This* was going to be interesting.

The bidding started. Discreetly, Felicia avoided looking in the direction of Mr Clancy. He wouldn't show his hand until later, anyway. He'd wait until the closing moments. A few of the dealers pitched in early, but they soon fell away. She peered at one man who was tweaking the rim of his cap… was that a bid? No, he was turning to speak to his wife. Across the room, then, to the phones. Betsy nodded, raised a hand. Bid. To the internet, poised, waiting. Then to the room, where an expectant hush had fallen, and finally, she allowed her gaze to fall on Mr Clancy's chair.

He wasn't there.

She felt a jolt of surprise go through her, one which she was sure must show on her face. Hastily rearranging her features, she pushed her confusion to the back of her mind, looking briskly back to the phones. Betsy nodded again.

"It's with the phones at £30,000," Felicia announced. The room looked back at her silently. The internet was blank. It was like a collective, indrawn breath. "Going... going..." Felicia paused, let it sit. "Gone!" The gavel hit the rostrum once more.

The breath was released. The room erupted into a furore of chatter and nervous laughter. Felicia noticed Mr Clancy slipping furtively back into his seat.

Someone ran up and handed Felicia a piece of paper. She frowned down at it.

"What's this?"

The messenger, a teenage boy in the green apron worn by the sale day staff, simply shrugged helplessly.

"It was just given to me. Sorry."

"All right," Felicia replied, sighing, before turning back to the room, leaning into her microphone. "Excuse me, everyone, there's been a slight last-minute addition to the catalogue. A Jacobean carved oak cupboard, circa 1600."

"It must be that over there," Amelia supplied in whisper, pointing to the wardrobe in the corner. "I heard Hugo mention that it only came in late last night. That's why they had to wedge it in like that. There was nowhere else for it to go."

"I really wish they wouldn't *do* this," Felicia muttered to herself. It wasn't unheard of for this sort of thing to happen, but just looked so amateurish, in her opinion. Clearly, some conniving dealer had managed to appeal to Hugo's softer side and convince him to put their item in at the last minute. Probably given him the whole sob story about how they were desperate for the cash, when in reality, they just didn't want to wait for the next sale.

"Shall we start the bidding, then? Will anyone give me £500?"

A few murmurs, then someone tentatively raised their bidding paddle. Felicia wasted no time.

"Excellent. Do I see £600 anywhere?"

A pause, and then, very slowly, Mr Clancy's hand began to move.

Afterwards, people would swear that from that moment, all hell seemed to break loose. The double doors to the saleroom crashed open, the cold April wind gusting within. Silhouetted in the doorway, a tall figure stalked into the room, accompanied by a flurry of blossom petals from the cherry tree outside.

"Stop the auction! Stop it *right* now!"

Felicia almost dropped the gavel in shock.

"Dexter!" She gasped.

Amelia spun around in her seat, eyes wide with horror.

"Isn't that… your husband?"

"My *ex*-husband," Felicia managed, in a strangled voice. "And he's going to be ex in more ways than one when I'm through with him. Dexter," she hissed, as he drew closer. "What the hell are you *playing* at? You can't just march in here and—"

"You can't sell it," he panted, stabbing a finger towards the wardrobe. "Felicia, you don't know what you're doing. You have absolutely no *idea*—"

"No, *you* have no idea!"She snapped. "There's a contract between ourselves and the vendor. I'm bound to sell this piece as agreed." She looked past his shoulder, eyes narrowing in disbelief as she spotted the round gleam of a lens. "Wait… are you *filming* this? For that ridiculous show of yours?"

The cameraman looked away awkwardly, hitching the equipment on his shoulder.

"It is *not*—" Dexter broke off with an effort. She actually heard his teeth grind down upon one another. When he spoke, his voice was more measured, although his eyes still snapped with fire. "I'm not going into this with you again."

"You're right, I think we covered everything in the divorce," she said icily.

"Dad?" Algernon had risen to his feet, confusion and delight fighting for dominance on his face. "What are you doing here?"

"I'll show you, Algie." Dexter strode up to the wardrobe, grasping the handles and throwing the doors open with a flourish.

A man fell out, thudding to the floor. Glassy eyes stared out at the room. Then, slowly, a pool of red began to spill from beneath his jacket.

Chapter Three

"So, let me go over this again, Mrs Grant," Detective Sergeant Pettifer of the Welland Police scratched behind his ear with a well-chewed pencil stub as he regarded his meagre notes.

"Ms," she interjected quickly, before he could continue. Her neatly manicured fingers squeezed the arm of the chair she was sitting in, then released with a visibly conscious effort. She crossed her hands daintily in her lap, instead, regarding him with a tight smile. "It's *Ms* Grant. Dexter and I are divorced."

"So you seem so keen to tell everybody," Dexter Grant lounged in the cracked leather armchair next to hers, a dry, slightly mocking smile upon his lips. "You've already announced it to half of Stamford this morning."

If a faint flush rose along Felicia's highly planed cheekbones, it was too well-hidden by either immaculate makeup or innate composure to show definitively. She tilted her chin.

"That wasn't my intention. I forgot that the microphone was still on. You did rather take me by surprise, bursting in like that and interrupting my auction with your idiotic—"

"Idiotic?" Dexter sat upright in his chair, eyes flashing. "So first it was ridiculous, now my work's idiotic. What next?"

Sergeant Pettifer groaned internally. He wasn't having a good day as it was. He was supposed to be on the sidelines of the school rugby pitch right now, watching his youngest. His first Saturday off work in four months; he'd promised, faithfully, that he'd be there.

And then, a murder. And not just any murder. A murder right here in Stamford.

Perhaps unsurprisingly, a murder wasn't a common occurrence in a quiet, genteel market town like this. So when it happened, the chief insisted upon absolutely *everyone* being dragged in to work on it. *Even* if it was their first Saturday off in four months.

In fact, everyone *was* here, with the notable exception of the chief himself, Sergeant Pettifer couldn't help but note darkly. Probably polishing off the important business of a leisurely brunch or a convivial round of golf first. No doubt he'd be along later, once the tedious groundwork was safely done.

Sergeant Pettifer drew himself up short, taken aback by the train of his own thoughts. Usually, he had a healthy respect for authority. But Detective Chief Inspector Heavenly was already proving to be no normal superior; Pettifer's charitable nature had already been sorely tested today, and that was even before he'd come up against these two sitting across the desk from him in the cluttered upstairs office.

He regarded them assessingly. They were a striking pair; even he could see that, with his prosaic eye. The husband, classically good-looking in that well-bred, clean-shaven sort of way, dark hair springing back from a high forehead. A rakishly arranged cravat bloomed at his tanned throat, contrasting with the rumpled linen shirt rolled carelessly to his elbows. Pettifer had him pinned down easily enough; urbane, a bit full of himself, the sort of man women seemed to like and other men found insufferable. He'd met the type plenty of times before; it was all very textbook... at least, the half of him that was *above* the desk was, Pettifer had to concede, with no small measure of irritation. The rest was another matter. Cargo trousers and heavy desert boots completed an outfit that, when put together, was almost stagey, costume-like. It didn't fit, and Pettifer didn't like things which didn't fit. They offended his straightforward sensibilities.

Having said that, he was but a minor puzzling inconvenience in the scheme of things, Pettifer thought, gritting his teeth and glaring down at his notes, whereas her… *she* was the one who posed the real problem here. She was the one he was going to have to watch.

She was a mass of almosts and not-quites. She was *almost* what you'd call beautiful, except she wasn't. She was far more interesting than that. Her face had a painterly, elusive quality, all soft lines and smudged hints of shadow. The eyes, *almost* almond-shaped, seemed to shift with light and mood, one moment placid silver-grey, the next dark and stormy. She had all the gloss and chilly poise of the Londoner she professed herself to be these days, and, yet, despite the fact that it shouldn't, something about her seemed to fit within this shabby, time-worn office in a provincial pocket of middle England. He sensed that there *was* some emotion there, beneath the tranquil surface, but she wasn't giving any of it away.

"This won't take long, I assure you." He spoke loudly, making them both turn to look at him. "I just need the facts."

And what facts they were, he thought dazedly. If he didn't have an auction room full of bidders to corroborate them, he'd never believe it. It sounded like the most ridiculous piece of fiction imaginable.

"You told my constable that this man simply…" he squinted at Constable Winters's distinctly erratic approach to cursive handwriting. "Fell out of a *wardrobe*? In the middle of the auction?"

"A Jacobean oak cupboard," she corrected him coolly, with a toss of her chestnut-coloured head.

Sergeant Pettifer blinked at her for several moments, trying to see what difference it made. In the end, he gave up.

"Uh, yes. Quite." He put aside the notebook, and with it, all pretence of consulting it. He preferred to get the facts himself first-hand anyway. Leaning forward in his chair—which creaked in a distinctly unflattering way as his weight shifted upon it—he interlaced his fingers on the desk, adopting his most interrogative look. It was time to get down to brass tacks. With these two, he could see them going around in circles for hours; they were just those kind of witnesses. "And you have absolutely *no* idea how he might have got inside there, or when?"

"I really couldn't say," she opened her palms to him, a fluttering, oddly helpless gesture, and one which he didn't believe for a moment. He wasn't sure of much yet, but this woman was anything but incapable. He'd stake his badge on that. "The saleroom's been open since nine o'clock this morning for last-minute viewings. People can walk in and out freely, and there's no guarantee that the staff over there would notice them all. They tend to man the upstairs, where the small, easily pocketable things are. The furniture, we're not so worried about, for obvious reasons." Then her eyes widened. "Of course, there's the CCTV system. I'm not sure how well the cameras cover that particular corner, but you'd certainly be able to see who entered through the doors and when."

Sergeant Pettifer raised an eyebrow.

"We'd already thought of that. Unfortunately, your staff informed us that the system has been out of use for some months now. Weren't you aware of the fact?"

There was a pause. She looked down, then just as quickly, her gaze flickered upwards again.

"No," she said at last. "No, I wasn't. But then, I really don't have much to do with the business these days. In fact, I haven't for some years now."

"I see, my apologies. I just assumed because of the way you referred to it. You said *we*…"

"Did I?" She said vaguely. "Well, it's an old habit, I suppose. A turn of phrase. I set this place up with my father, you see. But we parted company years ago. Business differences," she explained quickly, as he opened his mouth to ask. "Nothing which has mattered for a long time."

Sergeant Pettifer felt his mouth set in a firm line. He wasn't so sure that he believed that, but he wasn't about to press it right now. She'd shut him down very neatly.

"So, you see, I don't really know anything about the set-up of things here any more," she continued apologetically. "In fact, I only arrived in Stamford about three and a half hours ago."

"And why was that?"

"An emergency. My father broke his leg early this morning, so naturally he couldn't take the auction. I was a last-minute substitute."

"And you, sir?" Sergeant Pettifer turned to Dexter Grant, who'd been sprawling negligently in his chair, regarding a collection of bound leather volumes in the bookcase next to him. It was hard to tell if he'd even been following the course of the interview. "When did *you* arrive?"

He looked a little nonplussed by the question.

"Surely there isn't much doubt about *that*, Sergeant. Everyone saw me arrive." His mouth curved up on one side. "It was rather a dramatic entrance, even by my standards."

Next to him, Felicia's jaw tightened faintly. Pettifer noticed it with interest. So, the lady did have feelings after all, did she?

"Yes, well, we'll be getting to that," Sergeant Pettifer said ominously. "But I meant when did you arrive in *town*, sir? You gave your address as London as well, I believe."

"Indeed I did, although as a matter of fact, I came here straight from the airport. I've been in Southern Spain filming the latest series of my television show, *Treasure Seeker*." He seemed to sit up straighter then, his face brightening. "Perhaps you've caught it?"

A dent appeared between Felicia Grant's eyebrows.

"I'm afraid I'm not much of a one for documentaries," Sergeant Pettifer demurred politely. "More of a sports man, myself."

"Oh, it's far more swashbuckling than your average documentary," Dexter Grant said animatedly. He gazed off, apparently at the peeling plaster on the wall behind the sergeant's head, although he suspected that it was intended as what the film business described as the "middle distance". "It's action-packed stuff. The critics have likened me to a real-life Indiana Jones."

There was a strangled choking sound from the chair next to him. Sergeant Pettifer coughed discreetly, wondering how on earth he was going to get this interview back on track.

"I'm sure it's very entertaining, sir." Pettifer was trying *very* hard not to comment on the hat he'd just spotted hanging behind Dexter over the back of the chair. A battered leather fedora crowned with a knotted cord. He was starting to feel slightly hysterical, as though none of this could possibly be real. "But there's just one small matter I wanted to clear up. It was you who opened the wardrobe, was it not?"

A kind of wariness crept into Dexter's eyes. It was subtle, and the rest of his insouciant mien didn't alter, but Sergeant Pettifer had been doing this a long time. He didn't miss it.

"Yes, that's correct."

"And I understand that as you entered the auction room in the, er—manner which you did—your intention was to sabotage the sale of that very wardrobe?"

Dexter Grant sat bolt upright.

"Now see here, it wasn't *quite* like that."

"Then what was it like?" Sergeant Pettifer deliberately kept his tone genial. "Explain it to me. Because I understand that what you said was—," he broke off here, reaching for the notebook on the desk next to him and flipping through it leisurely. "Excuse me, I want to get the wording exactly right. Ah, yes, you said, 'You can't sell it. You don't know what you're doing.'" He glanced up sardonically. "Unless that was intended as a reflection on Ms Grant's professional capabilities."

Dark brows slanted downwards over deep blue eyes.

"Of course not. Felicia's very good at her job."

If the compliment was intended to soften the woman sitting next to him, it didn't quite land. She whirled on him now, a vision of beautifully controlled fury.

"An excellent question, Sergeant, and one I'd very much like to know the answer to myself."

They were disrupted at that moment by the cacophony of heavy boots thundering up the rickety stairs. Constable Winters puffed into view, hesitantly craning her head around the lintel.

"Sarge? Forensics are asking if they can turn the body."

Sergeant Pettifer felt his back teeth set together. Just when they'd been about to get somewhere.

"Sarge?" Winters prompted nervously. "What should I do? Give them the go ahead, or ought we to wait for the Chief?"

Sergeant Pettifer rubbed a calloused hand across the back of his short-cropped head and suppressed a sigh. He could understand her trepidation; this wasn't a decision he much fancied making himself. Chances were, he'd get it wrong either way. The chief inspector wasn't an easy man to please; in fact, he was nigh on impossible, despite what his elegant manners and solicitous demeanour might suggest.

He was also something of a Rottweiler when it came to interviews, with a tendency towards the dramatic flinging of accusations that would have been fine in a police drama, but wasn't quite so acceptable in real life. Sergeant Pettifer had lost count of the number of times he'd had to step in and soothe down a burgeoning libel case in the making. Which was why he had been so keen to get through this particular line of questioning before the inspector arrived on the scene.

Was it strange that Dexter Grant had singled out the particular item of furniture that the body was hidden in? Yes, it most certainly was. Even a layman would say that much. But it was hardly damning, especially at such an early stage in the investigation. Sergeant Pettifer was a measured man, and he didn't subscribe to the stereotypically uncompromising policeman's view that there was no such thing as a coincidence. Unfortunately, he knew from what already felt like long—and certainly suffering—experience that DCI Heavenly did.

Aware that three pairs of eyes were looking at him expectantly, Sergeant Pettifer cleared his throat decisively.

"Yes, Winters, tell them to turn him. We'll be down in a minute."

Felicia and Dexter Grant looked a bit startled at that pronouncement, but he didn't enlighten them immediately. Instead, he took his time gathering up his belongings, tucking the notebook into his inside jacket pocket. He glanced around the office, at the clustered comfortableness of it, the slanting, frozen light cleaved into wedges by the rafters. It was like pressing pause, stepping back in time into a Victorian cabinet of curiosities. Hard to imagine that a cold-blooded murder could occur in a place like this.

"I want to ask you to come across to the saleroom with me now, Ms Grant," he said idly, still looking around him. "Just for a moment. See if you can identify the man who was killed here today."

He heard her sharp intake of breath.

"But Sergeant, I've just told you that I haven't been here in years. I'm really not familiar with many of the local faces these days. I'm not sure I can be of much help."

He looked at her then, smiled kindly.

"Humour me, please."

She sighed reluctantly, but she was already getting up. In that moment, he felt a surge of admiration for her; he'd been braced for more in the way of squeamish protestations.

"All right, then. But I really ought to check on my son; I left him with Betsy, but... he was there when it happened." She looked at Dexter then, a glance the sergeant recognised, one parent to another. For a second, it seemed to transcend all the animosity between the two of them.

"He'll be all right, Fliss." Dexter's voice softened around the diminutive. "Children have a way of bouncing back from these things. Far better than adults do, in fact."

Sergeant Pettifer levered himself awkwardly out of the chair, into which he had become uncomfortably wedged.

"In that case, I won't keep you long. And, yes, Mr Grant, you'd better come, too."

Dexter's mouth, which had been open, crashed shut. Sergeant Pettifer smiled wryly.

"I had a feeling you were about to insist."

"Well..." Dexter looked flummoxed. "Yes, I was, actually. It's not something I feel Felicia ought to have to do on her own."

Back to Felicia, was it, then? The switch didn't go unobserved by the Sergeant. He was beginning to find the relationship between these two more and more interesting.

She looked momentarily as though she might be about to hotly protest the need for an escort, but then exhaustion swept across her face, and she simply shrugged.

Pettifer stepped aside, with a sweeping gesture towards the staircase.

"After you then, Ms Grant. Lead the way."

Chapter Four

Colin Creaton looked up at the bruised clouds overhead and hugged the precious cargo he carried closer to himself, tucking it carefully beneath the folds of his serviceable beige coat. And just in time; a large raindrop splashed onto the faded material, blooming outwards in a dark stain. Another one landed squarely on his head, trickling down the back of his collar. Outwardly he shivered, but another part of him scarcely noticed. It was somewhere else entirely.

He was in bliss. Celestial, auroral, glorious bliss. The kind where choirs of angels seemed to be singing in his head; a sweet, lilting melody of—

"Colin?" An abrasive, decidedly *un*angelic voice lashed through the escalating rumble of raindrops on cobblestones. "What are you faffing about for? We're about to get soaked!"

"Sorry, Margaret." Springing to attention, Colin fumbled in his pocket for the car keys whilst trying desperately not to expose the box under his arm to the elements in the process. *He* could get drenched right through; he wouldn't care a jot, so long as *it* stayed dry. After all these years of waiting, he couldn't bear to see one drop of moisture mar the pristine cardboard.

It was even more beautiful than he could have imagined, he thought, lost again to the dream state. Boxed for 45 years, as perfect as the day it came off the production line. No sticky childish hands had grasped and crumpled and mulched it. And within, the engine itself, undented by boisterous play, the teak and cream paint unscratched by careless tumbling into a basket with numerous other toys.

It was the Holy Grail, the one he'd been waiting for. Now, Colin thought mistily, he could die happy.

"*Colin!*" Margaret howled, yanking desperately at the passenger door handle. Her hair was plastered to her head, water running in rivulets down her face, dripping off the end of her nose. "Put that bloody thing down and open the car!"

Studiously ignoring that penultimate command, Colin flicked open the key—the electrics had failed not long after they brought the car home, something Margaret was still yet to forgive him for —and they both flung themselves within.

With a sense of timing—not to mention a certain puckishness —characteristic of English April weather, the rain stopped in tandem with the closing of the doors. They sat in deafening silence for a moment, gently steaming in the close confines of the car, as outside the sun burst resplendently back into view, scattering sparkles across the cobblestones with a generous hand.

Colin daren't risk looking at Margaret. Instead, he twisted around, carefully depositing the train on the back seat, buckling the seat belt across it so it wouldn't move. He tested the tension of the band with a frown. Maybe something to pad it out...

He reached up towards his neck, and his fingers stilled. Suddenly, he remembered the raindrop dripping down his collar. His *bare* collar. Slowly, with a mounting sense of trepidation, he turned.

"Um," he gulped. "Margaret, dear."

"Yes, Colin." She was staring straight ahead. The words were forced from between tightly clamped lips.

"It's just that, well, I seem to have misplaced my scarf. I must have left it at the auction."

There was a beat of silence. Her entire being seemed to still, then, slowly, her eyelids descended. Colin shrank back into his seat.

"Sorry, Margaret," he whispered, putting the key in the ignition. "We'll leave it. It doesn't matter."

Her eyes snapped open, sparking with a sudden fire.

"We most certainly will *not* leave it, Colin Creaton!" She said furiously, wrestling out of her seatbelt. "That's pure lambswool, that is, and I'll be damned if one of those shifty teenagers they call staff goes off with it." Her chin quivered in magnificent, righteous indignation. "You've no concept of economy, Colin, none at all! If you had to do the accounts each month like I do, you wouldn't be so careless." She flung open the car door. "Now, come along—and bring an umbrella this time!"

Colin hesitated, glancing anxiously at the box on the back seat. He was loathe to leave it in the car. What if someone stole it? The mere thought struck terror into his heart. Decisively, he reached for it—

"*Colin!*"

His hand retracted as though it had been burned.

"Coming, Margaret, coming," sacrificing his coat to the cause, he flung it across the back seat, hiding the train from prying eyes, and scuttled meekly after her as they retraced their steps back along Broad Street towards the auction house. Beyond the glistening slate rooftops, a rainbow was beginning to paint the sky in a sorbet-coloured wash.

He realised that something was wrong as soon as they walked into the cavernous foyer. It was completely empty. No receptionist at the desk, no flow of bidders coming in and out of the saleroom doors at the back, no staff running up and down the grand, curving staircase to the upstairs offices, wearing green aprons and harried expressions. There was just an echoing silence, strange and unreal-seeming. Colin felt that shiver run through him once more and wondered if he was coming down with a cold. Better not mention it to Margaret, mind; she'd only blame him for keeping them out in the rain.

Clearly, though, his wife was unaware of any such ominous atmosphere. Instead, she just looked irritated.

"Where on earth *is* everybody?" She barked, barrelling straight towards the double doors. "Honestly, the way they run this place. Not a staff member in sight!"

"Margaret, wait—" Colin began, but either she ignored him or it was too late. Out of long practice, Colin managed to catch the door before it swung back and smashed him in the face.

She hadn't got far, though. She was standing stock-still just inside the doorway. He almost walked into the back of her. He opened his mouth to ask what was going on, then looked up, and the question became suddenly unnecessary.

"Dear me," Margaret's voiced was hushed, shocked. "What a to-do."

It seemed like a slight understatement for the scene that greeted them.

His first impression was that they must have wandered into the theatre across the road by mistake. The tableau was familiar to any classic crime buff; the body slumped on the floor, the head twisted sideways at an awkward angle. The white-suited forensics team crouched over him. The burly, shabby-suited man watching on with a grim expression. A curt nod from him, and the forensics team carefully rolled the body over. It flopped like a landed fish, one arm flung outwards, bulging eyes staring straight at the ceiling.

A rather nondescript-looking individual, mind, Colin thought faintly. Not at all the sort of person who usually got murdered in books. His clothes were commonplace, a dark jacket and trousers, both of which looked to have seen better days. The hair was brushed across the top of the head at a slant that became necessary for a man after a certain age. The face, allowing for the pallor of death, was florid, a sign of too many long pub lunches and fireside nightcaps.

And then Colin saw the blood. Even that looked stagey, the neat pool creeping out from beneath the jacket, thick and bright like ink. Except, it could only be real. His eyes moved upwards, to where the wardrobe door gaped open. The same wardrobe he'd been standing next to earlier. The truth of what he was looking at came home to him in that moment, and unwittingly, he lurched forwards. But something stopped him; a resistance, pushing back against his waist. Looking down, he saw a band of white and blue police tape.

"My goodness, what *happened*?" He managed. "We were only here an hour ago. Standing right there, too." He shuddered. "The poor man could have been in there the whole time."

"So we were." There was something in Margaret's voice, a calculating quality that alarmed him. The next thing he knew, she was lifting up the tape, bending as though to duck underneath it. He plucked at her coat sleeve.

"What are you *doing*?" He whispered fretfully. "You can't go in there. It's a crime scene."

"And *we* have *vital* information," she retorted, drawing herself up to full height. Her already-ample chest swelled importantly. Her small, close-set eyes gleamed. Colin's heart promptly sank. "You said it yourself: we're *prime witnesses*. Isn't that what they call it in those books you read?"

There seemed little point in reminding her that he hadn't said anything of the kind. Instead, he took refuge in semantics.

"Primary witness," he corrected automatically in a whisper. And then, more to himself than her, "it's prime *suspect*." Something they'd probably swiftly become if Margaret went trampling all over the crime scene like a bull in a china shop.

They both turned their heads as activity occurred across the room. The scruffy-looking policeman was turning, speaking to someone behind him.

"If you wouldn't mind, Ms Grant. It'd be a great help."

A tall, slender woman stepped out of the shadows, her shoulder-length hair gleaming bronze beneath the lights. The auctioneer, Colin realised belatedly. It had taken him a moment to recognise her out of context.

"You had a key vantage point up there on the rostrum," the policeman continued, gesturing to the stage, which now had an empty, rather neglected air. "You could see the whole room for the entirety of the sale. I need to know if you noticed this man at any time." He gave her a searching look. "Take a moment. It's very important."

"I'm not sure," her voice was apologetic yet business-like. "It was a busy sale, and he's not very distinctive—" she broke off, then, and even from a distance, Colin saw the colour drain from her face. A finely-boned hand flew to her lips, which were parted in horror.

"What?" The policeman demanded sharply. "What is it?"

"It's…" she swallowed, wrapping her arms around herself protectively. "It's Barrington." The words seemed to come with an effort. She shook her head. "Barrington Clay. But… I don't understand. Why would anyone…" She swayed slightly on her feet, and a dark-haired man stepped up and caught her shoulder, putting an arm around her.

Next to him, Colin heard a soft gasp. Surprised, he glanced down at Margaret. She'd gone completely rigid. Her face had lost its ghoulish jubilation; it had closed in on itself. When she spoke, her voice was brittle, urgent.

"We have to leave, Colin. Now."

Colin, slightly nonplussed at the sudden change of tone, blinked.

"But… shouldn't we… I mean…" he flailed for a suitable

excuse, then settled rather pathetically upon, "what about my scarf?"

At that moment, one of the PCs on the scene, who had been busy scribbling on a notepad, looked up and noticed them. Her young face jolted in shock and annoyance, and she started towards them with a determined stride.

"I don't give a damn about the bloody *scarf!*" Margaret hissed shrilly. She grabbed his arm and hauled him away. "*Now*, Colin! Let's go."

By the time PC Jess Winters reached the police line, the older couple she'd seen lurking in the doorway had gone from view. Without breaking her stride, she ducked deftly beneath the tape, jogging through the foyer and out onto the steps that led down to the pavement, scanning the bustling street below with an expert eye. If anything, town had got busier in the intervening time, the morning local crowd beginning to be replaced by the more leisurely day-trippers intending to stop for a bit of lunch between perusing the shops. Jess's head swivelled left and right with an increasing sense of despair. An elderly couple in matching beige country attire didn't exactly stand out from the crowd. There were dozens of them.

Eventually, she had to concede that they'd disappeared. With a bitten-off curse, she turned to head back into the auction house, already dreading how she was going to break it to the sarge.

She pictured his tired expression, the dark circles beneath his eyes, the stress lines etched into his roughly-shaven skin, and winced. He was a good man, the sarge, but this wasn't just any case, and it wasn't just any *place*. This was Stamford, one of England's bastions of old-fashioned gentility. A place where people still wore tweed flat caps in the street without a hint of irony and the word of the local magazine functioned as gospel. A place of classical concerts in medieval churches and Georgian fairs on the meadows, of ancient, timbered hostelries with uneven floors and fanciful bridges under which the river swirled lazily.

The kind of place where people felt safe, cosseted from the harshness of the wider world.

And now, a murder. And not even the kind of murder that got buried in between the pages of the local papers: the heated argument behind closed doors that got out of hand, the mugging gone wrong in a pub car park. That was what most murders were; a moment of madness, often without much mystery to them. The sort of thing people flipped past, sympathetic but removed from.

But this... this was different. A calculated, audacious murder, on a sunny Saturday in the middle of a packed auction room, while mere feet away, people had been standing with spouses, parents, children. For once, it *could* have been them. And that changed things. It changed things a lot. The pressure to crack this case was going to be huge, all-encompassing.

And now she had to tell the sarge that they'd just lost two potential witnesses.

She had a feeling that this latest development wasn't going to go down well.

Chapter Five

Two streets away, in Stamford's resplendent Neoclassical town hall, Mayor Cassandra Lane was staring longingly at a plate of biscuits.

The plate in question was filled with a variety of offerings left over from a recent staff birthday. Artfully arranged by her teeth-grindingly efficient secretary, Gavin, it had been democratically placed right in the middle of the long meeting table.

So democratically, in fact, that from her position at the end, it was just out of reach. She would have to stretch across at least two other people. There was no way to do it inconspicuously; if there was, she'd know about it. She'd been working it out from every angle for the past twenty minutes.

It would have been all right, Cassie thought grumpily, if anyone else at these damned meetings ever actually *ate* the biscuits. But they seemed to think it was beneath them, somehow, or that it underlined the gravity of the meeting. They were all listening raptly now to a litany of clauses and objections—a list that had been going on for the past ten minutes and that only seemed to get more mind-numbing with each item. It was like Chinese water torture.

Cassie knew she ought to be grateful that she had such dedicated councillors on her team, but sometimes she just wished they'd all take it a *little* less seriously. They treated everything—from the banal to the downright ridiculous—as though it were life and death.

And she really wished they'd just eat the bloody *biscuits*, she thought, with a murderous, disproportionately savage swell of rage. It was all very well for *them*, with their quiet, orderly, retired existences, with fridges that weren't filled with nothing but formula milk and pots of fromage frais, with long, sweet night-times of uninterrupted sleep... oh God, she'd give anything for some *sleep*...

Realising that her head was beginning to loll against her shoulder at the mere notion, she blinked sharply, jolting herself upright. Sleep wasn't an option right now; sugar, however, was, if she could just get to it.

She assessed the positioning of a pink and white party ring with a calculating eye. It was right on the edge of the plate. Maybe if she dropped her pen like *so*, letting it roll quite accidentally in that direction...

She glanced up guiltily, but no one seemed to have noticed. They were all nodding along earnestly as the speaker droned on. She exhaled softly. All right, now maybe if she sort of *casually* reached across as though to retrieve it, and—

"What's your opinion, Madam Mayor?"

Twenty heads swivelled in her direction. Startled, Cassie jolted her arm back, knocking the plate flying in the process.

Biscuits soared through the air. Some landed with a clatter back on the desk, bursting into showers of crumbs on impact. A pink wafer landed in the Vice Chairman of the Finance Committee's cup of coffee, splashing hot liquid everywhere. The town clerk got hit in the side of the nose by a particularly velocious custard cream.

Following this cacophony was a rather weighty silence.

"Uh, well, I think it's a very, er…" Cassie tried to brazen it out, before petering off miserably. "What was the question again?"

The face across the table from her twisted into a barely-perceptible sneer. It was so fleeting, so faint, that most people would have said she was imagining things. But Cassie was more than aware of what Dennis Stanworthy thought of her; even if no one else appeared to see it.

When she'd taken on the role of mayor a year ago, she'd gone into it with her characteristic cheerful pragmatism, a trait honed by single motherhood for so many years and later, the appearance of three small sons close together. She'd sensibly prepared herself for the many potential pitfalls and annoyances that might come with the job.

What she'd never predicted was that her deputy would be the biggest of them all.

Oh, he'd been all courtly charm and sincere congratulations initially; so much so, that it had taken her longer than it ought to have done to flag the bitterness that broiled beneath it all. She'd even congratulated herself on how well she'd handled him, a memory that made her cringe now at how self-complacent she'd been.

She'd known that it was always going to be awkward, having a deputy who'd served on the council for over fifteen years to her mere two, who'd clearly thought himself a shoo-in for the job. But he'd seemed to take it with such good grace that it had been natural to swat away the odd unhelpful question directed towards her during a meeting, or an unflattering story that appeared in the local paper, apparently with no source. The first few times it happened, at least. After that, she'd had to revise her opinion.

The problem was what to *do* about it. Because there was nothing concrete, as such, that she could point the finger at. He was too clever for that. And so she just had to grit her teeth and put up with him subtly attempting to undermine her at every turn.

Unfortunately, in this case, she had to concede that she'd made it rather easy for him. Drawing herself up and brushing the crumbs off her lapel, she clasped her hands on the desk in front of her and attempted to look mayoral. Whatever *that* would look like.

"Red Lion Square, Madam Mayor," Councillor Jenkins, who headed up the planning committee, reiterated politely. Cassie tried valiantly not to notice that there was a garibaldi nestled amongst the soufflé of her frizzy grey hair. "The cobbles. There's been quite a division on the subject, as you know. The debate even featured on national radio last week." Her expression suggested that she didn't approve of the town's politics being aired to the wider world. "We feel it's time some decisions were made."

Cassie sighed inwardly, wondering, not for the first time, what had even possessed her to go into local politics in the first place, let alone run for mayor. Although, in truth, it hadn't possessed *her* at all, she thought darkly. It had all been Robyn's idea.

Robyn was seventeen, her eldest child, and a veritable force of nature. Some days, just looking at her daughter's boundless energy and determination was enough to make Cassie want to lie down in a darkened room with a cold compress. If there was anything to be done, Robyn would do it. If there was any cause to be championed, or change to be effected, Robyn was there. She would probably be prime minister one day, Cassie though hazily, with that awe one has as a parent, watching the baby they brought into the world surpass them in every way. But for now, she was living vicariously through her mother by shoving her headlong into the world of local politics. Whether the mother in question liked it or not.

All right, so that wasn't *quite* fair, Cassie acknowledged, with an immediate surge of guilt. She *had* been in dire need of a nudge. If she was being honest, she could understand a little of Robyn's drive; she'd once possessed no small amount of it herself. Back when it was just the two of them. With a master's degree in finance in one hand and a positive pregnancy test in the other, she'd known that she couldn't give up on either. So she'd done both. She'd worked her way up the corporate ladder with a child on her hip, and, when it had been made clear to her that she was knocking her head against the glass ceiling, she'd branched out and set up on her own.

And then, nine years ago, she'd met Alistair at a trade event. He'd loved her, loved Robyn, and for once, for the first time, it had just been so damned *nice* to be supported. To not have to carry it all by herself. She'd sunk into that feeling, revelled in something she'd never even had the chance to realise that she'd missed. When he'd asked her if she wanted more children, she'd discovered that she very much did, and the boys had followed in quick succession. She hadn't missed work at first; full-time motherhood had seemed exotic, exciting... until she'd begun to lose herself amongst the never-ending mountain of washing, the playdates, the tantrums. She'd never forget the day when she'd realised that the highlight of her week had become a solo trip to the supermarket.

She hadn't been *unhappy* as such, just... bored. Under-stimulated. And when Robyn had come home unexpectedly early from school one lunchtime and found her downing a glass of wine while the boys had their naps, she'd told her in no uncertain terms what she thought.

"You need a job, Mum," she'd said firmly. And because it was Robyn, that was exactly what had happened. The next thing Cassie had known, she was handing out leaflets with her face on them.

And to think at the time how she'd told herself it would be *easy*, she thought now, choking back a dismal laugh at her own naïveté. After all, she'd reasoned, it was a small town in Lincolnshire where nothing happened. How hard could it possibly *be*?

What she hadn't reckoned on was that small, beautiful, historic towns where nothing happened were some of the hardest to manage. Stamford had the accolade—much quoted in local tourist publications—of being Britain's first conservation town. Once one of the country's most important coaching stops on the Great North Road, its perfectly preserved jewel of a Georgian centre had been ensured by the creation of the railways in Victorian times, leaving the once-opulent and bustling settlement a veritable backwater.

These days, what that translated into was a haven for day-trippers and weekenders, an ideal meeting-in-the-middle spot for old friends coming from North and South respectively, and a magnet for both history-buffs and dreamers alike who wanted to step back in time for a while. What they didn't see was that behind the scenes, it was a place constantly engaged in a juggling act with the old and the new. Because it *wasn't* a film set —although it had moonlighted as one several times over the years—but a working, thriving town, and it needed to function as one.

On the other hand, Cassie acceded, there was no denying that its golden-stoned, sash-windowed elegance was important not just from a conservation point of view, but from an economic one as well. Stamford was fortunate in the fact that it benefitted from a wealthy, largely leisured population, but the bijou independent shops that dotted the various squares and lanes couldn't exist by the grace of 20,000 locals alone. Nor could the myriad coffee shops, which seemed to continue to swell in number with each passing month. Nor could the Arts Centre, with its independent stage and cinema, or the famous George Inn. In all, the town certainly punched above its weight for its size, and that was down to its visitor appeal.

Hence the discussion currently underway, and why the replacing of the olde-worlde yet suspension-wrecking granite setts in Red Lion Square with the more convenient yet undeniably less aesthetic tarmac option was the hottest topic in town.

"Well," Cassie cleared her throat, leaning back nonchalantly in her seat with a smile. "Yes, I agree, it's time we gave people some *concrete* answers on this one."

She waited expectantly, but her attempt to lighten the mood was only met with blank faces.

"Tough crowd," she muttered under her breath.

"Pardon, Madam Mayor?" Dennis enquired, from the far end of the table. "Did you say something?"

"No, it's just, it was a… never mind," she said gloomily. If they couldn't spot an excellent pun when it came their way, she certainly wasn't going to go to the effort of explaining it to them. Frankly, they didn't deserve it. "So, granite setts…"

At that moment, there was a commotion in the hallway outside, and the door burst open. Gavin, looking uncharacteristically ruffled, toppled into the room, panting for breath. Cassie got the impression he'd taken the stairs two at a time on his way up.

Alarmed, she rose to her feet.

"Gavin? What's going on?"

"I'm *so* sorry to interrupt your meeting, Madam Mayor," he gulped, tugging at his tie. "But I thought you should know… there's been a murder. Up at the auction house."

A collective gasp shivered around the table. Cassie felt every muscle in her body lock.

"Who?" She asked, surprised by how steady her voice sounded.

"It hasn't been released yet. But the word in town is that it's an auctioneer."

He'd barely got the last syllable out before she was pushing past him. The next thing he knew, the mayor of Stamford was gone, running out into the street. Gavin turned back to the room of shocked and confused faces arranged around the table. His eyes focused, then blinked.

"Councillor," he said, slowly. "Were you aware that you have a biscuit in your hair?"

Chapter Six

"You *lost* them?" Sergeant Pettifer bellowed.

PC Jess Winters flinched.

"I'm sorry, sir."

"They should never have got in here in the first place!" In the absence of his desk—his usual favourite spot upon which to thump his fist whilst making a point—he settled for the back of a nearby chaise longue. His hand bounced off it soundlessly, making the whole thing far less satisfying than usual. For some reason, that only made him feel even more annoyed. "The front entrance should have been taped off and manned. Why the hell wasn't it?"

Jess pulled herself up.

"I take full responsibility, sir. I was on my way to oversee it. I should have been there sooner." Fear flashed through her eyes, but she held her head high. "I understand that you'll have to inform DCI Heavenly about this."

Pettifer looked at her quivering chin and felt himself soften. It was a blunder they really could have done without, but in truth, it wasn't entirely her fault. Until the promised reinforcements from the county squad turned up, they were operating with only the handful of officers who manned the tiny Welland Police Station in town. Jess had been running around trying to do about three jobs at once all afternoon; she was a good officer, earnest and hard-working, but she was only human. It wasn't fair of him to take out his bitterness and frustration on her. Besides, he knew she'd reprimand herself about it far more furiously than he could ever do. There was no need to add to her misery.

"Now then, lass," he said, with gruff awkwardness. "I'm not sure that'll serve anyone well. We're short-staffed enough as it is." Knowing Heavenly's capricious temper, he'd probably have her suspended on the spot, or worse. He cleared his throat, raising his voice to a brisk, business-like level to signal that the subject was closed. "Any sign of the weapon yet?"

Relief and gratitude flooded her face like sunshine breaking through the clouds. She flipped eagerly through her notebook, clearly desperate to redeem herself.

"Not yet. Medical opinion says it was a long, thin blade. Not tapered, like you'd expect a knife to be. Something unusual. They can't say what at the moment." She held out a plastic bag. "By the way, I've got the contents of the dead man's pockets. Nothing very telling that I can see, though."

Pettifer looked around him dubiously.

"Well, if you want unusual, this is your place. They sell all sorts here, including weaponry. I suppose we'd better check there's nothing missing from any of the lots."

"Already on it," Jess said buoyantly. "I've asked one of the staff members to make a start on it. A Hugo Dappleton; he seems to know everything that's going on. Technically, he's the deputy valuer, but he seems to do most of the general running of the place on a day-to-day basis. Between you and me, I get the impression the old man's not been quite with it lately."

By that, he took her to mean Peter Grant, the absent auction owner with the broken leg. The *conveniently* broken leg, perhaps? Pettifer mused on this. It seemed a bit of a stretch, but his mind was used to following all of the rivulets of potential that came off a case.

"Hence the lack of working CCTV," he nodded upwards, to where a camera stared blankly at him from the corner.

"Quite. But it might not be the only thing he's let slide." She tapped her notes with a short-clipped fingernail. "Apparently the wardrobe was such a late addition, even Hugo Dappleton knew nothing about it. He got a call at about nine o'clock last night from Peter Grant, asking him to head into work to take in a last-minute consignment. When he got here, there was a hire van waiting with the wardrobe inside. He helped the men unload it, then locked up and left."

Pettifer frowned.

"Didn't he think it was odd? At that time of night?"

"He did rather, yes. Apparently it's not entirely unheard of for him to have to wait at the office a little later than usual, till about six or seven—if a client is coming from a distance and has got held up in traffic, say. But Peter Grant had never asked him to do anything like that before."

"Sounds like we're going to have to have a word with Mr Grant senior, then, doesn't it?" Pettifer said blandly. "He should be coming home from hospital this afternoon; I let Felicia and Dexter Grant go to collect him. They're staying at her father's cottage; I'll head over there later, talk to all of them. Kill two birds with one stone, as the saying goes." He gave the woman next to him an assessing glance as he handed the bag of effects back to her. She was right; there was nothing useful to them in there. Just a wallet, a mobile phone, a small torch, some keys, and a tube of mints. "Say, Jess, you're a local girl—you ever heard of this Barrington Clay? Apparently, he's a fellow auctioneer. Owns a string of places just like this one."

She gave him a funny look.

"Course I've heard of him. Have you never seen *Chase the Bargain*? It's an antiques show, on at lunchtime."

Pettifer sniffed disparagingly.

"I don't watch daytime television, Constable."

"Neither do I," she said defensively. "But you know, sometimes when you're ill..." she pulled her phone out of her pocket. "Look, I'll show you."

She brought up a clip that showed a man in a bright pink suit enthusiastically bargaining with a stallholder at an antiques fair.

"Come on," he was saying jovially. "Surely you can knock a couple of extra pounds off for an impecunious swain?"

The stallholder was a shrivelled old woman who didn't look to have smiled in years.

"All right," she muttered ungraciously. "If it'll get rid of you."

"You, my lady, are a charm," he declared, seizing her outstretched hand and dropping a courtly kiss onto it. For a moment, she looked stunned, then a faint blush began to fill her sunken cheeks.

"I suppose I might be able to do something on that carriage clock you were looking at, too," she ventured shyly. "For such a nice gentleman as yourself, like."

The video came to an abrupt end.

"Quite a character," Sergeant Pettifer said thoughtfully, looking across to the body sprawled on the floor. "You wouldn't think it, looking at him today. Must have been a good actor."

"If he was, he totally inhabited the part," Jess said. "I used to see him around locally sometimes. That pink suit was like his trademark. He wore it everywhere he went, even if he was off-duty. He seemed to like being recognised. He was a real showman."

"Or a shrewd businessman." Pettifer raised his eyebrows. "Seeing as you seem to be such a television aficionado, Winters, I don't suppose you happen to be familiar with our other star of the small screen's output, too? You ever seen this *Treasure Hunter* thing?"

"*Treasure Seeker*," she corrected him automatically, then looked sheepish. "I mean, I might have caught it once or…" She exhaled. "Oh, all right, yes, I watched the last series. In my defence, though, who didn't?"

"Me," Pettifer said stonily.

"It's very educational," she protested.

"Is it, indeed?" He said drily. It sounded like the most appalling load of tripe to him. He'd done a quick internet search, and it seemed to involve a lot of scrambling about in ruins with Dexter Grant doing a well-groomed action man impression. "Nothing to do with the fact that the host is good-looking and posh, then?"

Jess gave him a sly look.

"I didn't think other men noticed that sort of thing."

They did when they were neither of those things themselves, Pettifer thought. But he wasn't about to admit as much.

"Besides, he's really quite brilliant," Jess said dreamily. "He spent the whole of last series hunting down this famous Viking hoard. He went all the way to Denmark to find these stone carvings, then he unravelled what they meant using this helmet they have in the British Museum, then…"

"It sounds fascinating," Pettifer said sarcastically. Then, annoyed with himself but unable not to ask, "did he find it in the end?"

"Of course he did," Jess looked affronted that he'd even asked. "He's Dexter Grant."

Pettifer rolled his eyes to heaven.

"You can't think he had anything to do with this, Sarge?" Jess asked, aghast. "He's a professor."

He speared her with a stern glance.

"Being telegenic and scholarly doesn't preclude a person from murder, constable. He's yet to explain to me why he tried to stop the sale over the exact item which happened to have a body in. Until he can satisfy me on that score, he's a person of interest." He looked across to the back of the saleroom, where a wooden door was propped ajar. It led to a storage shed tacked onto the back of the building, which housed items waiting sale or collection—and, currently, about a hundred or so increasingly impatient auction-goers.

"We'll have to decide what to do with the rest of them," he said resignedly. "We can't keep them cooped up in there all day."

"They *are* getting a bit fractious," Jess admitted. "Some of the dealers are starting to make a fuss about getting back to London tonight."

Pettifer scrubbed a weary hand across his face.

"How many witness statements have we got through?"

"About a third of them. We're doing the families with children and the old people first, of course." She sighed. "I'll be honest with you, Sarge, they're not yielding much. It was rammed in there, everyone moving about, people coming and going, and of course, their attention was all on the front of the room." She shrugged. "We'll keep at it, but I'll admit I'm not hopeful."

Sergeant Pettifer gave a dour smile.

"Apparently, if you want to commit a murder, an auction room's the place to do it." He gave her a sideways look. "I'll level with you, Winters. What we have in there is less a hundred or so potential witnesses and more a hundred or so potential *suspects*. The truth is, any one of them could have easily moved around to the side of the wardrobe, inserted a blade through that split in the wood, and stabbed him." He eyed the crack that ran up the side of the wardrobe. Originating from a knot in the grain, it had expanded to a point where almost an entire fist could have fitted through it. "He'd have been a captive in there; you couldn't miss. I doubt it would even have taken much strength."

Although it would be a risky business, no doubt about it. That worried him a little, the sheer brazenness of it; there was something reckless, even slightly unbalanced about it.

"Well, I don't know about *that*, sir," Jess said cheerfully. "We might be able to rule out the babies. And I can't quite see one of the spaniels doing it; no opposable thumbs. Maybe if they banded together…"

"Very droll, Winters. Very droll."

"Well, someone has to keep a sense of humour around here."

Indeed, Pettifer thought grimly. And somehow, he didn't think that Chief Inspector Heavenly would be the one to take up the mantle. He could only thank God that he hadn't arrived yet and started throwing his weight around.

"You'd better hand some of those witness interviews over to me. We'll get through them faster if there are two of us at it."

She looked startled.

"But what about the Grants, sir?"

"The Grants can wait." He retrieved the chewed pencil stub from behind his ear and flipped to a fresh page in his notebook, bracing himself for an interminable afternoon. "They can answer my questions later." And he had a lot of them still to ask, a list that was only growing the further this investigation proceeded. "Every answer I get just seems to throw up more questions with that lot."

"Something's bothering you, isn't it, Sarge?" She raised her fair eyebrows. "Something they said to you earlier?"

He shook his head pensively.

"Something they *didn't* say."

She gave him a surprised, searching look, but he was already walking away.

Chapter Seven

"**A** murder?" Peter Grant roared. "I leave you in charge of my auction house for one morning and you manage to oversee a *murder*?"

They were sitting in the low-beamed kitchen of Peter's cottage on Water Street, the windows of which, appropriately enough, gazed out over the river. The wide green bank was swaying with clusters of daffodils, their stellated yellow faces splayed towards the late afternoon sun. Overhead, birds flitted between the blossom-laden branches, calling sweetly to one another. Felicia took a moment to drink in the view, carefully counting to ten before she turned to face the irate man glaring at her from a wheelchair, which, even positioned in the centre of the room, took up most of the available space. Peter's 17th century milliner's cottage had many selling points, but capaciousness certainly wasn't one of them.

"I'm fairly sure it would still have happened whoever was standing on the rostrum," she said reasonably.

"Hmph," Peter didn't look convinced. Clearly, he imagined that no murderer would dare to strike under his watch. "Still, at least they had the consideration to leave it till the last lot. You didn't manage to sell the cupboard, I suppose?" He added, hopefully.

Felicia almost choked on air.

"Strangely enough, Dad, no, I didn't. The dead body falling out of it rather halted proceedings. I felt it might be inappropriate to go on with the bidding at that point."

If Peter noticed her sarcasm, he didn't show it. Instead, he shook his head broodingly.

"Damn, and I promised old Batty so faithfully." He narrowed his eyes at his daughter. "It's bad enough that I had to wait until now to find out. My own business, as well! Can you imagine what it looks like, me being the last to know?"

He seemed to regard this omission as the biggest sin of all.

"You were in hospital having your leg set," Felicia eyed the plaster cast limb in exasperation. "I was *trying* to save you the stress."

"Well, I'm even more stressed now, knowing that this has been going on all day without my knowledge!" Peter snapped.

Felicia was on the verge of a choice retort when Algernon trailed in.

"Mum, I'm starving. Are there any biscuits?"

"In the tin, duck," Peter said, his broad face softening at the sight of his grandson. "I got those chocolate ones you like."

Felicia drew in a breath, grateful for the timely reminder that her father wasn't quite so heartless and irascible as he came across at times. A salt-of-the-earth Lincolnshire man, he'd had to fight his way up the rungs of life. That survivor's mentality ran deep, even now, when he was long past needing it. It was like a suit of armour he never seemed quite prepared to take off.

"*This* is why I can't leave anyone else in charge," Peter grumbled, shoving against the wheels on his chair. "I should be there now, sorting it all out."

"There's nothing you can do, Dad. I've left Hugo to watch over things, but the best thing is to let the police get on with their investigation."

"Investigation!" Peter went purple. "Trampling all over the place, more like, with their big flat feet. Poking about, disarraying everything. I know what they're like."

Felicia decided that it was better not to ask *how* her father was apparently so familiar with police intervention. Plausible deniability might be useful later.

"How the hell does this bloody thing— *Ahh!*" At an irate slap to the side, the wheelchair lurched forwards, almost steamrollering Godfrey, Peter's burly ginger tomcat, who'd just slunk into the kitchen like a guilty student returning from an all-nighter. He hissed, leaping up onto the table with an offended look, where he proceeded to wash himself passive-aggressively.

"Dad, careful!" Felicia grabbed at the chair before it could take out the rest of the kitchen. "You almost ran over the cat."

"Serve him right, after he put me in this blasted chair in the first place." He glared at the animal. "Mangy old thing," he said darkly. "Always creeping in and out, treats this place like a hotel. Don't know why I ever took him in in the first place. I've half a mind to boot him back out on his ear."

Godfrey snarled at him in response, before resuming his grooming regime. He clearly knew, as Felicia did, that nothing of the sort would ever happen, even if he knocked his owner down the stairs a dozen times. The two of them maintained a showy acrimony—one which she suspected they both enjoyed—but secretly, they were very well suited.

Perhaps, she reflected, looking from one cantankerous, brawny male to the other, because they were actually astonishingly alike.

She motioned to the wheelchair.

"Do you even know how to use this thing? Did they show you at the hospital?"

"They tried," Peter scoffed. "Told them I was fixing tractors on the farm before I could walk. There's nothing *they* can teach *me* about mechanics, I said. They quietened down after that, left me to it."

"I'll bet they did," Felicia murmured. It sounded like the nurses had correctly assessed that they were on a hiding to nothing with this particular patient. Unfortunately, wise as it might have been on their part, it didn't help *her* much. Visions of her father careering along the narrow, uneven Stamford pavements, sending unwary tourists flying in all directions, rose in front of her eyes, and she suppressed a shudder.

"Surely there must be a lock on this thing?" She muttered, fiddling with the mechanism on the side.

"Don't you dare," Peter roared, stirred into sudden, vociferous fury. "If I want to get to my auction house, I will, and if I die trying…"

"Chance would be a fine thing," Dexter said under his breath, from where he'd been sitting silently—uncharacteristically silently, Felicia thought, a touch peevishly—in the rocking chair by the range.

Peter's head swivelled, and he pinioned his former son-in-law with a withering glare.

"What's he doing here, anyway? No one's seen fit to explain it to me."

"No one's seen fit to explain it to *me*, either," Felicia said bitterly, with an accusatory sideways glance at Dexter.

"If you're all going to start arguing, I'm going outside," Algernon announced wearily.

No one paid him the slightest attention.

Felicia made a show of rummaging in her handbag for her phone.

"Well then, you leave me no choice, Dad. If I can't make you be sensible, I'll simply have to call Juliette instead."

The effect was immediate and, Felicia thought, rather satisfying. Peter blanched.

"Now then, duck, let's not be hasty," he said cajolingly. "I don't see that there's any need for *that*. I'm sure you and I can rub along just fine."

Felicia pocketed her phone with a concealed smile. Her younger sister was probably the only person on earth who could make their father quake in his size-twelve boots. Juliette saw herself as a nurturer, but she went about it in such a militant, overzealous manner that her tender ministrations felt more like a slow, painfully organised suffocation. She had a meticulously organised house, sat on every committee going, and presided over a brood of outwardly perfect, yet strangely haunted-looking children. Felicia privately amused herself by comparing them to over-pampered hamsters; tended to in every way, yet desperate only to escape.

"Can we?" Felicia asked her father now, with an arched brow. "I can't recall us ever doing so before."

"You take things to heart so, that's all," Peter said gruffly. "Just like your mother."

Seeing as Felicia's mother had run off with a Spanish cruise ship owner and currently spent most of the year circling the Balearics with a cocktail in hand, Felicia wasn't sure how she felt about the comparison. She was forever being likened to her mother; true, she had her looks—passed almost wholesale down to Algernon, with Dexter's genes scarcely making an appearance —and, even she had to admit, a little of her sense of drama. But she was, she hoped, not quite so capricious, so whimsical in her treatment of others' feelings.

Then again, she thought, as she watched a spaniel trotting dolefully along the river path with its owner, shivering against the biting April wind, sometimes she wondered if her mother might not be the sensible one after all.

"Besides, Juliette's got the children to think of," Peter continued. "She can't just up sticks and leave."

"*I've* got a child to think of," Felicia said testily. "Speaking of which, where is he?"

"Skulked off outside, probably," Dexter offered. "To get away from all the bickering. You know what he's like."

Felicia suppressed a sigh. Algernon was strangely sensitive about these things. In fact, he was strangely sensitive about a lot of things.

The truth was, she'd never really understood her son. It was her guilty mother's secret, the one that used to awaken her in the night, panicked, terrified that she was a terrible parent, as beside her, Dexter dozed on, oblivious. When she'd had a baby, she'd blithely assumed that he would be the best parts of both of them; Dexter's charisma mixed with her savoir vivre, his gregariousness with her way of putting people at ease. She'd anticipated a sunny, talkative child; instead, she'd got an unknown quantity, introspective and dreamy. He'd taken so long to utter his first word that she'd had to lie to the health visitor about it for fear they'd think something was wrong with him.

But there was nothing wrong with Algernon; she'd always known that. He was just… different. One minute a boy, the next an adult. He was funny and solemn at alternate turns, one moment filled with childish wonder, the next mature beyond all expectation. Sometimes, he was happy to be with others his own age; other times, he just wanted to be alone. He liked plenty of the things his friends did—cricket, iced buns at school teatime, conducting serious and clandestine swaps of luridly coloured playing cards in whatever latest incarnation had gripped his year group's imagination—but also plenty that they didn't. Classical music, poetry, spending his weekends sorting through boxes of dead people's possessions at a dusty auction house…

"I'll talk to him." She pulled on her coat, a pale-pink affair that matched the blossom on the trees outside. It had been hideously expensive and, she thought wryly, probably not designed with tramping around muddy river banks in mind. "You," she pointed sternly at Dexter. "Look after Dad. Make sure he doesn't go anywhere."

The two men eyed one another warily. Before there could be any protestations over the arrangement, Felicia pushed open the front door of the cottage, automatically ducking her head to pass beneath the deep lintel.

The low sun shone in her eyes as she stepped outside, and she raised a hand to shield them. The street was silent; by this point on a Saturday afternoon, the town entered an interval of stasis between the shutting of the shops and cafés and the opening of the pubs and restaurants for the evening. The day-trippers had trickled away, the weekenders had retreated to their B&Bs to rest their feet, and the dinner crowd hadn't arrived yet. It was a small breathing period, where the locals emerged to walk their dogs, post their letters, and enjoy the peace of their town once more.

"Algernon," she called softly, as she crossed the lane. As she stepped onto the wide strip of riverbank, her heels sunk immediately into the earth, fastening her in place.

"Damn," she muttered, twisting her foot this way and that. Unfortunately, that only caused her to sink even deeper. "Double damn."

"Need some help?"

She looked up, startled. Jack Riding was standing mere feet away, a camera in his hand and a look of polite query on his face.

Her first thought was how golden he appeared, with the sun spilling out from behind him. It meshed in his blond hair, gilded his tanned skin, slanted off the high planes of his face. The second was that she hadn't heard him approaching at all. The disconcerting idea occurred that perhaps he might have crept up on her, but she quickly dismissed that, cross with herself for entertaining something so histrionic. This was a public footpath, after all; the man had every right to be here. Today's events must be getting to her more than she'd realised.

She was about to accept his offer of assistance, when something stopped her. His face was perfectly devoid of expression; but, then, she looked into his eyes and immediately bristled.

Amused. He was actually *amused* by her predicament The knowledge made her feel disproportionately piqued.

"No, thank you," she said stiffly. "I'm quite all right."

"My apologies," he inclined his head gravely. "Of course, I should have seen that this is a deliberate attitude you're striking."

Felicia, whose legs were pinned at a splayed angle, forcing her torso backwards as she tried valiantly to keep balance, didn't quite know how to respond to that. Instead, she gave her foot a vehement tug.

"Whoa!" Jack was by her side in an instant, catching her by the waist as she toppled backwards. "What are you doing?"

"What does it look like?" She began, lowering her voice as a jogger went past, staring at them in unabashed curiosity. "I'm getting out of here."

Preferably before they became the town spectacle. On a slow news day, this would be enough to land them on the front page of the Stamford Mercury.

"Not like that you're not." His hand was still on the small of her back. The pressure was light; so much so that she could barely feel it through her coat, but she was strangely aware of it, nonetheless. It was distracting, disconcerting. "Do it again and we'll both be in the river."

"What do *you* suggest then?" Her tone was sharper than intended, but it didn't seem to perturb him.

"The way I see it, we have two options. One, you lose the shoes."

"What?" She was appalled at the suggestion. Squelching around on the riverbank barefoot was *not* something which appealed.

"All right, then, option two it is."

The next thing she knew, he'd swept her right off her feet.

Chapter Eight

Detective Sergeant Pettifer looked out over a twilit Stamford. A bat swooped low, a blurred whisk of darkness against the violet water that reflected the sky above.

What a day. And it wasn't even over yet. He still had to give a full briefing to DCI Heavenly.

Suddenly, the exhaustion swept over him, and he paused on the bridge, leaning on the railing. It was a fanciful confection, all delicate, scrolling ironwork painted in heritage shades of chalk white and sage green. It looked like it had been part of a set somewhere, left here by accident.

Jess had been right about the witnesses; no one had seen anything. Or, to be more specific, the ones which had didn't realise that they had, and the ones which hadn't seemed to be of the type to imagine that they had. There was nothing concrete to go on.

Except this. Turning his head, Pettifer gazed through the trees that graced the riverbank to the row of stone cottages on Water Street. Lights were coming on now, curtains drawing, the windows glowing boxes of illumination. Everything they had seemed to lead back to the Grants.

To conduct a murder at your own auction house… it was either incredibly stupid or fiendishly clever.

Felicia Grant wasn't stupid in the slightest; he was sure of that. Dexter was another matter; he might be a genius in his subject, but he'd come across to Pettifer as having little plain common sense outside of it. Peter Grant, he'd yet to meet.

A situation he had to remedy right now. He couldn't stand out here on the bridge for ever, inviting as the idea might be.

Hefting a sigh, he shuffled across to the far bank, descending the steps that lead onto the narrow path…

… and almost fell over something.

"*Jesus!*" Flinging out a hand, he braced himself against the trunk of the nearest tree and managed to stop himself from toppling right over. He squinted down into the gloaming, where a dark mass was just visible on the ground. "What the—"

The shape began to move, unfurling itself. And then a childlike voice said pleasantly, "Hello, Sergeant."

Pettifer blinked a couple of times, willing his eyes to adjust. Gradually, more details appeared; a pale, heart-shaped face, large grey eyes, a tousled thatch of chestnut hair, almost bronze in tone. Strange, ethereal colouring; the resemblance was so striking that he found himself doing a double take.

"You're Felicia's son, I presume?" He said, gruffly.

A vigorous nod confirmed this.

"And *you're* Sergeant Pettifer. You're investigating the murder, aren't you? I saw you earlier, at the auction."

"What are you doing out here at this time of night?"

The boy gave him an incredulous look.

"It's five-thirty."

Was it only? Sergeant Pettifer looked at his watch and winced. God, it had felt like a long day.

"Never mind that," he said, irritably. "Just answer the question, lad."

"Warblers."

The sergeant blinked, wondering if this was some kind of new derogatory slang word he'd yet to come across. Really, he couldn't keep up with them all these days.

"Pardon?"

The boy pointed directly upwards into the branches of the tree.

"You don't often get to hear the evening chorus in London. Too much traffic. There's a pair of blackcaps up there. Or there was," he added, slightly accusingly. "I think you've scared them off with your crashing about."

This had to be one of the strangest children he had ever come across, the sergeant thought faintly. He highly doubted that any of his brood would know what the evening chorus was, let alone come outside and sit under a tree in the gathering dark just to hear it. He folded his arms, looming over the boy.

"How old are you, anyway?"

"Twelve," was the proud pronouncement. "My birthday was last month."

Pettifer would have put him closer to ten; he was small, young-looking. But then, he was in a rather scrunched up position.

"Have you come to interview me?" The boy asked, eyes shining hopefully.

"Er …" Pettifer wasn't quite sure how to respond to that.

"Because your PC—the blonde lady—she was talking to everyone at the auction earlier, wasn't she? Asking them what they saw, and where they were. But she never asked me. I waited for her to, but she never did." The omission seemed to bemuse rather than affront him. He gazed up at Pettifer, his expression clearing. "So I assume that's why you're here; because she forgot. But it's all right, because I've remembered everything. I've been going over it all afternoon, making sure I don't forget."

Pettifer decided it was easier at this point to play along. If the boy wanted an interview, he could go through the motions. He pulled himself up, made himself look official.

"Well, then, er… What did you see?"

A serious grey gaze met his unwaveringly.

"Aren't you going to make notes?"

"Oh, yes." Chastened, Pettifer hastily fumbled in his breast pocket for his notebook, flipping it open to a fresh page. "Naturally."

"Well, it was a busy auction. And I was helping Betsy with the phone bids, so I wasn't looking all the time… which means I didn't see as much as I might have done," the lad explained, apologetically.

"That's all right," Pettifer said, in his best reassuring voice. The one he used for flustered little old ladies and other witnesses who he already knew wouldn't have anything useful to yield, but who he had to pay lip service to. "Just tell me what you can remember."

"All right," he hugged his knees to his chest, a faraway look on his young face. Pettifer could tell that he was unspooling backwards in his mind, picturing the auction room earlier in the day.

"Mum was annoyed when they gave her the wardrobe to sell at the last moment; she never shows it, but I could tell. I think she'd noticed it before, because she kept looking towards the back of the room. Although, that might have been because Jack was there… you know, the photographer? He always has a camera around his neck. He works for the auction sometimes, taking pictures for adverts and stuff. I like him; lots of people think he's quite rude, because he doesn't say much, but really it's just because he only says what he thinks needs to be said. He doesn't like chatting, which suits me, because sometimes I don't either. I noticed Mum was looking at him strangely, but then, she probably doesn't know who he is. She hasn't been to the auction in years, whereas I spend lots of time there. I'm going to take it over one day, you know."

Pettifer nodded numbly, trying to keep up with the torrent of information.

"So, this… Jack, was it? He was near the wardrobe during the sale? Is that what you're saying?"

Any faint hope of a lead was quickly quashed, however.

"Almost everyone was near it at some point. People move around a lot during an auction, you know." He paused, then added, "except me. I only got up twice during the whole thing. Once when Mrs Fielding dropped her stick—she's old and she doesn't move very well, so I picked it up for her—and once to go to the loo. I couldn't hold it any more," he explained, almost apologetically.

Pettifer, who hadn't felt the need for this insight into the machinations of the childish bladder, merely coughed awkwardly.

"Did anything go wrong during the sale? As in, any moments where things weren't quite as they should have been?"

The boy tapped his chin thoughtfully.

"Well, there was a moment when Hugo got up just at the beginning of the collectables section; he must have been taking a break. Only he ran off so quickly that there was a gap when there was no bidding clerk, and Mum had to wait until Amelia came and took over. She's nice, Amelia; she's away at university a lot of the time, but when she's back for the holidays she comes and works the sale."

Pettifer looked at him with renewed interest.

"He ran off, you say?" He'd spoken to Hugo Dappleton himself that afternoon, and he'd struck him as a conscientious sort of lad. Not at all the sort to leave his auctioneer in the lurch like that. "Now, what made him do that, do you reckon?"

It had been intended as a rhetorical question, but his companion was ready with an answer.

"Because of the wardrobe, I expect. He was staring into that corner, and then he got up and left. I watched him; he went straight over to it and started looking around, like he was expecting to see something. But whatever it was must have gone, because he moved away again quite quickly."

"You don't miss much, do you lad?" Pettifer was quietly impressed.

The boy shrugged.

"I just pay attention, that's all. Most people don't." He frowned. "I've been trying to think about what he might have seen, but the only people who had been standing near it recently were those two women."

"Which women?" Pettifer's tone had changed; it was no longer pleasantly patronising, but sharp, urgent. "Describe them to me."

"The ones who dressed the same. Sort of flowery dresses. One had a big floppy hat on. I hadn't seen them before."

Pettifer made a mental note to ask Jess about it. She'd know who he meant.

"Oh, and I thought I saw Gavin. Aunt Cassie's secretary. But I don't think I could have done."

Pettifer tried not to blanch at this unwelcome new information.

"Not… Cassandra Lane? The mayor? *She's* your aunt?"

He pictured their erstwhile mayor next to Felicia Grant. The family resemblance was utterly non-existent. Someone must have had an affair with the milkman if those two were supposed to be sisters.

"She's not *really* my aunt," Algernon explained. "I just call her that. She's my godmother, though."

Ah, that made more sense. No milkmen involved, then. Pettifer coughed awkwardly.

"Ah, I see. Go on with what you were saying… Why couldn't you have seen this Gavin?"

"Because Aunt Cassie said that she had a council meeting this afternoon; that's why she wasn't at the sale. So, Gavin couldn't possibly have been there; he would have been at the town hall, working. I must have made a mistake."

His small young face was troubled as he said it; Pettifer

understood that expression well. It was the same one he got when the evidence didn't seem to add up.

"And this was at the same time? You're sure?"

"Yes. I remember, because Betsy had a break between phone bids she was late back. I was starting to worry about it."

Pettifer looked out over the water once more, assimilating this information. He'd got more out of this child in five minutes than they'd managed to extract from a hundred other witnesses over the course of the afternoon. He turned back to the wide-eyed face, which had been watching him patiently.

"What's your name, lad?" He asked quietly.

"Algernon."

Pettifer almost choked on air.

"It's from the sixteenth century with roots in eleventh-century France," Algernon explained loftily, apparently unperturbed by the reaction. "But it's best known from *The Importance of Being Earnest*. By Oscar Wilde," he elaborated, as Pettifer showed no signs of recognition. "Are you familiar with it?"

"I… ah…" Pettifer experienced the same sinking sensation he recalled from school when a teacher had asked him if he'd done his homework. He flailed for a moment, then admitted reluctantly, "no, lad, afraid I'm not really one for novels."

Algernon gave him an innocent look.

"It's a play."

He was rapidly going off this child, Pettifer thought grimly. Good witness or not, he was a precocious little bugger.

"Have I been helpful, Sergeant?" Algernon gazed up at him hopefully. "Do you think this'll help you to crack the case?"

Pettifer hesitated, wondering how to handle this. On the one hand, he didn't want to give the lad ideas; the last thing he needed was him turning amateur detective. But on the other hand, he didn't want to trample all over his curiosity, either. It was probably a healthier response than dwelling on what he'd witnessed today. He looked at the boy, tried to imagine it was his own child, and wondered what he'd do.

"You did the right thing telling me," he said, then, as Algernon's eyes lit up, he continued in a quelling tone, "but a real police investigation isn't like it seems in books. It's hard work and diligence and following up a lot of leads that don't go anywhere. I'll look into what you've told me, but I don't want you to get your hopes up."

"All right," Algernon sighed. Then he reached into his coat pocket. There was a rustle, and he produced a crumpled paper bag, which he thrust under the sergeant's nose.

"Sherbet lemon?"

Slightly wrong-footed by the sudden change of tack, Sergeant Pettifer automatically accepted, even though normally he wouldn't have done. The cloying tartness fizzed on his tongue, and he rolled the sweet around his mouth, clicking it against his teeth. My, but these took him back. He used to eat these by the bag-load when he was a boy. Once upon a time, he would have bit down into it, cleaving it neatly in two, but these days...

Next to him, there was a satisfying crack as Algernon did just that.

"It releases the filling," he explained, catching the sergeant's eye. "You should try it."

"One day, lad, you'll come to realise that you've only got the one set of teeth to see you out," Sergeant Pettifer said dolefully, and a little resentfully.

"Grandad says the same thing," Algernon supplied. "I actually bought these for him, so we'd better stop eating them." The bag disappeared back into his pocket. "I thought he'd need some more, now he can't get them himself. He always has a bag of them on him somewhere. They're kind of like his trademark."

Trademark. The word sent an involuntary tingle up and down the sergeant's spine. It was a sensation he recognised all too well.

It meant that something was clicking into place, something he ought to have seen earlier.

An image swam into his mind, of Felicia Grant, looking down at the body with that lost, perplexed expression, saying, "I didn't recognise him for a moment."

Of course! That was what was wrong, what had been bothering him. He could have slapped himself on the forehead, like a buffoonish detective in a comedy play. He was acting like one; it would be no less that he'd deserve. How could he have missed something so obvious?

"I say, you've got a strange look on your face," Algernon said, eyeing him warily. "You haven't gone and swallowed it whole, have you? I did that once, when I was eight, and I wasn't allowed another boiled sweet for two whole years. Only wine gums and jelly babies."

His tone implied that it had felt like a very long two years.

"No, I'm all right, lad," Sergeant Pettifer said, trying to keep his tone casual. "Just an idea, that's all. I really do need to speak to your mother, though. Any idea where she might be?"

"She's probably come out to look for me." Algernon stood, dusting off his knees. "I have been quite a long time; she doesn't often notice for a while, but when she does she starts thinking all sorts of things might have happened to me. She's quite dramatic," he explained, matter-of-factly. "She doesn't like to think she is, but she is. I'd better come back with you."

Such an assessment of Felicia Grant's parenting style wasn't exactly surprising to Pettifer. Hands-off *and* melodramatic simultaneously? It fitted with the deepening mystery of the woman.

Algernon skipped nimbly over a protruding tree root.

"The house is this way."

Pettifer caught up with him, peeling aside the frondy drapery of the willow to form a doorway. They both stopped, looking at the framed scene that greeted them on the other side. Jack Riding was standing there on the riverbank, looking straight at them. And there, in his arms…

"Is that…" Pettifer managed, out of the side of his mouth. "Your mother?"

"Yes." Algernon sounded more weary than surprised. "I'm afraid so."

Chapter Nine

F or about half a second, Felicia was too stunned to react. The only other time she'd ever been held like this was by Dexter, when he'd carried her over the threshold after their honeymoon. It had not been a wholesale success. She'd had a lump on the back of her head for three days afterwards. Jack, she had to say, felt more reassuringly capable, but nevertheless, having her feet dangling in mid-air made her feel out of control, faintly panicked.

Then she looked up, and saw Algernon and Sergeant Pettifer staring at them from amongst the trees. To say that her heart sank would be an understatement.

"Put me down," she managed, in a strangled voice. Then, realising how ungracious she sounded, "*please*."

"As you wish." He deftly deposited her on the safety of the path.

"Thank you." She smoothed a hand over her hair, trying to regain some composure. "Good evening, Sergeant," she called pleasantly at the encroaching figure striding across the bank towards them, shapeless suit jacket billowing around him like a fractious bat. Despite his shambolic presence, the expression on his face was anything but comical. He looked grim, determined. Felicia swallowed. This couldn't be good.

"Ms Grant," he boomed, stepping over a gaggle of ducks with surprising deftness for a man of his build. "We need to talk. You haven't been entirely honest with me."

"Interesting as this sounds," Jack murmured in her ear. She started slightly; for a moment, she'd forgotten he was even there. "You'll have to excuse me. I've rather had enough of the police for one day."

She felt rather than heard him slip away, blending soundlessly into the twilight. She began to turn, perplexed, but Sergeant Pettifer was in front of her now, wheezing alarmingly from his short trudge across the grass.

"Ms Grant?" He probed. "We can do this here or at the station. Your choice."

"Yes, yes, all right," she said crisply, absorbing some of his irritation. "But come inside, won't you? Neither of us wants to see the finer details of your investigation all over town tomorrow."

But either he didn't hear her, or he chose to ignore it. He was looking with interest at a spot over her shoulder.

"Where's your friend gone to?"

"He is *not* my friend," she said indignantly, darting a nervous glance towards Algernon. "We've only just met."

Pettifer raised an unruly brow.

"That's how you greet people down your way, is it?"

"Algie, why don't you go on in?" She said, over-brightly. "I'll be there in a minute."

She hustled him away, waiting until his small form had disappeared through the front door of the cottage before turning to Pettifer, arms folded militantly.

"If you must know, this *is* my way. I grew up right here in Stamford."

"St George's Square?" He named one of the most opulent addresses in town. "Barn Hill?"

"Right here, actually," she said blandly, nodding towards the Lilliputian cottage behind them.

"What… a whole family?" Pettifer struggled to his astonishment.

"All four of us, yes. Plus two cats, a hamster, a three-legged rabbit and a tank full of stick insects." She threw him a glance of restrained amusement. "What, not what you were expecting, Sergeant? You of all people should know that appearances can be deceptive. This accent was bought at a price, sometimes one my parents struggled to pay. My growth was powered by a lot of cottage cheese and corned beef. Sometimes together." She tried to repress a retrospective shudder. "The lasagne was particularly memorable. So you see, whatever you think you know about me, you can forget it." She shrugged. "Dexter's the one with real breeding. I'm just a pretender."

To his credit, his expression didn't change. His slab-like face remained immovable.

"Can't be a lot worse than spam stuffed marrow," he said mildly. "We had that a lot when I was a kid, when my dad was between jobs."

It was an admission of apology, strangely cloaked, but she recognised it nonetheless. She felt herself softening slightly.

"What exactly was it you wanted to talk to me about?"

The atmosphere abruptly changed. The look he gave her was sharp as he remarked, "you said you never saw Mr Clay at the auction."

"That's correct."

"Is it?"

She frowned, not liking the implication in his tone.

"As far as I'm aware, yes, but you saw how many people were there—the room was packed when you arrived, and that was just those who'd stayed on until the end. There were people coming and going all day." She sighed, deciding that it was time to nip this in the bud. "Look, I know you want me to be a key witness, but the truth is, when I'm on the rostrum, it's just a sea of faces most of the time. It's rare that I notice anyone in particular. I don't know, maybe if he'd been—" She broke off, cursing herself for saying too much.

"If he'd been wearing his pink suit?" Sergeant Pettifer's voice was concerningly casual. She got the sense that this was a trap she'd walked neatly into. "Yes, it's funny about that. Everyone was so used to seeing him in it; it seemed part of his character. So larger than life. But out of it... well, he looked totally different. Almost unprepossessing. The sort of man you wouldn't notice if you passed him in the street." He gave her a searching look. "Must have been useful to be able to just switch his whole persona on like that... or off, for that matter."

Now, Felicia was starting to feel a prickle of real annoyance.

"What are you trying to say, exactly?"

"Nothing." His response was airy. "Nothing at all. Just that he clearly didn't want to be recognised, did he? Little bit of corporate espionage, perhaps? Or maybe he was planning to cause trouble at the sale?"

"You're looking at me like I ought to know," Felicia snapped. He was starting to make her feel flustered. This sudden, attacking style of interrogation was completely throwing her. She was beginning to realise how complacent she'd been, assuming that his non-threatening demeanour was the whole picture. This man wasn't the fool he made himself out to be. Nor was he slack at his job. It was only just beginning to dawn on her that he might actually be a far better detective than she'd given him credit for. "But may I remind you that I only arrived this morning?"

"Another interesting fact," Pettifer shoved his hands in his pockets of his shabby suit, one fist going straight through the bottom with a ripping sound. He valiantly ignored it, continuing, "tell me, Ms Grant, what exactly was your professional relationship like with the victim?"

"You mean my *father's* relationship. I don't work at Grant's any more, remember?"

"It's still your name above the door though, isn't it? You can't tell me that you have no interest in the place."

She opened her mouth to say something—she wasn't even sure what, exactly—but in any event decided against it. Apparently taking that as an assent, Pettifer pressed on.

"Well? And I'd recommend your being honest with me. I can find all of this out for myself, but it'll save a lot of time if you co-operate with me now."

She pressed a hand to her forehead, suddenly feeling engulfed by weariness.

"He was a competitor, Sergeant. All businesses have them."

"Yes, but were you on cordial terms?"

She gave a small smile at that.

"This is the antiques world. It's *all* very genteel and cordial… on the surface, at least." At his disbelieving look, she added, "all right, so there's a fair bit of rivalry between the lower-end dealers, but it's hardly what you'd call cutthroat. Besides, we're not talking about dealers here; we're talking about auctioneers. It's a totally different picture. The vast majority of them are old public school boys, for one thing. It's actually rather an exclusive club."

There was a twist of her lips as she said it. Pettifer watched her carefully, then asked an instinctive question.

"How many women auctioneers are there? Just out of interest."

"Not many," she admitted. "More than there used to be. It's getting better. When I began, I was one of only a handful in the country."

"Must have been a difficult way up," he observed softly.

"It had its moments." A small v-shaped crease appeared between her eyebrows. She looked at him, as though suddenly suspicious of the more sympathetic approach. He couldn't blame her for that; it had perhaps been underhand, to unleash such a grilling on her like that, but it had been necessary. He knew more where he stood with her now. Ultimately, the progress of the investigation had to come above her delicate sensibilities. "Look, Sergeant, if it's honesty you want, I'll happily give it to you. Barrington wasn't a popular figure in the industry. He put a lot of people's noses out of joint. There are certain subtle boundaries, codes of conduct all auction houses tacitly agree to. Barrington had a tendency to not only overstep them, but bulldoze them to the ground."

"In what way?" He was careful to ask more gently; he wanted to get her back on side now.

"Encroaching onto other auction houses' patches was the worst. Advertising in their local press, holding valuation days in town. He did them all the time when I was running Grant's, and he never so much as had courtesy to inform us. The first we'd know of it was the poster." She sighed. "All rather bad form, and somewhat vexing, but hardly a motive for killing the man, it that's what you're trying to not-so-subtly imply. Especially considering that I haven't even been involved in the antiques world for over eight years. It would have been a long time to wait for my revenge, don't you think?"

Plus I was up on the rostrum the whole time. It didn't need to be said; they both knew it. There was no way she could have done it… not on her own, at any rate.

"What is it you do now, exactly?" He asked, ignoring the last, rather sarcastic part of her speech.

"I manage an exclusive contemporary art gallery in London. We sell one-off works to private clients all over the world." It was rattled off so pat, it must have come straight out of a marketing leaflet.

"You travel a lot, then?"

She shook her head, jawline tightening.

"Not any more. I did, once. But then Dexter got his break in television and… well, we couldn't both be absent. Our son deserves at least one of us around."

"Do you enjoy it?"

She looked startled at the question, as though it had been shouted at her, when in reality, it had been spoken very quietly.

"What?"

"Do you *enjoy* it?" He reiterated. "Selling modern art?"

Her eyes, almost colourless in the dark, widened.

"It's… well…" She shook her head, exhaling frustratedly. When she spoke again, her voice was clipped: "Look. Was. That everything? Only, it's been rather a long day."

"Not quite, I'm afraid." In truth, he'd have loved to have let her go. She was right; it had been one hell of a day… for both of them. But duty called, and he had one more ace to play tonight. "It's come to our attention that your father was the one who ordered the last-minute inclusion of the wardrobe into the sale. Were you aware of that?"

Genuine surprise flickered across her face.

"No. I assumed it was Hugo. He can be soft-hearted like that; the dealers know how to play him. Dad would always say no to that sort of thing."

"Well, he made an exception this time. We have it from Mr Dappleton that your father rang him late last night asking him to oversee the unloading of it."

Her eyebrows raised.

"I'm going to need to speak to your father," Pettifer said gently. "I trust that he's well enough to talk?"

She cast him a sardonic glance.

"Oh, yes."

Something about her amusement sent a tremor of trepidation through Pettifer.

She inclined her head towards the cottage, a ghost of a smile playing across her lips.

"I'll take you to him."

"The man was a shark," grunted Peter.

"Dad!" Felicia admonished. "He's just been murdered."

"Well then he's unlikely to change his ways now," Peter retorted. "I'd say there'll be a lot of relief now he's dead."

Felicia caught Sergeant Pettifer's eye.

"He doesn't mean that," she said quickly. "He's still on quite a bit of pain medication."

"Of course I mean it!" Peter spluttered. "I don't hold truck with any of this nonsense about not speaking ill of the dead. What's the point in that? Besides, the Sergeant here wants to find his killer, doesn't he? And it's not going to make his job any easier if we're all sugar-coating the truth. He wants facts, not platitudes."

Sergeant Pettifer looked at him with a new kind of respect.

"To tell you the truth, sir, sometimes I wish more people would take your view."

Peter gave Felicia a triumphant, I-told-you-so look. She threw up her hands in surrender and went to fill the kettle. It seemed they were going to be here for a while.

"Barrington didn't come from much," Peter began, gesturing for Pettifer to take a seat. "He had to build what he'd got brick by brick. It gave him a hard edge, but I could understand that. I came by the same route myself; I know what it's like. You do what you have to do to survive, to prove them all wrong." He cast a pointed glance in Felicia's direction. "You have to have been through it to know; many times we've fallen out about what Felicia here calls my methods, but at least I can say that I've always been honest. I never hurt anyone, never swindled them, never trod on anyone on my way up. Barrington, suffice to say, was not of the same view. He upset many people along the way."

Pettifer leaned forwards. There was a gleam in his eyes, a light of interest.

"Are you saying that he cheated people?"

"I'm saying that there were a lot of coincidences which went his way. Dealers suddenly moving their allegiance, consignments which had been promised to another auction house diverted to his at the last minute. He was a megalomaniac; his reach was spreading by the year. More than once, a rival auction house which was occupying the patch he wanted mysteriously floundered and either closed completely or agreed to sell to him. I tried to talk to a couple of them about it afterwards; I knew the owners, knew they'd had no intention of giving up, but they wouldn't tell me what had changed. But there was something wrong in it, I could tell. He'd done something to force their hand."

"And was he interested in acquiring Grant's?"

Peter threw back his head and gave a booming laugh. Even Godfrey, who'd wound himself into a tight ball in the fruit bowl, looked up accusingly.

"Was he ever! He'd wanted Stamford since the year dot; drove him crazy that I'd got here first."

"Couldn't he have just set up here if he'd wanted to?"

"In a town this size?" Peter shook his head. "We'd have obliterated each other. He wasn't stupid; he knew it was all or nothing."

"And he never approached you about selling? Never tried to… uh… force your hand?"

"He wouldn't *dare*!" Peter snapped, apparently insulted at the mere suggestion. "He knows where I'd have told him to stick—"

"Tea, sergeant?" Felicia interjected desperately, plonking the chipped earthenware pot on the checked tablecloth in front of him. For a man who spent his life amongst fine antiques, it was a wonder so few of them seemed to make it into her father's own home, which instead fell securely into the serviceable time-warp category. It was like the seventies had never left.

Perhaps that was one of the main problems they'd had when running the business together, she brooded, as tea gushed sporadically from the repaired spout into the sergeant's cup. She genuinely loved beautiful things; her home in London was filled with treasures she'd collected over the years. A 17th-century four-poster bed she'd spent almost two months' wages on. A bronze lion she'd picked up in a market in southern France on her honeymoon with Dexter. A pair of fondant-hued Aesthetic-period paintings of Grecian women lolling on marble seats, bought back when such things were going for pennies. Their value had skyrocketed since then, but she couldn't bear to part with them. She couldn't part with any of it. It all meant something to her, far beyond material value. These things had a past; they had history. They had been loved and unloved, admired and ignored, collected and discarded. They'd seen things, absorbed the essence of the past. That enchanted her in a way that her father could never really understand. He liked antiques, esteemed them, and was certainly very knowledgeable about them, but it was ultimately a business for him. He'd gone into antiques because, at the time, the market was booming. He'd learned about them by osmosis, by necessity, as he went along. She sensed that it would have been the same with anything else he'd chosen.

Sergeant Pettifer discreetly watched her as she poured out the tea. Her expression was serene, as usual, her hand steady, but there was something of a tightness about the jaw that hinted at a certain tension—although, to be fair, that was nothing that couldn't be easily explained away by the presence of her father, Pettifer acceded, looking across at the man in question now. The accent sourced back to North Lincolnshire, maybe even not far from the border of his own native Yorkshire. Blunt to the point of awkwardness, as people from that part of the world could be. He could see why he might ruffle the feathers of some down here in softly-spoken Middle England, but Pettifer, a man who spoke his language, saw past the bluster. A self-made businessman, still a little rough around the edges, but no tyrant. All the same, it was clear why he would never see eye-to-eye with his daughter, with her cut-glass accent, her well-educated sense of poise and polish.

Pettifer didn't doubt that Peter Grant had had only the noblest of intentions when he'd scrimped to send his daughter to one of the country's most elite schools, but in doing so, he had created a huge chasm between them. They were literally from two different worlds.

"There is something else I need to ask you about, sir." Pettifer paused to take a slurp of his tea, calculating how best to approach this. Cautiously, he decided. Respectfully. Like it was no serious matter. Any hint of accusation, and Peter Grant would go on the attack. That was just his type. "A small matter to be cleared up, is all. I'm given to understand that the wardrobe in which the deceased was found only arrived at the auction late last night, under your instructions. Is that correct?"

"It is." Peter Grant eyed him over the rim of his cup. A certain wariness had crept into his tone. "No law against that, is there?"

"Of course not," Pettifer said jovially. "We'd just like to understand a bit more about the circumstances, that's all. For background," he added.

"Ah, well," Peter leaned back in his wheelchair. "It was a favour, you see. Old acquaintance of mine. Well, my father's, actually. The man's ninety-five if he's a day, but he's a good customer. Didn't feel I could say no when he asked, even if it was a bit irregular." He sighed. "But then, old Batty himself was always a bit irregular. I learned a long time ago not to question his whims."

Sergeant Pettifer looked up from his notes, incredulity etched onto his face.

"Did you say his name was Batty?"

"Not his real name, of course. No one ever called him Batty to his face. Name's Henry. Henry Bunting. Lives up on Barn Hill. Halliday House, it's called. Big, dilapidated old place with a carriage arch going through it."

Pettifer nodded.

"I know it."

It was one of the biggest mansions in town, in one of the best locations. Once, it would probably have been one of the most impressively opulent houses, too, but the years hadn't been kind to it. Unlike its neighbours, which had all been lovingly and expensively maintained and restored over the years, it had been essentially left to fall down.

"One of your officers will already have spoken to him," Peter continued. "He said he would be at the sale today. Seemed very keen to watch the thing go under the hammer."

"Any particular reason for that?"

Peter shrugged.

"People like watching auctions. They find them exciting. You'd be surprised how many people travel long distances to watch their stuff sell."

"He's a nice old man," Felicia added. "Like Dad said, a bit eccentric. Almost a recluse, really. There weren't many things he'd leave the house for, but the auction was one of them." She frowned at her father. "Having said that, I don't remember seeing him at all. Are you sure he said he'd be there?"

"He was adamant about it. You must have just missed him."

A keen look had sharpened the lines of Pettifer's face. He punched a key on his phone, holding it up to his ear with a murmured, "excuse me for a moment." His square form squeezed through the narrow doorway into the shadowed hall.

Peter watched him go.

"What's bitten him? Something we said?"

"He thinks he's got a new suspect to add to his list," Felicia replied tartly. "He's probably indulging in visions of old Mr Bunting stabbing a blade through his own wardrobe in a frenzied attack of post-consignment regret."

Peter started.

"Surely you don't think he seriously suspects—"

"He suspects all of us, Dad," Felicia said sharply. "Why else do you think he's here?"

"All right, all?" Dexter sauntered in, opening the fridge and peering hopefully inside. "Thought I'd stay out of the way until the coast was clear. Algie says that police sergeant was around here a while ago. The one who looks like a prop forward."

"I *was* a prop forward," Sergeant Pettifer said genially, from the doorway. "Until a sixteen stone lad from Barnsley landed on my neck." He tugged aside his collar to reveal a livid red scar. "Rather put paid to my hopes of making it professionally. I don't take it too hard, though; the police has its moments, even if not quite the same glamour. Or the pay," he added, dryly.

"Oh." Dexter craned around the fridge door, looking as sheepish as it was possible for Dexter to look. "Didn't see you there, Sergeant."

Pettifer looked squarely at Felicia and Peter.

"According to my constable, there was no Henry Bunting amongst the witnesses."

He seemed a little deflated by the news. Felicia tried not to feel too amused. Peter, on the other hand, appeared discomfited.

"Well, that's very odd, I must say." And then, almost more to himself than anyone else, "Batty's old school, a man of his word. I can't imagine why he'd—"

The rest of what he'd been about to say was lost forever. Because, for the second time that day, and with a suddenness that made them all jump, everything descended into chaos.

Chapter Ten

With a tremendous force, the front door exploded open, crashing against the wall as a hurricane swept inside the house, trailing bags, files, and a flapping scarf in its wake.

"Felicia?" The hurricane identified itself as female in strident, albeit panicked-sounding tones. "Are you here?"

"Cass?" Palpably confused, Felicia stepped forward, only to be rugby tackled by a billowing coat.

"You're alive," the coat gasped. "Oh God, you're *alive*!"

"Of course I'm alive," Felicia managed, all but disappeared beneath the voluminous material. "Although you're about to suffocate me."

"Sorry." The coat unwound itself from around her. An arm reached up and pulled back the hood, revealing a tangled mop of blonde curls. With this reference point to go on, the details became somewhat clearer to Sergeant Pettifer. What had seemed like an autonomous mass of clothing now took on a more logical form. A woman encased in a long black puffer coat. And not just any woman; Pettifer would know that head of hair anywhere.

"Mayor Lane," he boomed. "Care to tell me what's going on?"

She turned, her freckled face registering shock, then, following swiftly on, anger.

"I don't know," she put her hands on her hips. "Perhaps *you'd* care to tell *me* what's going on, Sergeant? Perhaps *you'd* care to tell me why I had to hear from my secretary that there'd been a murder at the auction house? Perhaps you'd care to tell *me* why, when I rushed over there, the officious oik on the door wouldn't give me any information? Even when I told him that the rumour in town was that the victim was an auctioneer, and that my best friend is an auctioneer?"

Pettifer bit back a groan. He'd have to be having words with someone later.

"Must have been one of the backups from the county force. I'm sorry, Madam Mayor, that shouldn't have happened."

She sniffed, turning to Felicia.

"And *then* I remembered about your father in hospital, so I raced over there, only to find that he'd been discharged. I didn't know what else to do, so I came here, and..." she raised a hand to her forehead, reaching for the back of a chair.

"Sit down, Cass," Felicia pulled out a chair. "You've had a shock. Dad, have you got any brandy in the house?"

"Not unless your mother left any of her cooking brandy in the cupboards when she left. Only thing the stuff's good for."

"Sherry, then?"

Peter looked appalled at the suggestion.

"*Sherry?*" He spluttered. "What kind of man do you think I am?"

Felicia glared at him until he grumbled, "there's some single malt in the living room. On the sideboard," he added, as Dexter leapt into service.

Pettifer waited patiently while a glass was pressed into Cassie's hand. She knocked it back in one go, the colour swiftly returning to her cheeks. Her gaze moved from Felicia to Pettifer, turning from concerned to interrogative in a moment. Despite himself, Pettifer tried not to flinch. He'd heard that their innocuously benign-looking mayor had a stare to freeze the blood in your veins, but he'd not personally been on the receiving end of it before. Suppressing a gulp, he tried to focus on the fact that she had odd earrings on instead. It made her seem fractionally less intimidating.

"So if it wasn't Felicia, who *was* it?" Cassie demanded. "What are the facts?"

"I don't have all of them yet," Pettifer demurred, declining the urge to add, officiously, "and it'll be none of your business when I do." The mayor seemed to have forgotten the ceremonial nature of her role temporarily, but it was something he could forgive; after all, she had spent the afternoon believing that it was her friend who'd been murdered, a misapprehension apparently not corrected by the police at the scene. He couldn't exactly blame her for being angry.

And so he wasn't surprised to discover that she wasn't about to be put aside that easily.

"What *do* you have, then? Surely you must have got *some*where?"

"It was Barrington," Felicia spoke up quietly.

"Barrington Clay?" Cassie spluttered incredulously. "At your auction? I'm amazed he dared show his face."

"He didn't," Dexter supplied, pouring himself a glass of whisky. "He was hiding in a wardrobe."

Cassie stared at him. Her eyes seemed to be struggling to focus.

"He was *what*?"

"Why do you say he wouldn't dare show his face, Madam Mayor?" Pettifer asked idly.

Felicia darted him a wary look.

"Just a figure of speech, I think."

"Oh, come off it, Fliss, you hated him." Cassie waved her glass expansively, almost sloshing amber-coloured liquid across the scrubbed pine table. "He said you were... what *was* it he said? Too *decorative* to be an auctioneer? That was it."

The colour was rising in her cheeks, lending them a rosy glow.

"That was a long time ago," Felicia said stiffly. "Back when I first started auctioneering. I was only twenty-three. And I *think*," she prised the glass gently from Cassie's hand. "You might have had enough steadying of the nerves for the time being. I'll make you some coffee instead."

Before you say anything else damning, was the silent addendum that only Pettifer heard. Despite himself, he was starting to feel a little sorry for Felicia Grant. She was doing her best to be cool-headed and circumspect, only for everyone around her to cheerfully throw out incriminating statements left, right and centre.

"Perhaps, Sergeant, we could do this tomorrow? It's been something of a day. For *all* of us," she added, with feeling.

Pettifer hesitated, then nodded.

"All right. I can see the sense in that. I trust you're not planning to go anywhere in the meantime?"

"You and Algie will stay here," Peter grunted. "There's the spare room. Twin beds, but it'll do for a night or two."

"And you, sir?" Pettifer turned a gimlet eye on Dexter Grant, who was propped against the cabinets, tinkling the ice in his glass. "You won't be haring off back to London?"

Dexter gave him a level look. For a moment, Pettifer had the fleeting impression that he wasn't quite as cavalierly empty-headed as he appeared to be.

"Is that a question or an order?"

"It's a request," Pettifer replied. "Let's leave it at that."

"Dad?" Algernon appeared in the doorway, face hopeful. "You're staying?"

"So it appears." Dexter looked at Felicia. "I can take a room at The George. I'll walk up now, see what they've got."

Algernon's face fell in disapprobation.

"You're not going to stay here with us?" He looked at his mother appealing. "Tell him, Mum. Tell him he can stay here. I'll sleep on the sofa; I don't mind."

Pettifer noted that Dexter looked far more amenable to the idea of sharing a room with his ex-wife than she did. One glance at her stony expression, however, and he coughed, rearranging his features.

"I'm not sure it's the best idea, Algie," he said gently. "Look, I'll come over to see you in the morning, take you out for breakfast. How does that sound?"

"Oh, let the man stay here, Felicia," Peter spoke irritably from the corner. "It's only for a night. Looks like I'll be camped out on the sofa bed down here for the foreseeable, anyway," he gestured to his plaster cast. "You'll share with the boy, mind," he added, quellingly, to his son-in-law. "And Felicia will take my room. I won't have any funny business under my roof. Even if you were once married, you're not now."

"Dad!" Felicia squawked, as Dexter choked on his drink. Behind her, Cassie covered her mouth to hide a grin.

Algernon was either blissfully unaware of any innuendo, or too pleased with the result to care. He'd moved to his father's side, looking up at him in adoration.

"Well, we seem to have come to an arrangement, at least," Felicia managed. "Does that satisfy you, Sergeant?"

"Perfectly." Pettifer checked his watch. "I'll leave you to it. I'll be back here in the morning, ten o'clock sharp. We'll conclude my questions then."

"I'll see you out," Felicia offered, following him to the doorway.

He paused beneath the lintel and turned, looking over her shoulder as though to check that none of the others in the kitchen were listening. When he spoke, his voice was little more than a low, conspiratorial rumble.

"Listen, it's not my place to say anything, but that new friend of yours, out on the riverbank just now?" he held up a hand to silence her as she opened her mouth to protest. "Listen… he's not…" he hefted a sigh, dropping his voice even lower. "Just be careful. That's all I'll say."

"That sounded ominous," Cassie observed, as the policeman departed, making an inordinate amount of noise in the hall as he went. For a heart-stopping moment, Felicia thought she'd overheard Pettifer's allusion to Jack, but then Cassie expanded, "about how he'd be back tomorrow with more questions? He doesn't think you're actually involved, does he?"

"Unfortunately, I think he does." Felicia busied herself with the cafetière, trying not to obsess about what that oblique warning might have meant. She could think about it later, when her head wasn't so clouded with exhaustion.

"And I told him that you hated Barrington!" Cassie's hand flew to her mouth, eyes widening in horror. "Oh, God, I'm *so* sorry. It's the first proper drink I've had since I stopped breastfeeding, and it just went…" she made an upwards whooshing motion. "Straight to my head. I'll never forgive myself."

"Cass, it's fine." Once Cassie started talking, often it was hard to stop her. Felicia did so in this case by plonking a cup of coffee firmly on the table in front of her. "I was on the rostrum the entire time, so I couldn't have done it myself. And I think he'll have a hard time proving that I was embroiled in some complex scheme which involved me luring Barrington into a cupboard in my own auction and arranging to have him bumped off while the sale was going on."

"You think he was in there voluntarily, then?"

Felicia stopped, sugar bowl in hand.

"What do you mean?"

"Well, as in, you think he got in there of his own accord? No one, say, shut him inside against his will?"

"I think that's unlikely. The cupboard wasn't locked; he could easily have got out if he'd wanted to. Besides, even if he couldn't, surely he would have made a sound; banged on the doors, called for help, that sort of thing."

"Maybe he was too afraid to." Cassie stirred her coffee with an excitable whisking motion, eyes alight with possibilities. "Maybe he was hiding from someone. Or maybe he was paralysed in there. Someone injected him with something before the sale, then…"

"Algernon, why don't you help your father make up the sofa for Grandad tonight?" Felicia interrupted loudly, funnelling them out of the room. Pushing the door to behind them, she gave Cassie a despairing look. "Cass! The last thing he needs after today is a load of gruesome conspiracy theories put into his head. He's probably traumatised enough as it is."

Somewhat to her chagrin, both Cassie and Peter started laughing.

"Traumatised my foot!" Wheezed Peter. "Does the lad look traumatised to you?"

"He's twelve years old, Fliss," Cassie explained, not unkindly. "He probably thinks it's the most exciting thing ever to have happened to him."

"Probably desperate to tell all his friends about it," Peter said fondly. "If it weren't for the excitement of his father being here, he'd be glued to his phone right now. You'd be lucky to get a word out of him all night."

Felicia whirled on him.

"Yes, and while we're on that subject, what were you *thinking*? Surely, you can't want Dexter here any more than I do."

Peter gave one of his patented harrumphs.

"I might be no fan of the man—can't see why you couldn't have married someone more sensible myself—but he *is* the boy's father, and they haven't seen each other properly in weeks. Give him a break, duck. For Algie's sake, we'll all just have to rub along."

Cassie raised her eyebrows over the rim of her cup.

"Should be interesting."

And for once, Felicia was inclined to agree.

Chapter Eleven

"**I**'m worried about Batty."

Felicia put the last of the pudding bowls into the dishwasher and straightened up with a sense of resignation. She'd known that there was something on her father's mind all throughout dinner; he'd been conspicuously quiet, toyed with the food on his plate—both very uncharacteristic acts. Perhaps if it had been her who'd done the cooking she might have been able to explain it away better—she was from the school of not being able to boil an egg—but Dexter had pronounced himself in charge, much to everyone's relief. If there was one thing she really missed about her ex-husband, it was the food, Felicia thought dreamily. Tonight, he'd made a chicken recipe he'd picked up whilst filming in Spain; baked in a casserole dish with rice, chorizo and orange slices, it had been almost enough to make her rethink her marriage.

With an effort, she pulled her mind back to the present issue.

"Because he wasn't at the auction? Dad, he's *old*. He probably just forgot."

"Since last night?" Peter said derisively. "He's not senile.

Besides, Batty never misses an appointment. Like clockwork, he is." He shook his head. "Something's wrong, I'm sure of it."

Felicia sighed inwardly.

"It's no good; I'm going to have to ask... why do you call him Batty?"

"Because he killed someone once." Algernon piped up from the doorway. Felicia and Peter both started in surprise.

"I thought you were in your room?" Felicia said, slightly accusingly. Honestly, how was she supposed to protect her son from adult conversations when he insisted upon creeping about the place so stealthily?

Following in the long-held tradition of teenage children, Algernon ignored his mother's question entirely. Instead, he just repeated, eagerly, "he *did*, he killed someone. Grandad told me all about it."

Peter shifted uneasily in his chair as Felicia turned an exasperated look on him.

"Well, look now, the boy's not a child any more!" He blustered. "He's old enough to hear about something which happened long ago. Besides," he reminded Algernon sternly, "I never said that he *actually* killed anyone; just that some folk got it into their heads that he did." He sighed heftily. "The police were content that the governess simply tripped and fell down the stairs; I don't know when the rumours started. Batty was a strapping lad of thirteen then; some people started suggesting that he'd never liked the governess, that he'd wanted a tutor instead, like other lads of his age. He thought it was embarrassing, being taught by a woman. But he was due to go away to Eton that autumn anyway!" Peter thumped his fist indignantly on the arm of the chair. "She would have been gone within months. There would have been no point..." he sat back in his chair with a creak. "The great irony is that he never did go away in the end. Illness, apparently. Consumption. He's been an invalid in that house ever since." He shook his head. "I don't know, it was all way before my time; way before anyone's time now, I'd wager. It was my father who told me the story. For my part, I can't believe it. Batty always seemed like such a gentle soul to me..." he broke off, looking shamefaced. "I suppose I oughtn't call him that... Batty... it was the name folk around here gave him afterwards, and it sort of stuck."

Felicia brought the old man to mind. It had been some years since she'd last seen him, but what she did recall was a softly spoken gentleman, filled with old courtly charm. Her father was right; it was hard to imagine anyone less threatening.

As though responding to her thoughts, Peter stirred suddenly, coming to a decision.

"I think I'll just nip over there, check everything's all right. It's just so unlike the old boy to break his word."

"Dad, no." Felicia put a hand on the armrest. "Look, it's dark, you're not used to this chair. Why not check in the morning?"

His florid face set in stubborn lines.

"It's no good, duck. I won't be able to rest thinking about it."

Felicia was experienced enough in dealing with her father to know when not to argue. When he got brooding on something, there was no satisfying him until action had been taken. So instead, she reached for her shoes, wincing as she eased her protesting feet into the sharp gradient.

"*I'll* go, then. How about that?"

"All right. But you're to take that husband of yours with you," he added firmly. "I won't have you wandering around after dark with some rampaging murderer on the loose."

"That's a bit dramatic, Dad, don't you think?" She caught herself about to say, "it's only been *one* murder" and wondered slightly hysterically how far her parameters must have shifted in the course of the afternoon. "But I'll take Dexter, if it makes you happier."

Peter huffed.

"Can't exactly say it does. Man's about as much good as a

chocolate teapot, if you ask me. But I suppose he's better than nothing."

And with that ringing endorsement, Felicia went to find her escort.

———

"It's a bit spooky, isn't it?" Dexter gazed up at the crumbling façade of Halliday House dubiously.

Felicia folded her arms across her body and shivered in the chill night air.

"Just knock on the door, and let's get this over with."

"There's no reason to get snippy just because you've got the wrong shoes on." He lifted the heavy lion's head knocker and let it fall. The sound could be heard reverberating within the cavernous interior. "The old codger's probably in bed by now; I doubt he'll be too pleased to be woken up over some wild goose chase."

"You can be the one to tell my dad that when we get back."

Dexter grimaced.

"I think not. He's not keen on me at the best of times." He cast her an accusing stare over his shoulder. "God only knows what you told him about the divorce."

"I didn't tell him anything," she retorted. "Whatever impression he's got of you, you gave it to him yourself." She stepped back and craned her neck to look up at the house, searching for signs of life behind the shuttered, crumbling windows. The street known as Barn Hill was a narrow, steeply cobbled incline lined with grand houses; it wound up away from the town's main intersection of All Saint's Place and Red Lion Square, shielded from both by the ancient stone walls of the church from which the Place took its name. It created a strange juxtaposition; up here, all was silent, empty, the only illumination provided by lines of soft lemon light peeking between the joins of the wooden window screens. Whereas, just down below, she could glimpse the red brake lights of cars, hear the laughter as people spilled out of the pubs, enveloped in the warm amber glow of Victorian streetlamps. Two different worlds, all within mere feet of one another. "And I hate to break it to you, but he never liked you much from the start. He always thought you were on the flamboyant side. A flâneur."

"Ponce" was actually the word that was used, but Felicia had decided on a tactful edit. After all, she wasn't cruel.

As it was, she probably went too far in the opposite direction, because Dexter looked rather flattered.

"A flâneur?" He stroked his chin. "I've never seen myself that way before… but, yes, I can see how he might draw the comparison. After all, some of our finest artists and thinkers…"

"Yes, well," Felicia said, hastily, reaching around him to bang on the door again before he could get too carried away with the idea. "He's not answering. Do you think we should try and get round the back?" She pointed to the carriage arch, which gaped in the centre of the stone façade. "There's a driveway in there. There'll be a side door somewhere. He might not even use this front part of the house any more."

Dexter looked startled.

"Surely you're not expecting me to go in there?"

She raised a brow.

"What, the buccaneering Dr Grant, too scared to go into an old house? Whatever *would* your fans think? Next they'll find out that you stay in a plush hotel when you're filming instead of camping out like you pretend to."

He scowled.

"I *told* you, it's to do with permits—"

"Hmm," with a smile, Felicia swept through the archway before he could continue to protest. "So you say. In every country you visit, too. Amazing, that."

"Yes, well," he muttered, trailing after her. "This modern world. Bureaucracy's gone wild."

If possible, the back of the house was in an even sorrier state than the front. A straggly wisteria, once no doubt resplendent, draped forlornly over the grimy windows. Dilapidated-looking stables sat to the rear of the courtyard, doors rotting off their hinges. Beyond the back wall of the house, an overgrown terrace was visible, together with the languid slope of what promised to be extensive lawns.

"God, this would be an amazing project," Dexter whistled, gazing around him wondrously, all trepidation apparently forgotten. "I bet there are people itching to get their hands on this."

"Just about every developer in town, I'd wager," Felicia responded dryly.

And probably quite a few individual buyers, too. Fixer-uppers were in perilously short supply in the centre, especially on a street like this one, where every other property had been done up to the nines. It stood out like a thorn amongst roses.

Then again, Felicia thought, as the glass in the side door shivered in its frame at her tentative knock, to call it a fixer-upper was something of an understatement. It was more of a full-scale restoration that this place needed, probably amounting to millions. Not a job for the faint-hearted, or for the shallow of pocket.

More out of impulse than any rational thought, Felicia moved her arm down and tried the handle. With a click, the door creaked open. She looked over her shoulder at Dexter, who merely shrugged at the query in her eyes.

"Well, we've come this far."

With no small amount of trepidation, Felicia stepped softly over the threshold, picking her way across the threadbare rug. Gaping holes in the fabric revealed the flagstones beneath, worn to a pebble-like lustre by centuries of footsteps.

Inside, the house was silent, frigid; Felicia could see her breath gathering in faint clouds in front of her face. She looked around, eyes adjusting to the gloom. It seemed her initial assumption had been correct; while once this would have been part of the servants' quarters, the room was clearly now being used as a makeshift kitchen, albeit one bizarrely stuffed with priceless antiques. They'd obviously been moved down from the upstairs apartments, where they'd been designed as opulent display items; now, they were being used like any other practical piece of furniture. It was hard to look at for an auctioneer, so Felicia tried not to. Instead, she moved through the narrow doorway into what proved an even narrower passage, craning her neck to see up the steep servants' staircase. For the briefest of moments, an image swam before her eyes, startlingly vivid in the gloom. A dark-clothed figure, sprawled on the floor at the foot of the stairs, submerged in a black pool of skirts and blood. She shivered, trying to push the image aside. She was being ridiculous; there were no ghosts here, just shadows, the same as any other old house.

"You know, if you creep around like that, you're likely going to scare the living daylights out of him," Dexter's voice behind her made her start. "He'll think we're burglars. Far better to crash about a bit, let him know we're here." He raised a hand to cup his mouth and bellowed, "Mr Bunting! Are you here?"

"Dexter!" Ears ringing, Felicia leapt backwards with a scowl. "You'll give the man a heart attack." A thought struck her. "What if he *is* asleep? Maybe this wasn't such a good idea after all. We should go."

"If he was, he's hardly going to be after that." Dexter caught her arm. There was a mischievous gleam in his eyes which alarmed her. "Come on. Faint heart, fair lady and all of that. We might as well finish the job. Besides, I'm intrigued to see a bit more of this house. I bet it's got some cracking state rooms."

"I believe there's an original Adams plasterwork ceiling somewhere," Felicia said reluctantly.

"And I'll bet you've always wanted to see it, too," Dexter coaxed.

She had, as a matter of fact, but she wasn't about to let him get carried away.

"This isn't one of your shows," she hissed. "Technically, we're trespassing. We're here for a specific reason; let's not get sidetracked."

But if afterwards, they happened to accidently-on-purpose get lost on the way out, she thought serenely... well, that would be understandable, wouldn't it? After all, it was a big house, everything was dark. There didn't seem to be a single light on in the whole place. To many people, that might have seemed strange, even disturbing, but an auctioneer got used to dealing with old people and their eccentricities. Mr Bunting would have lived through the war; they got used to blackouts and power cuts. For some, the habit never really left them. Her grandmother had been the same. Wandering around in the dark at night, it never even occurred to her to turn on a light. It was a wonder she'd never toppled down the stairs.

It dawned on her suddenly that the old man himself might be injured, lying in the dark having tripped and fallen. Emboldened by this thought, she grabbed the banister and moved swiftly up the stairs, calling out the elderly gentleman's name as she went.

The staircase ended at a door. Nudging it open, Felicia poked her head around, eyes widening. Moonlight spilled through the tall sash windows, casting the room in a silvery chequered pattern. Pale cream panelling lined the walls, finely moulded with a frieze of fruiting vines. High above their heads, an enormous crystal chandelier sprouted from the centre of an intricate plaster ceiling rose. The floor space was dominated in the centre by a colossal four poster bed, heavy tapestry curtains hanging loose.

They certainly weren't in the servants' quarters now.

"A hidden door," Dexter surveyed the doorway they'd just passed through, the front of which was decorated to match the wall that surrounded it. He let it go, and it closed soundlessly, melting seamlessly back into the plaster. Unless you knew where to look, the joins were almost impossible to see. "Very neat."

"Dexter, look," advancing into the room, Felicia pointed at the fire, the coals of which still glowed faintly in the grate. "Someone's been here recently."

"Well, they're not here now." Dexter strolled over to the high wing-backed armchair, which faced the fire. "So we might as well—"

Surprised at the way he broke off, Felicia turned to see him staring down at the chair, eyes wide in shock. Her heart jolted.

"Dexter?" She rasped, suddenly finding that her throat was tight with fear. "What... what is it?"

He reached behind the arm of the chair and picked up a bottle from the side table, looking at it reverently. "This is a Romanée-Conti; I never thought I'd get a chance to see one of these." Unstopping the cork, he selected a glass, examining it for signs of use before pouring some of the dark red liquid into it.

"Dexter!" Felicia admonished, surprised at how shaky her voice sounded. She couldn't decide whether she was more angry or relieved. "You can't just help yourself."

"The old boy won't mind," Dexter replied staunchly, holding the glass up to the light so that the liquid inside flashed like the coals in the fire behind him. "Wine buffs are generous sorts." He cast her a teasing look. "Why so jumpy all of a sudden? Did you think I'd found another body?"

"Very amusing," she folded her arms, not liking to admit that actually, a small part of her had been thinking just that. "Now, can we please just get out of here? He's clearly not at home. He must have gone out for a late walk or something."

Dexter looked slightly wistfully at the half-filled glass in his hand, but put it down.

"All right then. We've done our duty. Let's… Felicia?"

She was standing illuminated in the moonlight, frozen stock still. With her skin washed silver, the effect was uncannily statue-like.

"Dexter," she whispered. "Look."

He followed the line of her gaze, to where, emerging between the folds of the bed hangings, the pale shape of a hand was visible, fingers splayed, palm upwards to the ceiling.

Steeling himself, Dexter stepped forward, pulling back the heavy curtain.

"Bloody hell," he breathed. "Here we go again."

Chapter Twelve

"**R**ight you two. No more delays, no more excuses. I need answers. *Now.*"

Despite being shorter than both of them, Sergeant Pettifer nonetheless achieved the effect of looming over herself and Dexter quite successfully, Felicia thought weakly. Or perhaps it was just the force of his palpable ire, radiating out from him in waves, which created the impression.

Gone was the mild, even slightly comical figure of earlier, to be replaced by a menacing vision of law enforcement. Even Dexter, always one with a cavalier attitude to authority, suddenly appeared vaguely wary of putting a foot out of line.

They were standing out in the gardens at the back of the house. The lawns—every bit as vast as she'd suspected—were washed in moonlight. The moon was a hard, cold fist in the sky, so bright that it obscured any stars. The entire scene was rendered in stark greyscale; it filtered through the petals of the cherry blossom overhead, leaching it of all colour. Felicia suppressed a shiver, wondering if she dared ask what time it was. It felt like the middle of the night.

As if on cue, the bells at All Saints began to toll midnight.

"The Witching Hour," she murmured.

Sergeant Pettifer glared at her.

"What was that?"

"Nothing important." She pulled herself out of her reverie.

"*Nothing*—" Pettifer bit off, looking about ready to spontaneously combust. Dexter backed away infinitesimally. "Is *anything* of importance to you two? You just wander around finding two bodies in the space of an afternoon and that's just… what, a… *trifling* occurrence, is it? All in a day's work?"

His tirade ended in something of a squeak. There was a small pause.

"I don't think that's entirely fair, Sergeant," Dexter protested tentatively. "As we've explained, it was a total coincidence. We certainly didn't come here expecting to find a dead body."

"And what *did* you expect to find?"

"Honestly? A perturbed and slightly crotchety old man wondering why we were disturbing him at nine o'clock at night."

"So you didn't think there was anything amiss, then?"

"No, we didn't." Felicia jumped in, slightly testily. "We were humouring my father, that's all. It's generally easier than arguing with him."

Pettifer reflected that she was probably right. Peter Grant wasn't a man to cross. He coughed.

"Fair enough. So remind me, how did you get in?"

"The back door was unlocked."

Nothing noteworthy there, Pettifer acknowledged grimly. Stamford was the sort of place where some people still didn't bother to lock their doors, even in this day and age. And not just the older residents, either. PC Winters was always complaining about the two housemates she rented with on St Leonard's Street doing the same, and they were both in their twenties.

"To be honest, I almost didn't go in at all," Felicia admitted. "I was worried we might scare him to death, believe it or not." She gave an ironic smile.

"Well, it's a good thing you did," Pettifer conceded gruffly. Who knew how long the old boy might have been lying there otherwise? By all reports, no one ever entered the house. As it was, they'd found him only hours after he'd been murdered. It was a stroke of luck, really, from the policeman's point of view; this way, they still had a chance of getting some forensic evidence out of the scene. Really, he ought to be grateful to them; instead, he just felt this irrational annoyance.

"I suppose it was…" she looked like she didn't really want to ask the question. "The same weapon as earlier?"

Pettifer nodded.

"Looks like it. Unlikely there are two of whatever it is."

Which meant that someone had managed to smuggle it out of the auction somehow. And now they were roaming around Stamford with it. Pettifer tried not to dwell on the image of the body upstairs, but it seemed to be burned behind his eyelids. Sprawled on his back across the bed, the same glassy, wide-eyed stare, lips parted in a final gasp. The only difference was the angle of the attack; this time, the blade had gone in the front, pushed right between the ribs. Quick, ruthless, unhesitating. It told him something else about the killer. Because this wasn't the same as sidling up to a wardrobe and poking a blade through the wood. This was front on, looking the victim straight in the eye. Even Pettifer, seasoned policeman that he was, felt chilled by the thought.

"Your son tells me that your valuer, Hugo Dappleton, left you rather in the lurch earlier," he said, trying to bring his focus back to the interview at hand.

"You've spoken to Algernon?"

"*He* spoke to *me*."

She didn't seem to think that much amiss. She shrugged.

"Well, yes, he did rather. It was a bit of a tricky moment."

"Did it concern you?"

"I was more irritated than anything at the time. But now you mention it, it was very unlike him. He's normally so conscientious. I know how father relies on him, even if he won't admit it."

"No ideas as to why he might have done it?"

"To be honest, I was too busy in the moment to think much about it, and I can't say it's occupied my mind much since. A few other things have happened, in case you hadn't noticed."

A bit of exasperated frost had crept into her tone, which Pettifer ignored. He could well understand it; it was late, it was cold, and she'd just found her second body of the day. But he couldn't afford to feel any sympathy.

"Did you happen to notice anything else out of the ordinary? Anything at all?"

"Are these questions really necessary right now?" Dexter interjected. "Look, Sergeant, I appreciate you've got a job to do, but it's late, it's cold, and corpses seem to be jumping out at us left, right and centre. We've given you our statement for tonight. Do you think we could do this some other time?"

"No, I do *not*," Pettifer snapped, finally pushed over the edge of civility. "I'm not keen to be standing out here any more than you are, Mr Grant, but as you so astutely pointed out, there have now been two murders within the space of twelve hours. To say that things are beginning to escalate at an alarming rate would be an understatement, wouldn't you agree?" Without waiting for them to reply, he carried on, aware that his voice was rising angrily with every word, but not particularly caring. "Even if you two *aren't* involved somehow, which is starting to seem more improbable by the hour, you certainly seem to be at the centre of events. Now, there is nothing whatsoever preventing me from hauling you both down to the station and locking you up for the remainder of the night until I'm satisfied you've answered my questions—nothing, that is, save my good nature, and that's hanging by a *thread* at this point. So I would *suggest*," his voice was a dull roar by now, "that you tell me everything you know right now. Starting, Mr Grant, with what you were doing at the auction this afternoon. And *no* more prevaricating. I want the *truth*, or else."

"Well, it's not something I can really talk about," Dexter said haughtily. "My producers…"

Pettifer made a languid show of reaching for his handcuffs.

"All right, all right, there's no need for that." Dexter said hurriedly, backing away behind Felicia. He shoved his hands in his pockets, rocked back on his heels. Regarded Pettifer assessingly. "How much do you know about the history of this town, Sergeant?"

"Not a lot," Pettifer confessed, unabashed. "I haven't had much time for sight-seeing since I transferred."

"Well, there's plenty of it. About 1,000 years, to be exact. This might seem like a bucolic backwater these days, but it certainly hasn't always been the case. In the 1300s, this was amongst the ten biggest towns in England. It was also a major religious centre," he gestured towards the spire of All Saints', which was just peeking above the slate-tiled roof. "Hence why there are all these medieval churches dotted around the centre, some within mere metres of each other."

Pettifer raised an eyebrow, the closest he deigned to come to conceding interest.

"Your point, Mr Grant?"

"My *point* is that we talk a lot about the decline of Stamford after the Georgian period, but it wasn't the first major crest and trough this place has been through in its time. After the break with Rome under Henry VIII, the town suffered badly. There were a lot of Catholics here, and they didn't go away. They just went underground."

He paused atmospherically. Felicia tutted loudly. Pettifer scratched behind his ear. Looking somewhat disappointed in his audience, Dexter ploughed on regardless.

"Fast-forward to the Civil War; loyalties were split down the middle. The town was torn in two. Charles I knew he was losing; he went on the run from Oxford, disguised as a servant, then a clergyman, intending to surrender himself to the Scottish army at Newark. He thought they'd be more reasonable than the English Parliamentarians, and they'd agreed in advance that if he gave himself up to them, they'd protect him. He fled across the middle of the country, staying at various secret houses along the way. One night at a time, then gone. Where do you think he stayed, on his last night as a free man?" He spread his arms wide with a grin. "Right here in Stamford. In fact, rumour has it, right *here* in Barn Hill."

Pettifer looked around him dubiously.

"I know it's sometimes hard to envisage that anything existed here before the Georgians," Dexter said quietly. "But this has been a street since medieval times. People lived here. You might not be able to see their houses any more, but they still exist. Some broken into rubble which was then used to build what's here today." He patted the rough-hewn stone of the wall. As with many houses in Stamford, the front was faced, smoothed to the flattest surface possible, the joins between the bricks all but invisible to create the illusion of a seamless sheet of honey-coloured rock. But here, at the back, where it was less likely to be seen, the finish was rougher, the chisel marks still visible. "Others were simply swallowed into the build, perfectly encased within the new façade. Until you're inside, you'd never realise the older house was still there."

Felicia stirred then, turning to him, eyes wide.

"The parlour… where we went in." Her voice had a breathy, excited quality to it.

"Exactly. The front of the house, where we found the body, that's Georgian built all right. But the back, those old servants' quarters… that's a different story."

"Of course, I should have seen it myself." Animation coloured her voice. "Do you really think this might be it?"

A light frost was forming on the grass. Pettifer was suddenly, uncomfortably aware that freezing damp was soaking into his shoes.

"All very interesting, I'm sure, Mr Grant, but from my point of view, there's only one thing which matters, and that's what all of this has to do with a wardrobe for sale in a provincial auction house. You'll have to forgive my slowness, but I'm not quite seeing it."

Dexter looked at him for a long moment.

"It's probably easiest if I show you."

The auction house was shrouded in shadows, and eerily silent. Slabs of moonlight fell thickly upon the floor, and the tall windows shimmered with a coating of frost. The door banged behind them, the sound reverberating around the space like an endless lament. Felicia found herself flinching, then, catching Dexter looking at her, quickly kept moving.

She'd been here at night more times than she cared to count, often on her own. It was always slightly strange, a place like this after hours. It was designed for events, for bustle; there was something forlorn, wrong-feeling about it when it was empty, like a theatre between performances.

But it had never felt menacing before. The murder seemed to have changed something, affected the very atmosphere of the place. She could only hope it wouldn't be a permanent shift.

She had to steel herself as they approached the swing doors that led to the saleroom. She could feel a resistance, almost physical, pressing back against her, warning her not to go in there. But she ignored it, forcing herself to stay in place as Sergeant Pettifer unlocked the doors and ducked beneath the crime scene tape, holding it up for her.

She took a breath, and went in.

The worst of it was that everything looked so *normal*. The rostrum, the chairs arranged in rows, the furniture still crowding around the edges of the room. If it weren't for the forensic markers still dotted around, the dark stain on the floor, just visible in the moonlight, it would be as though nothing had happened at all. As though time had rewound, and it was the night before the sale. Everything arranged, everything waiting. She and Algernon would still be in London, Dexter would still be... well, wherever Dexter was, and none of this would have happened yet. This whole, hellish day would be as yet unwritten. Maybe it wouldn't happen like this at all. Maybe it would play out completely differently. One small tweak, a moment missed, and the butterfly effect would ripple outwards. Her father glancing down on the stairs, seeing the cat just in time. Then he would have taken the auction as usual; he would have been there earlier than she was. Maybe he would have gone to the cupboard, opened it up, looked inside, curious about this mysterious late addition from the eccentric old friend of his father's. Maybe he would have found Barrington in there, or prevented him from ending up in there in the first place. Maybe he would have saved him.

Or maybe it would all have been just the same. The truth was, she would never know, and there was no going back, no rewinding time. The cupboard in question gaped open in the corner, blending into the shadows, almost daring them to approach.

Dexter seemed to feel none of her qualms. He produced a torch from his pocket, clicking it on. A blue beam speared the darkness.

"Ultraviolet," Pettifer observed. It was phrased as an observation, but Dexter clearly heard the question in it, because he obliged with an answer.

"It's useful for seeing detail in dark objects."

"We use them for paintings where dirt and varnish have obscured parts of the image," Felicia added. "You'd be amazed what can get lost under there."

"Some things are meant to get lost, mind," Dexter shone the beam up into the interior of the cupboard. "At least, to those who don't know where to look."

Felicia and Pettifer craned to see. There, running along the join at the top, was a carved line of text, illuminated in ghostly blue light.

"*Dieu et Mon Droit*," Felicia read softly.

Pettifer frowned.

"Isn't that the royal motto?"

Dexter nodded.

"It translates as 'God and my right'. It refers to the idea that the sovereign of a country is placed in charge by God, and, therefore, answers only to Him… or Her," he added, somewhat nervously, at Felicia's raised eyebrows.

"The Divine Right of Kings," Pettifer said. Then, when his companions both looked somewhat surprised, he continued stiffly: "What? I did pay attention to the *odd* history lesson at school. I know what it means. And I also know that it's what caused all the problems between Charles I and Parliament."

"Not to interrupt your mansplaining, Dexter, but that motto was supposedly coined by William the Conqueror," Felicia pointed out sweetly. "It's been used by every monarch for over one thousand years. It's not unique to Charles I."

Dexter gave her a quelling look. Pettifer glanced at the ceiling.

"*This* is why I didn't marry a fellow police officer," he muttered.

"I'm well aware of that," Dexter said shortly. "But I hadn't quite finished. If you'll let me continue?"

"By all means," she replied, gesturing airily. Then, leaning across to Pettifer, she said, conspiratorially, "You have to put him in his place every now and again. His head gets very inflated, all those women hanging on his every word."

Pettifer suppressed a smile. Dexter looked as though he might be about to say something, then pursed his lips, moving the torch beam along the line of text.

"As discussed, although it's not *unique* to Charles I..."—a pointed glare here in Felicia's direction—"it *was* particularly pertinent in his case. It was the issue the entire Civil War rested upon. And there's this." The beam alighted upon the capitalised *N* of the word *Mon*.

Pettifer squinted.

"Is that... backwards?"

"It is." Dexter absently let the torch beam dip as he spoke, revealing a lurid violet splash on the floor of the wardrobe. Felicia swallowed at the unwelcome reminder of what had happened here only twelve hours ago. She remembered reading once that ultraviolet light could show up bloodstains for years after they'd been cleaned away, long after they'd ceased to be visible to the naked eye. Even with the body moved out, even once the room was put back to normal, this cupboard would forever hold the stain of murder. It was a chilling notion, and one she wasn't keen to dwell upon. Instead, she forced herself to focus on what Dexter was saying as he continued. "It could, of course, be a mistake. It's unlikely, but at a pinch, it could be an acceptable explanation... if it weren't for the fact that it's *not the only one*. There's a crest in York that has exactly the same feature." He brought up a photograph on his phone, turned the screen around to show them. "See? On a public building. There's no way *that* was a mistake. Someone did it deliberately. It *means* something."

Felicia noted with some minor amusement that Pettifer was leaning forward, hanging on to every word. Then she realised she was doing the same, and shook herself irritably. It killed her to admit it, but Dexter was *good* at this. He could spin a story like it was golden thread, drawing you into its dazzling embrace without you even noticing.

"What?" Pettifer demanded. *"What* does it mean?"

Dexter shrugged, stowing his phone away in his pocket.

"No idea."

It was like a bubble bursting. Pettifer's face fell in approbation.

"You don't *know*? But… you *must* know."

He looked like a child who'd just discovered that the Tooth Fairy wasn't real. Felicia half expected him to stamp his foot.

"We don't have *all* the answers, Sergeant," Dexter said. "History's like the cosmos; it's a huge, dark expanse, unknowable and unexplored. Occasionally, we uncover one small piece of it, but it's just that. One tiny piece; a fragment, if you will. The rest is still in the shadows, and maybe it always will be."

Pettifer lapsed into a crushed silence. Felicia decided it was time to get to the crux of the matter. They'd danced around it long enough.

"So, what is it, then?" She put her hands on her hips. "Come on, out with it. What's the big prize?"

"Pardon?" Dexter put on a good show of innocence when he wanted to. It could fool many people, but not ones who'd been married to him for ten years. She speared him with an unimpressed look.

"Oh, come off it. You were here with your cameraman, Dexter. This is for your show." She spoke very slowly and deliberately, her voice dripping with disdain. "Your *show*, in case you've forgotten, is called *Treasure Seeker*. Your viewers aren't going to be impressed by an old wardrobe with some carvings inside it." Then her face cleared as the truth emblazoned itself across her brain. "Oh, but wait. *Now* I see. But, no… you can't be serious."

"And why not?" Dexter said defensively. "Charles I was known for lavishing gifts on people who'd helped him. He did it all the time."

"So you think he was carting an enormous cupboard filled with treasure around with him as he fled for his life, do you?" Felicia's tone was derisive. "That's far-fetched even for you, Dexter."

"I think that it's not unreasonable to imagine a scenario where some weeks after he stayed here, a wardrobe gets delivered to the house," Dexter said stubbornly. "And if that wardrobe happened to be filled with priceless treasure... well, from the outside, who would be able to tell?"

"There's just one rather large problem," Felicia patted the wardrobe. "This is from the Jacobean era, Dexter. It's a whole generation too early for Charles I."

"Exactly!" Dexter looked triumphant. "What could be more unlikely to pass notice than an old-fashioned cupboard? It's actually rather ingenious. They would have known that his sympathisers were still being watched."

"Well, there's no treasure in it now," Pettifer, who was beginning to feel rather lost by the whole thing, nonetheless felt obliged to point out the obvious.

"No, but if this belongs to the *house*, and the house is still *there*..."

"Dexter, it was four hundred years ago," Felicia said gently. "What are the chances this wardrobe even belonged to that house originally?"

"Pretty damn high. You know as well as I do what old English families are. They keep their treasures close." Frustration coloured his tone. "What's happened to you, Fliss? Once you would have been in this with me."

He was right; she would have been. The thought tugged at her heartstrings, hit her with a longing that momentarily took her breath. Her hand in his, caught up in the mystery, his magnetic enthusiasm, the sheer romance of it all. It wouldn't have mattered what they found; it wouldn't have mattered if they could prove they were right. It was the adventure that had counted to them back then. But, now...

"Things have changed," she said dully. "*I've* grown up. I don't go on treasure hunts any more."

"I don't think you've changed that much," he said softly, stepping closer. His eyes were colourless in this light, but she knew them so well. A deep cobalt blue, like the deepest parts of the ocean seen from above. Hard to look away from, even now. Even after everything.

"It'll be fun," his voice was coaxing. "All we need are the old papers relating to the house. Inventories, ledgers…"

"No." Pettifer's voice rang out firmly, making them both start. "This is all very well and good, Mr Grant, but I can't afford to get carried away with fantasies. This is a very real, very *contemporary* murder investigation. One which I'm under a hell of a lot of pressure to solve."

Dexter's mouth dropped open. *No* wasn't a word he was used to hearing often.

"But…"

"No buts. If you want to see the paperwork, you'll have to take it up with the estate… *after* my investigation is over. In the meantime, I need you two to go home and stay out of trouble. You understand me?"

Dexter seemed about to protest, but Felicia jabbed him sharply in the side with her elbow. She knew when Pettifer meant business. Best to back off. For now.

"More than happy to. Dexter and I have had quite enough of murder, haven't we, Dexter?"

She gave him a meaningful look, and was just dragging him towards the door when Pettifer's voice made them both stop.

"Oh, Mr Grant?"

Dexter turned.

"Just out of interest…" Pettifer was staring into the cupboard, a frown scored into his features. "You said Charles spent his last night here as a *free* man. What happened after that?"

"He reached Newark and gave himself into the hands of the Scottish army as planned," Dexter said flatly. "He thought they would protect him; instead, they used him as a bartering tool. He wasn't actually executed for another three years, but after that, it was only ever really a matter of time." He gave a wry tilt of the head. "History's fairly brutal, Sergeant."

Pettifer nodded to himself.

"So is murder, Mr Grant, whenever it happens." With a heavy feeling of foreboding, he pushed the door closed on the wooden tomb where a man, trapped and defenceless, had met his bloodied end. "It seems to me that not a lot has changed."

Chapter Thirteen

The phone was ringing again, a muffled, yet still surprisingly shrill sound. Felicia groaned, put her hands over her ears, and tried to focus on the printed figures on the page in front of her.

"That'll be the Herald again." Hugo appeared at the top of the stairs, flushed and unusually dishevelled. His hair was sticking up in tufts as though he'd been yanking his fingers through it repeatedly, and his tie—this time patterned with a colourful array of tropical fish—was crooked. "I told them no comment, but they won't seem to take that for an answer. They're determined to speak to you personally."

She'd come to the office this morning hoping for a bit of peace and quiet in which to get a head start on the invoicing from yesterday's sale. Normally it wouldn't be done so promptly, but as she and Algernon would be leaving for London as soon as Sergeant Pettifer gave them the go ahead to do so, she felt it was only fair on her father that she did what she could while she was here. Or at least, that was the official reason, she conceded uneasily. The line she was trotting out to herself.

"Thanks." Then she ventured, "you know, it's Sunday; you really *don't* need to be here.... any of you."

She'd turned up this morning to find Hugo, Betsy and Amelia on the doorstep, all palpably exhausted but trying not to show it behind bright, determined faces. Thus far, she hadn't had the heart to turn them away.

"I know," Hugo fiddled with his tie hesitantly. "But... well, Sergeant Pettifer said we could be here, as the office isn't technically part of the crime scene; only the saleroom is. And we wanted to help; it felt right to come in."

Felicia could well understand. She suspected, in fact, that really it was because they felt like she did: helpless, afraid, and desperate to feel like they were doing something normal. So she said nothing, just nodded.

The phone stopped. Both Felicia and Hugo breathed a sigh of relief.

It started again. Then the other line started to ring, too, creating an echoing, off-beat canon.

"This is hopeless," she shouted, over the din. "We'll never get anything done like this. It's probably better if we all just go home."

Downstairs, the door sounded. One of the phones stopped ringing, to be replaced by the low rumbling of a male voice.

"Felicia?" Dexter's head appeared at the top of the stairs. "It's the Stamford Bugle. They want to know if you'd like to give an—"

"Bloody *no!*" Felicia and Hugo yelled in tandem. Dexter raised his eyebrows.

"Would you like me to communicate that verbatim, or ought I paraphrase into something more cordial?" He said dryly.

She waved him away irritably, turning back to Hugo.

"This is a disaster. I've no idea how they even got hold of the story so fast."

"They have their ways," Hugo said darkly. "And you can't exactly blame them for being interested. A country auctioneer finding two bodies in the same day in a quaint English town? And not just any auctioneer, but one who happens to have been married to Dexter Grant, Treasure Seeker? It's absolute fodder for them."

"Speaking of Dexter Grant, Treasure Seeker," Felicia said sardonically. "Surely he can't *still* be on the phone? I told him to get rid of any journalists as quickly as possible."

"If it's that editor from The Bugle, then I fear for him," Hugo shuddered. "I've dealt with her before. She's a frosty old bint."

From downstairs there came a rich, throaty laugh.

"Sounds like she's defrosted to me," Felicia observed tautly, stoically pretending to examine the invoices again.

There was a pause. Hugo gulped nervously.

Dexter came bounding up the stairs, tossing the phone onto a teetering pile of ring binders, from where it promptly slid straight back off and fell into the wastepaper basket.

"Rather a charming lady," he proclaimed, settling into the nearest chair and propping his booted feet up on the desk. He was still, to Felicia's acute embarrassment, wearing his Treasure Seeker costume, his bags having been sent straight on to London from the airport. "Has fourteen guinea pigs. She's invited me to dinner and a show."

"I'm sure she has," Felicia muttered.

"Come to think of it, I'm not certain that her motives were *entirely* in the pursuit of knowledge." Dexter frowned. "Perhaps I ought to have asked what kind of show." Then he shrugged, patting a yawn.

"Glad to see you exerting yourself," Felicia said acidly.

"In case you'd forgotten, dear heart, we *were* kept up for half the night by an unholy combination of corpses and your pet policeman. You can hardly wonder at me being tired." He reclined, tilting his hat over his eyes. "Maybe I'll just have forty winks, before he turns up again to terrorise us with more of his questions."

"Your nap will have to wait, Mr Grant," a rumbling voice emerged from the stairwell. "Her pet policeman's already here."

"How does he *do* that?" Dexter sat upright, looking aggrieved.

"A policeman's sixth sense, Mr Grant," Pettifer said ominously, appearing at the top of the stairs. His square form filled the doorway. "But you can relax, for the time being at least. I'm not here for you." He pointed a stubby finger at Hugo. "It's Mr Dappleton I've come to see. I went to your house; your parents said you were here." He raised his eyebrows. "Do you normally work on a Sunday?"

"Not unless there's been a murder, no," Hugo smiled, but it wavered unconvincingly. Felicia noticed that he'd wrapped his arms around himself, his fingers white as they dug into his sleeves. "I just wanted... *we* just wanted," he amended, as Betsy came bustling up the stairs, arms full of walking sticks. "To be here for Felicia. Do what we can."

Pettifer eyed Betsy disbelievingly.

"A very devoted staff you have here, Ms Grant."

"Felicia's always been extremely loyal to us," Betsy said staunchly. "And Peter. We try to repay where we can."

"I understand that you're in charge of the saleroom?" Pettifer asked her.

"It's mostly my domain, yes," Betsy deposited the sticks into an umbrella stand, dusting off her fluffy angora cardigan. "Everything in the sale goes past me, if that's what you're angling at. Felicia's told us how it was the same weapon which was used last night."

"Oh, she *did*, did she?" Pettifer gave Felicia a quelling look. She met his stare unrepentantly. "So you'll know that whatever it was won't be there now, if indeed it ever came from here in the first place. The murderer might have brought it with them."

"So you *do* think it was premeditated, then?" Felicia interjected sharply.

"To be truthful, Ms Grant, I have no idea. That's why it's so important to establish what, if anything, might be missing from the saleroom. If we can find out for certain whether the weapon did or didn't come from here, then it'll shed a lot of light upon the nature of the murder, which in turn will guide us on a lot of other factors. Motive, for example."

"I bet you've got quite a few of those," Hugo muttered under his breath. Then, when Pettifer looked at him searchingly, he blushed. "I mean, everyone knows he wasn't a nice man. That's all I meant."

"It's all right, Hugo," Felicia said soothingly. "Sergeant Pettifer's not about to drag you off in handcuffs for stating the obvious. Are you?" She shot at him.

"Of course not," Pettifer said irritably. He didn't appreciate being cast as the villain. "But I do need to ask you some questions about yesterday. Is there somewhere private we can go to talk?"

Hugo set his chin.

"I've nothing to hide, Sergeant. You can ask me anything right here."

Pettifer sighed internally. They always came to regret saying that in the end. But it wasn't his job to mollycoddle the lad.

"Some new information has come to light. A witness saw you leaving the rostrum in a hurry during the sale and moving towards the back of the room, where the wardrobe was. Can you explain to me what you were doing?"

A wary light entered Hugo's eyes.

"They must have been mistaken. I never—"

"You *did* leave the rostrum in a hurry, Hugo," Felicia said gently. "You can't deny that. Why don't you just tell us what happened?"

Hugo shifted.

"I just… thought I saw something, that's all. Someone. Hovering around by the wardrobe. I was worried they might be tampering with it, so I went to have a look. But by the time I got there, they'd gone."

"Who did you see?" Pettifer demanded.

"I don't know," Hugo said helplessly. "It's a dark corner."

"Tall? Short? Male? Female? You must have seen *something*."

"Just a figure, that's all. Afterwards, I wondered if it was even that. If it hadn't been a shadow or something and I'd just imagined it."

Pettifer's lips twisted in annoyance.

"That's not exactly helpful, Mr Dappleton."

"I'm sorry."

"Why would you think anyone would want to tamper with the wardrobe anyway?" Felicia asked.

Hugo and Betsy exchanged a look.

"What?" Felicia demanded, looking between them.

"Things have been a bit… up in the air lately," Hugo said reluctantly. "Nothing I wanted to worry you about, but…"

"I think we're past that now, Mr Dappleton," Pettifer said severely.

"It's nothing… really. Just a few incidents, that's all. We've been a bit understaffed. The ship's not as tight as it was. I'm just trying to be a bit more vigilant."

"What *sort* of incidents?" Felicia pressed. Hugo squirmed, tugging at his collar.

"Well… you know …client's paperwork going astray, lots being misplaced before the sale…"

"Stolen," Betsy choked out. "*Not* misplaced. Someone's been pinching things, Hugo. We've *talked* about this."

She swept away indignantly, leaving Hugo looking awkward.

"She's a bit sensitive about it," he explained quietly. "She's very protective of your father, Felicia. And of you. She can't bring herself to think…" he shook his head, suddenly looking weary, older than his years. "She'd rather believe that there's some nefarious conspiracy afoot."

The phone began to ring, a muffled sound emitting from the depths of the paper basket.

"Is there a phone in the bin?" Pettifer seemed momentarily distracted.

"Best place for it," Felicia said, with feeling.

"Was that all you wanted me for, Sergeant?" Hugo reached in and retrieved it. "Only, as you can see, we're today's big news."

Pettifer nodded curtly before turning to Felicia with a querying look. She shrugged.

"Like he said, we're flavour of the week. Everyone wants to know about the auctioneer who keeps falling over bodies. It's actually quite a nuisance."

"*What*?" Pettifer thundered, startling Dexter, who'd been surreptitiously dozing beneath his hat. "The press know about the second murder? Already?"

"Well, yes." Felicia blinked at him. "Am I to take it that it wasn't you who told them, then?"

"Certainly not," Pettifer fumed, scraping a hand across his squashed features. Felicia tried not to stare at his nose, which she found quite fascinating; it looked to have been broken in about three different places. "Christ, this is all I need: the whole bloody town in hysteria." He glared at Dexter. "If I find out that you had anything to do with this…"

"*Me*?" Dexter's face was the picture of righteous indignation. "Why would *I*…"

"I can think of lots of reasons," Pettifer said darkly. "Starting and ending with that dratted show of yours."

"Much as I'm inclined to agree with your estimation of my ex-husband's character," Felicia said dryly. "I can vouch for him on that one, Sergeant. He's been in my vicinity since last night."

"Felicia?" Amelia's voice preceded her light footsteps on the stairs. "Hugo said that the police were—oh," she faltered.

"Never fear, miss," Pettifer rumbled. "I was just leaving." He inclined a mocking nod towards Dexter.". "Until later, Dr Livingstone."

"Dr Livingstone?" Amelia looked charmingly confused. "I

thought you were meant to be the evil fiancé from George of the Jungle." At their blank looks, she persisted. "That *is* a fancy dress outfit, right? You *were* at a party?"

Felicia looked smugly at Dexter.

"*Not* one of your fans, I feel."

He glowered back.

"Seriously though, she's got a point." Felicia rose to her feet, gesturing for him to do the same. "We *really* need to take you shopping."

Felicia stood on the pavement of St Mary's Street and looked at her watch again. The slender thoroughfare, which ran adjacent to the High Street, was where most of the bijou shops were based, so it had seemed the most likely location for them both to find what they needed. Once here, she and Dexter had gone their separate ways temporarily; her to find a less ankle-breaking pair of shoes— something which she had done, she was impressed with herself to note, in fairly record time. It helped, she supposed, that there wasn't nearly so much choice as she was used to; it rather concentrated the mind. That said, if she'd been expecting to have to settle for a pair of galoshes or walking boots, she'd been utterly wrong. Stamford wasn't all country clothing stores any more. Although there were still plenty of places where you could buy a tweed flat cap and a quilted gilet, if you were so inclined, those shops were now interspersed by tiny artisan jewellers, sleek cafés, and craft bakeries. Somewhere in the time since she'd been gone, her town had gone boutique. It was, she had to admit, slightly disorientating.

Some things hadn't changed though. Stamford had always been something of a nucleus for the independent gentleman's outfitter. The sort of timber framed, gilt-lettered establishments with old-fashioned brass bells above the doorways and windows displaying tasteful arrangements of nattily patterned socks and whimsical cufflinks. A place where tweed was available, it seemed, in every conceivable hue, as were chinos and suede brogues. If something didn't quite fit, it could be tweaked, sometimes on the spot, by a brisk, non-nonsense seamstress. Meanwhile, a request to change buttons or shoelaces for a brighter option was met with barely a blink.

Dexter had disappeared into the beeswax-scented embrace of one of these, and as yet, hadn't emerged. If it was any other person, Felicia might have started to worry that something had befallen him, but as it was Dexter, she was just beginning to feel a reminiscent sort of annoyance. She'd lost count of the number of hours she'd wasted during her marriage just hanging around waiting for Dexter. Dexter, who had no real concept of time, who just sauntered along eventually and looked baffled when challenged about how long he'd been gone. *She'd* been the one standing at the altar waiting for *him*—despite assiduously observing the 'bride is always late' tradition—because he'd left his buttonhole behind. He'd almost missed Algernon's birth altogether because he'd got chatting to one of the neighbours about their spring border. Apparently he'd been invited in for a cup of tea and "didn't feel it would be polite to say no". All whilst she was ten centimetres dilated and trying desperately to hold back the urge to push.

Now here she was, still waiting. And she wasn't even *married* to the man any more. It really was insupportable.

She was distracting herself by admiring an array of particularly characterful ties in the shop window, wondering if it would be worth buying one for Hugo now to keep for Christmas, when a voice sounded over her shoulder.

"Still in those shoes, then? You must have a death wish."

She spun around to see Jack watching her, hands in his pockets. He was standing in the entrance to one of the several narrow, artery-like passageways that ran at intervals between the buildings down towards the meadows.

"Oh," she said flatly, her tone belying the sudden skip her heart gave. "It's you."

"I'm surprised you dared to break cover," he observed. "You *are* our current local celebrity, after all."

He had such a curiously expressionless way of speaking that she could never be certain whether he was being serious or not. Or worse, whether the joke, if there was one, was at her expense.

"No one's asked me for my autograph yet," she said crisply. She stood back to let a family of four pass, pressing herself against the stone wall of the outfitters. One of the parents glanced back, as though trying to place her, and she turned her face away, letting her hair fall across her cheek. "I'm surprised there are so many people here today. You'd think that two brutal murders would be enough to put them off."

"You're kidding?" One corner of his mouth tilted upwards. "That's why there are even more of them than usual. After all, what better activity to while away the Easter holidays? I can see the brochures already: Come to Stamford! Wander the cobbles, admire the blossom, browse the shops, have a spot of lunch, tour a murder scene or two…"

She eyed him warily.

"You're rather a strange sort of person, aren't you?"

"Funny, that. I would say the same about you." He tilted his head. "I've certainly never needed to pull anyone else out of the riverbank before. But maybe that's a common occurrence in London, I don't know."

She held up her wrist, from which the ribboned handles of the bag dangled.

"If you *must* know, I was just buying some different shoes."

His green eyes sharpened, focused intently on her face.

"So that means you're staying then?" He asked quietly.

"For the time being, I have to. The police haven't said we can leave." Being under his gaze was intense; she was starting to feel hot. "Have they spoken to you yet?"

Dark, angry emotion flashed across his face. It startled her so much that she went to take a step back, then realised she couldn't. The wall was right behind her; she could feel the rough, gritty texture of the stone against her bare forearm.

"Is that a trick question?" He said, very softly.

"N— no," she stuttered. For the first time, she felt uneasy. Not frightened, as such, more awed by the turbulence which seemed to be broiling beneath the surface of his finely-planed face. "Why should it be?"

Suddenly, he shook his head, raising a hand to his temple.

"I'm sorry. I shouldn't have… I'm just a bit edgy at the moment. I thought that you…" He turned towards the passage from which he'd come, then turned back to look squarely at her. "I really am sorry."

And then he was gone. Instinctively, she went to follow him, but a tall body blocked her way.

"Everything all right?" Dexter had stepped out of the doorway to the outfitters on her left and was looking down at her. For a moment, she was so disorientated that she scarcely noticed what he was wearing. Then her eyes refocused, travelling up and down.

He was sporting a geranium pink linen blazer over a mint green shirt with white pinstripes. His long legs were clad in stone-coloured chinos, finishing in a pair of tan shoes with pink laces. From his jacket pocket, a mint green handkerchief, the exact same colour as his shirt, flourished.

"*That's* what you went for?" She managed. "You look like a walking boiled sweet."

She neglected to add that he actually managed to make it look rather dashing. The thought flustered her, made her feel overly warm. Between this and her reaction to Jack, she was starting to wonder if she might be heading into an early menopause. It was the only explanation.

Then he produced a straw fedora from behind his back and clasped it on his head, and the sensation vanished.

"Seriously? Another hat?"

He shrugged.

"I've got rather used to them. The lovely lady in there—Phyllis —collects novelty sugar shakers—"

Felicia bit down on her tongue so hard that it smarted.

"She says I have a head for hats," he dusted off the sleeve of his jacket, looking insufferably pleased with himself. "Apparently, I have a remarkably well-formed skull."

"Remarkably well-formed for coshing," Felicia muttered darkly.

"Pardon?"

"Oh, nothing, nothing," she said breezily, taking his arm and leading him onwards down the street. Overhead, the bells of St John's, tucked into a crook around the corner, began to chime sweetly. "Come on, that's one o'clock. How about we get some lunch somewhere? We can stop in to pick up Algie on the way."

Chapter Fourteen

"Thanks for this, Cass," Felicia sank into the wing-backed chair in a secluded corner of The George Inn's tastefully-appointed lounge with a grateful sigh. "I needed to get out of the house, or I would have strangled someone."

"Someone being Juliette, I presume?" Cassie gave her a knowing smile over the tea menu.

"She would be top of the list, yes, but if I couldn't get at her, I probably would have settled for whoever else was in the vicinity," Felicia brushed a weary hand across her forehead, pushing her hair back. "She has that sort of catatonic effect on people."

"Nothing a pot of Duchess Grey and a cream tea can't fix," Cassie handed the menu across to her.

"That does sound heavenly." Felicia studied the extensive list with a sense of wonder. "You know, I haven't been out to tea in years."

She looked around the room, which was filled with a variety of sofas, chaises, and armchairs, all set at discreet angles around low tables. The colour scheme was pale and neutral, at odds with the rest of the building, which boasted dark oak panelling and low, mullioned windows, cosy nooks and secluded corners. In here, however, there was an open-ness to the layout, allowing for a certain degree of privacy, but also allowing for a good view of your fellow diners. It was a place to see and be seen. Already, Felicia could see several people she recognised. Evelina Fielding was holding court with a group of similarly smartly turned-out elderly ladies in the far corner, passing around a plate of pastel-coloured macarons. Over by the fireplace, Amelia was sharing a slab of tiffin with her mother, the sofa around them surrounded by shopping bags. And next to the window…

"Well, you know us here in Stamford. Stuck in the past," Cassie grinned.

"Not always a bad thing," Felicia said, watching enviously as an enormous wedge of Victoria sponge was set down at a table adjacent to them, filled with pillowy cream and fresh raspberries. "Not to dent your mood, but isn't that your deputy mayor over there in the window?"

"Dennis," Cassie hissed. She looked at Felicia hopefully. "I don't suppose there's any chance that he might have done it?"

"No such luck, Cass," Felicia laughed. "He was in the council meeting with you when it happened, remember?"

"Bugger, you're right." Then her face cleared. "He was late, though. Missed the first fifteen minutes entirely."

"You're sure this was yesterday?"

"Absolutely. He's never late. Likes to be there to show me up in person."

"Don't you think you're being a little paranoid? He's not the devil incarnate."

Cassie glared at her so ferociously that Felicia felt inclined to hide behind the tea menu.

"Whose side are you on, Fliss? If my own best friend won't even believe me…"

"I do, I do," Felicia said hastily, uncrossing her legs and tilting forwards so that she could lay a reassuring hand on Cassie's knee. "Sorry, that came out wrongly." Her lips twisted into an approximation of a smile. "After all, who else would have believed me when I said that my respected academic of a husband was dressing up as a desert explorer and gallivanting around chasing treasure?"

"It did seem rather far-fetched, I'll admit. But then, I've known Dexter for a long time. I knew there was a Peter Pan figure in him just waiting to burst out."

"Well, it's truly out of the bottle now."

"Fliss, listen…" a concerned frown crossed her friend's usually jovial face. "You do *know* that the show isn't the reason that everything… well, went the way it did, don't you?"

"What do you mean?"

"You know what I mean. I'm not saying that it wasn't unhelpful, with him suddenly off travelling all the time, and getting all wrapped up in his new stardom, but you'd been growing apart for a while. You must remember that. Dexter's been in your life since you were eighteen; that's twenty-two years ago now. It's only natural that you were both going to change in that time."

"I know," Felicia said. "It was me who ended it remember? *My* choice."

"Yes, but I think you've told yourself that it was forced upon you, and that's not true."

Felicia craned her neck around. "Dennis looks like he could do with some company. Shall I invite him to have tea with us?"

Cassie held up her hands in surrender.

"Fine! You're not going to talk about it; I can tell when there's no point. Just… leave Dennis where he is." She scratched gingerly at her neck. "Just being near the man brings me out in hives."

"Does anyone even actually *get* hives any more, Mum?"

"Robyn!" Felicia jumped to her feet, enveloping the slight frame. "How wonderful to see you. What are you doing here?"

"Working." She held up the notepad in her hand. "I waitress here now."

"But… I thought you worked at the library? And at the school in the holidays?"

"I still do. But I saw this going and thought I'd pick up something extra. All looks good on the CV."

"Ah, of course." Felicia nodded. "It's Oxford you're applying for, isn't it?"

Robyn smiled ruefully, brushing a strand of hair out of her eyes. She had the most fascinating hair, Felicia had always thought; the exact colour of the outside of a butternut squash.

"It's not just about getting the grades, even though everyone thinks it is. The truth is, thousands of people get the grades and apply, so it has to be about more than that. You have to show them that you're creative and industrious, too."

"Both of which you are," Felicia said promptly. Robyn didn't look reassured by the endorsement.

"You're my godmother; you have to say that."

"Not at all. At least, I don't remember making that promise when I stood over the font at your christening."

"You were probably hungover," Cassie supplied.

"Cass! That is not true."

"Oh, not just you. Everyone was hung over. All my friends, at least. That's what you get when you have a baby at twenty-two." She pointed at Robyn. "Darling, I love you and I don't regret a thing, but *don't do it*. Wait until you're at least thirty."

Robyn rolled her eyes.

"No fear, Mum." She tapped her pad with a pen. "But they'd better not catch me chatting. What are you having?"

"The usual, please," Cassie declared, reclining backwards like a blonde, unruly cat.

"I'll join her," Felicia added.

"Coming up." Robyn whisked away.

Felicia looked after her fondly.

"She's a firecracker these days, isn't she?"

"She makes me feel about a hundred years old," Cassie groaned.

"Algernon has the opposite effect on me," Felicia admitted. "Sometimes, I forget that I'm the adult and he's the child."

"Where is he this afternoon, anyway? You haven't left him in Juliette's clutches, have you? Because I think that would constitute child cruelty."

"I'm not *that* bad a mother," Felicia laughed. "He's with Betsy. They're having a baking afternoon. Apparently he wants to 'perfect his carrot cake'".

Cassie looked impressed.

"I wish one of mine would say that."

"Your boys are still only tiny, Cass. I think you can let them off."

"Hmm. And Robyn's too busy saving the world to do anything as frivolous as baking." Cassie flipped open her white linen napkin. "At any rate, at least Algernon's not brooding about what happened?"

"Not at all. In a way, I'd rather he was."

"What do you mean?"

"He's got it into his head to play detective. He's got this ivory inlay which Betsy found on the floor and gave to him—"

"Inlay? Like one of those little discs which slot into wooden objects for decoration?"

"So you *do* listen to my antiques-related waffle sometimes. Yes, you find them on all sorts of things. Anyway, he thinks it's some fabulous clue. It took all of my powers of persuasion to stop him from running straight to poor old Sergeant Pettifer with it."

Cassie appeared to find that uproariously funny.

"I'd loved to have seen DCI Heavenly's face if you'd let him. You've met our new pillar of law enforcement I suppose?"

"I haven't yet had the pleasure," Felicia said dryly, as Robyn reappeared with a tray. "But I'm starting to build up a picture. What's he like?"

"Down from London. Some sort of golden boy. We're all supposed to be oh-so cringingly grateful that he's deigned to bring his expertise out here to the sticks, etcetera, etcetera. Bowing and scraping and..." She looked up, a little guiltily. "All right, so I'm exaggerating just a bit, but you'll see what I mean. The man thinks he's God's gift. You know the type."

"I certainly do. I was married to one, remember?"

Cassie frowned.

"Yes, but Dexter's different. He may be an infuriating arse, but he's an arse with a heart, if you know what I mean."

"Not in the slightest," Felicia replied silently, trying not to picture the biology of it. But then, that wasn't unusual. Cassie's way with words had always been on the idiosyncratic side. But, eventually, you understood what she was getting at. You just had to wait, and...

"I mean, Dexter is what he is," Cassie continued. "He does what it says on the tin. Heavenly isn't like that. You never really know where you are with him. He's all charm on the surface, but underneath..." she shook her head. "I don't know, maybe I'm getting carried away. But sometimes I wonder..."

She trailed off, eyes widening, as an enormous, fruit-studded scone was placed before her, along with porcelain dishes of jam, honey, and clotted cream.

"Cass?" Felicia prodded, first verbally, then literally. "Concentrate. You were saying?"

"Sorry," Cassie blinked, emerging from her daze. "It was nothing, really. Forget I said anything. Think I've still got a bit of baby brain." She clapped her hands together excitedly, like a small child. "This looks amazing, Robyn. I think the scones get bigger every time."

Robyn looked shiftily from side to side, then leaned closer.

"This goes no further, but I snaffled the two biggest ones for you."

"First rule of politics," Cassie winked at Felicia. "It's who you know that matters."

Robyn rolled her eyes.

"Tea's on its way. I'll be back in a minute."

"Sometimes, she does things which make me think she *is* my daughter after all," Cassie said approvingly, splitting her scone down the middle with a mother-of-pearl handled butter knife. "And always just when I'm beginning to despair that's she too much of a goody-goody to be redeemed."

"I heard that." Robyn dived back into view. "And by the way, I meant to say: nice shoes, Aunt Fliss. Loving the new look on you."

Cassie looked down at Felicia's feet, crossed neatly over one another, and did a double take.

"Bloody hell, I hadn't noticed those. She's right; what's happened to you?"

"You never notice anything, Cass," Felicia said, with exasperated fondness, spooning jam onto her scone. "And they're only trainers."

"They're turquoise," Cassie retorted, then squinted. "Is that diamante?"

"Certainly not," Felicia said, starting to feel a touch defensive about the subject. "It's just the light." She looked down at her feet. Admittedly, they weren't the sort of thing she'd usually go for; they were flat, for one thing. And given the choice, she would have opted for a more neutral colourway. But there hadn't been a lot left in her size, and besides, they were lovely, in a lustrous velvet with matching beribboned laces. They reminded her of the sort of thing she'd used to wear once. "They're rather fun, don't you think?" At her friend's disbelieving look, she persisted peevishly, "I do *do* fun sometimes, Cass. I'm not a crusty old biddy just yet."

"Yes, but not in your wardrobe," Cassie protested. "That's usually more along the lines of elegant and expensive and... well, frankly, a lot of grey. Actually, so much grey I was beginning to think I might have to stage an intervention."

God, she made her sound depressing. Felicia piled extra cream onto the scone.

"You're not having some sort of breakdown, are you?" Cassie looked at her in concern. "Finding those bodies hasn't tipped you over the edge?"

"The edge of *what*?" Felicia tried not to feel affronted.

"And, of course, then there's all the press," Cassie said, sympathetically.

"Felicia, dear." Felicia looked up to see Evelina Fielding standing over her. Or rather, standing next to her. Stooped over her stick, she was so small that her head barely met the top of the wing-backed chair. Felicia was taken aback by how frail she appeared, and, yet, there was something about her, a familiar sparkle in her china blue eyes which spoke of the same vibrant health she'd always enjoyed. "How are you? I heard about your adventures last night. The girls and I were just discussing it." She indicated behind her, to where the gaggle of snowy-haired ladies —none of whom could have been described as "girls" for many a long year—were gathering up their belongings. "Such a terrible thing. I simply had to come over and check you were coping."

"I'm fine, thank you, Evelina," Felicia said warmly. "It was a shock, but I'm trying to stay busy." She held up her cake plate.

"Ah, yes. Tea is always an excellent tonic," Evelina said bracingly. "A good strong cup can steady even the weakest of nerves. And we're going to need it around here. What this town is coming to, I simply can't say. Why, we haven't had a murder here in years—decades, in fact. And now two!" She pointed at Felicia with her cane. "You *will* be careful dear, won't you?"

"Me?" Felicia stammered, moving her head out of the way of the stick. "Why should I—"

"Well, you're the key witness, aren't you? It's all over town. Everybody knows that the police have spoken to you several times. They must believe that you know something, *saw* something."

"But I didn't—"

Evelina held up her hand with a knowing smile.

"No need to tell *me*, my dear. I understand you want to keep your counsel. Just be careful, that's all I ask. I've known you since you were knee high to a grasshopper; I couldn't bear to see anything happen to you."One of her friends called over to her, and she turned her head. "Ah, but I must make a move, or I'll miss my lift up to the golf club. Most of the time, I don't regret selling the car—no need for one here in Stamford—but it does make one rather reliant on other people." She patted her hip. "But alas, the body spoke. At least there's more room in the garage for all of my auction buys," she twinkled mischievously at Felicia. "Anyway, must dash. You will remember what I said, Felicia dear."

Felicia watched her go, a dainty, limping figure, like an injured sprite.

"Surely she can't actually *play* golf?"

Cassie rolled her eyes over the top of her scone.

"Of course not. They hold a bridge club up there for all the old dears."

"I wouldn't like to come up against Evelina at the card table," Felicia murmured. "I bet she cleans them all out every week."

"I don't doubt it." Cassie looked after her fondly. "Hard to believe that she used to live under anyone's thumb, isn't it? She's such a character."

"Yes, well, unfortunately marriages were different back then. Men had much more power."

"Sorry, sorry," a rather flustered Robyn reappeared with a teapot and cups. "We're absolutely rammed in here today."

"Murder's obviously good for business," Cassie said cheerfully, lifting the lid of the teapot and peering inside. "Perhaps

I should suggest it to the tourist board. We could put murder spots on the visitor map."

"Mum!" Robyn was aghast. "That's a terrible thing to say."

"Just good business sense, darling. I bet Felicia agrees; it'd be wonderful publicity for the auction house, wouldn't it, Fliss?"

"Hmm?" Felicia dragged her unfocused gaze away from the tea strainer with a blink. "Sorry, it's just… someone else said something very similar to me this afternoon."

"You see?" Cassie thumped a palm flat against the table, sending tea sloshing out of the teapot's spout. "It's a cracking idea! I'll float it at the next council meeting."

Robyn slunk off with a dismayed expression.

"You shouldn't tease her, you know," Felicia said sternly, pouring out tea for them both. "She'll only take it seriously."

"She takes everything seriously," Cassie retorted, dumping a heaped spoon of sugar into her cup and stirring it with a bullish motion. "That's her curse; she takes after her father."

"Ah," Felicia said knowledgeably. "Your earnest, save-the-world phase."

"That's the problem with getting pregnant when you're young; your brief whims continue to haunt you. They're not supposed to do that. Like ra-ra skirts and poodle perms, they're meant to be consigned to an embarrassing memory."

The mention of her youth—and the eighties, which seemed a worryingly short amount of time ago—led her thoughts inexorably back to Jack. How old *was* he, she wondered? Would he even have been alive before the new millennium? He didn't look more than thirty. That was only a ten year age difference. Hardly cradle-snatching territory, not these days.

"You're not thinking about what Evelina said, are you? She's a nice old thing, but mad as a hatter. They all are at that age. They enjoy a bit of melodrama. I wouldn't pay any attention to it."

"No, you're right," Felicia said hastily, feeling a bit guilty about not telling Cassie the truth.

The paper in the adjacent seat lowered. A finely boned hand reached out to the plate of Victoria Sponge she'd been admiring earlier. But this time, it wasn't the cake that arrested her attention. The sliver of profile was enough; the horn-rimmed glasses, the Roman nose, the small head, and beneath it, an extravagantly tied silk cravat.

Felicia sat back in her chair and tried to listen as Cassie rattled on. But in truth, there was only one thing on her mind: a question, rolling around and around in her mind like a marble.

What was Mr Clancy still doing here in Stamford?

Chapter Fifteen

"Cass? You haven't been lacing your tea, have you?" Felicia grabbed her friend's arm as they walked out of the courtyard into the lilac-scented air. "The car park's this way."

"Sober as a nun," Cassie proclaimed, mock solemnly. Then she pulled a face. "No, I've got to go back to the town hall, pick up some papers for a bit of light bedtime reading. We've got a killer of a planning committee meeting tomorrow, and I'm in no way prepared."

"I'll walk you home, then," Felicia teased. "I've got a bit of time to kill."

"You might very well laugh," Cassie muttered darkly. "I feel like it *is* my home sometimes. Homework on a Sunday evening, I ask you. I swear, I was better off in finance. At least there was more wine involved."

"Ah, but when you're in politics, the wine's often free," Felicia reminded her, linking her arm through her best friend's as they crossed the town bridge. A swan was snoozing on its nest amongst the reeds below, neck tucked gracefully into its pearly feathers. Above the meadows, the sky was a tropical cocktail of pink, peach and gold, the stone of the houses around them a molten toffee. To say it was a beautiful evening would be an understatement, although the warmth of the scene was deceptive; there was a sharp chill to the air, a reminder that it was still firmly spring.

"True, although it's often the most dreadful cheap plonk at those events. And you have to be polite about it, too! It's a good thing I'm no connoisseur; Dennis looks like he's about to burst into tears sometimes." Cassie tilted her head with a grin. "Actually, it's the one thing that makes drinking it more bearable, knowing that he's probably thinking about his wine cellar at home while having to force the equivalent of paint stripper down his throat."

"You're cruel, Cassandra Lane," Felicia said, not without fondness.

"I get my kicks where I can." They'd reached the bottom of the steps that led up to the town hall. "You got a minute or two? What time are you picking up Algie again?"

"Not till six. And if I'm so much as a minute early, I'll feel the force of his censure."

"Come up and see my lair then." Cassie unlocked the doors with her key. "The view's cracking at this time of night."

A huge figure loomed out at her from behind the door. Felicia leapt back, stifling a cry just in time as her eyes adjusted to the shadows.

"Oh, don't mind Daniel," Cassie said merrily, flicking on the light switch and illuminating the sprawling, frock-coated waxwork figure. "He's harmless, really. We just put him there to scare people."

Felicia needed no introduction to Daniel Lambert. He'd been a bit of a Georgian celebrity, known for his vast 50-stone weight, and had exhibited himself all over the country as the fattest man on record. He was a popular historical figure in Stamford, having died here in 1809; apparently it had taken twenty men to get his coffin to its current resting place in St Martin's churchyard.

Several places in the town were named after him, including the local football team, known affectionately as "The Daniels".

"He certainly scared me," Felicia admitted, although the lightness in her tone belied the hammering of her heart against her ribcage. It wasn't exactly surprising that she was jumpy, not after the day she'd had yesterday, but still, she'd rather Cassie didn't know just *how* jumpy. The last thing she wanted was to add to her best friend's already overloaded plate of worry. She tried to avoid looking directly at his glassy stare and, instead, turned to follow Cassie's progress up the wide staircase and past a dizzying array of doors, until they came to one that looked exactly like the rest, save for a small brass plaque that read "Mayor Cassandra Lane".

"Here we go," Cassie proclaimed proudly, preceding Felicia inside and flinging herself behind the vast mahogany desk. "Do sit down."

Felicia looked around for somewhere to do just that. It seemed as though every surface was covered in something or other. Eventually, she selected a chair opposite Cassie's desk, scooping up the pile of papers on it and casting around uncertainly for where to put them.

"Oh, just shove them onto the floor," Cassie said airily, flinging open the shutters behind her to reveal what she'd correctly sold as a stunning view of the Stamford rooftops.

Felicia carefully put the pile down on the only visible patch of carpet she could see. Sitting on the now clear chair with a metallic sort of rustle. With a frown, she reached underneath the cushion, producing an old crisp packet. Cassie didn't seem to notice, occupied as she was in watching the window of the Arts Centre, through which she had a direct line of sight. There seemed to be a dance class of sorts going on; couples were twirling around the floor with what, Felicia had to admit, appeared to be varying degrees of expertise. One man was tripping over his wife's foot, almost causing a pile-up. She could see why Cassie found the view so entertaining.

"I'm surprised Gavin can stand it in here," she said dryly. She'd heard all about the oh-so-efficient Gavin from Cassie's rants over the phone, and, having walked through the anteroom where his painstakingly neat desk resided, she could imagine how the two of them might clash.

"Oh, it just *kills* him," Cassie said gleefully, kicking off her shoes and propping her stockinged feet upon the desk. "He's absolutely desperate to get in and tidy up. Sometimes, when I come back from lunch early, I catch him standing in the doorway, gazing longingly inside."

"I told you, it *wasn't* me!"

The voice rang out suddenly from the other side of the wall. With a look at one another, Felicia and Cassie were on their feet in tandem.

The anteroom was no longer empty. A young man was standing on the far side of the desk, a stack of files clasped protectively to his chest, his face white and taut. From the perfectly starched crispness of his shirt, the tastefully muted silver-grey tie, Felicia could match him immediately to Cassie's description.

But he wasn't the only person now occupying the pristine space.

"All right, lad," Pettifer said soothingly, breaking off from writing in his notepad to hold up a conciliatory hand. "No need to get tetchy. It's just a simple question, that's all, and one I've got to ask. Surely you can see that?"

"What's going on?" Cassie was suddenly in Mayoral mode, striding forth with her hands on her hips. The fact that she still had no shoes on didn't seem to faze her. "*Why* are you questioning my assistant, Sergeant? He was nowhere near the auction house yesterday."

"Well, that's just it, Madam Mayor," Pettifer said, scratching behind his ear with the chewed stub of his pencil. "We have a witness who claims to have seen him there, in the saleroom, during the window in which we believe the murder must have been committed."

"But… that's impossible!" Cassie spluttered. "He was *here*. We had a council meeting." She stared bullishly at Pettifer. "I saw him with my own eyes. He was in the room with us."

"For the entire duration?"

There was a pause.

"Well… no," she admitted, with visible reluctance. "He was here beforehand, setting up… I saw him then. And he came in later, to tell us about the murder. He'd heard about it and thought we should know. But other than that, he would have been right here in his office. It's part of his job."

"And here today as well," Pettifer said blandly. "Another one who toils on the Sabbath. What a work ethic we have here in Stamford."

"The events of yesterday rather threw our schedule out," Gavin said, with an attempt at haughtiness which was ruined by the slight shake in his voice. "I have a lot to catch up on."

"That, and the fact that you left the building while the meeting was going on. That can't have helped."

Cassie whirled on him.

"You *what*?"

"CCTV footage from the foyer," Pettifer explained. "I can show you if you want."

"No, that won't be necessary." Cassie held up a hand to her temple. "If you say he's on there, then it must be true." She turned to her assistant. "Gavin? What's going on?"

Gavin's eyes darted around, unable to settle on any one spot. He was looking pastier, if it were possible, than he had when they first walked in.

"I suppose I *might* have gone out for a walk."

Even he didn't sound very certain.

"A *walk*?" Disbelief saturated Cassie's question. "*Where?*"

"Nowhere, really. Just… around. It was getting rather stuffy in here and I wanted some fresh air. I wasn't gone for long."

"Three quarters of an hour," Pettifer clarified. "We saw you re-enter the building at five to one."

Gavin blinked dazedly.

"Was I really so long? I can't remember. As I said, I was just wandering around town."

"Not a very good alibi, is it?" Pettifer remarked quietly. "Are you sure you don't want to try again?"

Gavin visibly started, almost dropping the files in his arms.

"*Alibi*? Wait, whoever said anything about my needing an alibi?" He looked wildly, imploringly, at Cassie. "I thought we were just talking about my bunking off work for a few minutes."

"Sergeant, surely you can't really think that Gavin had anything to do with this?" Cassie moved closer to her charge like a protective lioness. "The very idea's ridiculous. Why on earth would he want to kill a random auctioneer? I don't think he's even ever *been* to an auction. He *hates* old things." She motioned around them. "Just look at his office, for heaven's sake; Le Corbusier himself would probably think it was a tad on the minimalist side."

Pettifer ignored her.

"Where were you yesterday afternoon, lad, between one and three?"

"Well, *here*." Gavin stammered. "For some of it. I was back in the building by about twenty to three. Then the meeting broke up after Mayor Lane…" he glanced sideways at Cassie. "After she… well, ran out."

Pettifer looked askance at Cassie.

"I thought Felicia was *dead*, remember?" She said defensively.

"So I stayed behind for a while, clearing up the room," Gavin continued. "I thought about sitting down to some of the work I wanted to catch up on, but… well, it didn't seem quite right, somehow. After what had happened. I couldn't concentrate, so I went home."

"And what time was that?"

"About three o'clock, maybe? I didn't look closely at the time." Then he frowned as something apparently occurred to him. It seemed to embolden him enough to give Pettifer a cool look. "Although surely you would know that, if you've been watching the CCTV footage. You'd have seen me go."

Pettifer smiled.

"Just checking your memory, that's all."

"Checking his veracity, more like," Cassie snapped. "Where are you going with this, Sergeant?"

"So, you went straight home?" Pettifer pressed Gavin. "Was there anyone else there?"

"No, I live alone. I have a flat on Star Lane, above one of the shops." Gavin looked suddenly overwhelmed by what was being asked of him. "I didn't see anyone, either. Oh God, that means no one can prove I was there. But I *was*. I didn't do anything, honestly." He looked at Cassie again. "You have to believe me."

"I'm not the enemy here, lad," Pettifer said awkwardly. Felicia, observing quietly, could tell that he wasn't relishing any of this. "I just want the truth. If you tell me what you were doing at the auction, it'll go no further—providing it has no bearing on the case." He hesitated, then ventured, in a coaxing, conspiratorial sort of way, "a bit of a romantic tryst, maybe? I've been your age once, lad. I remember what it was like. I noticed there was a girl there. Blonde, pretty, about your age. If you tell me that—"

Cassie snorted loudly. Pettifer's head whipped around, and he fixed her with a glare.

"Sorry," she said sheepishly. "It's just, nothing could be less likely."

"I'm not interested in women, Sergeant," Gavin explained simply. "Never have been. It's not something I've ever hidden."

"I see." The tips of Pettifer's cauliflower ears had gone quite pink, Felicia thought. "Well, that's as may be. But I still need an answer from you. What were you *doing* there?"

Gavin seemed to waver for a moment. There was a heartbeat of a pause; Felicia realised that she was holding her breath, waiting. But then, suddenly, his face shuttered, and he shook his head.

"I've told you, I *wasn't*. I went for a walk." He began to push folders into the bookcase which ran along the wall behind his desk, his back firmly to Pettifer. "Look, I have nothing else to say. If you don't believe what I've told you, then you'll have to arrest me."

Pettifer snapped his notebook shut with a billowing sigh.

"All right, let's leave it there, then. For now," he evidently felt compelled to add. With a nod at Felicia and Cassie, he exited in his usual shambolic fashion.

Gavin didn't turn, but as soon as the door banged shut behind the policeman, he sagged forwards, bracing his hands upon the shelf as though holding himself up. Felicia could see the tenseness of his shoulder blades beneath his shirt. There was a heavy silence, one which Felicia didn't feel it was her place to break.

"I really am sorry about leaving during the meeting," he said at last, in a quiet voice. "I don't know what came over me…"

"We'll be having words," Cassie said sternly.

"Of course." He swallowed, turning to gather up an armful of the remaining files. "You know, actually, these shouldn't really be up here…" he was already backing towards the door, clearly desperate to escape. "I'll just take them…"

He trailed off, not even bothering to finish the sentence as he scuttled out. His head was down, the expression on his face one of utter misery. Felicia felt her heart go out to him. She looked back at Cassie, who was watching him go, all pretence of angry disappointment gone. Now, she just looked worried.

"Do you believe him?" Felicia asked, in a low voice, mindful that he might be lingering just around the corner on the landing.

"What? Gavin?" Cassie didn't seem to be thinking along the same lines; she was operating at her usual mother-of-four-children volume. "Bunking off work in the middle of a council meeting to 'go for a walk'?" She appeared utterly derisive of the idea. "Pigs would sooner fly. I struggle to get him to take his allotted lunch hour. He's the only person I know who's as assiduous as Robyn." She sighed frustratedly. "I don't know what he thinks he's *playing* at. If he withholds something from the police, he'll be in a lot of trouble. He's worked so hard on his career; I can't watch him do this." She tossed a tangle of hair back off her forehead with an impatient gesture. "I suppose I'd better talk to him. He hasn't really got anyone else. No parental figure to do these things. No anyone, really. Not any more." Her lips twisted. "I know he can be a bit trying sometimes, and I moan about him a lot, but I don't know… there's something rather sad about him, something *alone* I feel *someone* has to be there."

Felicia smiled softly.

"You're a good person, Cass, you know that?"

"Lamentably, yes," Cassie grumbled. "Sometimes, I wish I weren't. Life would be much easier as a sociopath, one feels."

"But not as rewarding." Felicia kissed her friend's cheek. "You go and talk to him; I'll catch you later."

She dashed down the stairs and out onto the pavement, taking a moment to pat Daniel Lambert fondly on the head as she went. Looking to her left, she spotted Pettifer's unmistakable form shuffling down St Mary's Hill towards the bridge. She could just see The George from here, its brightly appointed hanging baskets swinging in the breeze.

"On your way home, are you?" She slipped into step with him. "Where's your car?"

He gave her a suspicious sideways glance.

"I'm parked at the Old Cattle Market."

"Great, well I'm picking up Algernon from Betsy's cottage on Bath Row, so I'll walk with you."

They crossed the road, passing beneath the ancient Norman archway set into the wall between two shops.

"So… I saw Mr Clancy in The George just now," she said, striving for a casual, disinterested tone. "I didn't know he was a person of interest to you."

Pettifer gave her a look that suggested that he was well aware of what she was getting at.

"He's not. I gave him the green light to head back to London; if he's still here, then it's his choice to be."

Aha! Some information at last. Felicia felt a giddy flush of triumph. Invigorated, she spun to face him.

"You don't think it's just a little bit *odd*?"

"Not at all." Crushingly, Pettifer's answer came back immediately, and without inflection. "I believe he said he has some business interests here. Besides, he's a wealthy man, The George is a nice hotel; why shouldn't he stay on if he wants to?"

"Oh." Feeling a little deflated, she said, "I didn't know he had any other connection to here. I thought he just came up for the sale."

"You *really* think he makes all that money from antique furniture? In today's climate?" Pettifer sounded incredulous.

"Well… *yes*." Belatedly realising how naïve that sounded, she persisted, "brown wooden furniture may be having a slump right now, but he specialises in French Baroque—think the Palace of Versailles, Marie Antoinette—and that still goes for tens, if not hundreds of thousands of pounds."

"That may well be," he didn't look impressed. "But men like that never put all their eggs in one basket, Ms Grant. They have their fingers in any number of pies. Believe me, I come across enough of them in my job. Some of them over-reach and end up in the fraud courts, but most, like your Mr Clancy, keep their heads and carry on quietly, raking in the money as they go." At the expression on her face, he raised an eyebrow. "That shocks you?"

"Actually, I'm marvelling at your range of metaphors," Felicia confessed, trying not to smile.

He gave her a sour look, stopping at the small footbridge that crossed the stream onto the town meadows.

"I believe this is where we part. Now be gone. Before I book you for interfering in my investigation... again."

She held up her hands.

"Believe me, I have absolutely no desire to get involved in a murder investigation. I'm just... asking the question." She looked him squarely in the eye. "Look, murder's all about people, surely? Why they do what they do. Well, the thing about being an auctioneer is that you get to know *people*; you see just about every sort there is, at all different stages of life and death. You never really look at a person on a superficial level again. You always find yourself seeing more than maybe most people would, looking deeper than perhaps you ought. It becomes a habit." She shrugged. "I can't even help it any more."

The look he gave her was not unsympathetic.

"I'm sure, but that's supposing that people are acting with some sort of accepted scale, a predictable sense of humanity. But to be honest, I'm starting to think we might be dealing with someone quite mad." He scrubbed a hand across his fatigued face, sounding resigned. "Why else would anyone kill someone in such a risky and public way, if not for the sheer thrill of it? And why murder a blameless old man, who couldn't have had much time left anyway? None of it makes any sense, and I'm beginning to think that's because it's not meant to."

"*Was* he blameless, though?" She blurted out. "I mean, if you'd just look into what my father said about—"

"I *did* look into it."

The pronouncement stunned her into a brief silence.

"Oh," she said at last, in a small voice. "I see."

"Heavenly would have my head if he knew about this," he muttered, apparently to himself.

"And?" She pressed. "What did you find?"

He spread his hands wide.

"Absolutely nothing."

Felicia felt the sense of anti-climax thud heavily into her stomach.

"Really? Nothing at *all*?"

"What? That's surprising?" His tone was harsh, sarcastic. "Because it's town lore, so it *must* be true? Where do you think fairy stories came from, Ms Grant? Bored villagers and one vaguely factual happenstance which gets embellished into something far more exciting than the sum of its parts, that's where." He kicked moodily at a stone balancing on the edge of the bridge. It fell into the shallow water with a tinny splash. "As much as I can tell from an eighty-year-old police report, everything was above board. Trauma to the head and body, but nothing which couldn't be consistent with falling down a flight of stairs. No indication he strangled her, no marks on her wrists where she might have been grabbed and thrown from the landing. Besides, by all accounts, the boy just wasn't the type. Shy, dreamy, even-tempered, not exactly quick-witted..." He looked at her face and seemed to relent a little. "Look, I'm sorry, but, between you and that husband of yours... royal treasure and aristocratic cover-ups might sound like a titillating solution to the casual bystander, but all they're doing is distracting me from solving the very unromantic murder case in front of me. A murder case which a lot of people are desperate for me to wrap up quickly. I owe it to them to focus on finding the truth."

Feeling both stung and ashamed, Felicia knew she shouldn't say any more. But...

"I just can't accept it," she said stubbornly. "I can't accept that it's like you said. There *has* to be a reason. There just... has to be."

"If there is, it'll be right in front of us, not in the depths of fantasy land. Murder's either very prosaic, or very random. The public likes to think that it's more often the former. It makes them feel safer to think that, so we let them." He brought himself up abruptly. "I shouldn't have said any of this to you. Go home, Ms Grant. Spend time with your family, get on with your life. Try not to think about murder, or what people will do to one another. Believe me, you'll be a lot happier that way."

And then he was gone, striding off across the expanse of grass, the pinkening twilight blurring his edges until he was scarcely visible.

Felicia watched him disappear, unable to deny that in this case, he was most probably right. Turning on the spot, she faced the incongruous cluster of edifices that made up Bath Row. Unsurprisingly, once the site of the old town swimming baths, the building itself still featured the Victorian painted sign declaring it as such, although it had long since been a private residence. At one end, a crumbling wall was all which remained of the old castle, at the other, a hodgepodge of quaint little cottages. Although not otherwise particularly noteworthy, they did possess the distinction of being some of the only houses in town to boast front gardens; something which the owners used to great effect. Now, they were a confectionery-like riot of pink and white blossom, daffodils and sweet violets. In the summer, it would be roses, the autumn, dahlias. Winter would see twinkling lights woven amongst the bare branches, and holly wreaths glistening with jewel-like berries on the front doors.

Felicia pushed open the wrought-iron gate that led to Betsy's cottage, careful not to crush the swathes of primroses that encroached over the edges of the path. The front door was painted a pale lilac with a brass knocker in the shape of a batter whisk. Felicia smiled as she raised it and let it fall, wondering who'd bought it for her. Betsy had so many friends.

"Felicia," a floury figure loomed in the doorway. "Just in time. Algernon and I were about to eat all of the cake."

"I take it it worked, then?" Felicia stepped inside. "It is…" She raised a dramatic hand to her forehead. "Perfected?"

At the kitchen island, an even more floury Algernon was eating buttercream out of the bowl.

"It is," he said happily.

Felicia patted his head, trying not to look alarmed as a cloud of white powder puffed out.

"Sorry about that," Betsy said sheepishly. "We got a bit carried away. Had a flour fight."

Felicia held up her hands.

"So long as he's had a good time. Thanks so much for looking after him, by the way."

"Oh, he's never any trouble," Betsy said fondly. "Besides, I like having someone young about the house. What with my own grandchildren…" her eyes misted, then she blinked firmly, recovering herself. "But never mind all of that. They've got a good life Down Under, and I've got plenty to be keeping myself busy with here. Now," she said briskly, in a tone that brooked no further discussion of the subject. "You'll be wanting to get him home for some dinner. If he can manage some after all of the cake batter and icing he's been eating."

"I think you'd be surprised," Felicia said dryly. Then, "Algie, have you got your things together? We'd better be leaving Betsy to her evening."

"Just a sec." He scrambled down off the high stool and disappeared into the other room.

"While he's out of earshot," Betsy said, lowering her voice. "I thought you should know that I've finished going through all of the lots from yesterday and I can't see anything missing. Nothing that would match the weapon the police have been looking for, at any rate. I even went back through all of the invoices that had been paid earlier in the day, before the murder… I mean, er… before the body was found."

"You mean, for people who'd already taken things away with them whilst the sale was still going on? Of course, that makes perfect sense. I mean, there's no reason why the killer would hang around until the end."

"That was my reasoning. Surely, I thought, you'd get it done and then leave with the weapon before anyone discovered what had happened."

"It's a great theory. But no luck, you say?"

"As far as I can tell, the weapon couldn't have come from the sale."

She said it confidently enough, but her lips were pursed unhappily.

"Something's bothering you, isn't it?" Felicia said quietly, as Algernon re-entered the kitchen.

"Just a feeling..." Betsy paused shook her head vigorously, causing her fluffy, lilac-toned curls to tremble. "But no, ignore me, duck. I'm being fanciful. I've been over it and over those lots until I could recite them in my sleep, and like I said, it's all accounted for."

"So, we're back to square one, then," Felicia concluded resignedly. "Sergeant Pettifer's going to be very disappointed."

"Mum, do you think Dad might stay around for a bit now? Maybe he could spend Easter with us."

Felicia hesitated as she ushered Algernon in front of her. The pavement on the town's main bridge—the only one that allowed cars—was notoriously narrow, even by Stamford's standards. It had to be undertaken in single file, unless you harboured a secret desire to get clipped by a fast-moving wing mirror or have your toes run over by a spinning tyre.

"I don't know," she confessed. Once upon a time, she'd felt she had to have an answer for everything, but these days, she saw no point in lying to him. Algie was twelve now, old enough to know where things stood between herself and Dexter. Old enough to understand that his father, whilst attentive and affectionate in so many ways, had become ever more unreliable in the past few years, as his priorities had skewed in the direction of fame and adulation.

Or was she being unfair again? Was Cassie right, and she used the all-encompassing demands of the show as an excuse for giving up on a marriage that, if not as sparkling as it might once have been, had hardly been in dire straits either? It was a question that still pricked at her sometimes, and now it was at the forefront of her mind again, uncomfortably insistent as she looked down into her son's hopeful, upturned face.

She'd been aware, as she and Dexter had strolled down St Mary's Street that afternoon, that they'd probably resembled any other couple out for a romantic Sunday. Once upon a time, they *had* been that couple; best friends in love, needing nothing but each other's company. The thought had made her rather wistful despite herself. And then at lunch with Algernon, the three of them together again... it had all seemed so natural. As if nothing had changed. Dexter and Algie had been joking together, boasting about who could order the most impressive pudding, and in that moment, watching them sitting side by side, she'd realised, perhaps for the first time, just how alike they were. She'd always thought of them as chalk and cheese; Dexter tall and dark, Algernon slight and ethereal, with his russet hair and wide-set silver eyes. Dexter so affable, so outgoing, always at the centre of any party, Algernon so quiet, so mysterious, always on the edges, always observing.

"I mean, now they've cancelled his programme, he hasn't got anything to rush off for, has he?" Algernon was saying, as they approached the crossroads upon which The George sat, its windows a patchwork of golden diamonds, like cat's eyes in the growing dark. "So he might as well stay and—"

"Wait... now they've *what*?" She stopped abruptly, grabbing his shoulder and spinning him around.

"They rang him earlier," Algernon shifted the cake tin, which he was over-protectively hugging to his chest. "From London. They said they didn't think it was right to carry on with it, after what happened yesterday. The murders," he added, as though she might mistakenly think he meant something else.

"How do you know all of this, anyway? Were you listening at doors?"

"Of course not." Algernon looked mortally offended. "But Grandad's cottage isn't very big, and Dad's voice is quite loud when he's cross. I worked it out from his side of the conversation."

"Oh, dear," Felicia sighed, looking both ways before steering him across the road onto Water Street. "I expect he's going to be in quite the mood when we get back."

"He was rather quiet when he dropped me off at Betsy's," Algernon ventured. "And Dad's not normally quiet, is he? Do you think he'll be really upset?"

"It is very important to him, Algie," Felicia said gently. "So yes, I imagine he will be."

"Oh." Algernon drooped for a moment, then brightened. "But in that case, it'll be good for him to stay with us for a while. We can distract him."

"Hmm…" Felicia said, noncommittally. She was peering into the dusk, trying to locate her father's cottage. With a wedge of inky-black riverbank on one side, the sole illumination came from a few small windows in the houses to their right. The only sound was the rustling of the weeping willows, emerging from somewhere within the thick darkness. It was strangely disorientating, even almost isolating, despite their being in the middle of town.

"You know, Grandad seemed to think it was all quite funny," Algernon was saying thoughtfully. "He said something about comeuppance."

"Yes, well," Felicia said hastily, making a mental note to speak to her father later about setting a good example. "It's probably the painkillers he's on, or something."

Suddenly, further down the street, headlights flicked on, throwing a glaring beam of harsh white light into their faces. Dazzled, Felicia held up an arm to shield her eyes, but it was too late.

With a screech of tyres, the car was speeding towards them.

Felicia acted on pure instinct. Grasping Algernon's shoulders, she yanked him backwards, just as the car shot past, so close that she felt the cold *whoosh* of metallic air roll over them like a wave. They toppled backwards, landing in a heap on top of a patch of Narcissi.

"Algernon?" She shook the limp form on top of her, heart in her mouth. "Algie?"

Suddenly, his head shot up, looking frantically from side to side.

"Is the cake all right?"

Spotting the tin wedged up on its side against a nearby tree stump, he scrambled over to it, prising open the lid.

"Good to know you've got your priorities sorted," Felicia said shakily, getting to her feet, then having to grab at the back of a bench to steady herself. She looked along the street, but the car was nowhere to be seen. "Come along, we'd better get inside, before anything else happens."

Chapter Sixteen

"And you think it was deliberate?"

Sergeant Pettifer's booming voice rang around the small, low-beamed kitchen. Felicia moved towards the cottage door, poking her head around before pushing it to and flicking down the latch.

"I don't want Algernon to hear any of this," she explained, in a low tone. "As far as he's concerned, it was an accident."

Twelve might be old enough to know some things, but not everything, Felicia told herself silently. The thoughts that were circulating around her head right now were things no child should ever have to confront.

Pettifer nodded, then proceeded in what, whilst was clearly intended to be a quieter voice, bore no discernible difference in volume.

"And the car drove straight at you, you say? It couldn't have been simply going too fast? It's a narrow road down here."

"It practically mounted the pavement, Sergeant."

"Fair enough." Pettifer made a jot in his notebook. She wondered what his handwriting was like; atrocious, if the shape of the squiggles he was making was anything to go by. She was starting to suspect that he wasn't making notes at all, but just did it for effect. "And you didn't get a good look at the car?"

"I didn't get *any* kind of look at the car," Felicia retorted. "I told you, they turned on their full beams. All I could see was headlights. I couldn't even tell you what colour it was."

"A curious thing, that." A silken voice emerged from behind her. "It interests me very much."

Felicia spun around to see a man standing in the open doorway.

He wasn't tall, but there was a proportional compactness about him, something neat, elegant... almost *willowy*, Felicia decided, slightly surprised by the choice of word. It wasn't one that would normally be used to describe a man, but here, it seemed to fit. His hair was silver in the true sense, swept backwards from a high, domed forehead, beneath which small, pointed features clustered close together in the centre of his face, flanked by two sharply sheered cheekbones. He didn't look old enough to have gone naturally grey yet—it was hard to say exactly how old he might be, but Felicia estimated 45 at most. His eyes were an ice blue, with just a touch of violet, and moved around little. He was dressed impeccably, in a pale-grey three-piece suit that toned in perfectly with his hair. The jacket was unbuttoned, his hands were in the pockets. He was oddly beautiful, in an uneasy, unpredictable way. He put her in mind of a fox—an arctic fox, silvered and silent, watchful from a distance. He stood there, waiting, as though he'd been there for hours, although of course he couldn't have been, Felicia noted, with a jolt. That was the door she'd *just* closed. She'd latched it only moments ago.

"And you are?" She managed, although in truth, she already knew.

"Of course, my manners." The man stepped forward, extending a hand. The kind of hand she'd been expecting; a pianist's hand, pale and long-fingered, with smooth, tapering nails. "Detective Chief Inspector Heavenly, at your service.

Apologies for not being here sooner. I was at a function and the message didn't reach me immediately." A small quirk of a muscle in his cheek revealed his displeasure at this. "But I came as soon as I heard. I knew this required my personal presence. Such a *distressing* incident for all of us. The whole town, in fact."

Felicia tried not to stare at him in open disbelief. For once, however, her innate civility failed her.

"And, yet, two murders *wasn't*?"

The words were out of her mouth before she could stop them, incredulous and accusing. Something flickered across his face, too quick to see, but the impression it left on her subconscious burned.

"I prefer to remain in the background during investigations, Mrs Grant." The obsequious tone was gone. In its place was something clipped, flinty. "It is my method. Unorthodox, I'll admit, but it's yielded results in its time."

"*Ms* Grant," she threw her hands up, finally pushed beyond all endurance. It was, perhaps, a fairly minor point in the circumstances, but after the night she'd had, it finally tipped her over the edge. "Grant is *my* name! It's always been *my* name. *Grant's* Auctioneers. Why does nobody seem to have got that?"

Ungratifyingly, no one looked particularly moved by her outburst... except she noted, with a surge of goodwill towards him, Sergeant Pettifer, who arranged his squashed features into a sheepish expression.

"Good point." He looked at Dexter. "It should have occurred to me that you must have taken her name."

It was probably in that pile of background information waiting for him on his desk at the station. Due to the speed at which events were progressing in this case, he hadn't even had the chance to run an eye over it yet.

"Dashed inconvenient it is, too," Dexter grumbled. "Even in this day and age. It's an administrative nightmare. Sometimes, I wish I'd never done it."

"Believe me, it was a good call," Felicia said, with feeling.

Pettifer immediately made a mental note to look up Dexter Grant's birth name. Just for a bit of light relief.

Heavenly, meanwhile, was looking supremely unimpressed by this digression.

"Can we get back to the matter at hand, please? Tell me… *Ms* Grant… why would anyone want to harm you, do you think?"

"Because of *this*," Felicia, clearly ready for the question, caught up the paper from the kitchen table and unfolded it with a snap, brandishing the front page. On it, the headline blared, AUCTIONEER CHIEF WITNESS IN DOUBLE MURDER.

"I'm not sure that's entirely correct," Dexter mused. "I mean, wouldn't a double murder be when two people were killed together, at the same time?"

Everyone in the room glared at him.

"Someone has to defend the English language," he muttered, receding into the corner.

Felicia turned back to Heavenly, tapping the paper.

"I was even warned about it today. Told I needed to be careful. I didn't really pay much attention, but now…"

"Now, what? Someone accelerates from a parking space a little too quickly? This town is filled with elderly drivers, Ms Grant. Half of them can hardly see over the steering wheel." He gave her a pitying look. "We mustn't let the events of the past couple of days send our imagination into overdrive."

Over his shoulder, Pettifer winced. Felicia Grant wasn't the kind of woman who took well to being patronised.

He was right; the transformation on her face was instantaneous. Like an icy wind sweeping over a landscape, freezing everything in its wake. When she spoke, her voice held that bite of frost he'd become accustomed to when you got on the wrong side of her.

"Why are you even *here*, Chief Inspector, if you believe this was just an accident?"

"I never said that, Ms Grant," Heavenly said silkily. "I only questioned your version of events, that's all."

There was a pause. Then—

"You think I'm making this *up*?" Felicia looked aghast. "Why would I do that?"

"I may have been invisible during this investigation, but I have not been idle." Heavenly had begun to pace, as he often did when he was starting to soliloquise. Pettifer suspected he thought it very Holmesian. As it was, in this case, he came up against the wall within three steps and was forced to turn, looking annoyed at having the effect curtailed by what 17th-century builders had considered adequate floor space. "I've read the files, the reports, the interview notes. And two people stand out very clearly to me in all of this. *Two* people who appeared suddenly in town on the morning of the first murder. *Two* people who stumbled rather conveniently upon the second body. *Two* people who, when questioned, have given consistently vague and at times, frankly, fantastical"—he looked pointedly at Dexter—"accounts as to what they were doing and why."

So *that's* what Heavenly was really doing here. Pettifer felt the foreboding that had been nagging at him since his superior had appeared in the doorway morph into cold, unwelcome clarity. Clearly, Felicia did, too, because her eyes widened in alarm. But it was Dexter who got in first. Not looking at all ruffled at the implication that he might be involved in two murders, he opened his palms wide and said reasonably:

"Look, Inspector, you can't be serious. We've been *over* this. Felicia couldn't possibly have done anything. She was on the rostrum the whole time."

Felicia cast him a look that bordered on gratitude, but apparently didn't wish to commit itself.

"Yes, but *you* weren't, were you, sir?" Heavenly whirled on him. There was a gleam of triumph in his eye. His lips were rolled back slightly, revealing shining white canines.

Sergeant Pettifer screwed his eyes shut and contemplated other career options.

Clearly, it finally dawned on Dexter that Heavenly was deadly serious, and for a moment, he actually seemed lost for words, which the sergeant didn't imagine happened regularly. He recovered himself quickly, though.

"Well, no, but everyone saw me arrive after the murder had taken place," he pointed out defiantly. "There's an entire roomful of people in there who will swear to it."

"What they *saw* was you bursting in making a big spectacle. There's nothing to say that you weren't there earlier, mingling unobtrusively in the crowd."

Briefly, Dexter's concern was overtaken by mortal offence at the notion that he could possibly go unnoticed.

"For all we know, you two could have been in cahoots." Heavenly was clearly warming to his theme, talking to himself more than anyone. He was pacing again, in truncated spurts. He appeared to be enjoying himself immensely. "Yes, that could work. All eyes on her while *he* quietly does the deed."

There was a beat of stunned silence. Sergeant Pettifer felt like putting his head in his hands.

"Cahoots?" Dexter spluttered disbelievingly.

"The deed?" Felicia murmured faintly.

Sergeant Pettifer looked up at the ceiling and wondered if that job at his wife's cousin's factory was still going begging.

"Just so we're absolutely clear on this," Felicia said quietly. "Are you actually accusing us of committing two murders?"

The atmosphere in the room had suddenly gone very still. It was like a farcical play, with all of them standing on their spots, frozen in place. And, yet, nothing about it was funny. Pettifer suddenly felt himself stir, come back to reality. He leapt into action.

"Of course not," he blurted out quickly, before Heavenly could respond. "We would never do anything so unprofessional, would we, sir?"

If possible, the air temperature seemed to drop several more degrees. Heavenly looked utterly furious, his eerily smooth skin stretched taut across his fox-like face. Felicia looked down at his hand and saw it clenched into a fist at his side, with a visible tremor he was clearly trying to suppress, and in that moment, she felt a flash of real disquiet. There was something about him that seemed to be held together only by the thin lacquer of his polished veneer.

He took a deep, slow breath. Then he opened his eyes and smiled thinly.

"Nothing so *dramatic*, Ms Grant." He was all unctuousness again; somehow, Felicia found that worse. She had to fight a very real urge to recoil. "You in the art world really do have *quite* the imagination; I find it *most* fascinating." A rather forced laugh here. "No, this was merely some casual questions. A slight experimental quirk of mine, I'll admit, but I like to think expansively in these cases. Show the town that I will leave no stone unturned, no question unasked, in my quest for the truth."

Dexter raised a dark brow.

"Yours?"

"Ours. The police. The families. The entire town. We all deserve answers, don't you think?"

"In which case, you still have a lot more stones to turn over." Suddenly, Felicia couldn't stand to have the man within ten feet of her for a moment longer. She moved pointedly to stand by the door. "We mustn't keep you from it."

The lines of his face tautened even more. Felicia noticed that the muscle in his cheek was twitching again. For a tense moment, she thought he was going to argue, but then he spun on his polished heel and stalked out, snapping at Pettifer to follow... which he did, but slowly, indicating with his head for Felicia to accompany him out into the hall. The front door was wide open, Heavenly having slammed it against the wall with a peevish lack of nominative determinism. Pettifer paused in the opening, the small outside lantern light above illuminating his features in a burnt orange glow.

"Is he always like that?" She made an attempt at levity. "Because if so, I can understand why you look perpetually stressed."

"Be careful," he said quietly, out of the corner of his mouth, and she knew that they weren't talking about Heavenly any more.

"So you *do* think that someone tried to—"

"I don't know what I think, all right? That's what worries me. Just… err on the side of caution, all right? Don't do anything reckless."

Any feeling of vindication that he at least half believed her was swiftly replaced by a less tender emotion. She folded her arms mutinously.

"Reckless like what exactly? Like trying to work out who might be trying to kill me *before* they have another go at it?" Her voice was hard, sarcastic. "That sort of thing, you mean? You'd rather I just sat around and politely waited to be bumped off, would you? *Much* more sensible."

"Look, I'll do what I can. But Heavenly has got himself involved now; my hands are tied. I can't help you as much as I might have done before."

He did seem genuinely contrite, and having seen Heavenly in action, she could understand what a tight spot he was now in. If he helped her, he'd have to go against his superior. His irascible, not-entirely-balanced superior, for that matter. His entire career could be on the line. She felt herself relenting slightly.

"You helped me tonight," she said softly. "Thanks for not letting us get arrested."

Pettifer gave a hefty shrug.

"He had no grounds for it anyway; it would have been a PR disaster. Not that *he'll* appreciate that," he added, with a rueful look out into the darkness, where presumably Heavenly was lurking impatiently. "He never does. I'll get the bollocking of my life the minute we're out of earshot."

Felicia winced.

"Sorry."

"Never mind all of that. You just do as I asked, all right?" He jabbed a stubby finger at her. "The last thing I want is to be finding your body somewhere."

"Getting fond of me, are we?" She joked weakly.

"Nah. Just don't fancy all the paperwork." He grinned, an expression that quickly turned to a grimace as a querulous voice shrieked, "Pettifer! Where *are* you?"

"Here we go," he muttered, disappearing into the night to join his superior. As they moved away, she could hear Heavenly hissing furiously, "You *will* suffer for this, Sergeant. How *dare* you interfere with my interrogation?"

She closed the front door, feeling a little guilty for leaving Pettifer to Heavenly's wrath, but knowing that there wasn't a lot she could do. That was his fight. Right now, she had her own to deal with.

"Are you going to listen to him?"

A quiet voice made her spin around. Dexter was leaning against the doorframe to the kitchen, hands in pockets, watching her steadily.

She tipped her chin defensively.

"Did no one tell you it's bad manners to eavesdrop?"

"So you're not." He nodded wearily. "I can't say I'm surprised. You've never been great at taking other people's advice."

"Turns out I'm not so great at sitting around waiting to be killed, either," she snapped, with a bravado that, truth be told, she didn't really feel. But it was better than the alternative, which was retreating under the duvet and succumbing to the terror and helplessness that was pawing at the edges of her consciousness.

"I've got to take some action. If the police aren't going to investigate it, then I'll do it myself."

She wasn't quite sure where that last pronouncement came from, but as she said it, she realised that she meant it. Unfortunately, Dexter chose that moment to echo her next thoughts.

"Oh, really, and how are you going to do *that*? You're an antiques valuer, Felicia, not a detective."

Later, she would tell herself that it was his tone that did it. That she might have backed out, might have changed her mind... if it weren't for the incredulous dismissiveness in his voice at that moment. It sparked a firework of reaction in her, an old stubbornness that steeled every bar of resolve in her body. She regarded him coolly.

"I'm used to being observant, asking the right questions. I'm sure the skills are fairly transferrable."

And besides, she reflected silently, as she swept off up the stairs, leaving him staring in her wake, what other choice did she really have?

It was a cold night. Stamford lay silent, the pubs having bolted their doors hours ago, the lights in the surrounding windows steadily clicking to black. The only illumination came from the low gleam of streetlamps, pooling in amber folds on the pavement. Up above, the moon was wrestling with the thin film of cloud that screened it from view, wreathing itself in a ghostly rainbow.

Even if anyone had been around to see the shadow dart across the cobbles of Red Lion Square, it was unlikely they would have noticed it. It was careful, skirting the edges of the light's reach, staying in the darkest recesses beneath the buildings. Even if anyone had been around to see it slip around the back of the church onto the steep incline of Barn Hill, it was unlikely they would have paid much attention, lost as they would have been in their own thoughts, their own desire to get home at such an hour. If anyone had been around to see it melt beneath the empty carriage archway of Halliday House... now, *that* might have given them pause. After all, everyone in town knew that the place was still a crime scene.

But as it was, it didn't matter. Because no one was around. No one saw. And the shadow moved soundlessly around to the back of the house, to where a small, meanly high window delineated the lowlier end of the servant's quarters. No view out across the garden for the scullery maids as they washed pots and peeled vegetables; the Georgian planners had seen to that.

The shadow paused for a moment, a splash of darkness against the pale stone wall. It was regarding the window thoughtfully. Then it seemed to come to a decision. It disappeared momentarily into the outbuildings, re-emerging with a rusted garden spade, which it jammed upwards into the crumbling wooden window frame. With a spongy splintering sound, the frame gave way in an instant, the window gusting open on a sudden breeze.

If anyone had been around at that moment, they would have seen the moon finally break free from its filmy prison, shedding cold silver light over the scene, melting the shadowy cloak of the figure below. Suddenly, it wasn't a vague shape any more, but a person. A person who was smiling to themselves.

But no one was around to see. And so the silvery figure braced itself against the rough stone wall and heaved itself upwards, slipping soundlessly through the opening to re-join the shadows within.

Chapter Seventeen

By midway through Monday morning, Felicia was forced to concede the decidedly galling fact that Dexter had, in fact, been right. Any bracing visions of herself as the gifted amateur sleuth applying their niche, career-based knowledge to the thorny subject of solving crimes was dissolving in front of her eyes faster than a sugar lump dropped into a glass of champagne as she surveyed the piles of useless and decidedly unrevealing information she'd gathered around her. There was no getting away from it; she had absolutely no idea what she was doing. Worse, she didn't even know where to *start*.

She'd been raking through the list of registered buyers from Saturday's sale, hoping desperately that something—or rather some*one*—would leap out at her. Someone who'd been in that room wanted to kill her, and she had absolutely no idea who. It was almost too paralysing to think about, so she forced her mind back onto the practicalities.

Surely, *someone* had to have been acting suspiciously, had to have given themselves away *somehow*. She screwed up her brow, forcing herself to think back. But all that she could come up with was that half the room had been acting in what most people would term a strange or shifty manner. That was an occupational hazard of hosting a room full of antique dealers.

So much for transferrable skills.

Felicia dropped her head onto a stack of old auction catalogues with a groan. This was hopeless.

"Not going well then, I take it?" Hugo popped his head nervously around the door, cup of tea in hand.

She hastily clicked off the screen, then realised how foolish that was. After all, there was no reason why she shouldn't be looking at the buyer's list. In fact, it was actively necessary in the aftermath of a sale. Hugo wouldn't have thought anything of it. Although now she was behaving in such a skittish manner, he might notice something was amiss; the very thing she'd been trying to avoid.

Indeed, he was looking at her curiously now.

"Are you all right? You know, you don't have to be here, Felicia. We can handle it between us. You've had one hell of a weekend; no one would blame you for taking a quiet day."

Felicia choked back a strangled laugh. A quiet day? With a double murderer on her back?

Although of course, Hugo didn't know about that last part. Nobody did. She thought it was something best kept to herself. Besides, if the police didn't even believe her, who else would? She'd just come across as unhinged.

And there was another small factor to consider. This person could be anyone. This was a market town, the kind where popping out for a morning's errand took 40 minutes rather than four due to the amount of acquaintances one became waylaid by. The high street on a weekday morning was a veritable hub, news spreading quickly over frothy coffees and freshly baked sourdough loaves wrapped in brown paper. People talking, openly and innocently, to someone they knew, could easily get back to whoever was doing this.

As far as her adversary was aware, Felicia thought last night's incident was nothing more than an accident. That seemed to be the natural assumption for the police, so the killer no doubt hoped the same could be said for her. It was an assumption she had no desire to disabuse them of. Let them think they were safe.

"Really, I'm better off here," she assured Hugo. Not least because it was where she felt most secure, she added silently. Her own territory. "Besides, I can't leave you in the lurch, not while Dad's out of action. The least I can do is answer some emails." Her eyes raked down the screen dubiously. "He's... er... banned quite a lot of people, hasn't he?"

Like a shop or a pub could refuse to serve a customer, auction houses had the discretion to refuse to accept a person's bids. Sometimes, it could be on suspicion of fraud, more often because the person hadn't paid for something they bought in a previous sale. Technically, bidding in an auction was a legally binding contract, but if someone simply refused to pay up afterwards, there wasn't a lot the auction house could do, save ban them from buying in future sales. It happened a lot with dealers, either because they didn't look at something properly beforehand, or because they left a bid on something then ran out of money in the interim.

"Oh, yes, he loves banning people," Hugo said cheerfully, taking a swig of his tea. Felicia noticed, somewhat to her chagrin, that the mug had the *Treasure Seeker* logo emblazoned across it. How the hell had *that* got here? "You know what it's like. Dealers running out of money and not paying for stuff. He chased old Dodger Wells out of here with a shotgun once. He still comes back, mind. Nothing puts him off."

"Life at a country auction," Felicia joked weakly, trying not to let her mind fill with the potential assault charge that might have been. "Move over, James Herriot. Someone should write a book about it."

"I think someone has." The phone started to ring downstairs, and Hugo pulled a face. "Here we go again. Everyone wants to know when they can come and get their purchases, and I don't know what to tell them. The police haven't given us any information about when we can release the items. I'm putting them all off with some waffle about how technically, they're still part of the crime scene."

"But surely if they now know that the weapon didn't come from here, then everything else is free to go?"

"You would think. But I don't fancy asking that Sergeant about it, do you? He's pretty intimidating."

"Oh, he's all right," Felicia said vaguely, feeling as though she ought to defend Pettifer. "He's all bark, really."

"If you say so," Hugo said doubtfully. "You know, you'd be amazed at who's the most persistent about getting hold of their stuff. You'd think it'd be the leathery dealers, but it isn't. It's the fluffy little old ladies! And those Belvedere sisters." At her blank look, he persisted, "You know, the sort of… wafty ones? They live at Kesteven Hall, just over the border. Their mother's Lady Fernleigh." He raised a sandy eyebrow. "Can't imagine they'd be in dire need, would you? But the way they carry on…"

"Kesteven Hall?" A behemoth in grey stone swam before Felicia's eyes. It was a local landmark, one of the oldest estates in the country. She'd known there were daughters; the last she'd heard, they were devil-may-care society types, drifting from one champagne reception to the next and getting entangled in the odd scandal along the way. "What would they be buying from us for? They've got a house full of Chippendale and old masters."

She'd even heard they had a Constable there. Just sitting on the wall in one of the corridors, surrounded by a load of ten-a-penny hunting prints. The thought was enough to make any self-respecting art historian swoon.

"They've set up an antiques business. The daughters, I mean. All online, of course. Flogging country stuff back to their London set at vastly inflated prices, I'd wager."

There was a depth of feeling in his voice that took her aback slightly; normally, Hugo was so mild, so slow to judge. It was one of the reasons he was such a good front-facing feature of the business. So different to her father, with his fiery temper, his inability to deal with even the smallest inconvenience without flying off the handle.

"I don't know how I'm going to put them off again," Hugo sighed dolefully. "They've already rang twice."

More on impulse than anything, Felicia clicked back onto the buyer's list, tapping the surname into the search box. It came up with a business name—Intaglio Vintage Homeware—registered to a Francesca and Olivia Belvedere at Kesteven Hall. She sat back in her chair thoughtfully. She remembered those two; somehow, they'd seemed to stand out to her more than anyone else from that day; perhaps because they literally *had* stood out, in their bright, flowing dresses, their wide-brimmed hats, their balayaged hair tonged into painstakingly natural-effect waves. She'd thought they looked like out-of-towners, and in a way, she'd been right. They'd certainly been everywhere during the sale; every time she'd looked up, they'd been in a different spot in the room. And hadn't she seen them over by the Jacobean cupboard at some point?

It was a bit of a long shot, admittedly. But right now, it was better than nothing. It was somewhere she could *start*.

Somehow, she seemed to have made the decision without even realising she'd done so. She was reaching for her phone, selecting a number from the recent calls list.

"Sergeant? It's Felicia Grant. I was wondering—pardon? Oh, yes, yes, I'm fine. No, no more… er, bodies. Listen, I was calling to ask about the lots in the saleroom. Considering that the murder weapon couldn't possibly have been amongst them, surely they can't be of any more use to your investigation? Can I release them to their rightful owners?" A pause, then, "thank you, that's very helpful. Yes, I'll call you if there are any more… incidents."

Hugo was looking at her with something approaching admiration. Feeling self-conscious, she rose briskly to her feet.

"Ask Amelia to box up their lots, will you? I'm going to do a bit of silver service for our ladies of the manor."

The trip to Kesteven Hall involved hopping over the border into the next county; not as intrepid as it sounded when your town sat on the threshold to four of the things. After navigating her car out of its boxed-in parking space on Water Street, it was simply a matter of wending her way across the bridge, around the crook of St Mary's Street, and out of the western edge of town, past the Italianate row of townhouses known as Rutland Terrace, with their wrought-iron balconies and arched windows. Beyond that lay Tinwell Road, with its detached mansions, and before she knew it, she was out of Lincolnshire altogether, a discreet sign at the side of the road quietly welcoming her to Rutland, England's smallest county and proud emblazoner of the motto *Multum in Parvo*, or, in more modern parlance, "much in little". Although it was a fairly accepted fact that not a lot happened in Rutland—at only a half an hour's drive across the entire breadth and boasting only two small market towns by way of civilisation, it had a long history of being absorbed into other counties, but had won back its independence in the 1970s—there was no denying that what Raddlemen, much like Stamfordians, were lacking in number, they made up for with a ferocious sense of local pride. And not without reason; just as Stamford was home to one of the most important Elizabethan estates in England—not to mention the world-famous horse trials that took place within its grounds each September—Rutland held at its heart the largest reservoir in the country in the form of Rutland Water. The huge lake, bisected by the rolling hills of the Hambleton peninsula, was a magnet for cyclists, walkers, water-sport enthusiasts, and conservationists.

It came into view now as she climbed up the long, tree-lined drive that led to the hall, a shining expanse of silver beneath the mid-morning sun. In a clever anticipation game designed by some 18th-century landscaper, the building itself didn't appear until the last minute, looming suddenly from behind a grassy knoll like a sheer cliff face rising from the earth. Despite its domestic-sounding epithet, it was a formidable structure, more castle than house-like, designed to cater to the concerns of Medieval warfare rather than the beauty or comfort any inhabitants might desire. It occupied an imposing spot on a rare piece of high ground that overlooked the surrounding countryside—rather *too* rare, as it happened, to be entirely convincing. Rutland's countryside was of the gently undulating, bucolic type, and Felicia suspected that the motte on which the building sat was rather more man-made than natural.

Nonetheless, it made for a wonderful view. Felicia stopped for a moment as she unbent from the car, unable not to take a moment. Green hills and blue sky were something the eyes never tired of, and she'd been in London for so long she couldn't remember a view that wasn't grey.

"Not bad, is it?"

Felicia turned to see a small woman carrying a wicker basket filled with a glorious profusion of ruffle-edged tulips in shades of raspberry ripple. On her head was a battered old straw hat, peppered with holes, beneath which lustrous dark hair tumbled to her slender shoulders. One hand, clad in a gardening glove, once a pink rose print but now so encrusted with soil that it was scarcely identifiable, clutched a pair of secateurs. The other was bare, revealing delicate fingers, the fourth of which was adorned with the biggest diamond Felicia had ever set eyes upon. The result was discombobulating, exuding a shabbiness yet a dazzling glamour simultaneously. There was, in Felicia's experience, only one class of person who could create such an impossible effect.

"It's beautiful," Felicia said truthfully. "You don't get many views like this, especially not around here."

"Yes, well, they got the situation right, at least," Lady Fernleigh said stridently. "About the only thing they did, mind." She looked up at the hall behind them with a resigned expression. "Still, they were only thinking about killing one another back then."

With her head tilted back, the light shining beneath the brim of her hat, Felicia finally got a proper look at her face. Well-preserved yet weary was the immediate impression she got.

"I'm from the auction house," Felicia said, indicating the box in her arms. "Your daughters bought some items from us on Saturday."

"Ah, yes, their little business. They seem to be doing rather nicely with it. I told them they had to do something; they were hanging around with rather a fast set in London. Giving them ideas. Lots of new money about these days, you see. Old money's all very well, but not if there isn't any of it left to speak of." She stubbed her toe against a stone of the hall. "All bound up in here, and draining like a sink all the time. That's their reality. I'm not going to do it forever. I told them, 'Get yourselves back here, learn some business sense, make some money. You'll need it when this place is yours.'" She hoisted the basket on her arm, regarded Felicia thoughtfully. "Say, what did you say your name was?"

Her voice was cultured, as you'd expect, but also throaty; the hallmark of a life spent out in the elements. Felicia found herself warming to the woman immediately. She could see how she might have gained her reputation for being something of a dragon, but from where Felicia was standing, her bullish frankness was rather more refreshing.

"Grant." Felicia was far too polite to point out that she hadn't in the first place. "Felicia Grant. From the auction in Stamford."

"Of course, Peter's daughter!" The green eyes seemed to light from within, glowing with reminiscence. She was still an attractive woman, but Felicia could see in that moment just how breathtakingly lovely she would have been once. It wasn't a wonder that she'd attracted the duke's eye, although many had been surprised at the time. The heir to one of the oldest estates in the land marrying a butcher's daughter from Northampton who'd just happened to be at the polo one day after some of her parents' customers gave them spare tickets... it was a well-known fairy tale around here. "My, he was a one when we were younger. Always a twinkle in those blue eyes of his. I haven't seen him in years; how is he?"

"Not quite so twinkly at the moment. He's broken his leg, and inaction isn't exactly his strong suit. We'll all be glad when he's up and about again."

"Dearest Peter," Lady Fernleigh was saying dreamily. Rather *too* dreamily, Felicia thought, looking at her with a sudden wariness. She decided to change the subject.

"We've had quite a busy few days, as you can imagine. After the murder..."

"Murder?" Lady Fernleigh blinked vaguely. "Oh, yes, the girls did mention something like that to me. I'm really quite insulated up here, quite out of things. Just me and my garden." She looked lovingly down at the tulips in her basket. "Something which is really *mine*. Although I've had to promise these to the flower arrangements; we've got a concert here later. Symphonies of Spring, they call it."

"I didn't realise. In which case, I'll drop these off and get out of your way. You must have so much to do."

"Oh, there's always something going on. People tramping around the house and garden. It's such a bore, but unfortunately events pay so well. Better than anything else." She sighed. "And one must be practical. I've had to be practical all my life. Monty was no good, bless him, so it had to be me. Sometimes, I've wondered, if I'd known... but one can't go back..." she broke off, gazing thoughtfully into the distance. Then, suddenly, she seemed to shake herself, bestowing upon Felicia such a brilliant smile that it took her quite aback. "But you must excuse my fancies. Now, where were we? The auction house, yes." She linked her free arm through Felicia's, guiding her towards the drawbridge that straddled the moat. "Such a fascinating thing, auctions. People are *so* interested. I wonder now… we've got an event here next month —a gala evening. An auction might be just the thing, don't you think? For charity, of course. It would be fabulous to have you doing it; you're *so* glamorous. You could spare a little evening, couldn't you? For *charity*?"

"Um…" feeling as though she'd just been pounced upon by a previously snoozing tiger, Felicia was temporarily lost for a response. She was rapidly beginning to rethink her initial assessment of the woman's bluntness. "Well, I mean, I wasn't actually *planning* on…"

"*Mother!*" A sharp voice emerged from the central courtyard. "Leave her alone. The poor woman doesn't want to be roped into one of your schemes."

"I wasn't!" The green eyes widened innocently, dark lashes fluttering. A dainty hand went limply to the wronged breast. "Felicia and I were just *talking*, weren't we, my dear?"

"Arrange your tulips, mother," the girl said sternly, drifting towards them in a cloud of jasmine perfume and floral-sprigged muslin.

Lady Fernleigh sighed theatrically.

"Do you have children?" She asked Felicia.

"I have a son. He's only twelve, though."

"Ah, then you still have all of this to come. You will find, in a few years' time, that, suddenly the balance changes. Where once you were the one in charge, you find yourself being shamefully bossed about. And the worst of it is, you're not even quite sure how it happened."

"*Mother*," the girl said again, warningly.

Lady Fernleigh held up her hands and glided elegantly away.

"I'm sorry about that," the girl said sincerely. "She's a pet, really, but she can be the most shameful scrounger. She's like a boa constrictor. She just keeps squeezing." She sighed. "I suppose it's not her fault, really. She's had to be like that, trying to keep this huge place going on absolutely no money. Daddy was absolutely useless when it came to anything worldly. If it weren't for Mummy, we'd have lost it all years ago." She gave Felicia a quick look. "You didn't actually *agree* to anything, did you?"

"I don't think so," Felicia said slowly. "But truthfully, it's hard to be sure."

"That's her secret. If nobody knows what they agreed to do, then she can bully them into whatever she likes." She eyed the box in Felicia's arms, her face lighting up. "Oh, are those our lots? Wonderful! We've been desperate for those. We've already got a buyer for that Majolica oil vessel. And the footstool."

"And the yellow glass cruet set," an identical blonde head popped around the studded wooden door. "I've just sold it to one of Bertie's cousins in Mayfair. Pending photos, of course."

"You can take them right now," her sister replied, indicating the box, which she still hadn't retrieved from Felicia's arms. Felicia was beginning to wonder if she'd be expected to carry it all the way into the hall, a fear that was soon confirmed.

"Come on in," said the sister in the doorway. "We'll show you where to put them."

Felicia followed them through the courtyard. If they weren't wearing slightly different colourways of what looked to her remarkably like the same dress, it would have been impossible to tell them apart. She and Juliette had never dressed alike; although, granted, they'd never even looked remotely similar, so there mightn't have been much point anyway. Juliette was all their father, stocky and fair-haired, with eyes so blue it was hard to believe they were gifted by nature. She had his solid, practical nature, too. Their family had been split down the middle, just as so many were. Cassie's had the big heads versus the little heads

(Cassie being one of the big heads), Dexter's had fair versus dark, and the Grant's… well, they had something less tangible. Worldly v. otherworldly, grounded v. airy, practical v. artistic… she and her mother were the wood nymphs, the blink-and-you'll-miss-thems. Her mother had certainly lived up to that, disappearing into the halcyon embrace of turquoise seas, cocktails on tap, and bronzed Spanish skin before anyone had known what was happening.

These sisters, however, were carbon copies of one another. It was slightly unnerving, especially when they stood side by side. They weren't as young as their clothes and mannerisms might make them seem, she realised now, seeing them in broad daylight. They had to be close on thirty-five.

The scene that greeted her inside the building couldn't have been more removed from the tranquillity without. Everything was activity, people scurrying backwards and forwards clutching clipboards, vases and various other paraphernalia. Someone was winding greenery through the banisters of the huge, sweeping staircase, another untangling yards of fairy lights. A porter rushed past, a stack of chairs wobbling precariously in his arms. Felicia craned her neck, peering through the doorway after him into the Great Hall. Round tables had been set out in the darkly panelled, high-ceilinged room. The walls were hung with such an array of antique arms that the effect was almost like an iron cage. Felicia decided it was better not to look too closely at what strange implements might be included in their number. Up in the minstrel's gallery, the orchestra were setting up their music stands. It made the bustle of auction day seem positively millpond-like. Felicia decided that she couldn't blame Lady Fernleigh for staying out of the way.

"Oh, don't mind all of them," the sister in the blue dress tossed back over her shoulder, as Felicia was nearly mown down by someone charging forth with an enormous silver candelabra. "They're from the events company." You'd better move Mummy's golf clubs," she said, with sudden biting imperiousness, to an unfortunate boy who happened to be passing at that moment, laden down with cutlery. "Before someone trips over them." She stepped over the bag that was slumped against the wall, sliding partway across the floor. She turned to glance back at Felicia with an apologetic look, her voice returning to its former sing-song tone. "Sorry. She's always leaving them all over the place."

They led her straight through the hall and out into the courtyard that formed the heart of the building. Protected by the walls on all four sides, it featured a serenely blooming garden of the well-behaved type, with neatly trimmed box hedging forming a knot garden and a tinkling lion's head fountain to the centre.

"Over here," the purple-dressed sister beckoned Felicia with a gel-manicured hand. "Mummy let us have one of the stables for our business."

The remark was a little disingenuous, seeing as "the stables" consisted of a monstrous block the breadth of a medium-sized mansion, complete with a whitewashed clock tower with a verdigrised dome and shining gilt face. But Felicia was too fed up by this point to care. Her arms were aching from carrying the box, and she was getting desperate to put it down. She did just that the minute they were inside the door, plonking it on the nearest workbench quickly before they could ask her to carry it anywhere else.

The room was still only half-finished, but what was there showed the promise of an impressive set-up. In the centre was a studio, with huge pastel backing boards forming the set of a room in which blond wood furniture was artfully arranged alongside rattan and chintz. The rest of the space around the studio was filled with shelving, upon which a variety of homeware items sat cheek-by-jowl. There was lots of retro-coloured glass and naively painted pottery; the sort of stuff you couldn't seem to give away at auction any more. Clearly, their business revolved around reinventing these pieces in a millennial-flavoured packaging. Felicia had to admit that it was ingenious.

"Sorry about the delay in getting this to you." Considering there had only been Sunday in between, there hadn't really been any delay at all, but Felicia was unabashed about the lie. As she'd anticipated, they didn't bat an eyelid. She carried on, in a casual voice, "the murder's rather held things up, as you can imagine."

"Oh, yes," they both started nodding earnestly. They reminded Felicia of those dogs that used to sit on car dashboards.

"Terrible, wasn't it, Francesca?" This from the blue dress, who Felicia could now identify, by process of elimination, as Olivia.

"Awful," Francesca—the purple dress—agreed feverishly. "We were *so* shaken by it."

Felicia, seeing her opening, couldn't keep the sharpness out of her voice.

"So, you knew him, then?"

Immediately, the atmosphere changed, tautened. They blanched in tandem. Olivia, who Felicia could already tell was the more forthright of the two—but only by a whisker—recovered herself first.

"What?" She stammered. "I mean, no. Not at all. We never met him."

Anyone could tell they were lying. Felicia took a step closer, feeling the frisson of a huntress approaching her quarry.

"Are you absolutely sure about that?" She asked softly.

"She knows, Olivia!" Francesca whispered, plucking at her sleeve. "I don't know how, but she *knows!*"

"Shut up, Fran!" Olivia snapped desperately. She looked up at Felicia, and her eyes were huge, frightened. "Look, why are you really here? What do you want from us?"

"Just the truth, that's all." Felicia kept her voice gentle, unthreatening, even though inside, her heart was pounding with a kind of exultation. Was *this* why Pettifer did it? For this moment, when you finally got to the truth, when the mystery unravelled? "Why don't you tell me about it?"

"We didn't *mean* to do it," Francesca blurted out on a wail. "It was a mistake. *Honestly*. We never—"

"*Fran!*" Olivia looked wild now, like a trapped animal. Her hand was gripping the edge of the half-finished workbench, where a hammer was resting. Her fingers were mere centimetres from it.

At the sight of it, Felicia felt herself go very cold. Suddenly, she wasn't feeling so ebullient, so clever. Quite the opposite. For the first time, it struck her just how foolish she'd been, coming out here all alone.

On instinct, she began to edge back towards the door.

"Once you've started... it just doesn't end," Francesca was moaning. "The lies. You can't imagine."

She could feel the breeze from outside against her back. She was so close to freedom. It was the moment to turn and run, to save her life. And, yet, she stopped.

Afterwards, she'd tell herself how crazy that had been. How reckless. But in that moment, she'd realised that she still had to know. She just *had* to know the truth.

"Why did you do it?" Her voice was shaking, but she held her gaze steady. "Why did you kill Barrington?"

Chapter Eighteen

"Kill him?" Olivia stared at her, eyes bulging. "What on earth are you talking about? We *bought* from him."

"It was an accident," Francesca whimpered, wringing the hem of her dress in her hands. "But he had the most *marvellous* enamel égouttoir in his sale. It was just perfect. We even knew who we'd sell it to."

"We agonised about it for *days*, didn't we, Francesca?"

"Days," Francesca repeated solemnly.

"In the end we said we'd just watch the auction online. We promised ourselves."

"*Promised*," Francesca breathed earnestly.

"But then…" Olivia sagged back against the workbench. "It just *happened*."

"We clicked the 'bid' button." Francesca's face disappeared behind fingers festooned with bejewelled stacking rings.

"We felt awful about it," Olivia explained hastily. "But by then it was too late. We'd bought it."

"*Awful*," Francesca gave a muffled moan.

"It did sell well, mind," Francesca sighed wistfully. "It was a good buy. And, then… well, you know how these things are: once you've done it once, it's so easy to..." she leaned forward conspiratorially, then whispered, "… do it again."

"And again," Francesca intoned miserably. "If Mummy knew about it then she'd have a fit. She'd never forgive us."

Felicia, who'd been watching this whole farcical exchange with a mounting sense of unreality and disbelief, forced herself to breathe out slowly. Her heart rate was returning to normal, at least, but her nerves were still jangling, her mouth dry with the remnants of fear. She couldn't work out if she wanted to hug them both for not murdering her or strangle them herself for being so astonishingly asinine.

"Why not?" She managed not to do either, and instead rasped out what seemed to be the pertinent question.

They looked uncertainly at each other. In the end, as usual, Olivia took the decision.

"They're in the middle of a legal dispute," she explained quietly. "Mummy's going to take him to court. No one's supposed to know; it's all very embarrassing for her."

Felicia, suddenly interested, folded her arms and looked expectant. Olivia swallowed, then continued, with visible reluctance:

"Money was tight last year. We'd had that washout summer, and most of the outdoor events had to be cancelled. Then the roof started leaking. *Again*." A strained smile was summoned at this. "The estate didn't have the money to pay for it. So, Mummy had to do what she always does in that situation: she sells something."

"A painting, a piece of furniture, a vase…" Francesca piped up. "Something from a dark corner. Nothing that anyone would notice."

"There was this painting…there'd always been this family rumour that it might be a Constable. Such a small, dark little picture really. It didn't look like much. Anyway, it had been sitting in the servant's corridor for generations, and several people had been out to look at it. No one was very confident, so she decided it was time to sell it. She got Barrington Clay around to value it for her. He agreed that it wasn't likely, said he'd check with some of his London contacts. In the end, he told her it was probably "school of". She agreed to sell it with him—anonymously, of course," Olivia added, with a nervous look at Felicia. "No one must *ever* know that we do this. It would ruin the whole image."

Felicia dipped her chin in a nod of assent, encouraging them to continue.

"But then it appeared again at one of the London auctions six months ago. New evidence had certified it a Constable. It sold for £5 million."

Felicia remembered it well. It had caused quite a stir at the time, in part because no-one could find out who it had belonged to. Everything had been very secretive; now, she knew why.

"I hardly dare ask this, but how much did it originally sell for at Clay's?"

There was a pause. Then:

"A couple of hundred thousand," Francesca said, in a small voice. "We actually thought it had done pretty well, considering."

Felicia winced.

"Anyway, Mummy was absolutely *livid* with Barrington Clay. She thinks that he knew more than he told her. She said that the person he sold it to was probably someone he knew, and he took a cut of the profits when it sold again in London. But that sort of thing doesn't really *happen*, does it?" They both looked beseechingly at her.

Felicia made a noncommittal sound. The truth was, it wasn't entirely unheard of. It was the art world, after all; all manner of "things" happened every day, half of which the average person wouldn't believe.

"And anyway, why would he want to do it?" Olivia pressed, clearly not buoyed by Felicia's silence. "Wouldn't it have been better for him if he'd said it *was* a Constable? He would have got all the publicity for it *and* more commission from the sale."

Or, in all probability, nothing at all. It was a weary acceptance amongst provincial auction houses that as soon as you said anything was of high value, people all too often immediately wanted to whisk it away to London, where they thought it would fetch a higher price. In reality, this wasn't always the case—it was a big fish, small pond sort of scenario, and the lower commission tended to equal things out on the final statement—but getting people to accept that was often a losing battle. Many times in her days at Grant's had Felicia done hours of research on something only to watch it walk back out of the door. So, even though she could never sanction what Barrington had potentially done, she could see why he might have been tempted to do it. The certainty of a generous cut would have appeared seductive when compared to the very real prospect of ending up empty-handed.

"Anyway, I don't suppose we'll ever know now, will we?" Francesca looked doleful. "Not now he's dead and all."

"N-o," Felicia said slowly. "I don't suppose we ever shall."

She was crunching back across the gravel towards her car when her phone rang. It was Hugo.

"How'd it go? You get out of there all right? I hear Lady Fernleigh is a little on the airy-fairy side. Inclined to keep people there for hours."

"Oh, she's not all she pretends to be. Sharp as a tack, if you ask me, and a *very* shrewd operator."

"And the daughters?"

"I'd say not quite so much. You were right about their business, by the way. They seem to be selling a lot to their friends."

"And does Mummy know that?"

"Mummy does *not*. She'll be in for an unpleasant surprise when she finds out."

Felicia found that she actually felt quite sorry for the woman. She admired her, in a vaguely wary sort of way. She was tough, she'd known sadness, she carried a huge burden each day which wasn't even really her own, but she got on with it. Now, she thought she was handing over her life's work into safe hands; personally, Felicia wasn't so sure.

But it wasn't her problem. What was it that Dexter was always saying to Algernon? You can't worry about everyone; it's people's responsibility to look after themselves. Dexter could be surprisingly sage when he chose to be. It was just a shame about the other 99 per cent of the time.

"Anyway," she told Hugo. "I'm on my way back to the office now, so if there's any…"

"Actually, that's why I called. I was hoping I'd catch you while you were still out and about. Do you mind making a detour on your way back? We've had a…well, it's a bit of a strange thing, really."

"I'm listening."

"Magda Clay called here asking about a valuation for probate."

Felicia's usually reliable poise momentarily deserted her, resulting in her almost tripping over her own feet.

"As in… Barrington's wife? *That* Magda Clay?"

"Not likely to be many people with that name knocking around," Hugo pointed out.

"I suppose you're right. But it doesn't make any sense. Why *us*? More to the point, why *now*? The man's not in the ground yet; the police haven't even released his body, as far as I'm aware."

Probate, or the valuation of a person's estate for calculating inheritance tax, was an arduous, follicle-ripping process that could drag on for months, if not years. It certainly wasn't something worth rushing into. Magda Clay must have known that; she was an auctioneer's wife, after all.

"And she wants us to go now?" Felicia asked slowly.

"No, she wants *you* to go now. She specifically requested it; she doesn't want anyone else to do it."

Curiouser and curiouser, Felicia thought, with a little tingle of anticipation only mildly tempered by the sheepish realisation that she clearly hadn't learnt anything from the last twenty minutes. Logic cautioned that it was madness to head over there alone, and, yet... she couldn't *not* go and see what all of this was about, could she?

"Do you want the address? It's..."

"No need, I know exactly where it is." Out of the corner of her eye, she became aware of a car pulling towards her. A sleek black car, gliding across the gravel. "Er... I'll see you later."

She was just stowing the phone in her pocket when the car doors swung open and, from each side, a trousered leg emerged. But that was where the mirror image ended. One was dapperly attired, with a neat pinstripe and shining Oxfords, the other shabby and dusty, the hem unravelling, the shoes scuffed with broken laces that had been reknotted. Only two people could pull off such an incongruous double act, except maybe Dexter and herself.

"My," she said jauntily. "If it isn't our pillars of law enforcement. Good to see you out and about in the community. We wouldn't want people to feel unsafe now, would we?"

Pettifer looked uneasy, but Heavenly's expression was stony.

"What are you doing here, Ms Grant?"

"Working. The ladies here bought some things from the auction. I was just dropping them off." She held up her hands. "Nothing sinister, I assure you. You'll find them both in there safe and well. I haven't murdered them with a medieval mace I've pulled off the wall or anything like that."

"Murder isn't something to be amused by, Ms Grant." Heavenly was snappish, irritable, like an unusually sleek terrier.

"I didn't much think so myself. That's why I came to you last night." There was a hardness beneath her jaunty tone, a small tell of the anger she still felt towards him. It was his fault that she was here in the first place. If he'd just taken her *seriously*…she pulled herself up short, knowing that there was no point going down that road. What was done was done. He wasn't going to change his mind…unless she could change it for him. "Anyway, you know why *I'm* here. What brings you this way?"

"Lady Fernleigh…" Pettifer began, at the same time as Heavenly snapped, "that's police business." They looked at one another. Or rather, Pettifer looked. Heavenly glared venomously.

"Ah," Felicia nodded sagely. "So, you've found out about the legal case Lady Fernleigh was pursuing against Barrington, have you? I was wondering how long that would take you."

Pettifer gave her a searching, even slightly amused look. With Heavenly, on the other hand, there was no ambiguity. He was simply apoplectic.

"How did you come by that information?"

She opened her eyes wide.

"It's not a crime to be talked to, is it? *I* can't help it if people tell me things." Unlocking her car, she folded herself into the seat with a glib, "well, I'd better be off. Places to be. Good luck with your enquiries, gentlemen."

She pulled the door closed, but Heavenly rapped imperiously on the window. Suppressing a sigh, she wound it down.

"And where do you think you're going now?"

He sounded like the father of a wayward teenager. Felicia wondered briefly if he had children, then swiftly dismissed it. He didn't have the hard-won patience, nor the worry lines.

"If you must know, I have another appointment. With Mrs Clay. She wants me to value some things at the house. Unless, of course, that would constitute my profiting from a crime?" She added smoothly, with a delicately arched brow.

Without waiting for an answer, she pulled away, executing a sweeping turn before speeding off down the drive.

Sergeant Pettifer watched her go with ill-disguised admiration.

"She's quite something, that Ms Grant."

"Hmm." By his side, Chief Inspector Heavenly looked thunderous. The vein was popping frantically in his cheek. "That *something* might just be the accomplice to cold-blooded murder."

Pettifer sidled a glance at his superior.

"Do you really believe that, sir?"

"Of that woman, I'd believe anything," was the biting reply. "I haven't been a policeman all of these years not to know bad news when I see it."

And then he was stalking off across the drawbridge, leaving Pettifer no choice but to sigh and follow in his expensively scented wake.

Chapter Nineteen

Despite his business being some fifteen minutes out into Cambridgeshire, Barrington had lived for years in Stamford. Felicia had always thought it a slightly antagonistic move, his presence encroaching on the town that he coveted as the epicentre of his empire. She'd passed his house on the way out of town but had, by some sort of ingrained superstition, studiously avoided glancing at it.

Most of the houses on Tinwell Road were unexceptional in style, mostly dating from the mid-century onwards. What made them notable was their size; huge mansions nestled on generous plots, with sprawling gardens and set back façades, all perched on a long bank high above the road, affording them campestral views over the valley that dropped away into countryside beyond. It wasn't hard to see why they were such a popular choice for the moneyed craving some space in a town where, by dint of the fact that the street plans hadn't changed an inch in several hundred years, it was otherwise sorely lacking. Not for the residents of Tinwell Road the headache of having to scramble for one of the permit parking spaces in streets that were designed for carriages rather than cars, something which Felicia had to own to appreciating as she pulled onto the curving driveway in front of the Clay's house.

Not every house on the road was modern; down at the end closest to town existed a few Victorian survivors, flamboyantly neo gothic in style with steep, spiky gables, moodily bowed windows, and the generally forbidding, hulking haunted-house look that the period excelled at so unabashedly. It was on one of these that Felicia found herself raising the grimacing gargoyle's head knocker, letting it fall with a dull, ominous-sounding thud that could be heard reverberating around the hall within.

Nothing happened for a few moments; so long, in fact, that Felicia stepped back, shielding her eyes against the sun to look up at the windows. There were no signs of life, but then, that wasn't too telling; most people tended to prefer their day-to-day living areas at the back of the house these days. Just as she was contemplating knocking again, there was the sound of bolts being drawn back, and the vast arched front door—supposedly meant to look ecclesiastical but in reality, more reminiscent of the sort found in a dungeon—swung open.

Felicia tried not to stare at the woman standing in the opening, but it wasn't easy. Suddenly, she realised how curious she'd been to set eyes on Magda Clay, interested to find out what sort of woman could co-exist with Barrington for almost 40 years. He'd been the sort of man you'd have expected to boast a string of divorces to his name. In his TV career, he was well-known for the twinkle in his eye, the roguish, flirty banter, the slightly overfamiliar way he slung his arm around the younger, more attractive female contestants on his team. And, yet, it was also known that at the end of the filming day, he went back home to Magda. The blurry figure in the background, never seen, but a powerful presence, nonetheless. The impression given was of a forthright, characterful woman, willing to accept her husband's impish persona on screen but brooking no nonsense in reality.

Now, standing in front of her, Felicia realised she didn't quite know what to make of what she was seeing. Because the most remarkable thing about Magda Clay was how utterly *un*remarkable she was. Her hair—the colour of a wild rabbit's pelt —was worn in a severe bob that grazed her chin. Her face was pale, unmade-up, her eyes an indistinct wash of blue and grey. Deep grooves bracketed her bloodless lips. Her hands were small, fine, the nails neatly trimmed, cuticles pressed back. She was dressed exclusively in grey. Felicia thought back to what Cassie had said about her own wardrobe and concurred that she might have been right about the need for an intervention.

"Good afternoon," Felicia recovered from her surprise—and, she had to admit, a certain sense of anticlimax—and hurriedly held out her hand, hoping the other woman hadn't noticed her staring. "I'm—"

"I know who you are," she smiled thinly, but there was no malice in it, only, Felicia thought, a sort of weariness. The pale eyes that looked back at her were without expression, but it was impossible not to notice the pink rims, the slightly puffed lids. "I've seen your picture many times. You're quite distinctive."

Felicia tried not to wonder if she meant that in a good way.

"Apparently you wanted to speak to me about valuations for probate?" she ventured gently, as Magda Clay opened the door wider, gesturing for her to come inside. "You understand that it's only early? You don't need to make any decisions just yet."

She wasn't as small as she'd appeared a moment ago, Felicia realised now. It was simply an optical illusion, the door dwarfing her by sheer comparison. She was bolting it carefully behind them, and didn't answer for a moment.

"The decision's already made." Her voice was quiet. Then she turned, and her eyes were bright, glittering. "I know what I want, and that's it gone. Every bit of it." She looked around at the darkly panelled hallway, with its studded war chest beneath the window, the oak hall stand draped in coats and hats, the tiled fireplace flanked by two bulbous dragoon vases that reached almost up to the mantelpiece, and her expression was blank, like she didn't recognise any of it. "I've half a mind to burn the lot." Then she saw Felicia's startled expression, and gave a sudden, jarring bark of a laugh. "Oh, don't *worry*, I won't. No, I'm far too sensible for that. Besides, I think I'm owed as much as I can get. I certainly earned it."

The bitterness, burst free from its restraints, was rolling off her in waves now, almost shocking in its intensity. Felicia found herself wanting to step back.

She'd seen many things in her time as an antiques valuer; she'd faced countless families and spouses in the aftermath of a loved one's passing, and they certainly hadn't all exuded the quiet, dignified grief one might expect. Death did strange things to the living; it brought their own existence sharply into focus, and the effect it had varied from person to person. Some were relieved and trying not to show it, some felt guilty and lashed out, others just wanted what they could get while they were still alive to make use of it. Reality suspended for a while, and people lost themselves in the midst of it.

Magda Clay must have either really hated her husband, or really loved him. It was often surprising how those two emotions manifested in such similar ways.

"Mrs Clay," Felicia ventured, eyeing her client warily. She took her breath. This next part had to be said, and to be honest, the sooner the better. She was suddenly feeling rather keen to be out of here. She tried not to think about the bolted door. "I understand how difficult this must be for you, and I want to help, but... well, you *are* aware that it was *my* auction house where your husband was..." Good God, no, *don't* use the word murdered "... I mean, where the ... incident... happened?"

Something flickered across her face, something self-satisfied and cruel...but also, Felicia thought, something desperately sad. The question seemed to have sparked something, though; she regarded Felicia as though finally really seeing her, head tilted on one side in thought. Then, without answering, she turned and walked through the doorway into the rest of the house. Sensing that she was probably expected to follow, Felicia did.

She found herself emerging from the dark hall into a large, unexpectedly bright drawing room with deep, floor-to-ceiling bays that provided a rich view of the garden. Magda Clay was in front of the open drinks cabinet in the corner, unstopping a glass decanter, which she waved in Felicia's direction.

"You want one?"

"Better not," Felicia held up her Dictaphone by way of explanation. "I'm on duty."

The mouth twisted. Felicia got the sense that she'd disappointed her somehow.

"Yes, I suppose you are." Her voice was flat, bored. Whatever confidential sort of mood she'd been in previously, it was gone now. She poured a large tot of brandy into a balloon glass, not looking at Felicia again. The spark of interest had gone. "Start wherever you like, it doesn't bother me. And anything you want to sell, consider it yours. When everything's settled, obviously."

She was raising the drink to her lips just as the doorbell rang, a shrill, startling echo around the large house. It was almost enough to make Felicia jump, but Mrs Clay barely blinked. Instead, she just looked faintly irritated.

"That'll be some solicitor or another, no doubt, if not the police. Deathly dull, the lot of them." She smiled faintly at her own joke, placing her glass on the coffee table with a careless clunk. "The amount of tradesmen death seems to accumulate, you wouldn't believe."

Felicia had a horrible feeling she was classed as one of the "tradesmen" herself. A clerk of death. What a thought.

Voices floated through from the hall. A high-pitched exclamation of surprise, followed by a deeper baritone. More indistinct murmuring, followed by the sound of the door opening wider, footsteps on the wooden floorboards. Advancing towards her. Hastily, Felicia fumbled for the clipboard she'd left on the sideboard, spinning around and pretending to be absorbed in an astoundingly ugly—and surprisingly modern, given its owner—painting of a horse on the wall. She was almost inclined to believe that it had to be one of Magda's choices, although she didn't look to be an animal lover. She didn't seem to be much of an *anything* lover, truth be told. Certainly not of her husband, the man she'd shared her life with for so many decades. Felicia was still feeling faintly discombobulated by the woman she'd encountered, so unlike the grieving widow she'd been anticipating.

"So kind of you to call," Mrs Clay was simpering—wait, *simpering*? It took everything in Felicia not to crane her neck around in astonishment. "A real celebrity, taking the time to—but here I am chattering away. *Do* come through; I've got someone in for the probate, but don't mind her. You'll have a drink, won't you?"

Felicia feigned a flourished scribble on the pad, then turned casually, about to say that she'd start upstairs after all, only to discover that she would be addressing a walking profusion of blooms. Roses, lilies, frothing gypsophila. All that was visible above the foliage was a sliver of forehead crowned with thick dark hair.

It was a forehead she'd know anywhere.

Chapter Twenty

The words she'd been about to say died on her lips. In fact, her entire face seemed to freeze.

"Felicia," Dexter said cheerfully, popping his head around a particularly blowsy flower. "Fancy seeing you here."

"Fancy," she managed, through gritted teeth, trying to decide if she was more confused, irritated or just plain cross.

Mrs Clay was darting quick looks between them, then her face cleared.

"Hang on," she said slowly to Dexter. "*Grant...*" She turned to Felicia, somewhat accusingly, as though she was guilty of a grievous and deliberate deception. "Aren't you two..."

"Married?" Supplied Dexter. "Well, yes, I suppose we are, rather."

Mrs Clay looked distinctly disappointed. Felicia did a double take.

"We *were* married," she corrected, with a meaningful glare at Dexter. "Not any more."

Mrs Clay looked markedly more buoyant.

"I see," she purred, and Felicia tried not to look as taken aback as she felt. It was like a conjuring trick, where one woman had gone to answer the door and a completely different one had returned. "Won't you sit down? How about that drink?"

"Sounds delightful," Dexter replied, and Felicia rolled her eyes. Of course *he* would. Never mind that it was scarcely midday.

"I'll just put these in a vase. Make yourself at home." Arms overflowing with flowers, Magda disappeared through a doorway on the right.

Felicia waited until she was safely out of sight before whirling on Dexter with a hissed, "what the *hell* are you doing?"

He looked at her innocently.

"Paying my respects to the widow. What else?"

She folded her arms and fixed him with an interrogative stare. He sighed.

"All *right*, Hugo told me you were coming here."

"And?"

"*And* I didn't think you should come alone. Someone out there tried to *kill* you, Felicia." He was starting to get rattled; his brows were drawn down, his mouth tight. "Look, I've been thinking about what you said yesterday evening, after the sergeant left… and I've concluded that you're right. We can't just sit around and wait. We need to find out who did this before they try again."

"*We?*" She was flabbergasted, and, if she was being honest, faintly horrified.

"Yes, *we*. I can help. I *want* to help." At her expression, he scowled. "Damn it, Felicia, now's not the time to be stubborn."

He probably had a point, but that only made her feel even more unreasonably irritated with him, which in turn, made her dig her heels in all the more. She told herself it was because he'd been so dismissive of her last night, nothing more. Certainly nothing to do with the way Magda Clay had just been gazing at him. That would just be… well, it would be ridiculous. Nothing more, nothing less.

"And why, *exactly*, are you suddenly so keen to help?" She bit back. She was feeling hot, cross with herself, ready to take it out on him. "Nothing to do with them cancelling your show, by any chance? This whole pesky unsolved murder thing is turning into a real professional headache for you, isn't it?"

His jaw dropped. It was strangely satisfying, Felicia thought. It was a rare occurrence to get Dexter on the back foot.

"How the *devil* did you find out about that?"

"Algernon heard you on the phone."

"Bloody *hell*," he fumed savagely, gripping the back of the velvet-upholstered sofa. "Is *nothing* in this family private?"

"Not while we're all packed into that shoebox of a cottage, no." She frowned. "And you shouldn't blame Algie. He was worried about you. You might try talking to him for once, instead of brushing everything under the carpet."

"*Me*?" He spluttered, whirling around. "*I'm* not the one who's sneaking around trying to track down a double murderer on my own. What kind of responsible parenting is that?"

Their voices were rising, eyes locked. They hadn't got into an argument like this in years. Felicia realised belatedly that her hands were scrunched into her fists at her sides.

"Oh, and bringing a pampered history professor along for the ride is going to make it all *so* much safer, is it?" She flared, her voice thick with sarcasm.

The stared each other down for a moment, silently furious.

"Everything all right?" Mrs Clay was back, watching them suspiciously.

They both snapped to attention simultaneously.

"Of course, absolutely," Dexter, as ever speedy to recover, treated her to his most disarming smile, ushering her towards the sofa. "Just a little, er, logistical planning, that's all. Now, where were we? Ah, drinks. No, you sit down. I'll do it. I've been around a few bars in my time."

Mrs Clay, obviously mollified, tittered. Felicia choked on a strangled cough. The other woman's head swivelled around like an owl's, and she fixed her with a piercing look.

"Why don't you start upstairs?" She said coldly. It wasn't a suggestion.

Felicia opened her mouth, then closed it again as she realised that she had no reasonable way of refusing. Despite having been about to propose just the same thing herself, she found that suddenly, she wasn't all that keen to leave. And now Dexter was looking at her, with that infuriatingly smug expression that reminded her why she'd divorced him in the first place. Suppressing a scowl, she gathered up her paraphernalia and moved away into the hall, making as though to go up the stairs. But she didn't go all of the way. The staircase had a double turn, and she stopped on the first of these, the banisters effectively blocking her from the view of anyone who might happen to glance through the open doorway.

"This must all have been a terrible shock for you," Dexter was saying sympathetically, the clinking of ice suggesting that he was busying himself at the bar. "To be on your own after…how many years were you married?"

"Thirty-seven. But my marriage never offered much in the way of companionship." A pause—rather a calculated one, from Felicia's point of view—and then, "The truth is, it was all over long ago. I've been on my own for years, really." She sighed. "I can't *tell* you how lonely I've been."

There was a creaking sound as Dexter installed himself on the leather sofa.

"I can only imagine," he murmured.

Felicia thought she might gag.

"Of course, being divorced, I'm sure you understand. In fact," there was another pause, *another* creak, and she breathed, "I feel absolutely sure that you do. The need for comfort…companionship."

To hell with this. Felicia stuck her head around the dogleg, peering through the banisters. Magda Clay was sitting very close to Dexter, far closer than was polite. And her hand…

Felicia felt her eyebrows shoot up... was placed proprietorially on his knee.

"Uh, yes." Looking somewhat discomfited, Dexter patted the hand awkwardly before returning it to her own lap. "But we... um... well, we have our son. It keeps things cordial between us."

"*I* wanted children," she said dully, staring into her drink. "When I was younger, I dreamed of a big family. But Barrington kept saying that it wasn't time. There was always a new deal, a new scheme, a new acquisition. He always had just *one* more thing he wanted to do first. And, then, before I knew it, it was too late. I wonder now if that was deliberate, if he never really ever planned to give me children at all." She sucked in a quavering breath. "But then, I'm beginning to question everything. My marriage, our life together, everything I thought I knew... it's driving me mad. *Mad*."

She was crying openly now, the tears making ghostly tracks down her face. Dexter looked like a rabbit in the headlights; for once, even he didn't seem to know quite what to say next. But as it turned out, he didn't need to. She was continuing, the words a gathering torrent, falling over one another in their haste to be heard.

"Do you know what they're saying now? The police? Do you know what they told me?" Her hand was shaking, rattling the ice in her glass, but she didn't seem to notice. "They're telling me that my husband was a crook. A *criminal*. Oh, not in so many words, of course." Her smile was bitter, ugly. "They're being very cagey about it, very gentle. Pretending it's all just routine questioning. But I'm not as stupid as I look; I know what they're getting at, what they're *suggesting*." She drew to a pause with a shudder of emotion. "I used to work as a secretary at a solicitor's, before my marriage. It was only for a while, but I learned a thing or two about how the police work. I know what it means when they turn his business inside out. When they ask me if there's a hidden safe in the house. Offshore assets in my name."

"How dreadful," Dexter was patting her shoulder, having regained some of his usual flair for handling the fairer sex. "And you really had no idea?"

"None," she said quickly. *Too* quickly. She sidled him a look. "I mean, don't get me wrong, I knew he was…well, a bit of a jack-the-lad. Always has been. He was working the market stall when we met, and within a couple of years, we had enough money to marry, put down a deposit on a house…I suppose I *wondered*, even then. But he said everything was all right, above board, and I…" her face crumpled. "Well, I believed him, didn't I? I loved him, trusted him. Why shouldn't I?"

An indistinct murmur of sympathy from Dexter. Felicia, who'd ducked back out of sight, could only hope that he wasn't slowly suffocating in her embrace.

"I suppose, if I'm being completely honest, perhaps it suited me not to know." Her voice was unsteady; Felicia thought she detected the first tremors of hysteria thrumming beneath it like an underground stream. "I liked all of *this*," a sloshing sound, presumably as she gesticulated at her ornate surroundings. "I mean, who wouldn't? The luxury, the comfort. The prestige. Things I never dared hope for, growing up. And then suddenly, all mine. But now I think, for what? What's it worth, if it was all a lie? If it was built on blackmail and intimidation and backhanders? Misery and deception. Just a sordid house of cards, all of it. I'd rather be back in the bedsit where he found me. At least there was integrity in that."

A pause whilst she gulped some of her drink, and then she was off again, every word burning with emotion.

"I used to be a blonde, you know. When we met. I loved it. But Barrington preferred me as a brunette. He never encouraged me to look glamorous. At the time, I told myself it was because he loved me as I was. Now, I see what it was really all about. The respectable, mousy, country town wife. Doing the flowers at the church, joining the WI, shopping at the Friday market for dinners to entertain his friends…" she choked on a sob. "The perfect cover for all of those dodgy deals, that was me. Just part of the show. *Useful*."

The last word was uttered with such venom that Felicia, even from her safe distance, shivered in response.

"And there was *nothing* strange about him lately?" Dexter had lost some of his suavity; there was a hint of desperation in his voice. He was clearly fast giving up on this interview yielding anything valuable. Not that Felicia blamed him; she was of the same mind herself. " Nothing… different?"

A rustle indicated Magda's shake of the head.

"I mean, he was a bit excitable lately, highly strung. At the time, I didn't think much of it. I mean, he was that sort of character. Always on the edge of his seat. Always a new scheme." She sighed. "I almost wish I *could* give the police something. It would serve him right. It would give *me* some closure, at least. I've been searching everywhere I can think of, hoping I'll find something. Things they might have missed."

"And have you?" An audible creak as Dexter leaned forward. She could imagine his eyes, inky and intense, so arresting that it was impossible to look anywhere else. "Found anything, I mean?"

Suddenly, a splitting creak rent the air. It seemed to ricochet around the stark space like a gunshot. Felicia looked down at her foot and bit her lip in annoyance. Instinctively, she'd been leaning forward, craning to hear more, her weight pressing into a loose floorboard at the top of the stairs.

It seemed to shake Magda Clay out of whatever trance she'd been in. She blinked, as though surprised to find herself where she was. With some small embarrassment, she shifted subtly away from Dexter on the sofa, looking at her glass accusingly as she placed it gently on the coffee table.

"I really should see what's going on up there." She said stiffly. "After all, you can't be too careful."

"Of course." Dexter took the hint seamlessly, reaching for his hat, which had been reclining on the back of the sofa. "You have a lot to attend to. I mustn't keep you."

"Thank you for the flowers…truly, they're lovely." She seemed almost abashed, shooing him towards the door. She couldn't wait to get rid of him; that much was apparent.

They were in the hall now; only a slight turn of the head, and Magda would see her. Felicia backed silently up the stairs, thanking God she'd swapped out her heels.

She slipped through the nearest doorway, into a room that was immediately recognisable. Tapestries lined the burgundy-painted walls. A vast bureau plat squatted on the Persian carpet. A globe sat serenely on the desk, the curling font describing placenames that no longer existed. The air was hushed, thick with the scent of old paper and cigar smoke. It was a gentleman's study in the purest sense, following the template that had existed for generations.

In an instant, Felicia forgot what had driven her in here in the first place. She'd unwittingly walked straight into Barrington's sanctuary, his private space. Surely, if there was anything incriminating he wouldn't want to keep at his offices, this is where it would end up.

She crossed to the desk, making an experimental tug on one of the drawers. She was fully expecting it to be locked, so it was much to her surprise when it slid straight open. Inside was a row of colour-coded folders. With a rising sense of excitement, she pulled one slightly out.

Health Insurance, the label read. Bewildered, she reached for the next one, then the next, flipping through with increasing frustration. House Documents. Building Work. ISAs. Surely this couldn't be it? This was the desk of an everyman, someone who had nothing to hide. Not the shady business figure everyone painted him as.

Then she shook herself. Of *course*, it wouldn't be here. Hadn't Magda Clay just said that the police had been over everything?

That she'd done just the same? This was the first place both of them would have looked.

Feeling rather stupid, Felicia sat back on her heels. As she did so, her eye became level with the ornately carved leg of the desk. And what she saw there made her smile.

It would never have occurred to the police to look for a secret drawer in the desk. They probably thought that was the sort of villainous feature that only existed in films.

But she wasn't the police. *She* was an auctioneer. And she knew otherwise.

"Everything all right in there?"

Magda Clay's voice, advancing up the stairs. With a muffled curse, Felicia pushed the drawer to with her hip, snatching at the nearest object just as the door opened.

"Oh, yes. I was just…trying to get a closer look at the mark on this." Felicia cavalierly flipped the figurine upside down to demonstrate, then saw that it was an early Sèvres and blanched, putting it down with exaggerated care.

Her heart was thumping, and not just because she'd almost dropped a valuable ceramic. She'd only had a few seconds to see the contents of that drawer, but it had been enough. Enough to know that the rumours were true, at any rate. More than anyone could have imagined.

There was no doubt about it.

Barrington Clay had been in it all the way up to his neck.

Chapter Twenty-One

Cassie Lane had always been firmly self-aware. She knew that, whilst she had many good qualities—determined, loyal, able to exist on almost no sleep, to name a few—there were also certain things that would forever remain hopelessly out of her grasp: sleek hair, tights that didn't ladder whenever she so much as looked at them, the ability to dunk a biscuit without it collapsing into her tea... and being quiet. In any sense of the word.

As such, she'd never been under the illusion that she'd make a good spy. Not even as a child, when most of her contemporaries were dreaming of such future career paths. Cassie had known, even then, that it was a non-starter for her.

She was reflecting on that right now as she stood in the doorway to her office, chewing her lower lip, and starting at every sound from within the creaking old building. She could hear printers spluttering on the floor above, the coffee machine whirring from the staff kitchen across the hall, phones ringing tinnily in the reception area below. But most of all, she could hear the hammering of her heart, the blood singing in her ears as she stared at the unflinchingly sparse, polished surface of the desk that filled most of the space in the anteroom.

This was wrong. She shouldn't be doing this. She shouldn't even be contemplating it.

And, yet... what other choice did she have?

Steeling herself, she padded as stealthily as she was able across the floor. She'd taken her shoes off—a clever move, she'd thought, rather proudly—although now she realised with a sense of deflation that the plush carpet made the distinction almost negligible. A regret that was only intensified moments later as she stubbed her toe on a discarded iron doorstop that was lying in her path. Biting off a bellowed curse she hopped around furiously for the next half a minute, sucking in air whilst tears swam before her eyes.

The pain having finally subsided to a burning throbbing, she hobbled the rest of the distance towards the desk, keener than ever to get this short-lived espionage career of hers over and done with. Grasping the brass handle of the topmost drawer, she yanked it open quickly, thanking God that Gavin was evangelical about the application of WD-40 on a regular basis. It slid open without a sound, although, to be honest, she was starting to think that speed might actually be the more effective strategy.

The contents were, it had to be said, more than a little disappointing. In fact, potentially a little alarming, Cassie thought, eyeing the rows of meticulously arranged stationery. Did the man *really* organise his paperclips into different colours? When this whole murder business was cleared up, perhaps she'd need to have a maternal talk with him about...well, getting a life. He was never going to meet a nice boy if...

She froze as a footstep rang on the staircase outside. Eyes wide, breath held, she waited.

Another footstep. Definitely a man's. Her lungs were beginning to burn. She squeezed her eyes shut, praying it wasn't Gavin. She had no idea how she was going to explain this to him.

She'd told him that she believed him, of course. What else could she say? He hadn't been willing to divulge anything more to her than he'd given the police; just the same story about how he'd been walking around town. So she'd nodded, and told him it'd be all right. And he'd looked so *relieved*…if he found out now that she'd lied, that she didn't really trust him at all…well, it didn't bear thinking about. She'd feel awful, like she'd failed him in the worst possible way.

In that moment, she knew she just couldn't do it. She couldn't betray him like this. Feeling shamefaced, she nudged the drawer gently closed.

The footsteps carried on past the door.

Cassie sagged heavily against the desk, almost knocking a hole punch off the edge in the process. She caught it just in time, although it trapped her finger in the mechanism, scraping off the top layer of skin. Sucking the offending digit resignedly, Cassie opened the bottom drawer. She knew that Gavin kept a full first aid kit in here; come to think of it, that would have been quite a good cover story if he *had* caught her, she thought wryly. Trust her to only think of it when it was too late.

The first aid kit was housed in a green plastic briefcase. Cassie was faintly gratified to see that this drawer was less tidy. In fact, it seemed to be a languishing spot for all manner of homeless items. There was a bundle of purple-patterned fabric in the corner, which, for one heart-stopping moment, Cassie was afraid might be a pair of pants, but on closer inspection, turned out to be only a tie. There was also an old Valentine's card—maybe she didn't need to have the talk with him after all—a secret stash of chocolate biscuits (she knew it! She *knew* no one could possibly be that worthy. All of that snootily turning down the variety box whilst picking at an undressed salad indeed) and a few golf balls.

Feeling even guiltier that she'd ever suspected she might find something incriminating in here, Cassie pulled out the green case, and as she did so, a scrap of paper dislodged itself from between the closure and fluttered to the floor. Automatically, she bent down to pick it up… and for the second time that afternoon, her eyes widened, the breath leaving her lungs in a rush.

The number scrawled across the surface of the paper was familiar to her. But even if it hadn't been, she would have recognised that handwriting anywhere. Normally, she would probably have been overjoyed to see it linked to something suspicious. But not now. Not like this. Not when it created a connection between the two people who both lacked an alibi for at least part of the council meeting on Saturday.

Cassie wrapped a plaster around her finger and wondered how she was going to bring herself to tell the police that her assistant was in secret contact with her deputy mayor.

Chapter Twenty-Two

F elicia crossed the hard tarmacked driveway, feeling her shoulders drop with every step she took further away from Barrington's house. She'd been in some strange properties in her time—one filled entirely with dolls had been particularly memorable—but this had an atmosphere even she couldn't shake off easily. She thought it had something to do with the woman in there, tragic and humiliated, torn between love and hate. Felicia couldn't imagine what it must be like, discovering that everything you'd thought was real had been nothing more than a convenient lie.

There was a presence behind her now, a shadow. The hairs on the back of her neck rose, but she didn't turn around. She didn't need to.

"God, I thought you were *never* going to finish." Dexter peeled away from the side of the house, where he'd been lurking as unobtrusively as someone dressed like a pick 'n' mix counter could possibly hope to. "How long does it take to look at a few old knick-knacks?"

"I'm not sure that Barrington would have appreciated his expertly and painstakingly acquired collection being described thus," Felicia replied, although somewhat begrudgingly. Truthfully, he'd had some exquisite pieces; she couldn't fault his taste. In fact, she had to admit to a certain amount of envy. "Besides, I was as fast as I could be. I didn't know you were waiting."

She'd actually rushed the job far more than was professionally acceptable. By rights, she ought to have been in there all afternoon. But Magda Clay's frosty presence had made it unbearable; she'd lingered in the doorway after Dexter had left, watching Felicia beadily as though suddenly distrustful of her motives. The memory of that stare on her back was enough to make Felicia shiver involuntarily, despite the mildness of the day.

She unlocked the car, then stared at Dexter as he hopped blithely into the passenger seat.

"What do you think you're *doing*?"

"Cadging a lift, obviously." He tossed his hat into the back and started rummaging around down the side of his seat. "I had to walk here; in case you'd forgotten, my transport was summoned back to London, along with all the support for my new series. I am officially without a vehicle. Both metaphorically and literally." He was trying to sound jovial about it, but she could tell it still smarted. "And besides, I'd say you owe me one. Didn't do half badly in there, did I, for a useless history professor? Got her to open up very nicely, I thought."

"Oh, yes, she was certainly opening up," Felicia said edgily, yanking her seatbelt across her body. Any more *open* and he probably would have found himself in a compromising position.

The inference was lost on him in any event. With an exclamation of triumph, he gave the lever a sharp tug, flipping the seat back into a reclined position. Felicia put the car into neutral, biting down on a caustic comment. He could never just sit still in someone's car; he *always* had to fiddle around and change things. It was maddening.

"Admit it, Fliss," he was saying smugly, as he adopted a

recumbent position. "I got more out of her than you were ever going to. You needed my help back there."

Felicia started the engine with a savage twist of the key, hoping that the dull roar would negate the need for a response. Because he was right, damn the man. If nothing else, they now had more of a sense of what Barrington's criminal résumé had included, and more than that, that he'd potentially been in the middle of something when he'd died. Something which had got him excited, Magda had said. Could that explain the inexplicable, the question no one could answer? Surely, if they could just find out what he was doing in the cupboard in the first place, then everything else would make sense. Or was that just the product of increasingly desperate thinking?

But she didn't admit any of this aloud. Dexter being right was invariably insufferable; one never got to hear the end of it.

They drove on in silence, funnelling up the narrow channel of Rutland Terrace, which morphed without warning into St Peter's Street. Stamford was filled with roads like that, narrowing, veering round a corner, and sneakily changing name. It was very confusing for the tourists. It could be pretty confusing for the locals, too. Sometimes, you weren't quite sure which road you were on, even if you'd traversed it a thousand times.

As they passed the empty mound of grass where St Peter's church had once stood, and which was now home to carpets of wildflowers, Dexter, obviously incapable of going any longer without hearing the sound of his own voice, turned to her eagerly.

"Listen...I've been having a think about the investigation. Going over it. See if there's anything I can add. Something no one else has thought of. Use my unique perspective, so to speak."

Felicia focused very hard on the road ahead and didn't respond. It didn't deter him, alas. He leaned forward, eyes shining.

"And the thing which strikes *me* is this...if the weapon didn't come from the sale, where *did* it come from?"

There was a lull following this startling insight. Felicia glanced derisively to the side, but he was looking at her so earnestly that she found she didn't have the heart to make a cutting comment. Instead she shrugged.

"Your guess is as good as mine."

"Well, I think I've *got* a pretty good guess..." he paused dramatically, then looked disappointed when she didn't respond with the requisite breathless anticipation. Rallying himself, he answered the question she'd never asked. "*Bunting's house up on Barn Hill!* You were inside the place, Felicia; *you* saw how many strange and archaic objects he had just lying about." He slapped the dashboard conclusively. "If you ask me, I'd say there's a jolly good chance that what the police are looking for came from there."

Then he sat back, looking very pleased with himself.

"You mean, someone stole it, took it to the sale, killed Barrington with it, then came back and killed its original owner with it?" Felicia said slowly.

"Maybe they thought the best place to hide it was back where it came from," Dexter said. "I mean, let's face it, it would be like a needle in a haystack in there. But the plan went wrong; old Batty caught them in the act, so they had to kill him."

"Why would they go to the trouble of breaking in there twice just to use a weapon from his house? They could get a weapon anywhere."

"To *frame* him! It was his cupboard, wasn't it? Or..." his face lit up. "Oh, this is even better." He clapped his hands together. "What time did they say Bunting died?"

"Somewhere between one and three, they think."

"And what time did we find Barrington?"

"About ten past one."

"So it *could* have been him," Dexter murmured, tapping his chin. "Yes, it would have been a close-run thing, but..."

Felicia veered into a free parking space in front of the auction house, slamming on the brake. She twisted in her seat to face him.

"Hang on, Dexter, let me just...are you *seriously* trying to suggest that Henry Bunting killed Barrington?"

"And why not? Isn't he the most likely suspect? He had a house full of sinister objects, any one of which could have doubled as a weapon. He would have known about the split in the side of the cupboard—because it was *his* cupboard! Not to mention that there's a decent chance this wasn't his first go at murder—"

"And afterwards, in a fit of remorse, madness, or perhaps both, he came straight home and shoved a blade between his ribs?" She interjected sarcastically.

"Maybe he thought it a poetic end," Dexter said, with a sulky frown.

"So poetic that the weapon just vanished into thin air afterwards?"

He paused for a moment, considering that, then visibly deflated.

"Ah, yes. I hadn't factored in that part," he said, in a small voice.

Of course he hadn't. Felicia unclipped her seat belt, wondering why the whole thing needled her so much. Dexter, trying to involve himself in the investigation—however ineptly he might be going about it. Was it because it reminded her uncomfortably of the fact that Algernon would do the same thing, given half a chance? That this whole business was starting to drag more than just herself into danger, and that she couldn't always protect the people close to her?

"I say, what's going on there?" Dexter was craning to see through the windscreen. Suddenly, Felicia became aware of a cacophony emerging from the doorway of Grant's. A shabby-coated dealer was shouting angrily, slamming the door behind him and stalking off down the steps.

"No idea." Felicia was already halfway out of the car. "But I intend to find out."

Inside, Betsy was at the desk, white-faced. Hugo was standing over her, murmuring something. When he saw Felicia, he visibly started, straightening with a slightly forced-looking smile.

"How'd it go with Mrs Clay? You've been quicker than I expected."

"What was all that about?" She gestured behind her towards the doorway.

"Ah, you saw that, did you." It wasn't a question. Felicia thought he seemed to sag slightly around the shoulders. "It's really nothing to worry about. Just a small misunderstanding. You know what these dealers are like; they can be so impatient and hot-headed. Won't listen to reason." Seeing that she wasn't mollified by that, he elaborated reluctantly. "There was a mix-up with one of the lots he bought. You know how it happens. It was supposed to be a lot of five walking sticks and two sword sticks; instead, it's six walking sticks and one sword stick. Nothing in there was particularly valuable, so it's not of huge importance. He's just blowing off steam, throwing his weight about. I didn't want to concern you with it."

The silence was broken by a muffled ringing. Hugo fished his mobile from his pocket, glancing quickly at the screen before holding it to his chest.

"I'm sorry, it's a…personal call. D'you mind?"

Felicia waved him on.

"I'll stand in for a minute."

Dexter stretched and yawned, making his way towards the stairs.

"Never a dull moment around here, is there? Time for a cup of tea, I think. Perk me back up after all of that whisky. God, that woman can sink a bit."

"All in the name of investigation, of course," Felicia muttered, then jumped as she turned to find Betsy standing right behind her.

"Is…er, everything all right? Did you want me?"

Betsy was twisting her wedding ring around and around her finger, not meeting her eye. Her normally jolly face was creased with indecision.

"I'm not sure. Look, can I…talk to you about something?"

"Of course."Hiding her curiosity as best she could, Felicia gestured up towards the office. "Shall we…"

"Not here." The words were blurted out. "It's too…" As if to illustrate her point, the doors swung open and a middle-aged couple staggered in, each at one end of a huge Grecian urn. In an instant, Betsy switched her sunny professional smile on. "Good afternoon. I take it you're here for a valuation?"

"I'll do it." Felicia leaned across the desk, ostensibly for a pen, but in reality so she could say, in a low voice, "how about later, after closing? At The George?"

Betsy nodded infinitesimally.

Nothing. Absolutely nothing. And after all of that work, too.

Police Constable Jess Winters rubbed her eyes, flopping back in her lumpy computer chair with a sigh. The chair was a hand-me-down, having made its way through almost every member of the force before finally ending up, inevitably, at the desk of the newest and most junior member. The fabric was fraying, it was anything but comfortable—there was a particular spring that poked her in the hip every time she moved—and the mechanism had long since broken, meaning that it was fixed at an uncomfortably low height. But at least she *had* a chair of her own, Jess reflected, with the same attempt at pragmatic optimism with which she tackled every aspect of her career. She had a desk of her own, too, even if it *was* shoved into a corner and possessed a wonky leg that had to be propped up on a pile of old photocopying. Really, she wasn't doing all that badly. There were contemporaries of hers in other forces who could put claim to less.

Jess cradled her—now cold—cup of coffee while she looked around the small room that constituted the beating heart of operations at the Welland Police Station. In fact, it constituted pretty much all of the Welland Police Station full stop. Apart from what she could see from her desk, there was only a small kitchenette, a communal loo—which didn't sound great, but was a great improvement on the outside privy, apparently, which had still been in use until only five years ago—and an evidence cupboard. The evidence had to share space with the cleaning equipment and everyone's coats, which had almost given DCI Heavenly an apoplexy when he'd first arrived, but as there wasn't really anywhere else to put it, he'd had no choice but to leave things as they were.

Like just about everyone else at the station, Jess wasn't entirely sure what DCI Heavenly was doing here. He'd given some vague, jargon-laden explanation in his inaugural speech—held in the office, with everyone standing around with mugs of tea and confused expressions, wondering what on earth he was on about —and no one had really dared ask him more about it since. Heavenly wasn't a man who invited questions of any sort.

Then again, she couldn't exactly criticise him for that. She was well-aware that her colleagues probably wondered the same about her; why a bright, promising young police officer who'd graduated top of her intake would choose to start her career at a backwater station like this.

Little did she know, in fact, just how much they wondered. How they looked curiously at her from time to time, discussed it in whispers beneath the sound cover of the boiling kettle, occasionally advanced the odd theory about it in the pub after a shift. The force of the Welland Police Station rarely had much of a mystery on their hands, so they relished whatever thrilling enigma came their way. But somehow, no one ever just *asked* her.

Because despite her chirpy, can-do openness, it was the one subject she seemed strangely reticent on. She wasn't like Heavenly; she hadn't spouted any flowery justifications. She'd just...never said anything at all. And so her fellow officers steered clear; they knew when to leave well alone.

Jess took a sip of her coffee and shuddered at the cold, slimy texture, then shrugged and drank it anyway. She couldn't be bothered to get up and make another; she'd only let *that* go cold, too. She scrolled once more through the documents on her screen; a triumph of hope over expectation, as she knew full well that there was nothing there. She'd been over it all with a fine toothcomb.

Background checks nearly always threw up something, particularly when they were on the victim of a murder. After all, most people got themselves murdered for a reason. Some were just in the wrong place at the wrong time, true, but with something like this—something premeditated, deliberate—there had to be an aim behind it. An aim that, presumably, started with something about the victim. Something they'd seen, something they'd done, something they were *about* to do...the list went on, but the essence was the same. It all came back to one question: why? Why *that* person?

It was a question Jess had every intention of answering. But thus far, it felt like one step forward, two steps back.

With Barrington Clay, it was transparently simple. The man was a crook. He'd swindled, blackmailed, and humiliated a vast amount of people in his time. The problem there wasn't finding out who might have wanted to kill him, but who *wouldn't*. The net was almost *too* wide, to be honest. But with Henry Bunting...

It was a blank page. Not quite literally, but almost. It might as well have been. For a man who'd lived almost 94 years in the same town, he'd left next to no discernible imprint. He really had been a recluse, in the truest sense. Just rattling around in his house, rarely venturing out except to the monthly auction at

Grant's, or to The George occasionally for a nightcap by the inglenook fireplace, or to the market on a Friday morning for fresh fish wrapped in paper and a bunch of asparagus. His financials were yet to come back; she could only hope that they might yield something of interest, because right now, she couldn't see how anybody might benefit from the death of an already very old man who couldn't have gone on for much longer anyway. A man who'd led an utterly blameless, chronically uneventful life…save one exception. Someone had died in his house. But it had been 80 years ago, and an accident, to all intents and purposes. She was grasping at straws, and she knew it.

She'd even rung Evelina Fielding, such was her desperation to get at something useful. Her—she had to admit, embarrassingly tenuous—logic was that as another old person, who also attended the auction on a regular basis, she might have known the man to speak to, maybe found out a bit more about him in that wittering, coaxing way elderly ladies had about them.

At least, if she'd succeeded at nothing else, Jess acceded wryly, she'd made a nonagenarian's day. Evelina had been utterly thrilled to be questioned. So thrilled, in fact, that Jess had almost started to wonder if the old dear hadn't done the murders herself just for a bit of titillation. She'd kept asking if it was a formal interrogation, and had seemed heartily disappointed when Jess had told her that no, she wasn't about to be dragged off to the station in handcuffs.

Not that it would have done much good even if she had been. It turned out that even though she'd been living in town all those years ago, she'd never known the Bunting family all that well— "not my class, dear; between you and I, I landed on my feet when I married my husband"—although she did remember the death of the governess well enough, and the rumours that had abounded afterwards.

"A lot of idle gossip, if you ask me," had been her crisp verdict. "Oh, it was all very thrilling at the time; I can see why everyone got swept up in it. I was only a child, and I'm ashamed to say I probably did, too. But with the benefit of maturity… well, it was all rather foolish and hysterical. After all, why should it have been anything other than an accident? That's far more likely, isn't it?"

Jess had agreed that yes, really, it was, and that had been that, more or less. Evelina had explained, with palpable regret in her voice, that she'd moved away after she'd married, and hadn't returned to town until twenty years ago, when she'd become widowed. Then, with that uncanny knack old people had of turning the conversation on a ninepin, she'd begun asking Jess all about herself. Was that a hint of a Southern accent she could hear? Yes, Jess had confessed; she'd grown up in Dorset, near Lyme. How lovely, Evelina had enthused. She'd always wanted to see that part of the world, but her husband hadn't liked anywhere with cliffs, so they hadn't been able to go. They'd been to Whitby once though; now, that had been nice, although rather chilly in March. She imagined that the Southern coast was much milder, although they did say that the beaches were very under-rated up North…

It had taken Jess a full fifteen minutes after that to get off the phone. When she had, she'd been overwhelmingly relieved—but also, she'd realised to her surprise, smiling.

A ping now signalled the arrival of a new email. Resurrecting her monitor, which had been quietly snoozing, she clicked on it to find the results of a financial check she'd requested. Not Henry Bunting's, though. Someone else's.

She blinked, rubbed her eyes again, then refocused her gaze. Everything stayed exactly the same; she wasn't hallucinating, at least.

She sat back with a low whistle, waiting for the elation to come. Which it did, cautiously, the grin spreading across her face, dimpling her cheeks. Finally, she had something good to tell the sarge. And not before time.

It would seem that they had a lead.

Chapter Twenty-Three

F elicia fiddled with the stem of her glass of rosé and resisted the urge to check her watch for the umpteenth time.

She'd be here. She was just running a bit late, that was all. She'd probably stopped in at home and got sidetracked by something. Maybe one of her grandchildren had rung just as she was fetching her coat. Felicia could imagine that Betsy would drop anything for one of her beloved brood.

Felicia took a sip of her wine, casting an eye around the courtyard. It was looking lovely tonight, the flagstoned space filled with potted topiary around which white fairy lights were wound, creating a twinkling effect in the evening light. At the tables, people sat beneath parasols, laughing and clinking glasses. The whole atmosphere was convivial, relaxed, refined. It was one of Felicia's favourite places in the world.

It was just a shame that she couldn't enjoy it as she normally would. She felt edgy, unable to settle, even to distract herself with some idle people watching as she might usually do.

"More wine, Aunt Fliss?" Robyn was at her side, fresh-faced and crisp in a white blouse with a scalloped collar. How she always looked so perky and energetic, Felicia would never know.

Youth, she supposed. But most teenagers at least needed sleep; she had it on good authority from Cassie that Robyn hardly ever closed her eyes.

She looked at her glass, surprised to see that it was empty. She must have downed it distractedly.

"Please." She pushed it across to Robyn. "Just a small one, though."

"You waiting for Mum?" Robyn put the glass on the tray she had balanced on one hand.

"No, not tonight. Someone from work…" Felicia's sentence trailed off as she watched a familiar dark blond head disappear into the dark interior of the inn.

"Ah, the mysterious Jack," Robyn said, following her gaze with a knowing smile. "I didn't know you had a crush on him, Aunt Fliss."

"Robyn!" Felicia whirled around, aghast. "I do *not* have a… that's ridiculous."

"So you *do*." Robyn grinned impishly. "The lady doth protest too much. Shows every time."

"Fiend," Felicia fumed, furious with herself for falling into such an obvious trap. "I want that silver pendant I gave you for your Christening back."

"I think the returns period might have expired after seventeen years." Robyn laughed. "Look, I'm not blaming you, Aunt Fliss. He's pretty easy on the eye. But alas, to be admired from afar, I think."

Felicia frowned.

"Why d'you say that?"

Robyn gave her a strange look.

"Well, I mean…everyone *knows* that Jack's trouble. The police are forever on at him for something or other."

Felicia felt something inside her go cold.

"I'm surprised he's still walking about, to be honest." Robyn continued, shifting her weight from one hip to the other. "I'd have thought they'd arrest him right from the off. He's an obvious suspect, from their point of view." At Felicia's blank expression, she said slowly, "you know, because he had all of that history with Barrington Clay, didn't he? How he fired him for stealing? He couldn't get another job for ages afterwards." She gave Felicia an exasperated look. "Honestly, Aunt Fliss, doesn't *anyone* tell you *anything*?"

"Apparently not," Felicia said softly.

Things were starting to slot into place, things that hadn't made sense before. Pettifer's obscure parting shot, that night in her father's cottage. Jack's frostiness when she'd asked if he'd been spoken to by the police. No wonder he'd been on the defensive; he'd probably thought she was making a pointed remark. She felt like dropping her head into her hands just thinking about it. God, how utterly mortifying.

Someone at one of the other tables was trying to get Robyn's attention. She glanced across, then back at Felicia apologetically.

"I'd better not ignore him. He's one of our regular residents."

Felicia watched her go, weaving deftly between the twinkling topiary trees. Then she did a double take, sitting bolt upright in her chair. Before she could talk herself out of it, she quickly rose to her feet, following the same path Robyn had to the table in the corner. She paused behind a fortuitously tall topiary spiral, waiting until her goddaughter had scribbled the order down and scuttled away before stepping into view.

"Mr Clancy?" She hovered in the appealingly self-effacing way that had proved itself the most useful product of her expensive education. As the dealer looked up, she placed a hand lightly against her breastbone. "Felicia Grant. From the auction?"

His face cleared.

"Ah, of course. The auctioneer. I remember you from the rostrum on Saturday."

"Well, I'm not *usually* an auctioneer," she admitted. "Not any more, anyway. That was my first sale for years."

He raised a surprised eyebrow.

"You wouldn't have known it." He picked up the folded newspaper from the chair next to him, gesturing for her to sit with a courtly sweep of the arm. "Please, join me. I was just having a quick aperitif." He raised a hand infinitesimally at a waiter on the other side of the courtyard with the air of someone fully expecting to be obeyed. Sure enough, the waiter's head swivelled, as though pulled by an invisible string. "What'll you have?"

"Thank you, but I've already got a rosé on order." As if on cue, Robyn appeared with a tray and began setting down their drinks, very professionally unfazed by Felicia's sudden change of table. Mr Clancy was having a glass of port, Felicia noticed. It seemed fitting for a man who almost appeared to belong to the century he specialised in. She didn't know a lot about him—he was famously fond of discretion—but she'd seen a photograph of him standing in the drawing room at his London townhouse once, accompanying a rare interview in an antiques magazine. She couldn't recall a word of the text now, but she still remembered the room, how stunningly beautiful it had been. He'd had the whole thing painstakingly restored to its 18th-century glory, from the gilt-and-plasterwork ceiling to the finest pieces of furniture from the period. Clearly, the Bourbon era was more than just a lucrative business model for him; it was an all-consuming passion.

"It must have been quite a weekend for you. I trust that the auction's not too badly affected?" He was watching her over the rim of his glass. For the first time, she noticed what a curiously large head he had in relation to his body. With an effort, she focused her attention on the exquisitely tied silk cravat that flowered at his throat. Dexter would be jealous of that cravat, she decided. She'd certainly never seen one tied quite like that before. Did Mr Clancy have a book, she wondered? A poster on the wall, detailing all the different styles and how to do them? Or did he just have a valet? He was the sort of man who would.

"We're coping," she said, with a demure lift of the shoulders.

"It's still a crime scene, but the police have allowed us to release the purchased lots." She swirled the blush-coloured liquid in her glass, striving for a casual tone. "I'm surprised to see that you're still in town. I sincerely hope they aren't keeping you here."

"Oh, no." He had small teeth, closely set. The bottom row was revealed when he smiled. "I'm here of my own volition. I'm a regular visitor to Stamford, as it happens. I have various business interests here." He crossed one leg over the other, revealing poppy-red socks. "More than that, the golf club's excellent."

Felicia waited for him to say more, but he just sipped his port languidly. A signet ring glinted on his small, paw-like hand.

At once, it came back to her in a rush. The crowded saleroom, the blur of faces, and, on the front row, a hand about to raise... a hand with a ring that flashed gold beneath the lights...

"You were about to bid on the Jacobean cupboard, weren't you?" She blurted out.

On the surface, his blandly polite expression didn't change. But then she saw it. A small muscle at the corner of his mouth twitched irritably.

"I'm not sure where you'd get that idea."

"I *saw* you," she pointed out, slightly shakily. "Just before it all happened...you were going to bid at £600. There's no point lying about it; I remember perfectly."

The muscle twitched again, more violently this time. The eyes behind the heavy tortoiseshell frames were now openly hostile.

"I fail to see what concern it is of yours."

"I suggest that you answer her question, sir." Pettifer's deep voice rumbled from behind Felicia's shoulder, his square shadow falling over their drinks. "Because if you don't, next it'll be mine."

Chapter Twenty-Four

He retrieved a chair from a nearby table and collapsed onto it heavily, giving Mr Clancy a hard look. "And my interrogations don't generally take place in such refined surroundings." He eyed the glass of port distastefully. "The catering's certainly not as good. Tepid tea in a polystyrene cup's about all we can stretch to."

Mr Clancy leaned back in his chair, regarding Felicia as though reassessing her. She could practically see the thoughts going through his head, wondering where this new balance of power had come from, what exactly her relationship with the police was.

"And so what if I was going to bid? A man can have his whims, can't he?" He shrugged lightly. "It was going cheaply; I decided to have a go. It happens all the time at auction. You come out with something you didn't expect to buy. It's part of the experience." His eyes met Felicia's, several degrees cooler than the genial tone of his voice. "As Ms Grant of all people ought to know."

"It's not really your line, though, is it?" She pressed, refusing to be drawn into the trap. "You're an eighteenth century furniture specialist."

"If you must know, it was for myself." His eyes narrowed. "Look, I haven't committed any crime. And I find this... ambush... rather insulting." His voice thrummed with anger. "Is this how the local police force usually operates, Sergeant? By sending in a civilian honeytrap to ask your questions for you?"

"We're not together," Felicia said, at the same time as Pettifer uttered shortly, "certainly not." They looked at one another.

"Very convincing." Clancy smiled mockingly, rising to his feet. "What a pair you make. Now, if you'll excuse me..." He flung his jacket over his arm, picking up the newspaper. "I think I'll move my dinner reservation. This unpleasant display has left rather a sour taste in my mouth."

Felicia watched him go for a moment, before turning back to Pettifer, saying quickly, "thanks for the help back there. I didn't think he was going to..."

She trailed off as she discovered the seat next to her was empty.

Luckily for her, he'd left a trail. The narrow avenue of topiary now rocking back and forth in their pots revealed that he'd gone in the direction of the carriage archway. Flinging down some money haphazardly on the table—she'd settle up properly with Robyn later, she told herself—she rushed after him.

As usual, she caught him in about ten seconds flat.

"Where are you going?" She puffed.

He didn't turn his head.

"Back to my car. Where else?"

She winced at the clipped tone.

"All right, so I'm getting the slightest sensation that you *might* be annoyed with me...but listen"

"Bloody *hell*, Felicia," he barked, with such velocity that it almost made her jump. He stopped in the shadowy cradle of the archway, glaring at her. "That was supposed to be *my* interrogation. *Mine*, as in, the police. As in, the people who are *actually* employed to solve crimes. The people who are *trained* to solve crimes. I know that doesn't seem to mean much to you armchair detectives; you all seem to think you can do our job just as well as we can, if not better. But the training, the procedure… it's there for a reason, as you've just demonstrated so indubitably tonight." He thrust an arm angrily back in the direction of the inn, its windows now glowing amber in the dusk. "I had questions to ask that man. Now, thanks to your incompetence, he's been spooked. More than that, he's furious. Not to mention that, he's just the sort of entitled, highly-connected person who's likely to contact the chief constable to complain." He sighed raggedly. "Quite aside from hindering the investigation into two murders, do you have *any* idea how much trouble you might have just got me into?"

Felicia blinked, taken aback. She'd never seen Pettifer lose his temper like that before. He was normally so benign, it was easy to forget what a big man he was, how intimidating he had the potential to be. She held up her hands contritely.

"I'm sorry, really."

"Are you?" He shook his head and walked off, veering to the left through the door in the wall that led through to the inn's gardens.

"Look, I didn't come here meaning to ask him any questions. I didn't even know he was still in town. It was just…a spur of the moment thing," she called after him helplessly.

"It always is with you," he threw back over his shoulder. "That's your problem. And if you're not more careful, it might get you killed."

She hesitated for a moment, then followed him. As she passed through the doorway into the walled garden, the hubbub from the terrace next door was swallowed by a hushed, verdant atmosphere. The scent of the wisteria, released with the dusk, was heady. The white-planted borders glowed vividly against the dark that surrounded them.

He'd stopped in the middle of the lawn, looking up at the

canopy of stars overhead. She wondered if he'd been waiting for her, or if he really was just admiring the heavens. She reached his side and tilted her head back.

"You never really see the stars much in London," she said softly. "It's one of the things I've always missed."

"They're not bad here. They're better back home in Yorkshire. Out in the dales, with no light pollution, you can see the Milky Way sometimes."

She smiled dryly.

"I bet you think everything's better in Yorkshire."

"God's own country," he quipped heartily. "But no, seriously, it's not too shabby here in Stamford. When I got the transfer, I wasn't all that keen. Thought it was going to be all fancy cafés serving frothy coffees and poncey, overpriced furniture shops... and it is," he acceded, with a touch of humour. "But it's also a lot more than that. I don't know, there's just something special about the place. It's not just the architecture; it's the atmosphere. I wouldn't be anywhere else now." He cast her a sideways look. "And if you ever tell anyone else at the station that I said anything so bloody airy-fairy, I'll have you arrested before you can blink. Understood?"

Felicia was actually desperate to ask what was so unforgivable about frothy coffees, but she refrained, instead saying, "don't worry, your secret's safe with me."

"Glad to hear it." He returned his gaze to the sky.

Feeling that they'd achieved a truce of sorts, Felicia decided to press home her advantage.

"So...what were you going to ask Mr Clancy about?"

"I know what you're doing," he rumbled, but without much conviction. "It won't work."

"Because you know, he lied about wanting to buy the cupboard for himself. I've seen inside his home, and it's a perfect replica of a Louis XIV interior, gilt and enamel everywhere. Not a piece of dark oak in sight. And he *definitely* didn't go for it on a whim, either. He sat through the entire sale and didn't bid on a single thing; there was nothing else he wanted. He must have been waiting for that cupboard all along, and…"

"That bloody *cupboard*!" Pettifer sounded exasperated. "Leave it alone, Felicia. It's nothing but a distraction, a fantasy story put into everyone's head by that ex-husband of yours. No, I've long suspected that our murder was committed for a much more prosaic reason. Money, in all likelihood. It usually is."

Felicia blinked, taken aback.

"From what I've seen, Barrington didn't have much money. Not officially, at least. He was mortgaged up to the eyeballs."

"I won't ask how you know that."

"Best not to. It involves some underhand dealings. You wouldn't approve."

He harrumphed.

"Yes, he was in deep trouble—on the surface. Everything they owned jointly was poured back into the business, which he was over-expanding at an unsustainable rate. The bailiffs would have come knocking any day now. Mrs Clay's going to be in for a horrible shock, if she doesn't know already."

"Does she have an alibi for Saturday afternoon?" Felicia asked instinctively.

"At home painting her nails," he answered automatically. "They had a dinner party booked that evening."

All afternoon? How many fingers and toes did the woman have? Felicia looked askance at Pettifer, but he was brooding away to himself: "but I'm *sure* he must have had a secret nest-egg stashed somewhere. Something hidden from his wife—and which always will be, if we can't dig it up. God knows, she's earned it." He thumped a fist into the other palm. "I know he was involved in dodgy deals; I *know* it, for Christ's sake! But I just can't find the proof."

Felicia coughed delicately.

"You…um, might try the desk in his study."

Pettifer eyed her in derision.

"It has a secret drawer," she elucidated. "Everything you need is in there."

He threw up his hands.

"Of *course* there's a secret drawer! Why wouldn't there be? Everything else about this place is barmy, after all. Next you'll tell me I have to solve a cryptogram, navigate a collapsing temple, and press the mysterious weapon which killed them both into a perfectly-sized slot in a secret door. Only *then* may I finally solve the case. Is that about the measure of it?"

"Actually, secret drawers are a fairly commonplace feature of antique desks," she said flatly. "So no, not really."

"Ah." He looked a bit sheepish. "I see. Well, er… thank you…"

There was a brief pause. Then he admitted, "But, actually, it wasn't Clay's money I meant. It was Bunting's." At her expectant glance, he continued: "We're still waiting on the official financial reports, but in a small town like this… well, there are certain shortcuts. I had a quiet word with the bank manager, who told me —*without* telling me, naturally—" he slanted her a look—"that, not only was he sitting on a family fortune which, thanks to his hermit-like way of existence, he'd barely made a dent in, but also a veritable gold-mine of a house, which he owned outright. I asked you earlier why anyone would want to kill an eccentric old man; well, now I have the answer to that. Several possible answers, in fact. His death will benefit a good many people, in one way or another."

"You mean his will?"

"No such luck," Pettifer grimaced. "The man was barmy until the end. No will in sight. Nothing he gave to his solicitors, anyway. Chances are, he scribbled something on the back of an envelope one day and shoved it behind a painting somewhere. He was from that sort of stock."

"I'm not sure who he would have left it to anyway. As far as I'm aware, he's always been a recluse. He knew my grandfather—

I *suppose* you'd call them friends, but really all it amounted to was a meal and a game of chess in the pub a few times a year. I don't think he had any real relationships. I suppose he has some natural heirs somewhere, though?"

"Everyone does *somewhere*. They'll have to trace them, mind. No near relations, and in these cases it tends to get very complicated."

"You don't have to tell me," Felicia groaned. "Auction houses do valuations for probate, remember? If someone dies intestate—without a will—and with no obvious heirs in the running, the process can go on for years."

"Exactly. So even if someone was hoping to inherit, they'll be waiting a long time yet."

"And even when they do, they may have to split the proceeds between dozens of other people," Felicia concluded dejectedly. "Not exactly much of a motive, then."

For the first time, she was beginning to feel the first fissures of doubt as to whether they would ever get to the bottom of all of this. Everywhere they turned in this case, they seemed to come up against a brick wall. Or—she eyed the façade of The George, rising up beyond the garden—maybe that should be a *stone* wall. A honey-coloured ironstone wall. It was as though Stamford itself was closing in upon its secrets, as it had for so many centuries prior.

"Well, I wouldn't quite say *that*." At her quizzical glance, Pettifer continued, "come on, this is your department. What happens in this sort of situation, where there are so many people involved, most of whom live far away and never even met the deceased? How do they decide who gets what?"

"They don't," Felicia replied. "The solicitor generally sells off all the assets on behalf of the estate and puts the money made into a big pot, which can then be shared out equally."

"*All* of the assets, first and foremost being the house."

"There are certainly a lot of people who'd like to get their hands on that house," she said vaguely, then she stared at him in dawning comprehension. "Wait, you're not thinking…"

"That suddenly, Mr Bunting's death looks very convenient for quite a few people? Yes, I am. The man was a creaking gate; he could have dragged on for years. Perhaps someone got bored of the wait. Someone like your Mr Clancy in there." He jerked a thumb back towards the courtyard. "Were you aware that he owns dozens of properties in town?"

"No, I wasn't."

"I'm not surprised; he's kept it very dark. But the police have access to this sort of information; if it's legal, you can't hide it from our financial checks. Been buying them up on the quiet for years now; a mix of commercial and residential. He owns most of the High Street, not that anyone renting the shops probably realises. I'd wager that's where most of his money comes from these days; the antiques are just a hobby."

So *those* were the business interests he was being so cagey about, Felicia thought. Things were starting to make a little more sense, at least.

They carried on walking, passing out through the gate at the far end of the garden that led to the tree-lined car park. One of the cars lit up as it was unlocked from afar, and a crunching of gravel morphed into the form of Jack as he passed in front of the headlight beams. He climbed in, placing his camera on the passenger seat.

"Our Mr Riding does get around rather, doesn't he?" Pettifer said quietly.

They'd paused by the gate, the shadows swallowing them, making them invisible. Felicia watched as the car pulled out onto the road, wondering if she had the courage to ask what was on her mind.

"Is he…a suspect?"

Pettifer didn't seem surprised at her question.

"You do remember what I said to you the other night, don't you?"

"I remember the vagueness of it," she replied, rather tartly.

He shrugged, unrepentant.

"I figured you'd find out more for yourself."

She didn't like to tell him that in reality, she'd hardly found out anything at all. And that perhaps a part of her didn't *want* to know more. So instead she just repeated her question firmly.

"*Is* he a suspect?"

Pettifer sighed.

"For most things which go bump in the night, yes. His name tends to get called up quite a bit. Old sins, long shadows and all of that. But for this?" He looked upwards, to where the colourless trees rustled overhead. "Well, he certainly had a motive, for the first murder at least. His animosity with the victim was known. And he was well-placed to do it. After all, who ever notices the photographer?"

She had, Felicia thought. But she didn't voice it.

"You haven't arrested him though," she persisted.

"It's all far too circumstantial. Besides, he couldn't have done Bunting. He was still being held at the auction house with the other witnesses."

The news made Felicia feel relieved in a way she couldn't explain.

"So he's clear then?"

"Unless he had an accomplice for the second one." He tilted his head towards her with a half-smile. "Heavenly thinks it's you, by the way."

Felicia rolled her eyes.

"Of course he does."

"You know, in all seriousness, Heavenly isn't a man you want to cross. You might want to be more circumspect about riling him."

"Oh, he deserves it," she scoffed. "Besides, what's he going to do, slam me in Stamford jail for impertinence?"

"There isn't a Stamford jail," Pettifer said, po-faced.

She'd forgotten how literally he took everything. But before she could reply, his phone began to ring. Felicia waited, feeling strangely tense, while he listened for a moment to whoever was on the other end of the line. His stony expression wasn't encouraging to start with, and when he swore loudly, her stomach flipped. Bad news, then.

He didn't even wait for her to ask.

"Bunting's house...it's been broken into."

Shock rolled through her, mingling with relief. At least it wasn't another body.

"What, just now?"

"They don't know." His jaw was tight. "No one's been at the crime scene since yesterday morning."

"Well, wouldn't someone have *heard* something?" She asked breathlessly. "Breaking glass? I'm sure you can narrow it down." She paused, then added, "Unless...I mean, you *did* lock it all up, didn't you? When you left? You didn't... um... forget?"

"*Of course I didn't bloody forget!*" He exploded. "But you've seen the place. One of the window casements around the back was rotten; it didn't fit in its frame. All they had to do was slide it up. Bloody *hell*," he spat out, looking very much like he'd like to thwack the nearest tree trunk, but refraining at the last moment. "This is the *last* thing we need."

"What is?"

They both looked across, then down. Algernon was standing there, watching them with that animatedly curious expression he wore so well.

"Where did *you* come from?" Felicia asked, looking around in bemusement. There was gravel everywhere; how on earth had he managed to creep up on them like that? "More to the point, where have you *been*? It's almost dark."

She could feel Pettifer's eyes on her; no doubt he was silently judging her lax parenting. She strove to ignore him.

"Just walking around," Algernon replied. "I went to Burghley Park. Did you know they have a herd of fallow deer there?"

"I did," she said sternly. "They've had them since…wait," she blinked, seeing his torn jumper. "What happened there?"

"Oh, nothing." He rubbed his arm absently. "I just fell."

"Probably wandering around looking up as usual, not at where you're putting your feet," Felicia said, although the intended note of rebuke came out more like resignation.

"You should be more careful, lad," Pettifer rumbled from next to her. "It's a big space out there. If you were really hurt, no one might find you for a long time."

There was a strange, uncomfortable pause.

"Well, come along, let's get you home," Felicia said brightly, giving Pettifer a quelling look over her shoulder. What was he trying to do, give them *both* nightmares?

She took Algernon's arm, but he wouldn't budge. He just stood there, staring up enquiringly at Pettifer.

"Is there a problem with the case? You sounded angry just now."

"Yes, well, that was wrong of me," Pettifer said diplomatically. "There are snags in every investigation, lad. Nothing to worry about. We'll sort it in the end. We're tracking down several leads as we speak."

Algernon looked deeply unimpressed with that answer, and Felicia couldn't blame him. She knew placatory semantics when she heard them.

"Whatever happened to those witnesses from the sale, by the way?" She asked suddenly. "Did Hugo ever manage to trace them for you?"

Algernon's ears pricked up.

"Witnesses? What witnesses?"

Pettifer glared at her. She held up her hands in apology.

"You'd better tell him now," she advised. "He won't leave it alone until you do. Trust me."

Pettifer sighed, then addressed Algernon.

"There were a couple at the auction on Saturday. An elderly couple. I don't suppose you'd remember them; from what my PC recalls, they wouldn't have stood out in any way. Tweed country coats, him in a flat cap…"

"There were five old couples there who would fit that description," Algernon said promptly. "Have you got anything else to narrow it down?"

Pettifer seemed temporarily lost for words. Then he cleared his throat.

"Uh, well, yes. Maybe. There was a red scarf left behind; it didn't belong to anyone else there. I don't suppose you remember…"

"I thought so," Algernon nodded. "They were standing by the wardrobe when the auction started. They left after the toys section. He bought a train. Teak and cream." He looked at Felicia expectantly, like a teacher waiting for a slow pupil to catch on.

And she did, after a second or two's delay.

"Algie, you're a *genius*!" She hugged him, turning to Pettifer to explain. "If we know what he bought, we can find his details from the bidding form. Everyone has to fill one in before they can take a bidding number."

Pettifer's expression lightened.

"Your mother's right, lad. You *are* a genius. More than that, you might have just provided a vital link in this case." He ruffled Algernon's hair. "Well done. That being said, though," he added warningly, as Algernon grinned, "what I said before still stands. You're to leave it to the police now." His gaze travelled up to meet Felicia's. "Both of you."

Algernon and Felicia looked at one another, and then back at him. Pettifer, from his vantage point, watched as their faces formed into mirrored expressions of dismay. In that moment, he thought they'd never looked more alike.

"But…" Felicia began to protest, but he cut her off.

"I *mean* it this time. No more poking around, you hear me? I don't want to see you anywhere near my investigation, not even if…"

"I was just going to say," she said serenely. "That you'll be wanting me to call Hugo and ask him to look through the bidders to get the details of who bought that train."

Pettifer's mouth opened, then closed. He had the unpleasant premonition that he looked like a goldfish.

"Yes, well," he blustered. "If you could, that would be very… helpful. Thank you," he added, somewhat begrudgingly. "But *after* that…"

"We'll stay well out of it," Felicia finished solemnly.

"Definitely," Algernon was nodding earnestly.

Pettifer looked at them both, knowing he should feel satisfied. Instead, he felt an all-too-familiar sinking sensation.

Frankly, he'd never felt less reassured in his life.

Chapter Twenty-Five

The cottage on Water Street was in total darkness as they walked back along the riverbank. In contrast to the warmly illuminated, lamplit windows of the surrounding dwellings, her father's house was rendered almost invisible, a watery smudge of pale stone melting into the purpling twilight.

They were passing the place where it had happened now, Felicia realised, feeling herself tensing recollectively. Almost twenty-four hours ago exactly. She looked at the verge where they'd fallen, half expecting it to show some mark there, some sign of what had occurred. But there was nothing; not so much as a dent in the grass. Everything looked exactly the same, even through the lens of her heightened emotions. No sinister atmosphere lingered, no stain of ominous foreboding. It was just the same peaceful, pretty stretch of riverbank. The trees still rustled soothingly, the ducks flapped and splashed in the water…

…And her son was still chattering brightly away, having apparently not even noticed that he was standing in almost exactly the same spot where he almost got mown down yesterday.

"Mum, d'you think Sergeant Pettifer will follow up on what I said?"

Oh, to be young and not dwell upon things, Felicia thought wistfully.

"I'm certain he will. I'll speak to Hugo about it when we get inside; he said he'd be staying on a bit tonight. We'll ask him to check before he goes home."

Algernon sighed in a world-weary sort of way.

"It's a shame. I might have made quite a good detective."

She gave him a strange look.

"You still could be. You're twelve, not a hundred and twelve. You can be whatever you want."

He rolled his eyes.

"But I already know what I'm going to do. I'm going to be an auctioneer, like you and Grandad."

Felicia felt her heart sink.

"Yes, well, you've got plenty of time to think about it. There's no need to rush."

He frowned.

"You're not listen—"

She ploughed on as though he hadn't spoken.

"You never know, you might change your mind."

"I *won't*, Mum." There were two high spots of colour appearing on his pale cheeks; always a sign he was entering a rare state of agitation. "I'm not like you."

The accusation in his voice felt like a dull blow to the chest. Suddenly, she had the disorientating sensation that they were no longer just talking about her career as an auctioneer, but something else entirely.

She looked down at the top of Algernon's head. He was studiously watching his feet as he walked, avoiding the cracks in the pavement. Immediately, she began to doubt her earlier reaction. Was she just being paranoid? Was she—God forbid—entering that "sensitive age" that her mother had occupied with staunch relish from the age of about 40 onwards? She'd assumed at the time that her father had been referring to the menopause when he called it that; later, she'd realised that it had nothing to do with biology and everything to do with her mother's flair for martyrdom.

"Mum, why are all the lights off?"

Algie's voice broke into her thoughts. He'd stopped in front of the cottage and was looking up at her, concern etched onto his small, pointed face.

"Maybe Grandad's gone out."

"In the dark?" Algernon was disbelieving. "In his wheelchair?"

Fair point, Felicia conceded. For all of her father's threats, she didn't think he would actually be able to get very far in that thing. He struggled enough just getting between the rooms in the cottage, which all had little steps going up and down into them.

"Unless..." Algernon's face brightened. "Maybe Auntie Juliette took him out?"

Privately, Felicia didn't think that was very likely. Juliette was always complaining that Felicia never told her anything; a failing that she drove home by scrupulously and pointedly detailing her every move. She'd even set up one of those synchronised calendars for them both to share whilst Peter was indisposed. Felicia had muted the notifications after the first hour. It was either that or go swiftly insane.

Having said that, though...

Hating herself for stooping to participate in the ridiculous thing, Felicia opened the calendar app and scrolled through.

"She couldn't have done," she told Algie. "She's got a PA meeting tonight."

No doubt involving pipe cleaners, she finished silently. Why every single thing in her sister's life seemed to involve pipe cleaners, Felicia would never know. *She'd* managed to get this far in motherhood whilst barely laying a finger on one of the infernal contraptions. It was just one of the many factors, no doubt, that rendered her a terrible parent in Juliette's exacting eyes.

Felicia pushed gingerly on the front door of the cottage. It swung open.

"Dad?" She called, stepping into the hall, her voice bouncing off the narrow walls on either side of her. "Are you here?"

The silence that greeted her was deafening. At least, it was initially; after a couple of moments, her ears began to pick up other sounds. The clock ticking on the mantelpiece in the living room, the familiar creaks of the house moving...and something else. A steady dripping. Coming from her right. The kitchen.

Motioning for Algernon to stay where he was, she moved slowly towards the kitchen doorway. The dripping was getting louder now, a slow, rhythmic drumbeat that made her heart beat harder in response.

"Dexter?" She ventured, on an afterthought. Unlikely as it seemed, she reassured herself by picturing them out together somewhere—hopefully indulging in some long-overdue bonding rather than killing one another.

She was just about to poke her head through the doorway into the kitchen when a tap on her shoulder made her swing around. Algernon was right behind her, gravely proffering a folded umbrella. She took it somewhat dubiously, not sure how effective it would prove as a weapon if needed but grateful that at least one of them was thinking on their feet. She chose not to dwell upon the fact that it probably ought to have been her, as the adult in the equation.

Umbrella held aloft, she inched around the corner. The kitchen was, if possible, even darker than the rest of the house, the small cottage window providing little in the way of illumination. The dripping sound was reverberating around the diminutive space, coming from a source she couldn't see.

And then, out of the corner of her eye, she sensed a flurry of movement. Reacting instantly, she raised the umbrella above her head and slashed downwards.

There was a hiss, followed by the scrabbling of claws on metal as a furry shape launched itself off the draining board.

"Sorry, Godfrey," Felicia gasped, as green eyes glared accusingly at her through the gloom. "I thought you were—" she shook her head, reaching over to turn off the tap, which she could now just about make out, her eyes having adjusted better to the dark. Immediately, the dripping ceased. "God knows what I thought."

For the first time, she began to entertain the uneasy idea that all of this might have sent her paranoid. What if—perish the thought—Heavenly might actually have been *right*, and she'd been spooked into seeing things that weren't there? What if…?

And then she saw it, and every thought drained from her head.

Light was glinting off the spokes of two motionless wheels. A dark shape was slumped in the chair, the head twisted at an unnatural angle.

Felicia's hands flew to her mouth.

"Oh my God," she whispered. "*Dad*."

Chapter Twenty-Six

The dark mass let out a shuddering snore, the head snapping upright.

"Oh, so you're back, are you?" It harrumphed. "Although what kind of time you call this, I'd very much like to know."

Felicia sagged against the sink, too breathless with relief to speak. She'd never been so thrilled to hear that acerbic, accusatory tone in all her life.

"Grandad?" Algernon's head appeared around the doorframe. Then, at Felicia's look of disapproval, he shrugged. "What? I knew it was safe to come out. No one else in the world snores quite like that."

"Snoring?" Peter boomed indignantly. "I wasn't snoring, you cheeky bugger. Sitting here watching that door I've been, all this time. Haven't so much as rested my eyes."

Felicia and Algernon, after a shared glance of tacit agreement, declined to contradict him.

"Waiting for someone to deign to remember about the old cripple alone at home, that's what I've been doing," Peter grumbled. "Chance'd be a fine thing, though, it turns out. Doesn't bode well for when I'm in my dotage, does it? I'll starve to death while you're all out gallivanting."

"I thought something might have happened to you," Felicia persisted, refusing to be drawn into that particular scenario. Her father at 70 was quite cantankerous enough; the thought of him at 90 was too much for her nerves at the moment. "Why on Earth are you sitting here in the dark?"

"It's not by choice, duck. You all buggered off out and it didn't seem to occur to any of you that I can't reach the light switches from this thing." He slapped the arm of the wheelchair irritably.

"You could have got yourself something to reach them with," Algernon pointed out, with that innocent, face-value helpfulness that made even Felicia want to kill him sometimes.

Peter gave him a flat stare.

"I'm well aware of that, lad. I was on my way to get a spatula when I got my wheels jammed in this corner. Been stuck like this for hours."

Felicia, who was beginning to feel rather guilty despite herself, moved to flick on the under-counter lights.

"Where's Dexter? I thought he'd have stayed with you."

Immediately, she regretted the question. Her father's expression, now clearly visible with the benefit of illumination, was not an impressed one.

"Him? Slunk off ages ago. Always coming and going, that one. What he's about, I've no idea." He wagged a finger at Felicia. "Shifty, haven't I always told you? Didn't I say that when you married him?"

Felicia glanced uneasily at Algernon, expecting him to look upset at such a character assassination of his father, but he barely blinked. With a sinking sensation, it occurred to her that he'd probably heard it all before. Peter had never been one for shielding children—or mollycoddling, as he so derisively called it —from the complicated reality of adult relationships. That attitude had coloured her own childhood, and she'd always striven not to replicate it, but she had to admit that in the increasingly tangled web of their family situation, it was getting harder and harder of late.

Even so, she wasn't about to have this argument with her father again; certainly not in front of Algernon. Not least because Peter's criteria for labelling another man as shifty was arbitrary in the extreme, coming down to whether they were a) a southerner, and b) wearing suede shoes. She'd never even bothered to challenge either, the former being so ingrained in the psyche of anyone who hailed from above Cambridge that it required no explanation, and the latter because she suspected it had something to do with the high-maintenance impracticality of the material in a damp, grass-covered country such as England.

Besides, she told herself, as a glance at the clock prompted her to open the fridge and peer unenthusiastically inside, to call Dexter shifty was so ridiculous that it scarcely warranted an argument anyway. The man was about as mysterious as a teaspoon.

"He left you in the dark?" Algernon was saying behind her. He sounded incredulous and, at the same time, not overly surprised. Which told you everything you needed to know, Felicia thought.

"Well, to be fair, it was still light then," Peter admitted grudgingly. "And I will say this; he made me a truly cracking cup of tea before he went; could have stood a spoon in it," he added, with what might even have been called a hint of pride. "We're teaching the man well. Another couple of days here in Lincolnshire and we'll have him sorted all right."

"Mum," Algernon said slowly, as she began to pull items out of the fridge. "What are you doing?"

"Someone's got to make dinner. We can't eat your cakes for every meal."

There was a silence. She turned to see them both staring at her in horror.

"What?" She said.

"It's just…er, well that tea was rather filling." Peter patted his stomach. "I'm not sure I could…"

"It's *pasta*," Felicia said, defensively. "Even *I* can't get pasta wrong."

Neither of them looked convinced. Felicia was beginning to feel rather irritated.

"I'm not *that* incompetent," she snapped, opening the cupboard to get a pan out and almost knocking her head on the cupboard. "Algie, put the kettle on, will you?"

With the air of one going to the gallows, Algernon obeyed.

"How was the auction today?" Peter asked, as she began throwing handfuls of fusilli haphazardly into the pan. "Everything all right after the sale?"

There was a sharpness to the question; she could feel his eyes boring into her back and made a noncommittal sound—"Mmm" —pretending to fiddle around with the bag of pasta. She really didn't want to get into this now.

"What's that?" Peter barked, apparently not about to be fobbed off. "Don't mumble at me, duck. Say what you mean, like I raised you to."

The kettle began to whistle on the range, a plume of steam billowing upwards, pooling under the low ceiling. Felicia sighed. Clearly, she was going to have to go there.

"Algie, why don't you go outside?" She suggested. He looked at her in approbation.

"But it's dark!"

"Upstairs, then."

"No, outside's fine," Algernon said glumly. "Just don't argue for too long. Promise?"

"Dinner'll be ten minutes," she promised.

His face fell.

"Actually, if you want to take your time…"

"Just *go*," she said, ferrying him out exasperatedly.

"Well?" Peter demanded, before she'd even had the chance to

turn back to face him. "What's all this about, then? What have you done now?"

Because of course it *would* be her fault. Felicia crashed the saucepan lid down and whirled around, hands gripping the cold metal bar on the range behind her.

"I haven't done anything, except try to keep things running smoothly. It's not been an easy experience, I can tell you. In fact, it's been quite an eye-opener."

His startlingly blue eyes narrowed to slits.

"And what is that supposed to mean?"

"It means CCTV which doesn't work on sale days. It means client's lots going missing during viewings. It means accounts which don't make any sense. The poor staff are trying to keep the business afloat when every day it's shifting beneath them. It's impossible."

His face paled beneath its weather-beaten rosiness.

"Those buggers! What have they been saying?"

"Nothing; that's just the point. They're far too loyal to say how much they're struggling. Or how worried they are—about you, Dad. So don't you dare blame them for this." The pasta was bubbling over, starchy froth hissing onto the hot plate. Irritably, she tilted the lid, no longer caring if dinner was a disaster. "What's going on, Dad? How did it all get into such a state?"

His lips flattened bullishly.

"It's fine. Nothing for you to worry about."

"Nothing—" she choked on a disbelieving laugh. "Nothing for me to worry about? When you've employed a criminal at the very place where your grandson spends his weekends?"

Peter frowned.

"Jack's not—"

"So you know who I mean then? You know all about it?" There went any faint hope that it might just have been a case of lacklustre diligence. Her father was of the old school; he didn't do interviews, or background checks. Generally, he just hired the first person who walked through the door asking for a job; the only test to pass was if he liked the look of them or not. He went on instinct, and infuriatingly, he was usually proved right. But this... this took it too far. "Are you completely and utterly insane?" She spluttered. "What were you thinking?"

"I was *thinking*," Peter said doggedly, "that he seemed like a decent sort of lad. Which, as you seem to have conveniently forgotten, is exactly the same basis you hired Hugo on, and that hasn't turned out too badly, has it? Besides, Jack is *not* a criminal. Well, not any more, at any rate," he conceded. "That's all long behind him now."

"Oh, so that makes it all right then, does it?" Felicia threw up her hands. "Let's just have felons roaming freely around the workplace then, shall we? Why not? Come one, come all." She broke off, shaking her head. "No wonder we've had a murder."

She'd have expected her father to be angered by her sarcasm, but instead, he looked faintly entertained.

"Dangerous?" He scoffed. "Jack's not dangerous. What are you harping on at, duck?"

His accent was getting thicker, as it always did when he was exercised. He was beginning to sound almost like Sergeant Pettifer now, the voice broadening and flattening in that distinct characteristic of where wold met dale.

"He has a record," Felicia ground out, rather irritated by his cavalier attitude.

"So that's enough to make him a potential murderer, is it?" Peter scowled, no longer amused. "A criminal's a criminal, that's it, is it? Good God, girl, I never raised any daughter of mine to be so bigoted. You're as bad as the police! Always on at him, they are, whenever anything's happened." He settled back in his chair with a harrumph. "They were round here just earlier, you know, asking me all about him; wanting to trip me up, no doubt. Trying to get me to say something they can use against him. Well, I told them just what I thought; especially that jumped-up little twerp of a man. Throwing his weight about; well, I tossed him right out of my house!"

Felicia was beginning to feel an all-too-familiar sinking feeling.

"Which policeman did you say it was?"

"Can't recall the name. Grey haired. Snappy dresser. Suede shoes," Peter added darkly. "Never trust a man wearing—"

"Heavenly?" Felicia choked out.

"Aye, that's the one. Knew it was a funny name."

"*Dad*," Felicia clapped a hand to her forehead and groaned. "He's the detective chief inspector!"

"I don't care if he's the bloody Prince of Wales!" Peter said stoutly. "I won't have him harassing my staff, and I told him as much."

No wonder the man had it in for them. Felicia took a deep breath.

"Dad, I need you to be totally honest with me here." She met his eye squarely. "Is something going on at the auction which shouldn't be? Something… not completely above board?"

And then she braced herself for an explosion.

She wasn't disappointed.

"How bloody *dare* you, lass?" Peter roared, almost vaulting out of his wheelchair. "Are you saying that I'm into something dodgy? That I'm a crook?"

Algernon chose that unfortunate moment to reappear in the doorway.

"It's been ten minutes, Mum. The pasta'll be…" He trailed off as he took in their faces, beating a tactical retreat with a mumbled, "Never mind."

Felicia glared at Peter.

"I dare, Dad, because two people are dead. Two people who are connected with your auction. I dare because the police are circling, and everything you say and do just seems to make us look more and more suspect." As he opened his mouth to protest, she cut him off with a frustrated motion. "So no, I don't have time right now to protect your delicate sensibilities. I need to know the truth. You need to *tell* me the truth. Before the police get there first."

"I told you, there's nothing to tell. Everything's fine." He was putting on a good show, but some of the assurance had left his tone.

"Then why does client paperwork keep going missing? Why can't I find half of the accounts? Why was a supposed competitor hiding in a wardrobe in the middle of our sale?"

"I don't *know*, I tell you!" The words were raw, ripped from him in a yell. "I don't understand any of it. Is that what you want to hear, that your old man's losing it, that he can't handle it on his own?" He sagged in his chair, looking utterly dejected. "By God, you'd just love that, wouldn't you?"

There was a silence, during which the pasta spat and broiled like a purgatorial geyser. Neither of them seemed to notice.

"How can you say that?" Felicia managed, at last, in a husky voice. "How can you ever think..."

"Because you'd be proven right after all of these years." He wouldn't look at her. "That it should have been me who'd left, and not you. That you'd have done it all so much better."

"It's not a competition, Dad." Felicia was shocked.

"Isn't it?" He shot back. "Are you telling me you've never looked at it and thought how much more successful it could be if I'd just listened to your fancy ideas..."

"I wanted to modernise, that's all." Beneath the exasperation, there was a sliver of guilt. Because yes, she had thought just that. "Expand. That's what businesses do. They're supposed to change." She'd pleaded with him at the time, trying to get him to see her point of view, but he just couldn't. It had been exclusively his baby for too long, and, different as they were in so many ways, in that instance, they'd just been far too much alike. Too stubborn, too opinionated, perhaps even a shade too egotistical. They'd clashed from day one of working together, and they hadn't stopped since. Even now, long after it was all over, it remained between them, a chasm of resentment and recrimination and hurt pride. It had changed everything, and she didn't know how to begin to get it back. She'd long since given up hope of ever doing so. "But this isn't about us, and it's not about what's happened in the past. I just want to help you, Dad."

"Well, I don't need it." The colour was flooding back into his cheeks. She knew that look; it meant he was closing off, hiding behind his usual bullish demeanour. "We're doing quite nicely at the auction without you; always have done. You needn't trouble yourself about me." He looked away, out of the low window beyond which the river scintillated beneath the evening's first stars. "In fact, you know what? I think I'll be all right now. You and Algernon can be on your way tomorrow."

She stared at him in confusion.

"Is that...what you want? For us to leave?"

"You've got your life in London, haven't you?" His face was in profile, shadowed and forbidding. "That's where you want to be. It's not for an old man like me to keep you stuck here. Juliette's said she'll pop in once a day; I'll be fine."

"But the investigation..."

"Also none of your concern." He nodded towards her phone, which was sitting on the table. The screen was illuminated, showing a new message. "Looks like there really is nothing for you here now." He wheeled his chair towards the door. "I'll call the boy for dinner."

Felicia picked up the phone. The message was from Pettifer; it was simple to the point of curtness, and its meaning couldn't be mistaken.

The police no longer required her to remain local.

She was free to go home.

Her father was right; there was no reason left for her to stay. She ought to be overjoyed. She *was* overjoyed; she told herself sternly, as she dumped the pasta into the colander that was waiting in the sink. This was exactly what she'd wanted.

A blurry film was obscuring her vision, hot and stinging. She blinked it away. Just the rising steam, that was all. Nothing more than that.

Chapter Twenty-Seven

Dinner was, as everyone had feared, a glutinous, borderline inedible affair, but no one seemed particularly to notice. Felicia and Peter stared determinedly at their plates, Algernon darting worried, quizzical looks between them. The atmosphere was enough to stem even his chirpy chatter, and a strained silence prevailed.

Not surprisingly, the meal was finished in record time, and within five minutes of sitting down, Felicia was up again, loading pans and cutlery into the dishwasher.

"You'd better go up and start packing, Algie." She focused studiously on the forks, which she was arranging into perfectly straight rows. "We're leaving in the morning."

The silence seemed to intensify, if such a thing were possible. Felicia resisted the natural urge to look up, knowing that she couldn't bear to see the expression on his face. She heard Peter stir uneasily in his chair, and hoped, rather pettily, that his leg was bothering him as well as his conscience.

Eventually, Algernon spoke, in a small voice.

"But…we just got here."

"We were only supposed to be coming down for the day," she reminded him, closing the dishwasher door.

"This is because you've fallen out, isn't it?"

Felicia finally turned. He was looking at them both accusingly, as though unsure who to blame more.

"The police have said we can go," Felicia said wearily. "Come on, Algie, don't make this difficult."

"Why shouldn't I?" He stood abruptly, scraping back his chair. He was as close to shouting as Felicia had ever heard him. "When it's not my fault? It's *never* my fault, and, yet, I'm expected to just take it. How is that fair?"

Felicia watched, open mouthed, as he stormed out of the kitchen, slamming his way through the front door.

"Well," Peter said, after a moment. "It's like having you as a teenager back, that is."

She gave him an unimpressed look.

"You'd best go after him, then," Peter said briskly.

"What happened to 'leave the lad be'?" She said sarcastically. "I thought that was your parenting mantra."

"He doesn't want you to leave him be," Peter retorted. "You'll learn the difference soon enough, duck. Once the hormones start kicking in, you need to become a veritable bloody mind reader. Especially if he's anything like you, you'll be in for a hell of a time. You were a right bugger, all the way through. Your sister, now," he became misty. "She was much simpler. If only we'd had two of her."

"Thanks, Dad," she said dryly. "Good to know your thoughts."

She found Algernon on the bridge, as she'd expected to. He was staring down into the water, chin resting on his forearms. Despite her father's confident assertion, she approached with caution.

"Algie, I'm sorry, but it's time. We've got to go back home."

He didn't turn his head.

"This *is* home."

He sounded utterly miserable. She felt her heart twist, mingling with a distinct feeling of exasperation.

"No, it isn't, it's..." What was it Pettifer had said? "It's a fantasy, Algie. Just look at it." She gestured around. "It doesn't even *look* real."

"But it is, Mum." He looked at her, eyes two opaque pools. "You grew up here, and you were happy. Weren't you?"

She hesitated, unable to answer him immediately. *Had* she been happy? The question threw her in a way it perhaps ought not to have done. Crammed into that house, her father working all the hours God sent, her mother juggling everything, but resentfully, in a martyrish way, making them all feel the ways in which they held her back. Cottage cheese and corned-beef lasagne. It didn't *sound* happy, when it was all laid out like that.

Except, it was. It had been. Because there'd been more to it than all of that; there'd been Stamford.

Her mind reeled backwards, flicking through the snapshotted memories. Picnics on the meadows, running across the bridges to feed the ducks on the way home from school. The Mid-Lent Fair that took over the town in the springtime. Bike rides at Burghley Park. Watching her father play cricket on Sunday afternoons. Tea in The George as a special treat after an exam. She'd loved living here, even secretly as a teenager when comradeship was formed by moaning loudly about being stuck in a small backwater town where nothing ever happened. People had boasted about how they couldn't wait to leave; now most of them were back, raising teenagers of their own.

Felicia had followed the path set out for her. She'd tripped off to university, dutifully gone on to London to work a minimum wage internship at a museum. And she had enjoyed it. But when her father had suggested setting up an auction house together in her old hometown, she'd needed no persuading. Something about it had felt right. Coming home had felt right.

But it hadn't lasted. She'd wound up back in London, self-exiled in a place she didn't really want to be. She'd done a lot of work over the years to convince herself otherwise. She'd thrown herself back into London life, told herself all the ways in which it was better for Algernon, all the opportunities it afforded him.

And, yet, despite it all, Algernon was happier here. She hadn't even needed him to tell her so, if she was being honest with herself. She'd known it for a long time now. It was written all over his face every time he returned from a weekend with his grandfather. He was brighter eyed, pinker cheeked, covered in not only auction dust but with a glow of satisfaction she recognised and envied. It was the feeling of having done a good day's work, of knowing that you'd created something worthwhile.

"We can't afford to fall under some romantic spell, Algie," she said gently, ignoring the feeling of guilt which was nudging at her. "We've got to be practical. We can't just uproot everything."

"Why not?"

The question was issued as a challenge. His chin was tilted in that stubborn way which she knew he'd inherited from her. She sighed.

"You haven't thought this through, darling. What about school, for one thing?"

"I'll go to school here. I don't mind moving."

The answer had come back so immediately that she thought he must have rehearsed it beforehand.

"But…all your friends?"

"Will still be my friends. I've been talking to them all the time we've been here." He held up his phone as proof. "It's not like it used to be, Mum."

"All right, well…" she was beginning to flounder. 'What about my job?" She demanded, triumphantly.

"You hate your job, Mum," Algernon said bluntly.

"I don't…" she faltered. Oh my goodness, was he right? "I don't…*hate* it," she stuttered feebly. "It's just…"

"Yes, you do. You think it's boring." He put his hands on his hips and looked up at her in a way that, for an alarming moment, reminded her horribly of her sister. "What else?"

She was beginning to feel uncomfortable under the spotlight of his uncompromising gaze.

"Well, it's not just a case of quitting my job. What would I *do* here? I can't just sit around and drink tea in The George all day."

"You'll work at the auction," Algernon declared, and she knew for certain in that moment that he'd plotted this all out. "You can run it, be the auctioneer, like you used to be."

"I can't just waltz back in, Algie," she said, a touch crossly. Because he was making it all sound so simple, in that way children did, when in fact, it was nothing of the kind.

"Of *course* you can. They need you and they know it."Seeing that she was about to interject, he continued hurriedly, "and before you mention Dad as a reason, he's been off travelling so much we probably wouldn't see him any less living here than we do in London. He can come and stay for weekends."

Felicia looked out across the water, not wanting to meet her son's all-too-perceptive grey gaze. Was this what Lady Fernleigh had meant, about them getting to an age where they started calling you out on things, where you no longer basked in the divine right of parents to be…well, always right?

"You're thinking about it, aren't you?"

She looked down into his face, and in that moment she saw Dexter, so powerfully and completely that it almost took her breath away. She'd always thought of Algernon, secretly, as her child; after all, he looked exactly like her. And, yet, suddenly, it could have been his father standing in front of her, giving her that exact same engaging grin, daring her to make a leap.

"Don't try and second-guess me, Algie," she said irritably.

"You *are*!" He flung his arms around her waist with the kind of abandon he used to when he was a small boy, then winced, drawing back.

"What is it?" He was cradling his elbow, and she grasped it

gently, turning it towards her. A livid purple bruise was blooming across the surface of his pale skin. "God, Algie. When you said you'd hurt yourself...I didn't realise it was that bad."

"It isn't." He was already tugging away. "It looks worse than it is. You should see the one on my shoulder."

"Your *shoulder*? How have you hurt that? I thought you fell over!"

"I did, but I got hit by the golf ball first."

"*What*?"

"Mum!" He was starting to look really embarrassed, his eyes darting around as though afraid someone might overhear. "It was nothing, all right? Someone's shot must have gone wild. I was unlucky, that's all. It hit me in the shoulder and knocked me off balance. I've taken far worse in cricket practise. Besides, Jack was there. He made sure I wasn't really hurt."

Felicia drew back.

"Jack was with you?"

Algernon looked as though he very much regretted saying anything.

"No...not exactly. I mean he sort of...appeared. Out of the trees. And he asked me if I was all right, helped me up."

Felicia felt a cold sensation run through her.

Her child had been alone, in a remote corner of the parkland, with a man she barely knew. A man with a criminal record. While a double murderer was still roaming at large.

And nothing had happened. It had been fine. Algie was fine.

But somehow, that didn't seem to be the point.

Suddenly, everything was starkly clear to her. She saw the situation as though from the outside looking in.

It was crazy to even entertain staying here. Pettifer was right; her father was right. They all were. What had she been *thinking*?

She turned to her son abruptly.

"Go inside and pack, Algie, like I asked you to."

His face fell.

"But..."

"No buts. We're leaving first thing in the morning." As he opened his mouth to object, she held up a silencing hand. "It's not up for discussion. London is our home. That's where we belong." *And you'll be safe there. Anywhere but here.* "Now go."

He stood his ground for a moment, then shook his head in what looked horribly to Felicia like disappointment. When he spoke, his voice was level, mature beyond his years.

"It's not really Stamford you're cross with, Mum; it's Grandad. And Dad, too. And your job, and everything you wish had gone differently. But I think we could have been happy here; both of us."

And then he brushed past her, crossing the grass and disappearing into the cottage without looking back. Felicia stayed on the bridge for a moment, watching the lights play along the surface of the water.

"I wonder if you might be right," she said softly.

Chapter Twenty-Eight

S he awoke with a start. Golden pink light was pressing against the curtains. Outside, she could hear the first fluted warm-up notes of the dawn chorus.

She lay there for a moment, listening, wondering what had woken her. But everything was peaceful. It was only when she rolled over to go back to sleep that she discovered that it wasn't coming from outside at all. Something was tugging at her, an insistent feeling that wouldn't let her rest. It was like a physical force, pulling her from the bed, urging her to do something.

She followed it, getting dressed swiftly, picking up her new turquoise plimsolls in one hand and moving softly down the stairs, muscle memory telling her feet exactly where to step to avoid the spots that creaked.

She slipped on the shoes in the hall, took her pale pink coat down off the hook and shrugged it over her shoulders whilst automatically turning to look in the mirror by the door. Her eyes were a bright, cool grey, looking back at her with an unreadable expression. She turned away, twisting the door handle and stepping out into the fresh morning air.

It was only when she was halfway around the curve of Water

Street, heading up towards the wrought-iron gates of Burghley Park, that she realised where her feet were subconsciously taking her. The insistent feeling, far from abating, was only getting more intense with every step closer she took. Putting her head down, she forged onwards up the hill.

She passed through the gates, shaded on either side by a small copse. The trees were just beginning to burst into leaf at this time of year, a fresh, almost luminous green as the new shoots unfurled on the tips of the branches. The parkland spread out before her, a rolling blanket of sparkling dew-covered lawn intersected here and there by paths and grazing sheep. In front of her was the avenue, a stately approach flanked by mature trees that led—via some aristocratic meandering designed to build suspense—up to the great Elizabethan house, currently hidden from view behind a well-positioned bank. To her right, another, much smaller path wound off towards the cricket pitch, neatly delineated from the rest of the grounds by a wooden post-and-rail fence. The pavilion was a chocolate box painter's dream, a gloriously whimsical pastiche of thatched roof and white-plastered walls.

She walked in that direction, skirting the edge of the pitch and heading for the perimeter of the park, which was bordered by a thick wedge of woodland. All was quiet at this time in the morning; most of Stamford had barely woken up. There were a few early birds out and about, some getting in a bleary-eyed jog before work, others trudging along obediently behind wagging-tailed dogs who were thrilled to be embarking on a new day and all of the exciting scents it brought with it. But they all receded further into the distance as she walked towards this little-used corner of the park, away from the main paths and trails. Soon, she had the sensation of being completely on her own. Half-shaded by the overhanging branches of the wood, she would be scarcely visible to anyone passing by.

The thought that Algernon had been walking along here in the falling darkness…it was enough to make any mother come out in goosebumps.

Even in the clear morning light, the woods were shrouded, a dense block of shadows. Felicia didn't hesitate at the gate with its polite 'private' sign; in one fluid movement, she vaulted it, landing on the spongy leaf-mould covered floor. Her steps made no sound as she made her way deeper into the trees.

And then, without warning, she was spat out into the light as suddenly as she'd been swallowed into the darkness. The tree trunks parted, and she found herself looking out over the smooth, manicured expanse of a putting green. A portly man in a fuchsia-pink polo shirt that matched the hue of his well-supped countenance was in the process of painstakingly lining up a shot. As his club connected with the ball, he looked up, saw Felicia standing there, and started violently, sending the ball looping vertiginously up into the air. There was a small glugging sound as it landed in the water.

"Oh, er…sorry." Felicia backed away into the trees once more, holding up her hands in apology. "That was my fault. I'd take that one again if I were you. I don't think anyone was looking."

As she turned to go, she saw him glancing furtively this way and that before surreptitiously dropping another ball out of his pocket onto the green. Usually, the sight might have amused her, but right now, she had other things preoccupying her mind. Worrying things. This little excursion hadn't been wasted; now she knew what it was that had been bothering her all night.

Although in a way, she wished that she didn't.

She took a breath, trying to order her racing thoughts. The birds were singing here in the woods, shafts of light piercing the gloom and landing in pools on the leaf-strewn floor. A sense of peace pervaded, a reminder that it wasn't the wood itself that was a sinister place, even if what had been attempted here might have been.

Because there was no way that a shot from the golf course,

however wild, could possibly have penetrated these dense trees and ended up in the parkland on the other side. Even Felicia's decidedly lacklustre knowledge of physics told her that much.

Which could only mean one thing. This had been no accident.

A picture of Algernon flashed into her mind. The fair skin, the bronze hair. He was getting more like her every day. And from a distance, in the fading light…

The realisation sent the blood rushing to her head, making it swim. She listed to one side, almost fell, only managing to right herself by bracing her palm against a nearby tree trunk. Then, she opened her eyes, and drew in a breath.

Something was glinting through the bracken on the forest floor. Something silver, illuminated in flashes by a beam of sunlight. As the dizziness subsided, she became aware of a throbbing in her left big toe, and realised that she hadn't swooned at all; instead, she'd tripped over something. Something metal. Something which looked very much like…

Slowly, with a sense of foreboding, she reached down and picked it up, the leaves shedding from it like a second skin as she lifted it.

Then she heard something behind her. The soft swish of dried leaves, the scrunching sound as a damp twig snapped underfoot.

She turned.

And in that moment, all of her worst suspicions came true.

Chapter Twenty-Nine

"**D**on't come any closer." Felicia backed away, golf club pointed outwards like a sword. "I mean it."

Jack stopped in his tracks.

"Okay. I'll stay here, then." He sat down on a nearby tree trunk, looking faintly wary. "Is everything... all right? Lost your ball, have you?"

"I know what you're doing here." Her voice was beginning to tremble, which she hated. She readjusted her grip on the club, strengthened her stance. She refused to show any signs of fear. "You were looking for this." Then, when he didn't reply immediately, she demanded, slightly shrilly, *"Weren't* you?"

"Er... no." He was looking less wary now, more bemused. "I'm not much of a golfer myself. Too many pointless rules and regulations. And I don't own a collared shirt." He rubbed the back of his neck, which was shown to distractingly golden advantage against the cerulean blue of his t-shirt. Despising herself for noticing, she looked determinedly at his feet instead as he continued, "if you must know, I was looking for squirrels."

That knocked her off track for a minute. She blinked, stared at him, wondering if she really was going mad.

"Did you say…*squirrels*?"

"Yes, I find them very relaxing to shoot." At her horrified expression, he laughed, holding up his camera. "With *this*. God, Felicia, what's the matter with you today? You're looking at me like I'm some kind of…"

He trailed off, the smile vanishing from his face. She watched it happen, the moment the realisation hit. It was strangely awful to watch. But she steeled herself against it. She couldn't afford to drop her guard.

"So that's it, is it?" He said softly. "You've got me pegged as Stamford's crazed killer, have you? Well, I suppose I ought to have seen that coming. It would be very convenient for everyone. After all, it's not like I'd be much of a loss to society, is it?"

He sounded angry, but also resigned. Exhausted. For the first time, Felicia's conviction began to falter. After all, he seemed so genuine, so plausible. But then, who said that a murderer couldn't be plausible? Wasn't that how so many of them got away with it?

Even so, for a reason she couldn't say, she felt the arm holding the golf club drop to her side.

"You don't have children, do you?" At his quizzical glance, she continued, "my son was injured here last night. He thinks it was an accident; *I* don't. Attacking me is one thing; attacking my child is quite another. I won't rest until I know that whoever did it is behind bars." She looked at him levelly. "This needs to end, Jack. I need the truth from you. From everyone."

"And you've had it from me. I had nothing to do with any of this. Yes, I found Algernon last night…"

"And now you're here again this morning. Surely you can see how suspicious that looks? Why I'm thinking the way I am?" She folded her arms. "You'll have to give me a damn good reason if you want to change my mind."

He raised a surprised eyebrow.

"Felicia, I live here," he said slowly. "Didn't you know that?"

For a moment, she was lost for words. She just looked around her dazedly.

"Not *here* here," he sounded exasperated. "On the estate. I rent one of the Bottle Lodges. Would you feel better if I proved it to you?" He fished a key out of his pocket and held it up, then hesitated before venturing, "come on, I'll make you a cup of tea. You look like you could use one. And we can talk about all of this somewhere less...arboreal. With actual chairs." He rose from the tree stump.

Immediately, her arms shot up and she brandished the golf club in both hands. He sighed.

"It's all right, I'm not going to add you to my list of victims." When she didn't look reassured, he added, "all right, how about this? Bring that thing with you, if you like. Then if I do anything menacing or criminal, you can cosh me over the head with it. Seem like a fair deal?"

Felicia bit her lip, feeling torn. In all honesty, it was madness itself to even consider going anywhere private with him. Then again, she acceded, with a glance around her, they were *already* somewhere pretty secluded. No one knew she was here, and it wasn't as though anyone else was likely to wander past. These woods were private; technically, both she and Jack were trespassing. If he really wanted to murder her, this was probably a good place to do it. Better than in his own house, certainly.

"Fine," she said curtly. But she held the golf club tightly in front of her as they left the wood, her following him back over the gate and into the sunlit parkland. The day was really getting going now, the sky a wash of pale lemon in front of which the two Bottle Lodges—with their striking resemblance to a baby's bottle—rose in a perfectly symmetrical pair on either side of the park gates.

Jack unlocked the door of the left-hand lodge. On the other side of the gateway, a lady was emerging from the doorway of the other lodge, bending down to pick up her milk. Upon straightening, she waved at Jack, who responded with a nod.

"There you go," he told Felicia—rather mock solemnly, she thought—"that's my neighbour, Pam. She's seen us go in together. Now, if you disappear in mysterious circumstances, she'll say that you were here, they'll search the place, find your mangled remains chopped up in the wood store, and my reign of terror will end. I'll get my comeuppance, and you'll have done a good thing for society. How's about that?"

She glared at him.

"Are you this flippant about everything?"

"Not everything, no." He filled the kettle and took down two mugs, turning to her with a suddenly serious expression. "Now, why don't you tell me what's going on? Why on earth would you think that I'd try and hurt Algernon?"

He sounded genuinely hurt, and she found that suddenly, she couldn't quite meet his eye. She prevaricated by looking around the kitchen. It was a small, square room, taking up the entire ground floor of the tower. Felicia assumed the living room was upstairs, and then the bedroom above that. It must be a strange property to live in.

"I didn't," she said at last. "I mean, I think it was an accident. I think it was me they were really after."

And then, in a breath, she told him.

"So, you think that someone's trying to kill you, and your first reaction is to go plunging off into some dark, isolated woods all on your own?" He didn't seem terribly impressed.

"Well, I knew they weren't going to still be there."

"You thought it might be me, and *I* was still there."

"Look, will you stop doing that?" She sat down on a kitchen chair, putting her head in her hands. "Twisting everything around? I suppose I wasn't really thinking."

"No," he said dryly. "That does seem to be something of a problem with you. Tell me, are you always this impetuous?"

"My son would say no, but only because he's worse than I am." She sat back in her chair. The kitchen was warm, homely. Inviting. It encouraged confidences. "He wants us to stay here, you know. For good."

Jack put a mug of tea in front of her.

"And you?"

"I don't know," she said, being honest for the first time. "I'm not sure you can ever really go back."

He drew up a chair opposite her.

"You're right about that. But then, you wouldn't be going back, would you? You'd be going forward."

She sipped her tea—strong builder's, her father would approve—and considered that notion. Jack had a way of putting things that could seem odd at first, but actually, upon reflection, made perfect simple sense. She liked that about him.

In fact, if she was being honest, she liked a few things about him. His steady gaze, his tousled curls, the blond stubble that shaded his chin. The way all of his clothes were falling to pieces. She even liked his house. All of which was astonishing in itself, because he couldn't possibly be further from her usual type.

But it wasn't that which unnerved her.

It was the fact that she didn't know him at all. She literally knew *nothing* about him. And, yet, he knew all about her.

And that frightened her. Because she couldn't afford to trust anyone she didn't know. Not right now.

"I... I should go." She started to rise to her feet. At once, it seemed to hit her what she was doing. What a foolish, dangerous game she was playing. "This was a mistake. I shouldn't be here."

He stared at her, in disbelief but not surprise.

"You still can't quite bring yourself to trust me, can you?"

"Would *you* trust you?" She shot back, before she could stop herself.

There was a pause.

"Ah, I see. You've been listening to tales about me." He was

285

angry, she could tell, although his voice was smooth. Reflexively, her fingers flexed towards the golf club propped against her chair. He saw it, and his brow darkened. "Oh, come off it, Felicia. I'm not going to hurt you. Surely you know that by now?"

"Why not?" Her temper was rising to match his. "You're a criminal, aren't you?"

"Oh, and we're all just the same, I suppose? That's like saying something's antique; it could be from 1901 or 1101. Would you say *that's* the same thing?" When she didn't respond, he shook his head in disgust. "Just as I thought. You haven't actually bothered to find out any real details, have you?" He snatched up her cup and stalked off to the sink. "You've just heard some vague gossip and made your mind up."

Felicia was about to protest hotly before realising, with some sense of shame, that he was right. That was exactly what she'd done.

"So why don't you tell me?" She said softly. "Give me your version of events. I'm listening." She sat down. "I'll stay for as long as it takes."

He swirled water around the cups and dumped them in the sink. Then he stood, looking out of the window. For a moment, she thought he wasn't going to say anything. But then he started to speak.

"There really isn't much to tell. It's a fairly common story. My parents got divorced and I moved with my mum to Stamford. I hated being uprooted, hated leaving my friends…hated the fact that they thought putting me in a fancy private school could make up for all of it. I acted out, fell in with the wrong crowd, got up to a few mild pranks—all smoothed over, of course. Any bottom-rung therapist would tell you it was a bid to get my parents' attention. Anyway, I managed to get myself expelled in the end. Set the headmaster's study on fire…accidentally, in my defence," he added, as her eyes widened. "It was meant to be a few fireworks in the wastepaper bin, that's all. He'd walk in, the whole lot'd go up... singed eyebrows, nothing more. Unfortunately, one landed in the curtains. It took them days to put the blaze out."

His lips twisted ruefully. "The great irony of it was that it only made things worse between my parents. They each blamed the other for how I'd 'turned out'." He looked out of the window, at where a bank of buttermilk yellow daffodils fluttered in the breeze, but she sensed that he wasn't really seeing the view outside. He was in the past, inside his head.

"I got away with it, legally at least. I mean, I got a record, nothing worse. But my parents never forgave me, and neither did anyone else. Everyone thought I was bad news. No decent university would take me. I was essentially stuck here, with all these people who hated me. In the end, you kind of end up playing up to it, just to spite them. You think you can't win, so why not just have fun while you're at it?" He shrugged. "I got up to a few things over the next couple of years...nothing that bad, in the scheme of things, but a small town's definition of 'nothing that bad' is set much lower than in a lot of other places." He braced his hands on the edge of the sink. "And then my mum got ill. It was a shock to the system, probably one which I needed. I sorted myself out, took the first good job I could get."

"At Clay's Auctions?" Felicia guessed.

He nodded.

"At first, I mean, I thought Barrington was all right. A bit slippery, maybe, prone to temper rages... not at all the image he presented to the world. But I was just a porter; I didn't see much of him. Truth be told, I didn't much care. It was an honest wage, and I had Mum to look after. But soon... I don't know, things started to seem... off. He was careful, but he couldn't control everything. People would turn up at the auction from time to time; I could see that they were desperate. He'd be angry when he found out, tell us not to let them in again. He was always disappearing to take mysterious phone calls, or out on meetings that weren't in the diary. In the end, I started to suspect that there was a side business going on; something far more profitable and far less legal than the bread-and-butter front of the auction house."

"It seems that you were right." Felicia toyed with the strap of the camera, which was sitting next to her on the table. "But I just can't understand why he'd do it. He had a career, a reputation, all of those fans...."

"Why does anyone do these things?" Jack had turned to face her. "Money, power...but more than that, I think it was about being somebody. You wouldn't have known, but at the time, he was being squeezed in all directions. You know how many auction houses there are in this small area; competition's tight, uncomfortable. Sometimes, there's not enough to go around. And you'd not long joined your father at Grant's—Barrington was furious about that. It gave it a future, and he'd been poised to take it over. He had Chase the Bargain, this image at the top of daytime antiques...I think he loved the attention, the adulation. But there were murmurs about replacing him, bringing in someone younger, more dynamic. I think in his head he was fighting all the time to stay relevant, to stay on top."

"Hence his obsession with expansion," Felicia said thoughtfully. "And why he was so determined to dominate the area, to take over everyone else's businesses."

"All of which required a lot of money," Jack agreed. "More than he was going to get honestly from the bank."

"So what happened? How did you get involved?"

"I wasn't *involved*, Felicia." Jack scowled. "I caught him on the phone one day, plotting to con an old lady out of a Chinese vase."

"Oh." Felicia felt rather sheepish. "Sorry."

"I might have been no saint at the time," he gave her a pointed look. "But that felt wrong even to me. I confronted him about it, told him what I thought. Threatened to go to the police, even." A self-deprecating smile here. "That was ambitious of me; as if they'd listen to anything *I* said. By then, I was firmly cemented in their minds as the local ne'er-do-well."

Felicia decided it was better if she ventured nothing. She'd only put her foot in it again.

"The next thing I knew, I'd been fired for stealing." Jack folded his arms, leaned back against the counter. "Silver and jewellery were found in the boot of my car, and in our house, too." He smiled, but there was no humour in it. "That was a nice extra touch. Well thought out. Of course, Barrington very magnanimously refused to press charges. It was actually a pretty great opportunity for him. Two birds with one stone. Guaranteed that nothing I ever told anyone about his practises would be believed whilst also painting himself as the great philanthropist."

"Anything you said would be put down to spite," Felicia concluded. "That must have been hard, knowing the truth but not being able to say anything."

"I can't say I really cared what people in town thought of me by that stage, but Mum…" something flashed across his face, a spasm of pain. "She said she believed me, but I don't think she ever really did. She thought I was back to my old ways. It broke her heart; she didn't last long after that. Just…faded away."

"I can understand why you must have hated him," Felicia said quietly.

"I wasn't his biggest fan, no. But in a funny sort of way, I've made peace with it. I've learned that sometimes in life, it's not all black and white. What Barrington did to me—and Mum—was awful, and I'll never forgive him for it. But at the same time, I can appreciate what it did for me. If it weren't for that, I wouldn't be doing what I do now." At her puzzled expression, he explained. "That was the nail in the coffin for me, as it were. No one around here would spit on me if I was on fire, let alone give me a job. It forced me to be creative, set up on my own. I taught myself photography, found I was good at it. It gave me a purpose again."

"You can really feel that way?"

Her disbelief must have been audible, because he smiled.

"It didn't happen overnight, that's for sure. But one gets philosophical as one gets older. Don't get me wrong, Felicia. Once, I would have gladly killed him...but not for some time now. I'd rather have brought him to account in a different way, in a more earthly court." He shrugged. "If I'm being totally honest, it's a shame for me that he died when he did. It means he got away with it. He'll never have to face the music."

Felicia sat back, trying to consolidate what she'd just heard. After everything she'd discovered about her old rival in the past couple of days—not to mention what she'd suspected for years—it shouldn't have been particularly shocking. And, yet, it was. Because here was someone whose life had well and truly been ruined by Barrington Clay. And yet, he seemed so calm about it, so resolute. How could that be possible... unless he'd already enacted his revenge?

A more earthly court. What did that even *mean*?

She looked Jack straight in the eye, holding his gaze so that he couldn't look away. Not that she'd ever known him to.

"There's something else, isn't there? Something you're not telling me."

He tilted his head for a moment, as though considering it. Then slowly, thoughtfully, he shook his head.

"You know, no one's got this many words out of me for a long time. You have quite the way with you, Ms Grant."

"Jack," she pressed, with a rising urgency. "If you know something...you could be in danger."

"Not so long ago, you seemed to think I *was* the danger." His words were clipped, final. "He strode to the door and opened it, letting the cold April air billow inside. He looked at her with something almost like regret.

"I'm sorry, Felicia, but confession's over."

Chapter Thirty

Colin Creaton's hand shook as he spooned tea leaves into the waiting pot. Steadying his nerve, he took a breath, brushing the spilled leaves into his hand before turning to face the two people sitting at the kitchen table behind him.

"Sorry, what was the question again?" He asked tremulously, pressing his foot onto the pedal of the bin and dusting his hands over the opening.

The sergeant, a burly, remarkably square-shaped man with a face that appeared to have met with the business end of a cricket bat at some point in its history, regarded him blandly.

"What time did you arrive at the auction, sir?"

The young PC with him looked up expectantly, pen poised over her thickly marked notepad. Colin gulped, wondering what she was finding to write so much about. Was it an intimidation tactic? He'd read about those. How policemen pretended to be writing reams of notes to put the suspect off their—

Wait… *suspect*? Surely, he wasn't… he couldn't be…

Colin barely suppressed a squeak of horror, sloshing water all over the counter—with some, mercifully, making it into the pot; they'd just have to be small cups of tea—as the idea struck him in full, terrifying Technicolor. His mind ran away with images: him being dragged off in handcuffs, pleading his innocence to stony-faced, impervious officers, flung into the back of a police van as, in the doorway to their marital home, Margaret was left alone, watching helplessly, tears trickling down her—

The flagrant unlikeliness of that last addition brought Colin back to earth with a jarring bump. He wasn't being dragged away anywhere; instead, he was standing in his rather tired-looking suburban kitchen, with the faux sandstone that didn't really look anything like sandstone but had been cheap and, importantly, from Margaret's point of view, beige, and the tea caddy that they'd had as a wedding present 50 years ago and that he hadn't really liked then. He'd managed to accidently smash the matching coffee canister during a shelving incident not long after the honeymoon, but the tea caddy had proven stubbornly unbreakable, taunting him with that longevity that the ugliest of items always enjoy. The police officers weren't granite-faced monsters after all, but two perfectly normal, reasonable-seeming people just doing their job, sitting at his kitchen awaiting tea with an increasing look of concern on their faces.

"Is… everything all right, sir?" The blonde PC asked hesitantly.

"Oh, yes." Feeling flustered and foolish, Colin began to mop up the flood of kettle water with a commemorative Diamond Jubilee tea towel, glad that Margaret wasn't here to see what a mess he was making, both of the kitchen and of the interview. The thought of her sobbing at his departure seemed more ridiculous than ever, he realised; she'd be far more likely to be angrily scolding him for being so inconsiderate as to get himself arrested, and had he *forgotten* that the Robinson's were supposed to be coming over for coffee and a look at the wormery later? Now she'd have to do it *all* on her own; *just* like him to leave her in the lurch… "It's just… hmm, now let me think. It's so difficult to be precise about times; when you're retired…" he gave a nervous laugh, reaching for the biscuit tin and proffering it towards the young PC.

She looked at the two fig rolls slowly desiccating in the bottom and visibly tried not to wrinkle her nose.

"Um, no, thank you. I've not long had breakfast."

Colin couldn't say he blamed her. He didn't much like fig rolls himself—apparently nobody did, hence the fact that they were eternally on offer and as such, eternally in Margaret's shopping basket. The one time Colin had dared to voice dissent, she'd snapped that he should thank his lucky stars that he was still getting biscuits at all at his age, that only last month Susan Moncrieff's husband had had all sugared products forcibly removed from the house after a pre-diabetic warning from the doctor, and would Colin prefer *that*?

Mindful of this conversation, Colin dutifully bit down on a stale fig roll now, glad at least that he wasn't married to Susan Moncrieff.

"I'm going to have to ask you to try and be a bit more specific than that," the burly Sergeant was saying patiently. "Were you there for the beginning of the sale, for instance?"

"Yes." Relieved that there was one question he could answer, the word shot from Colin's lips in a breathy rush. "Yes, we got there just in time. They were a bit late starting, I think."

"And you stayed until…when?"

"Ooh, I'm not sure. My lot was quite early, so … eleven… -ish?"

His voice rose in pitch on the final syllable. The policeman didn't blink.

"Interesting," was all he said.

Colin, who'd been stirring the tea, jolted, the spoon clattering against the neck of the teapot.

"Because the auction house records show that you bid on a lot at twenty to one," the sergeant continued evenly. "So one of you must be mistaken."

Bugger. Colin felt the blood drain from his face as he remembered. Margaret, having spent all morning expressing loud and frequent disgust over what she termed "old used tat" had found herself entranced by a large collection of Tupperware, evidently from a house clearance.

"So useful," she'd purred. "All the lids are there, too. And we can give the ones we don't want to your niece as a wedding present."

Her fury and indignation when she'd been outbid had known no bounds. Now, Colin cursed that blasted Tupperware to the skies, and not just for the diatribe he'd endured for the entirety of Saturday evening on the subject of selfish other bidders and the irresponsibly vagarious nature of the entire auction system.

While Colin was still flailing for a suitable answer, the sergeant was hefting to his feet with an audible creak.

"Don't mind if I have a quick look around while the brew's on, do you?"

The question was phrased mildly—was it just him, or had that broad, friendly Yorkshire brogue suddenly got more pronounced? But all the same, it made heat prickle beneath Colin's polyester mix collar.

"Well, I'm not sure…" he flustered. "I mean, my wife…I don't think she'd like it much." That was an understatement, he thought, with an involuntary quiver. He glanced at the clock, realising with a nasty jolt that she was due back any minute. The heat beneath his collar became a blazing inferno; he tugged it away from his neck, desperate for cool air. "She's very particular about the house, you see…"

Feeling rather proud of his protest—feeble though it might have been—he turned, only to find that he was alone in the kitchen, effectively talking to himself. He scuttled into the hallway, where the young PC was opening the cupboard under the stairs, peering inquisitively inside.

"Where is your wife, sir?" the sergeant was watching him from the glass double doors that led into the lounge.

"She chairs the neighbourhood watch meeting on Tuesday mornings," Colin responded obediently, privately rather ashamed of his failure to stand up for his rights. "She's very, er... community minded, my Margaret."

Although whether the community wished she were otherwise was a different matter.

There was a dainty tinkling of porcelain over his left shoulder. Colin's head whipped around in dismay to see the PC holding an adenoidal-looking bone china shepherdess, looking at it in perplexed fascination.

"Be careful with that!" Heart in his mouth, he took it gingerly from her, holding it as though it were an injured butterfly. "Margaret's very particular about her figurines." He set it back down carefully on the radiator shelf, tweaking it to the exact angle it had been at before in the hope that she wouldn't notice, all the while reflecting gloomily that she almost certainly would. When he turned around, the sergeant had disappeared, just the heel of his scuffed shoe disappearing around the turn of the stairs. Colin looked accusingly at the PC, who gazed back at him with such doe-eyed innocence that he knew he'd just been set up.

For the first time, Colin felt outrage rising up in his chest, eclipsing the fear. Stalking up the stairs in the policeman's wake, he puffed out his chest, preparing to be sterner than he ever had in his life. This, Colin felt, was his moment.

"Now, *see* here," he admonished. "This really isn't—"

"What's in here?" The sergeant interrupted, rattling the handle on the door to the spare room. "It's locked."

Slightly deflated that his moment of bravado had been so summarily ignored—and now appeared to be ebbing away as swiftly as it had come—Colin replied dolefully, "That's Margaret's cleaning room."

"Not your trains?" The policeman raised an unruly brow. "I understood you to be a collector."

"Oh, I am. But I have a shed outside for all of that. Margaret doesn't like... well, she prefers them kept out of the house..." "as do I" being the unspoken part of that sentence, which now hung awkwardly between them.

"I'm going to need to take a look inside," said the Sergeant at last, almost kindly.

"But it's nothing." Colin could feel his stammer surfacing, threatening to trip his tongue, the way it always did when he was acutely stressed. "I told you, it's just a cleaning room. It's where she keeps her..." he daren't admit that he wasn't sure exactly what she did keep in there. "Well, you know what women are."

The sergeant looked unmoved. He held out a slab-like palm, saying firmly:

"The key, please, sir."

"I don't have it," Colin whispered.

A parade of emotions swept across the sergeant's face, first surprise, then disbelief, then comprehension. There was a strained silence before he spoke.

"Are you telling me, sir, that you don't have access to this room?"

The response was a mute nod, head angled downwards towards the cheap beige carpet. In that moment, Pettifer's irritation promptly gave way to something less policeman-like and more human. He couldn't help pitying the man, so pale and colourless that he almost blended into the bland décor all around him. Stooped under the weight of something which wasn't just age.

From downstairs came the sound of the front door slamming.

"*Colin!*" A strident voice hollered. "Colin, where are you?"

Upstairs, two pairs of eyes met. Pettifer watched the older man's Adam's apple travel slowly up, then down the line of his throat before he answered, somewhat hoarsely.

"Up here, Margaret."

"Well, what are you doing up there?" The voice was peevish now. "Come and help me with these things."

"I think it would be better if you came up here." Colin's eyes didn't leave Pettifer's.

With a thunderous harrumph, heavy footsteps ascended the stairs.

"There's a very suspicious car outside. *Very* suspicious." The voice sounded pleased. "Black, doesn't look to have been cleaned in donkey's years. Always suspect, these dirty cars. Wonder what they're hiding behind those grimy windows. I think we should take down the numberplate. A car like that could only belong to a shifty sort."

"Or a policeman," Pettifer said lightly, as she rounded the newel post and came into view.

For a moment, the effect was priceless. Her eyes bulged, fleshy lips opening and closing soundlessly. Then she listed backwards, and suddenly Pettifer had an abrupt vision of the paperwork involved if she fell down the stairs. With quick reflexes few would have imagined he possessed, he shot out a hand and gripped her elbow, steadying her.

"Just the lady I wanted to see," he remarked conversationally.

With a scowl, she wrenched her arm away.

"What are you doing here? What do you want?"

"Recognise me, do you? Or perhaps my constable here?" He indicated Jess, who was looking on silently from the foot of the stairs. "It was she you ran away from at the crime scene on Saturday."

Margaret drew herself up hotly, bosom trembling.

"We did no such thing!"

"Ah, so you admit that you were there, then?"

She eyed him levelly.

"If you're here, then you must know that we were."

No flies on this one, Pettifer acknowledged, with grudging

respect. Not like her doltish husband, scared half witless by some simple questions into a ludicrous lie that only made him look more suspicious, not less. He was just lucky that it was Pettifer he'd been talking to rather than someone like Heavenly, who wouldn't have taken such a sympathetic view of lying to the police.

"So why didn't you come forward?" Respect for her faculties aside, Pettifer couldn't keep the exasperation out of his voice. "Why did you evade questioning?"

"I told you, we did no such thing." She thrust her chin forward. "A person's got a right to come and go as they please."

"Not when they're part of a police investigation, they haven't." He was starting to get annoyed.

"It's nothing to do with us." She folded her arms. "We weren't even there when he was stabbed."

"So you know all about it, then?" Pettifer shot out.

She gave a derisive snort at that.

"Who doesn't? It's all over the papers, isn't it? Stabbed with an unknown weapon in the very cupboard we were standing next to." A ghoulish gleam had come into her eye. Pettifer watched her carefully, an idea coming to him. He took a punt.

"It's a great story, I'll admit." He allowed just the right amount of awe to enter his voice. "I must have missed the interview in the papers this weekend."

She gave him a sharp look.

"What interview?"

"Well…," he gestured to her, affecting perplexity. "I mean, with a tale like that…you must have been approached by the press? They'll be clamouring for an eye-witness account of that sort."

"You think so?" She'd perked right up, a calculated yet also—rather alarmingly—starry look on her face as she contemplated it. "You *really* think so?"

"Of course," Pettifer said deferentially, trying to ignore Jess, who he could see out of the corner of his eye giving him a very strange look. "Why do you think we're so keen to talk to you? Someone at the centre of things…well, you're a very important witness, Margaret. Surely your story deserves to be told?"

"It does," she said breathily. Then, abruptly, she seemed to gather herself, her face shuttering as she said harshly, "but no, like I said. It's none of our business. I want no part of it. Neither of us saw anything which can help you, so you'd best be on your way. I don't know what he's been telling you…"

"Nothing, Margaret, I swear!" Colin jabbered. "They forced their way in…they intimidated me…"

Pettifer gave him a look of distaste, feeling any sense of pity for the man vanish. With the forbearance of experience, he didn't defend himself, but Jess, still in possession of youth's impetuous sense of right and wrong, piped up accusingly:

"Hardly! You were offering us tea and fig rolls only five minutes ago."

Colin shrank back.

"They gave me no choice, Margaret. They insisted on seeing your cleaning room, even though I told them…"

"Certainly not!" Her voice was like a whip. Pettifer noticed that she was trembling, her hands clenched at her sides as her jaw set in indignation. "You have no right to come poking around my house, no right at all!"

"It's a perfectly reasonable request," Pettifer said softly.

"Well, I don't see it that way! Barbaric police behaviour, that's what this is. If good, honest citizens can't feel safe in their homes…"

"I can get a warrant," Pettifer said, through gritted teeth. "But I'd rather not. And it won't look good for you."

"Then you'll have to get one." The answer came immediately, shrill and uncompromising. "Because I won't have you in my house a minute longer until you do. Out, both of you! *Out!*"

"Did you mean it, Sarge?" Jess asked, as they sat in the car several moments later. "About the warrant, I mean?"

"Oh, yes," the reply was quiet, eyes looking straight ahead as he fastened his seatbelt. Jess got the distinct impression that underneath the inscrutable exterior, her superior was more furious than she had ever seen him. "I meant every word."

"But will you actually get it?" The question was blurted out before she could think better of it, and she gulped, fiddling frantically with the small silver star in her earlobe, turning it around and around as she always did when nervous. Feeling as though she was suddenly on very thin ice, but that she'd come too far to turn back now, she elaborated hesitantly, "because, well... they're not *really* suspects, are they? We don't have anything on them, except the fact that they ran away from the scene; which, yes, was an odd thing to do, but then old couples can be like that, can't they? Odd, I mean."

Pettifer looked at her reflection in the dashboard, feeling amused despite himself.

"Yes, they can. Especially in a small place like this. It's easy for the world to pass you by." He put the key in the ignition, reflecting that Margaret Creaton had been right about one thing; the car really was filthy. "And you're right, I did throw the warrant out there in the heat of the moment. But all the same, I *am* going to try to get it." At her quizzical look, he expanded, "you know when I spoke to her about an interview with the press? Telling her story?"

"Yes, I did wonder where you were going with that."

"A bit of a fishing expedition. I had a hunch." He put the car in gear, reversing out of the tarmac square of driveway, exactly the same as every other house on the cul-de-sac possessed. Even though they were safely in the car, he still wanted to put some distance between him and the cluster of blank, identical façades that stared at them from all sides. The curtains tended to have ears on estates like this one. "I got the measure of her pretty quickly;

bit of a Hyacinth Bucket type, likes to stick her nose in everything, know what's going on, terrorises her husband…there's a need for importance there, or an illusion of it, at least. That's the sort of person who'd usually relish any opportunity to be in the limelight. I'd have expected her to be touting it all over town, but instead, she's coy, secretive. Why?"

"You're right," Jess was looking pensive. "I hadn't thought of that."

"And did you see the way she was shaking? She passed it off as anger, but I think it was something else." He drove back towards the main road, his tyres soundless on the smooth surface. Made a change from cobbles, he thought approvingly, then immediately wondered what was happening to him. "That's a woman who's afraid of something. And I intend to find out what." He looked both ways, turning to the right. "Oh, and Constable? One more thing…"

She looked at him anxiously, chewing her lip.

"Don't ever be afraid to question your superiors," he said softly. "A good partnership should always be accountable."

And with that, he focused on the road ahead as it wound back towards the golden spires of town.

Chapter Thirty-One

As last night's pink sky had promised, it was turning into a glorious April day, the heavens a clear wash of blue, the temperature just balmy enough to cross the tacit threshold where the English are prepared to throw off their layers, slip into a pair of inappropriately brief shorts, and declare it summer. Felicia had fallen prey to the same childish optimism—although mercifully not the shorts—and had stepped out without a coat for the first time since October. It was a move she was already regretting as she crossed the meadows now, the wide open space proving a playing ground for the wind to whip across and slap any exposed skin with a chilly blast in a stern warning that, sunshine notwithstanding, it was still firmly spring. Not that anyone else seemed put off; the riverbanks were already dotted with brightly patterned blankets, the ice cream van was parked up by the bridge and apparently doing a roaring trade, the ducks were sunning themselves beneath the wooden picnic benches, one eye beadily open for any food that might happen to drop from above.

The most besieged of these tables was the one which Felicia was making a beeline for now. She navigated a gaggle of plump green bodies, swinging a leg over the bench and trying not to kick anything in the orange bill while she was at it.

"Quite an entourage you've got here," she remarked.

"One chip," Pettifer said defensively, holding up a stubby finger to illustrate. "I dropped *one* chip." He shook his head exasperatedly, pushing the open crumple of newspaper towards her. "Help yourself, by the way."

She raised an eyebrow interrogatively.

"Salt and vinegar?"

"Of course," he looked offended. "Anything else is unnatural."

She selected one and bit into it, letting the flavours tingle and burst on her tongue. It had just the right amount of sogginess that any self-respecting chip shop chip ought to possess.

"I sincerely hope that this isn't your breakfast, by the way."

"More of an early lunch."

"At ten thirty?"

"I was up at dawn," he protested. "And it's your fault, so don't you start. I was paying a visit to those magnificent vanishing witnesses of Algernon's."

Felicia was so intrigued that she paused, a chip halfway to her mouth.

"And? Anything come of it?"

He filled her in as they polished off the chips.

"So," he said at last, crumpling the newspaper into a ball. "Now we have the pleasantries out of the way, how about you tell me why you wanted to meet? I sense that it wasn't just to pinch half of my lunch."

Felicia wiped her fingers on a napkin, finding herself suddenly hesitant. She'd debated with herself for almost two hours this morning before finally picking up the phone. After all, he'd told her in no uncertain terms that there was nothing more he could do to help her, so what would be the point? But then, didn't she have a civic duty to report what she knew?

Eventually, it hadn't been logic that had decided her; it had been fear. She was out of her depth, and she knew it. The notion that she might ever have been able to handle an investigation like this seemed ludicrous now. In truth, she was still no closer to answers than she had been at the beginning; if anything, she felt further away than ever. She needed all of the help and reassurance she could get, even if it had to come from a man who'd made it clear he wanted her out of the way.

Pettifer must have picked up on her hesitation, because he began to squeeze himself out from under the bench.

"Come on, I'll buy you a Flake 99. You can tell me all about it then."

Feeling her arteries furring up already, Felicia followed him across to the snaking queue that had formed at the side of the violently coloured ice-cream van. Pettifer didn't say anything while they waited, but as soon as they reached the hatch, he struck up an animated conversation with the owner, whom he seemed to know everything about. Felicia watched, feeling about four years' old again, as whipped ice cream was piped into the cone and a chocolate flake stuck into the resulting pillowy spiral at a rakish angle.

"Come here often, do you?" She asked dryly, as they reclaimed their bench swiftly before it was swooped upon by a hopeful-looking family clutching tinfoil sandwiches.

He gave her a level look.

"Felicia, I have three kids. Give it long enough and you'll be on intimate terms with the Stamford ice-cream man, too."

"Chance'd be a fine thing." She went to fold her arms, then remembered that she was holding an ice cream, so settled for a glare instead. "You've ordered me to leave town, in case you'd forgotten."

His expression didn't change.

"Didn't work though, did it?"

"Did you think it would?"

"Not really. But I thought it was my duty to recommend it."

"Through my father, though? That was a low move." She tried not to let the lingering, irrational sense of hurt show in her voice. "You could have just said it to my face."

He sighed.

"So you're annoyed with me. Fine. But you called me, remember? Whatever it is you're keeping back, you obviously want to tell me. I'm happy to wait."

And then he sat back and proceeded to demolish his ice cream.

Men were so obnoxious when they were right. She huffed.

"You know how Algernon said that he'd fallen over yesterday?" She paused. "Well, it turns out that there was...a bit more to it than that."

He was alert now, his gaze sharp.

"How much more?"

"Apparently a golf ball came out of nowhere and nearly hit him on the head."

"You're sure it wasn't an accident? The course-pitch-thing is over in that direction, isn't it?"

"Not much of a golfer, are you?" She guessed wryly.

"No, I leave that to Heavenly. But why would...ah," his face cleared. "I see. You think..."

He was the one person she didn't have to explain it to. She could see that he understood immediately. His eyes darkened, and he swore softly beneath his breath.

"This is getting really dangerous now, Felicia. You *need* to leave town."

"I know. I'd come to that same conclusion myself. Not because you told me to, though," she added quickly.

"Of course not. What a thought."

"In fact, we should have been on our way now, but I..." she reached for the brown paper-wrapped parcel which was propped up under the bench. "It's probably easier if I show you."

He looked on interestedly.

"I was wondering when we'd get to that. I suppose it's too much to hope that that's my missing murder weapon?"

"Sorry, no. But it might be important, all the same." She began to unwind the paper. "Something about what Algernon had said was bothering me, so I went up to the park early this morning, to the spot where he said it had happened…"

"Wait," Pettifer almost vaulted off the bench. "You went into a crime scene? *Again*?"

"I didn't know it was a crime scene then, did I? All I knew is that from my memory, the golf course was right on the other side of a bank of trees. So I checked, and it would be impossible for even the wildest shot to get through and accidently hit someone in the parkland, although clearly that's what someone wanted it to look like. I realised that the shot had to have come from much closer quarters, from within the trees themselves. And I was right." She revealed the golf club and handed it to him, careful to keep the paper between her fingers and the metal. "I'd say it's a man's, wouldn't you?"

He took it gingerly. Then, his gaze flickered up to meet hers.

"There's something I should tell you. Barrington was in regular contact with Henry Bunting before the day they died. The records show regular phone calls between them."

"Okay." Felicia wasn't quite following. "Does that mean anything?"

"I'm not sure. But it fits with a new theory I'm building." He put the club down on the table between them. "It's been bothering me all along, how Bunting was so insistent about putting that cupboard in at the last minute…yes, I know you'd all written it off as senility, but my policeman's brain tells me it's suspicious. And now, coupled with that contact between the two of them…" he leaned forward, lowering his voice. "What if they were in something together? Some sort of scam involving antiques? That sort of thing was right up Clay's street. And we know that

Bunting wasn't exactly all there. He would have been suggestible, easy to persuade… initially, at least."

"So you're wondering if he might have got cold feet," Felicia said slowly. "And Barrington killed him to cover his tracks. In theory, I can see it." But then she shook her head regretfully. "But he couldn't have done; it just isn't possible with the timings. Unless your forensics team made a mistake…"

"I won't tell them you suggested that," Pettifer said, with a small smile. "But, no, there's no mistake, and you're right. It's impossible that it happened that way." He spread his arms wide. "Welcome to deduction 101. If one theory doesn't fit the facts, we try something else, and then something else, until we find what does."

"I suppose Bunting could have killed Barrington, at a pinch," Felicia mused. "Set him up somehow, knowing he'd be in that cupboard at that time." She couldn't say that she liked that solution; the gentle old man she'd known was a stubbornly enduring image in her mind. "But that still wouldn't explain who killed him afterwards. Or who's coming after me now."

"Exactly my conundrum. But then I thought… what if there was someone else in on it?" He drummed the table with his fingers. "From what we've managed to glean, some of Clay's schemes were ambitious—far too much so for the, frankly, rather small-fry conman he really was. He wasn't exactly a criminal mastermind; you and your father were on to him years ago, and you weren't the only ones. No, to my mind, there must have been someone else in the shadows, pulling the strings…" He paused. "Someone who killed them both when they became a liability, perhaps."

Felicia thought back to what Jack had told her. Hadn't there been a hint, between the lines, of someone else's involvement? Someone on the end of the phone, someone who Barrington dropped everything to sidle off to clandestine meetings with. Someone restrained, patient, powerful…

Almost instinctively, she reached for the club, turning it over, looking for the metal ring that joined the shaft to the handle. If there was going to be anything, it would be there.

The sunlight shone off two small letters, engraved in simple script. They could almost have been dismissed as a logo. Except they weren't.

C. C.—Christopher Clancy.

Pettifer followed her gaze, then looked back up at her with a raised eyebrow. Felicia gave a weak shrug.

"Well, you *did* say he was holding something back."

Chapter Thirty-Two

"**Y**es, that's my club. Where the devil did you find it?"

Mr Clancy paused mid-swing, looking at them with a renewed interest. The antiques dealer hadn't originally been too thrilled to have his mid-morning round of golf interrupted, and he'd made no attempts to hide it. He'd greeted their presence on the fifth green with an uncooperative, almost monosyllabic defiance.

Until Pettifer had produced the golf club, that was. Now, he was alert, ball forgotten on the tee at his feet.

Pettifer remained customarily stoical.

"We're not at liberty to—"

"In the woods," Felicia blurted out. Then, ignoring Pettifer's glower, she pressed, "over there, right at the edge of the course. But then, you probably know that. After all, you're a member here, aren't you? Bit strange, isn't it, given that it's so far from home?"

Clancy crossed one checked leg over the other, leaning on his golf club. He looked at Pettifer with a sardonic expression.

"Still indulging the lady detective, are we, Sergeant? You must have a soft spot for bored, pampered women. Alas, I don't."

"Just answer the question, please, sir," Pettifer said, although he sounded weary.

Clancy turned back to Felicia with a mock bow.

"Sorry to disappoint my lady, but as it happens, no, not strange at all. Not for me. I'm a member at several clubs across the country." His lip curled upwards. "I can afford it. Why shouldn't I be?" He held out a hand. "And now, I think I've answered quite enough unwarranted questions. I've only humoured you thus far out of gratitude for the return of my club. I've been missing it dreadfully since it went missing."

Pettifer had gone very still.

"Let me just be clear, sir," he said slowly. "You're claiming that this club went missing? That it hasn't been in your possession recently?"

"You're not hearing me, Sergeant," Clancy said, in a bored voice, returning to his game. He lined up against the tee, swung backwards. "My patience is wearing thin with your antics. If there's anything more you want to ask me from now on, you'll need to do it through my solicitor."

What happened next startled even Felicia. Pettifer's arm shot out and grabbed the handle of Clancy's club, stopping the swing in mid-air. Clancy staggered backwards, staring at him slack-jawed.

"No, *you're* not hearing *me*." Pettifer said, with a sudden ferocity. "I'm not playing games here, sir. This club," he held up the paper-wrapped object. "Is a weapon in an attempted assault, possibly even murder. Someone out there used it to aim at a twelve-year-old boy."

"Well, wait now, that wasn't me." Clancy was ashen-faced now, stammering, all bravado gone. "Look, I told you; I lost it."

"You're going to have to do a lot better than that, I'm afraid."

"But I can prove it, I swear. Ask them at the hotel; they know all about it. In fact, they've taken a vested interest, given that the bag was in their care when the theft happened."

"Go on." Pettifer had released him, and was folding his arms, looking about as intimidating as Felicia had seen him. "When was this exactly?"

"Well, I'm not exactly sure..." as Pettifer's expression darkened, Clancy hastened on, "it was Sunday afternoon when I asked them to put the bag behind the reception desk. I was planning to have a quick drink in the bar before getting off for a short round here. But I changed my mind, decided to stay on for an early dinner and play the following afternoon instead. Well, at three o'clock yesterday the bag was still there, where I'd left it. I collected it, came here; it wasn't until I was partway around the course that I noticed my fairway wood was missing." They obviously looked unconvinced, because he elaborated, "it's not a standard club; you don't use it on every hole."

Pettifer looked at him for a long moment. Then he turned his head towards Felicia.

"Do you think he's telling the truth?"

Felicia felt about as taken aback as Mr Clancy looked. Knowing that Pettifer was probably going somewhere with this, though, she tried to sound confident as she replied:

"Well, the hotel will be able to confirm that he left his bag there as he said."

"True," Pettifer agreed. "And you've seen what it's like there, people coming and going all over the place. The bag would have been visible to those passing through the foyer. Anyone who timed it cleverly could easily have nipped behind the desk when it was empty and steal the club. It would be a risky move, but our murderer doesn't exactly seem shy of risk."

"Exactly," Clancy exclaimed eagerly. "So you see..."

Pettifer held up a silencing finger.

"But I can think of something more likely, and that's that Mr Clancy here took it himself before he even gave the bag to reception. Let's face it, they were hardly going to notice how many clubs were in it to begin with, were they? There's only his word for it that there was one fewer yesterday afternoon than when he handed it in on Sunday."

"Now, steady *on*," Clancy spluttered. "That's outrageous."

"Is it?" Pettifer stared him down. "Because what I'm looking at is a man who's consistently evaded our questions. I'm looking at a man who's stayed in town for spurious reasons despite the fact that I gave him leave to go."

"I *explained* that," Clancy ground out. The skin around his lips was so taut it had gone completely white. "I've had business to attend to."

"And, yet the staff at the hotel told me that you've met with no one since you've been here. That's unusual, apparently. As is the fact that every round you've played here at the club has been a solo one. Which leads me to wonder what you're really staying on for. And then I find that your golf club has been linked to a serious crime. A crime that just happened to take place whilst you were here at the course yesterday evening."

"I didn't go near those woods. I swear."

"But no one can corroborate that, can they, sir? You were here on your own, and at that time, with the light failing, I can't imagine there were many others out on the course."

"Well, no, but…"

"Do you know what Ms Grant here thinks?" Pettifer said, his tone suddenly conversational.

Clancy stared at Felicia, small eyes bulging.

"She thinks that you were in league with Barrington Clay. That something criminal was going on involving the sale. She thinks that's why you were there that day. That you lured Clay into that cupboard so that you could kill him."

Felicia tried to keep her face impassive. She wouldn't normally have been happy to have words put in her mouth, but she trusted Pettifer on this. He knew what he was doing. Or at least, she hoped he did. Otherwise she was probably heading for one hell of a libel case.

"She also thinks that you roped in Henry Bunting to help you. And that when he became a liability, you killed him, too."

"Now, just wait." Clancy was shaking. He was leaning on the golf club so heavily now she thought it might snap. "That is *completely* untrue. I never…"

"Then how do you explain the contact between yourself and Mr Bunting the evening before the sale?" Pettifer demanded. Tension was rolling off him in waves; he was closing in on his quarry. Felicia felt the hairs on the back of her neck stir. "It's all on record. He called you on Friday evening."

"Yes, he did." Clancy was almost shouting now, his self-control completely beginning to crack. "*He* called *me*." He looked between them wildly, head swivelling. "Don't you see what that *means*? Am I going to have to spell it out for you?"

When neither of them responded, he gave a strangled laugh.

"*I* was the one who was hired by *him*, not the other way around. The private client I was bidding on the cupboard for… was Mr Bunting himself."

Chapter Thirty-Three

"You've got to be kidding me," Pettifer said in exasperated amusement, as they stood watching Mr Clancy being helped into the back of Welland Police's single marked car by Jess.

It was the first sentence he'd uttered in some minutes, and, coming as it did without context, it earned him a surprised glance from Felicia.

"What?"

"You actually believe him, don't you?"

Felicia shifted defensively.

"Well, yes, as a matter of fact, I do."

"On what grounds?"

"Just…a feeling. Plus a knowledge of people, I suppose."

"That's why you're an auctioneer, and I'm the policeman," said Pettifer, stifling a yawn. "God, I'm glad this case is almost over."

She gave him a sharp look.

"You're charging him then?"

"Goodness, no, not yet. It's all far too woolly and circumstantial at the moment. But we'll get the hard evidence soon enough, now we know where to concentrate our efforts." He placed a hand on her shoulder. She had the sense he was trying to do it lightly, but it almost made her legs buckle all the same. "Well done, Felicia. I mean it. Finding that golf club…well, look, on the record, it was a bloody stupid thing to do, going in there alone, and I should be rapping you across the knuckles for it. But off…" he grinned. "You provided the key to the whole thing, and in a place which, I'll admit, we would never have thought to look. I'm not saying you should give up the day job, mind," he added, as a hasty afterthought. She rolled her eyes.

"Don't worry, I'll stick to the antiques. At least they don't murder each other."

"Good lass." Further down the slope, Jess was beckoning. "Right, best be off. It's not over till you've got the confession, as they say."

And he sauntered away towards the waiting car, looking, she had to admit, almost light-hearted. Which was nice for him, she supposed, but she couldn't quite feel the same way. Perhaps it was the knowledge that catching the killer didn't change the horrors that had happened; it was a relief, certainly, but could one ever call it something to be *happy* about?

Or then again, maybe it was simpler than that. Maybe it was more to do with the doubt that was hanging heavily over her, like the atmosphere just before it rains.

"This looks interesting. What's going on?"

She started, turning to see Jack standing on the edge of the woods, framed by two trees.

"You have rather a habit of creeping up on people, don't you?" She said crisply.

"Not at all. It's more that every time I see you, you're distracted by something." He tilted his head, regarding her with amusement. "You're not very observant, you know, considering your profession."

"I'm observant when it comes to small things," she said defensively. "Details. I'm good with those."

"Just not big things, then. Like…whole people appearing in

318

front of you." He was smiling at her, but there was nothing mocking in it. He seemed to be in a good mood. That made for everyone, then, except herself, Felicia thought. Was she over-thinking things? Seeing problems that weren't there?

"Are you here for a reason?" She said, a touch haughtily.

"You know me. Just lurking. Being dodgy and suspicious, as is my remit. I am a criminal, remember?" Ignoring her unimpressed look, he angled his head towards the police car. "Who is it, then? Because clearly, it isn't you or I. Which is surprising, seeing as we were the top suspects at one point."

"It's Mr Clancy," she said. "You know, the furniture dealer from London? Turns out it was his golf club I found in the woods. Apparently he was the one in league with Barrington. They were planning some sort of con together revolving around the sale."

He didn't reply, and she turned to look at him. He was staring at her, all amusement gone from his face.

"They're making a mistake," he said hoarsely. "The police. You need to tell them."

"What do you mean?"

"It wasn't him who was working with Barrington."

"How do you—" Then, slowly, she began to see. "Because you know who *was*. Because…you were following Barrington around, weren't you? Watching him. That's what you meant by bringing him to justice. You wanted to expose him. To prove your innocence."

"*No*," the word rang out loudly. "It was never about that. I've long since stopped caring what people think of me. But I…I didn't want anyone else to suffer because of what he did. What he was." He rubbed a hand across his face, looking suddenly jaded. "I always thought that if I could just catch him…and I was prepared to wait. I'm always around town; nobody really notices me any more. I'm just a photographer out working; they're used to seeing me in strange places at strange times. It's amazing what you can get away with if you're looking into a camera lens. It doesn't occur to people that you might still be listening, still be watching."

"Go on."

He did, but with visible reluctance.

"I overheard him on the phone when I was in town one day. I'd recognise his voice anywhere. He didn't see me; he'd ducked into one of the passageways to take the call. But from what he was saying, I knew he was up to something. He sounded excited, furtive. He was talking about a game-changing find. Said if they could just get the old man out of their way…"

"That's what you were doing at the auction? You'd followed him there?" She took a breath, looked straight up into his eyes. They were the colour of moss on a woodland floor. "Jack…did you know he was in that cupboard?"

"No. Absolutely not." He looked horrified, and she felt her shoulders drop with relief. "I followed him in there, yes. But the crowd was already building. One minute, I had him in my sights, the next, I'd lost him. He'd just…disappeared. I actually thought he must have left."

"But you stayed anyway," she said, guessing yet knowing that she was right. "Because you were waiting for the person he was meant to be meeting. The person on the phone."

He just nodded. She pressed on.

"And…did they turn up?"

"Yes."

A single word. He didn't elaborate. She felt her temper ignite.

"What exactly is it you're trying to *do*, Jack? Are you trying to help me or not? I can't even work out if you're on my side."

Something flickered across his face.

"I am. Believe me."

"Well, you don't act like it. You're always hovering around, you throw about vague hints, but you don't actually *give* me anything." She was trembling now with a rage she didn't know she could possess. "If I find out that someone had the chance to nearly put my son in hospital because you thought it was more important to be bloody *mysterious*…"

His eyes widened.

"Felicia, if I'd have known it would put you or Algernon in danger, of course I would have said something. But I…" he shifted awkwardly. "Well, I had my reasons; besides, I was certain you would be safe."

"*How?* How could you *possibly* be sure of that?"

He looked at her for a long moment. Then he sighed, sagging back against the tree trunk behind him.

"You're right, I'm sorry. I should have told you this earlier; I made a mistake, but I just… I couldn't quite face it. And I don't think you've been able to either."

She felt herself go still.

"What do you mean?"

"Come on, Felicia. You're an intelligent woman, aren't you? You've worked a load of stuff out already. And, yet, you miss what ought to be the one glaring inconsistency from that whole morning." He was starting to sound frustrated now. "You're hiding from the truth, not letting yourself see what's right in front of you." When she remained silent, his expression hardened in disbelief. "You're really going to make me spell it out for you? Fine, then. How about this? The cupboard was a last-minute addition; it wasn't in the catalogue. Therefore, no one could have known that it was going to be in the sale beforehand. Am I right?"

She nodded slowly.

"Apart from people involved in the sale. My father, the auction staff. Bunting, of course; he consigned it. And Barrington obviously found out, too, somehow."

"And one other person." He watched her carefully. "Come on, Felicia, think. *How can you stop the auction of an item you had absolutely no way of knowing about?*"

It took a moment. Then, in a wave, it rolled through her. She felt all of the sensation go from her legs.

"No," she whispered.

"I'm sorry," was all he said.

———————

She walked back to the cottage in a daze, her feet taking her along the familiar route on autopilot. Water Street was achingly beautiful on a day like this, the low boughs of blossom skimming the sparkling surface of the water, loose frills of petals drifting, confetti-like, on the current. Ducks snoozed gently on the daffodil-strewn bank, bright bills tucked neatly beneath their wing. Up on the bridge, children were leaning through the green iron railings, pointing excitedly as they spotted a silver fish between the billowing reeds. The row of cottages looked storybook-like in association, their bowed slate roofs like a too-large cap falling over the eyes of the wearer, diamond-paned windows peeking out from beneath the brim.

Felicia pushed on the front door, having long stopped expecting it to be locked. It swung open, and with a sense of wading through treacle, she moved slowly down the hallway.

He was in the kitchen, framed in the sunlit window, his back to her. She stopped in the doorway, just looking at him. At the curve of the back of his neck, the way the dark hair curled against the collar. It was a place she'd often rested her hand when they were together, and suddenly, in that moment, it felt as though her heart was breaking all over again. After all of this time, she'd thought he'd lost the power to hurt her.

How wrong she'd been. How naïve.

She wasn't aware of making a sound, but something must have alerted him to her presence, because he turned.

"Felicia, you're back." Then he saw her face, and frowned. "What's the matter?"

That was almost enough to get a hysterical laugh out of her. What a question. What indeed? Where to begin? Three and a half days in Stamford and so far she'd clocked up two dead bodies, a stalker, altercations with both her father and Algernon…and now this. Just when she'd thought it couldn't possibly get any worse, there was *this*. She hadn't realised until this moment just how much she'd trusted Dexter, how she'd *needed* to trust him. To lean into their shared history, the comfort of truly knowing someone. Now, it seemed that she hadn't known him as well as she'd thought. The shock and humiliation was like a physical blow to the chest, squeezing all of the air from her lungs.

"We need to talk." She sat down at the kitchen table and clasped her hands in front of her, mainly to disguise how much her hands were shaking.

"Okay." He turned back to the coffee he was making, switching on the little electric whisk that frothed up the milk. "I'm listening."

He sounded so normal, so unconcerned, and at once, Felicia realised that she didn't know where to start. How *did* one broach a subject like this?

"It's about you and…I mean, what you've been…" The whisk was vibrating with a tinny buzzing sound, like a wasp in her ear, making it impossible to concentrate on anything else, stretching her nerves until she snapped, the anger that had been held at bay exploding across the kitchen.

"Will you turn that bloody thing *off*?" Then another thought occurred to her, as she looked around her father's old-fashioned kitchen. "Where did you even *find* it? Jesus, did you actually buy it while you've been here?"

"I like foam," he said, a shade defensively. "What's your problem today? You're like a bear with a sore head."

"*You!*" She burst out. "*You're* my problem. You and your poncey coffees"—Oh God, now she sounded exactly like her father—"and your boiled sweet jackets and your flirting and…" her voice broke. "How could you *do* it, Dexter? Just… how *could* you?"

"Felicia, I think you'd better tell me what's going on." For the first time, he looked wary. "Because I have absolutely no idea what you're talking about."

"I know you were colluding with Barrington Clay. There's no point denying it."

"Ah." He put the whisk down, staring into the bottom of the coffee cup. She could only see his face in partial profile; the rest was obscured by a blaze of light from the window behind. "In which case, I won't."

Felicia sat back, emotions rocketing through her. Having it confirmed wasn't a shock, but it was still hard to hear. A small part of her, she supposed, had been hoping that he'd have come out with some flamboyant excuse, and explanation so implausible that only Dexter could make it true. Something which would make it all right somehow.

"And you broke into Barrington's house?" It hadn't occurred to her before, but as the words left her mouth, she knew it was true. "That was you as well, wasn't it?"

He closed his eyes briefly.

"I would hardly call it breaking in, but yes."

Felicia put her head in her hands, forcing herself to breathe.

"I don't suppose it matters to you that it was Algernon who almost got killed last night instead of me?"

"Wait...*what*?" He spun around, face ashen. "Something happened to Algie? But he..."

"The only thing which is keeping me from putting a kitchen knife in you right now," she said, amazed at how calm she sounded, "is knowing that you couldn't have done the murders yourself. You didn't arrive at the sale until after Barrington was killed, and you were with me for Bunting's." She looked straight at him. "But I might be tempted to change my mind, unless you tell me who was responsible *right now*."

"Oh my God," his mouth went slack. "I know that face.

You're… you're actually *serious*, aren't you? You genuinely think I had something to do with all of this. How could you even…"

He trailed off, looking too upset to continue. But that only hardened Felicia's resolve.

"How? I'll tell you how. Because you've consistently lied, to both me and the police. Because you broke into a crime scene. Because you've admitted you were involved in some scam with Barrington…"

"Wait *right* there," he held out a hand. "I certainly have not. I don't know where you've got that from. All I said was that we were doing business together. That's *all*. Look, Barrington called me. He said he's come across something truly exciting, potentially history-changing. He wanted my opinion."

"The ex-husband of his business rival?" She said sceptically.

"And the foremost academic on the subject of Royalist symbolism," Dexter ground out. "Believe it or not, Felicia, to some people I am more than just your old cast offs."

He did have a point there, but Felicia was still too furious to feel abashed. Instead, she folded her arms and glared at him as he continued.

"He called me again on Friday evening. Said the old man who'd promised him the cupboard had gone and pulled a fast one on him—his words, not mine," Dexter added, with a self-deprecating smile. "By putting it up for sale. Naturally, he was fairly livid; he said he was going to head over to the viewing early on Saturday and get a better look at it. Suggested I meet him there. So I got on the first flight…"

"You trusted him that much?" Felicia was incredulous.

"Whatever he might have been as a man, Clay was a first-rate antiques expert," Dexter said shortly. "So yes, I did as he asked. But, as you already know, I arrived too late."

"And you didn't think that the police might find any of this helpful?" Angry sarcasm radiated through her tone.

"What, and implicate myself? Jesus, Felicia, if even you don't believe me, what are the police likely to think?"

"I want to believe you." You have no idea just how much. "But I can't deny the facts, Dexter. If you're as innocent and uninvolved as you claim, then why did you break into Bunting's house?"

He looked uncomfortable.

"That was…something different. Personal."

"The library. Of course." The memory slotted into place; Pettifer telling her that the thief had broken into the library. She'd thought it odd at the time. "You were looking for the house documents which the police wouldn't let you see." She stood abruptly, facing him down across the table. "It was never about being implicated at all, was it? You didn't tell the police what you knew because you wanted to protect your reputation! This is all about your bloody *career*, isn't it?"

"You make it sound so sordid," he actually had the nerve to sound disapproving. "This is important historical…"

"I don't care about *history*, Dexter!" She exploded. "I care that your actions put me, and by extension, our son, in mortal danger." Her voice trembled. "I can never forgive you for that."

There was a commotion in the hall as the front door banged open, heavy footsteps thudding towards the kitchen. Pettifer appeared in the doorway, claret-faced and wheezing heavily.

"I got your message," he gasped, bent double. "Are you all right? When you said we'd got the wrong man, I…" he broke off, registering the scene in confusion.

"May I suggest," Felicia said calmly. "That you arrest my ex-husband instead?"

Dexter's mouth dropped open.

"Felicia! You can't be serious. You know I had nothing to do with this."

She couldn't bear to look at him, so she stared at a spot over his shoulder instead.

"I don't know what to believe any more, Dexter. Not from

you." She turned to Pettifer, explaining, "he's admitted that he was the one in business with Barrington. And there are a few other things he needs to tell you, too."

Pettifer cleared his throat apologetically.

"I'm sorry, sir, but we *are* going to need you to come down to the station for questioning."

Dexter's response was drowned out by another crash outside, followed by decidedly lighter and swifter footsteps in the hall. Jess Winters appeared in the doorway, pale-faced and frantic.

"Sir, thank God you're here. There's another one."

Pettifer looked up sharply.

"Who this time?"

Felicia felt her whole body go cold with dread.

"W-well, that's t-the thing... sir," Jess stammered. She looked a bit dazed. "You're not going to believe this, but it's... t-the murderer."

Chapter Thirty-Four

S he was lying flat on her back, one arm draped over the edge
of the sofa, fingertips brushing the carpet. In contrast to the
glassy-eyed stare of the first two bodies, her eyes were closed. She
could easily have been asleep. If it weren't for the chalky pallor,
the unnatural stillness…

"That's far enough, Felicia," Pettifer murmured gently, as he
ducked beneath the now horribly familiar blue-and-white striped
tape. "I know it's hard, but remember it's a crime scene."

She nodded, swallowed, unable to take her eyes off the figure
on the sofa. How different it was, when it was someone you knew
well. And when it was like this…

The empty sleeping pill bottle was open on the table, next to
the empty teacup. Both had little numbers propped up next to
them, marking them as evidence. Felicia knew there would be
more of them in the kitchen. That's where she'd crushed them up
first, apparently, before bringing the cup through here to finish it.
Her favourite room, surrounded by everything she most loved.
The place she'd wanted to die.

Dexter, standing just behind her, put a hand on her shoulder, and she didn't protest. She was still too shocked, too numb. The warmth of his skin through the silky fabric of her top felt like the only thing anchoring her to reality right now.

"I don't understand," she said hollowly. "Why would she do this?"

"The note she left explains a little of her state of mind," Pettifer replied. "In fact," he scratched his neck, looking suddenly uncomfortable. "You should probably see it, if you think you can face it. It's addressed to you."

"Me?" Felicia stared at him, astonished.

He handed her a plastic bag with a torn-off piece of paper inside. Lilac notepaper, with small watermarked roses running along the top. The sight of it made her throat close with emotion, but she made herself read the words.

> *Dear Felicia,*
>
> *I'm writing to you because I want you to know the truth. I've been so afraid of this moment for so long, but things have gone too far, and I know that I can no longer keep quiet, no matter what it might mean for me. You and your father have been so kind to me always, and deceiving you has been one of the most terrible things I've ever had to endure. I hope and pray that you can, if not understand, at least forgive me for what I've done.*

And here it ended abruptly, underscored by a jagged edge of paper. Felicia blinked, turning it over, but it was blank.

"Is that it?"

"Suicide notes tend to be fairly short," Pettifer said. "I know it's difficult for the people left behind to understand why they didn't say more, but..."

"No, I didn't mean that. It's more...why didn't she *sign* it? And why use a torn-off piece of paper? That wasn't like her at all."

"Because people *do*," Pettifer was clearly trying to be gentle, but his impatience to get on with the case was starting to show. "They're not exactly in a logical frame of mind."

"But she was supposed to meet me. Why would she arrange that if she was intending to…" Felicia broke off, unable to voice it.

Pettifer looked up sharply.

"When was this?"

"Last night. She's who I was waiting for at The George."

"That ties in," Pettifer said thoughtfully. "In fact, I'd say it pretty much seals it. Time of death is estimated at early yesterday evening." He looked at the note. "Clearly she decided at the last minute that she couldn't face telling you in person, so she…"

"Telling me what? I don't *understand* any of this." She waved the plastic-encased paper in hopeless frustration. "As far as I know, she just wanted to talk to me about the business."

"She did. Just…probably not in the way you think." He looked at her for a long moment, clearly weighing something up in his mind. Then he sighed heavily. "Look, I can't keep this from you. It'll be public knowledge soon enough; maybe already is, knowing the way the grapevine operates in small towns." He met her gaze steadily. "All of those anomalies at the auction—"

"My father," she blurted out, not meaning to interrupt but so consumed by gratitude that it wasn't the shock she'd been bracing herself for. "Yes, I know about that. He's been letting things slide a bit lately, but…"

Pettifer didn't blink.

"Not your father, Felicia. And not a case of absent-mindedness, either. Everything was being carefully engineered…by someone working for Barrington Clay."

And then he turned to look over his shoulder.

Felicia discovered that she was shaking her head vigorously, back and forth. It was making her dizzy, but she couldn't seem to stop.

"*No.* Not Betsy, there must be some…" she trailed off as she saw the pitying look on his face. "Mistake," she whispered.

"Why?" Dexter's voice, strong and confident, even though it sounded as though it was coming down a long tunnel. It brought her back to reality. "Why would she do that? She was always so happy at Grant's."

"If it's any consolation, she didn't do it strictly by choice. He was blackmailing her."

"It is and it isn't," Felicia said dazedly. While it was at least something to know that it hadn't been a purely cold-hearted betrayal of their trust, the thought of the kind, grandmotherly lady with the fondness for lilac and cross-stitch being coerced and frightened was almost worse, somehow. "I suppose I shouldn't ask—it's none of my business, really—but what…"

As usual, Pettifer seemed to know what she was saying without her needing to finish the sentence. He nodded stiffly.

"On the contrary, I'd say you have a right to know. It's all here in the correspondence between them." He picked up another plastic bag, this time with a purple mobile in it. Betsy's phone. Seeing it like that, wrapped up as evidence, made Felicia feel nauseous all over again. She focussed on breathing evenly as Pettifer scrolled though the messages.

"Obviously, it's out of context, but it's pretty obvious what happened. She passed him some information once—that, I'm afraid, seems to have been done by her own free choice; there was clearly a financial reward of some kind. She thought it would just be a one-off, wanted nothing more to do with it. But of course, that's not how he saw it. He wouldn't let her go after that."

Of course he wouldn't. Felicia closed her eyes. Poor, naïve Betsy. Barrington Clay must have thought all of his Christmases had come at once when he saw her coming. No doubt that first requested piece of information had been something quite innocuous, not even particularly useful to him. Something she'd see no real harm in handing over, not realising that in doing so, she was indebting herself to him forever.

"He'd got the measure of her, it seems," Pettifer said softly.

"The hold he had on her was pretty flimsy, after all. She hadn't done anything really criminal. The worst she'd get is sacked from her job at the auction. But clearly, she couldn't bear the thought of you or your father knowing what she'd done; reading between the lines, I think the shame of disappointing you both was worse to her than the thought of being reported to us."

Felicia looked over at Betsy, lying so peacefully in a nest of hand-embroidered cushions, and tried not to dwell on the inner torment and loneliness her friend must have been suffering to feel that this was the only way out. But it was impossible; the guilt was swelling in her throat, threatening to choke her.

"I should have known something was wrong when she didn't turn up last night. Why didn't I *check* on her? Why didn't I *think*?"

"Because it's not *normal* to think like that," Pettifer said, almost harshly. "Because you shouldn't have to think that just because someone doesn't turn up for a drink, they must be lying dead somewhere. It's *not* normal. So don't you go down that road, lass."

He was angry with himself, she could tell. He was taking it personally, blaming himself for failing to solve the case in time. To stop this from happening. She wished that she could comfort him, reassure him, but as she knew from her own feelings right now, culpability wasn't something which could simply be reasoned away.

"So… she killed Barrington to break his hold over her?" Dexter ventured.

"She must have felt desperate, trapped. Whether it was planned or not, we'll never know now. But Algernon told me that she was late back from her break during the sale; that must have been when she did it."

"And the weapon?"

"We'll see if it turns up here, of course. But in all likelihood she tossed it once the coast was clear. She would have known where to hide it while we were searching the saleroom; after all, it was her domain."

"And Bunting?" Felicia spoke for the first time in several minutes. "Why would she want to kill him?"

"There are several possibilities I can think of. We know that he was in with Clay on something; perhaps he also knew about Betsy's little side line? Or maybe he did go up to the auction that morning after all? Just because no one remembers seeing him doesn't mean that he wasn't there. What if he turned up just at the wrong moment, saw the murder take place?" He cast a regretful look at the body. "Like I said, though, ultimately there are questions we'll have to accept never having the answers to. But the confession's there; at least we can call it case closed, if nothing else." As she opened her mouth, he held up a quelling hand. "I know that look. You're about to argue with me, point out how I might have got it wrong." His voice dropped, softened. "Go home, Felicia. Relax. Have a cup of tea. I know it probably doesn't feel like much of a relief now, but it will, I promise. It just needs to sink in."

Felicia knew that tone. It meant that she was being summarily dismissed. Anything else she said would fall on deaf ears; there was simply no point wasting the energy.

At that moment, one of the forensics team got up, moving aside to reveal a small figure sitting on the other side of the kitchen doorway, a blanket wrapped around her frail shoulders. She was watching the swarming activity around her with a frightened, stunned look.

"That's the neighbour," Pettifer explained. "She's the one who found her."

"I know who she is." The sight of Evelina jolted Felicia into action. "Does she really need to still be here? She's a very old lady."

Looking slightly taken aback at the brusqueness of her tone, Pettifer stuttered, "well, I mean, initial statement's been taken, although I might have some more…"

"Then you can ask them later. In her *own* house." Felicia

moved towards the kitchen. "She's over ninety, Sergeant. It's not like she's going to go far. You'll know exactly where to find her."

"You're very kind, my dear, to see me home."

"Not at all," Felicia said honestly. It was actually a relief to have something practical to do. It kept her mind off the awful scene still playing out two doors away. "You must be in terrible shock. Did they make you a cup of tea?"

"Oh, yes, the young PC is a *very* nice girl. She made sure I was well looked after. But then she had to go and attend to something else and…well, it *was* rather awful, sitting there so near to where it all happened. I'm glad to be out of the place." She looked at Felicia with beseeching lupin-blue eyes. "Oh dear. Does that sound very heartless of me?"

"Of course not. It's only natural." They were standing on the front step. Felicia waited for Evelina to produce a key to the door, then realised that in typical Stamford fashion, it wouldn't be locked. A turn of the handle proved her correct. She ushered Evelina inside, glancing up as she did so. There was a security camera nestled amongst the profusion of wisteria, and she bit her lip guiltily. The murders must have made the old lady more afraid than she'd let on; and with good reason, it turned out. Felicia had been so wrapped up in herself it hadn't occurred to her to check in, a fact that she now regretted.

"My sons are very protective," Evelina said, catching Felicia's upwards look. "They don't live locally, you see."

"That must be hard sometimes," Felicia added, feeling worse than ever.

"Oh, *no*, dear," Evelina said brightly. "You mustn't feel like that. I've got plenty to be getting along with. Not like dear Betsy." Her face dimmed in recollection. "Such a *nice* neighbour, she was. Not *prying*, you understand, but around when one needed her. I used to ask her for tea every now and again. She was very lonely, you see; all of those grandchildren on the other side of the world. The police wouldn't tell me why she… well, you know—But I suspect it must be something to do with that. She didn't have much of a life outside them, you see, whereas mine is really *quite* full; fuller than it was when my husband was alive. He wasn't much of a one for society; he liked to be at home quietly. We lived out in the countryside, then."

"You chose this house, then?" Felicia guided her into the drawing room, trying to induce the old lady to stop moving for a moment. But she seemed determined to chatter on, clearly thrilled to have a guest, despite what she'd just said.

"Oh, *yes*. I wanted to come back into town. I lived here when I was young, you see. Just around the corner on Melancholy Walk. My father owned an ironmonger's." She finally allowed herself to be settled in a velvet chaise longue, which was enviably positioned in front of the deep bay window. Unlike Betsy's cottage, Evelina's house was of grand proportions, furnished in an elegant if slightly old-fashioned style. The drawing room itself was a beautiful room, double aspect, with French doors at the far end looking out onto the garden. "Not prosperous days, but ones I hold very dearly in my heart. Children weren't mollycoddled then, you see. We were turned out into the streets and told not to come back until supper time." She chuckled. "Oh, the things we got up to. Very innocent by today's standards, no doubt."

Felicia fetched a blanket from the back of the sofa and draped it over her.

"You'd better rest while you can. The police will be back to ask more questions later."

The old lady's eyes, which had been closed, suddenly opened again. Felicia was startled by how piercingly blue they were; she'd read once that people's eye colour faded as they aged, but apparently not Evelina's.

"That letter she left… she didn't say…"

"There's nothing you could have done," Felicia assured her gently. "You mustn't blame yourself."

Evelina visibly relaxed.

"I suppose it's true what they say. One never really knows what's going on in the hearts of those around them." She shook her head sadly. "When you've been alive as long as I have, you've seen almost everything. But to know that someone was so desperate…"

"I think people are often more complicated than we realise," Felicia said gently, then tried to lighten her tone, not wanting the old lady to dwell too much on it once she'd gone. "Now, is there anything I can get you before I leave? Someone I can call? Will you be all right on your own?"

"Oh, yes, dear. I've been on my own for twenty years. But are you *sure* you won't stay? I feel I should offer you some refreshment."

"Thank you, but I must go. I have to tell my son what's happened before he hears it from anyone else." Her composure wobbled temporarily. "He and Betsy were…very close."

"Of course," Evelina said sympathetically. "I've seen him coming to visit her. It was good of him to keep her company."

"It was mutual, in truth. They used to bake together. She was teaching him all of her recipes."

"Well then," Evelina fluffed the cushion behind her head and sank back against it. "I must dig out my old family scone recipe for him. It's really rather superb, if I do say so myself."

"That's very kind."

"Nonsense." The eyes were drifting closed again. "It's good for an old lady to have something to think about."

Felicia watched her as she dozed, filled with admiration. She'd often thought of Betsy as an old lady—grandmotherly, slightly fluffy—but in reality, she'd really only been in her late sixties. Not so old at all these days. Whereas, Evelina—well, she really *was* an old lady, by anyone's standards, and, yet, she had a vitality, a sparkle that made it easy to forget.

Ensconced in the chair, Evelina emitted an earth-rattling snore.

Well, sometimes, at least, Felicia amended with a faint smile, creeping quietly out of the room.

Chapter Thirty-Five

"Earl Grey, no sugar, and—though it pained me to do it—a splash of milk." A dainty white and gold teacup and saucer appeared in front of Felicia's eyes, blocking her view of the river. "Just what the doctor ordered."

"And served by the mayor herself, no less," Felicia summoned up a teasing smile, taking the cup from her friend's outstretched hand. "Whatever did I do to deserve such an honour?"

"You've done plenty this week, Fliss. You've more than earned it."

But not quite enough. The words were on the tip of her tongue, but Felicia held them back, determined not to put a dampener on the party. After the time of it they'd all had recently, everyone deserved a bit of light relief.

It was Saturday, a full week now since the auction, and four days since Betsy had been carried away in a body bag. Three days since the police had officially declared the case solved and Stamford had settled back into something approaching its bucolic, untroubled normality. Felicia wished that she could say the same about herself.

It had been a natural decision to stay on for a few more days.

After all, there were still things to be sorted at the auction—especially now they were minus a staff member—and with the imminent danger gone, she could see no good excuse to rush away. It was easier just to keep busy, to tell herself that she was needed, and pretend that she wasn't just delaying the moment when she would have to tell her son that it really *was* time to go. It was Easter Sunday tomorrow; the holidays were drawing to a close, and soon they would have to return to the life they'd had before. If that was even possible after everything that had happened. She wasn't sure that she would ever be quite the same again.

Shaking herself free of maudlin thoughts, she put an arm around Cassie's shoulder and gave it a squeeze.

"Come on, let's get some cake." She paused. "I take it there *is* cake?"

"Wouldn't be much of a tea party without it," Cassie pointed out, then reconsidered. "Actually, it wouldn't be any party of mine without it."

Felicia laughed as they moved away from the water's edge back onto the centre of the grassy bank in front of the cottages, where the party was currently in full swing. A hotchpotch of her father's furniture had been requisitioned for the occasion, dragged out into the sunshine and covered with an assortment of tablecloths and cushions. The weather had proven too good to resist in the end, the chill spring-like edge of the wind mellowing to a balmy breeze finally more reminiscent of the approaching summer than of the winter left behind.

Cassie had been desperate to throw Felicia a leaving party, but, with her diplomatic hat on, had realised that anything too overtly celebratory would have been inappropriate. After all, the case might be solved, but no one felt especially good about it. A woman they'd all known and liked, driven to kill through shame and despair...it wasn't the kind of catharsis anyone had hoped for when the murderer was finally caught.

So, Cassie had adapted her plans. Out went the champagne, in came the tea; it wasn't *technically* a party, she told herself, but a gathering. And after all, no one could possibly object to tea, that most reserved, English of drinks. Thoroughly unshowy; nothing *heartless* about it.

Nonetheless, despite her conviction, as Cassie watched her oldest friend perusing the array of cakes now, she couldn't deny the slightest frisson of concern. Felicia was always pale—it was part of her waifish charm—but she was paler than ever today, with violet smudges beneath her eyes, and Cassie wondered how much she'd been sleeping. She knew it was troubling her, the way things had ended, that she felt responsible for not going and checking on Betsy, even though Sergeant Pettifer had been firm about the fact that it would already have been too late to save her.

Cassie looked across at the man in question now, who was seated on a checked blanket in that awkward way men have at a picnic, stiff-kneed and uncomfortable-looking. He'd dropped in on the way home from his shift—to check on Felicia, Cassie half suspected, although he currently seemed to be more interested in the enormous wedge of coffee and walnut cake he was inhaling. Robyn had pounced on him, and was earnestly trying to engage him on local issues, her legs crossed gaminely beneath her with the flexible ease of youth.

At the other end of the blanket, Dexter was gesturing with a half-eaten shortcake finger as he regaled a starstruck-looking Amelia—a belated but apparently now very firm fan—with his various escapades from around the world. He'd studiously been avoiding Felicia all afternoon, Cassie had noticed. She got the distinct sense that something had happened between them, but even she knew when sometimes it was better not to ask. Instead, she continued to move her gaze around the assembled company, to where, beneath the frothing pink canopy of the cherry tree, Peter was established in his wheelchair—brake firmly on given the gradient of the riverbank—animatedly discussing the contents of the latest issue of *Top Gavel* magazine with Hugo. Gavin was looking on indulgently as they debated, his arm draped around his lover's waist.

"They make a nice couple, don't they?" Felicia had followed her gaze.

"Hmm," Cassie mumbled, making an acute study of a tower of fairy cakes. Felicia sidled her an amused glance.

"You're still put out about being the last to know, aren't you?"

"I should have worked it out!" Cassie burst out petulantly. "I saw that bloody tie in his drawer with my own eyes; it should have been obvious. Of course, it might have *helped* if you'd told me that Hugo was gay from the start," she added pointedly.

"I didn't know!" Felicia protested, then amended, "well, all right, so I might have guessed. But he's always been so private; I couldn't exactly march up to him and ask." She selected a slice of cherry cake and put it on her plate. "Besides, you shouldn't be so hard on yourself. You were distracted by other things, remember?" She dropped her voice. "I don't suppose you've mentioned anything to Gavin about finding Dennis's number in his desk?"

"Not yet, no." Cassie bit into a pikelet. "I didn't feel that now was the time. And truthfully, I'm just so relieved that he didn't have anything to do with the murders. That puts things in perspective a little." She frowned. "I suppose that's what he was doing at the auction, then? He went to see Hugo... but why on earth didn't he just *say* so? He could have saved himself from falling under suspicion."

"Love," Felicia said, simply. "He and Hugo had had a huge row about their relationship. Gavin's been out for years, as you know, but Hugo's always kept it a secret; even his family didn't know. That's why Gavin skipped out on the meeting; he was desperate to see Hugo, to make it up, but when he got there, he realised it wasn't the time or place, so he left again."

"And that's what Hugo saw at the back of the room? What he was being so cagey about?"

"He was trying to protect Gavin; if it was known that he'd been there, then he would have automatically become a suspect. Although, as it was, the police found out anyway. And Gavin couldn't bear to betray Hugo's wishes by making their relationship public knowledge."

"So *that's* why he wouldn't defend himself," Cassie breathed.

"He was an idiot." They both turned to see Hugo grinning at them, Gavin looking bashful at his side. "He could have been arrested over it. I was furious with him when I found out."

"Some things are more important," Gavin said stubbornly.

"Yes," Hugo gazed at him softly. "They are. I realised that when he finally told me what he'd done." He shook his head. "I can't hide any more. If my family doesn't like who I am, then…" his voice shook, but he steadied it. "Well, that's their problem, not mine."

"They will." Gavin gave him a reassuring squeeze. "We'll bring them around. I promise. It's just a case of time."

Hugo smiled hopefully back at him.

"We're going to look for a house," he told Felicia and Cassie. "After all, Gavin hates his flat, and I'm well overdue to move out of my parents' house. We've wasted quite enough time already."

"Well, I'm really happy for you both," Felicia said sincerely.

"Me, too," Cassie said, around a mouthful of pikelet. "I mean, I kind of knew all along, but…"

Felicia rolled her eyes, then turned as a meaty hand clamped down on her shoulder and a deep voice rumbled, "where's the other guest of honour, then? I wouldn't have thought he'd want to miss out on the cake."

"Normally wild horses couldn't keep him away," Felicia said ruefully. "But he's been different lately; since Betsy died…"

Pettifer's gaze sharpened.

"He's taken it badly?"

"He just can't believe it. They were very close. She was like a grandmother to him. And the thought that it was she who...well, who was trying to kill me." Felicia managed to get the words out, although it wasn't easy. "It's been a lot for both of us to take in." She took a breath. "And everyone around us keeps saying that it's over..."

"But you don't feel like it is?" Pettifer said, then, at her surprised look. "Believe it or not, Felicia, I do understand. It's the same on the other side of the investigation, too, you know. I don't always get the closure I'd like. But it won't always feel this way. One day soon you'll wake up and realise that yes, it really *is* all over."

"Is it, though?" She studied him over the gilt rim of her teacup. "All of it?"

He turned to look over his shoulder at Dexter, who was now reclining back on the picnic blanket, having his cup of tea refilled by Cassie.

"If you mean am I going to charge him for obstructing my investigation, then no. I don't think it would have altered the outcome of the case, and besides, you've helped me out here and there along the way." He grinned. "Reckon I owe you one. In fact, speaking of the erstwhile husband of yours, I have something for him."

Flipping open the battered satchel that lay against his side, he produced an overstuffed file, dropping it onto the rug beside Dexter, who looked up at him in wonderment.

"Is that..."

"All the old paperwork relating to the house, yes," Pettifer said gruffly. "But you're on the clock; I've got to get it back this afternoon, before it's missed."

Dexter looked very much as though he'd like to leap up and hug him. Pettifer edged away warily.

"This is incredible," Dexter eagerly began taking documents out, spreading them across the blanket, weighing them down with plates and teacups he commandeered regardless of whether their owner was finished with them or not. "I don't know how to thank you. The whole historical community…"

"Yes, well," Pettifer said hastily, evidently not keen to hear the thoughts of the whole historical community. "Just be sure that this never gets back to Heavenly; that'll be thanks enough."

"I meant to ask you, Sergeant," Cassie appeared, teapot in hand. "Whatever happened to the strange old couple with the mysterious cleaning room?"

Pettifer began to give Felicia a reprimanding look, then visibly gave up.

"No idea." He slurped his tea. "Never got the warrant through. But it would seem that they really *are* just a strange old couple."

Felicia's eyes widened in mock astonishment.

"You mean your hunch was wrong?"

"Everyone's hunches are wrong sometimes," he said. "Anyone who denies that isn't only deluded; they're dangerous."

Algernon knew that he ought to be getting back. He'd promised Mum that he was only going for a short walk. He'd needed some breathing space from the party; everyone was so happy, so relieved, so normal, when he still felt anything but.

Mum had understood, but she'd be getting worried by now. He must have been gone for… he squinted at the clock on the mantelpiece, but the face was strangely blurred. Giving up with a yawn, he set the empty glass on the table, letting his head fall back against the sofa cushions. Maybe he'd rest here…just for a moment. *Then* he would go back.

He was so indescribably tired. He'd never felt a tiredness like it. Like he could go to sleep for ever.

In time, his eyes closed, his breathing slowing to the faintest pulse. His arm was stretched out, fingers curled in on themselves. Half hidden within his palm, the ivory disc gleamed.

"Good grief!" Dexter was holding up a small piece of card. The back, which was all Felicia could see, was stained and foxed, the edges curling. Then Dexter turned it around to reveal a grainy black and white photograph. It contained a sombre-looking line of people gathered in a collective, blank-faced stare at the camera. Dexter tapped at a boy seated in the centre. "This must be Bunting. Hard to imagine that he was ever young, but here's the proof."

"Hang on." Something was prickling at her, the feeling that something was important here, something just beyond the reach of her consciousness. She plucked the photo from Dexter's hand, moving it closer to her face. "That girl there...she looks like Evelina."

She was at the edge of the group, small, younger than Bunting by several years, but there was no mistaking that bone structure. Or those eyes; despite the blurriness of the image, Felicia could feel them boring into her, reaching across the chasm of years. Even though the image was monochrome, she could almost see the brightness of the blue irises.

Pettifer shrugged.

"They were contemporaries, I suppose."

"Yes, but she told me that she didn't know him. She said they weren't allowed to mix." Then her eyes travelled along the row of figures, and her heart seemed to stop. "Oh my God," she whispered.

Pettifer was at her side in an instant.

"What? What do you see?"

She pointed at a woman dressed in a distinctive uniform of

black dress and starched white collar, her hair scraped back in a severe bun. "The governess."

"She's looking at Evelina."

"Not looking. *Staring*." The expression on her face was watchful, sharp, distrustful...and there was something else, too, something which took Felicia a moment to identify, but when she did, it made her whole body freeze.

Fear. That expression...it was *fear*.

"Sergeant," she said slowly, trying to keep her voice level. "You know what you said about hunches..."

"Forget what I said." He was already putting down his teacup, his expression grim. "Let's go."

She didn't need telling twice. She was already halfway across the bridge, heading in the direction of the meadows, and the wisteria-smothered house that overlooked them.

Chapter Thirty-Six

Soft footsteps crossed the room, at first cautiously, then becoming more confident. A light frame perched soundlessly on the edge of the sofa, scarcely making a dent in the plush velvet seat cushion.

Evelina Fielding looked down at the unconscious boy lying in her drawing room and sighed. Then she reached out a sinewy hand and tenderly stroked the unruly bronze hair away from his forehead.

"I *am* sorry about this, my dear," she murmured. "You seem like a sweet child, and I really am *so* fond of your mother. But needs must, and if it reassures you, I stayed with Betsy while the pills took effect, and she really did seem so peaceful, no pain at all, just…slipped away. I bore her no ill will, you see; I simply… needed her gone. Just as now I need *you* gone." Peeling his finger back gently, she retrieved the ivory inlay, holding it up to the light, turning it this way and that. "I've come too far to leave loose ends, my dear. You're a bright boy; I'm sure you understand."

He didn't stir. She shook her head remorsefully.

"Of course, it will be *very* hard on your mother. Your disappearance, I mean. No suicide for *you*; that would never wash.

But if, in the aftermath of Betsy's death, you were to, say...run away... and never be found..."

She turned to look out of the window, beyond which the town she loved rose in a haze of gold above the meadows.

"Yes, it'll be hard on your mother," she said, pensively. "That's the one thing I regret."

Chapter Thirty-Seven

Felicia ran through town, urged on by a feeling she couldn't quite explain, but which she knew without a doubt was right; the instinct of a mother knowing that her child was in imminent danger. Behind her, she could hear the thudding footsteps of Pettifer on her tail.

She raced across the footbridge that linked the meadows to Bath Row, scattering indignant ducks into the water with a cacophony of quacking. The wrought-iron gate into Evelina's front garden was ajar, and Felicia shoved it aside, only then stopping to look behind her. Pettifer was a pinprick in the distance, having fallen far behind.

She drew against the front door of the house, out of sight of the windows, catching her breath and trying to think clearly. By rights, she knew it was the sensible thing to wait for him; after all, he was the one experienced at this sort of thing. If she went barging in there all guns blazing, she might only make everything worse.

Vaguely impressed with herself on tamping down her natural impetuousness for once, she eased aside a trail of wisteria to peek in at the window.

What she saw in there made her blood chill in her veins.

And she knew in that moment that she couldn't possibly wait for Sergeant Pettifer.

———

Pettifer stopped at the open garden gate, doubled over, his breath coming in jagged, hefting gasps. Being stationed in Stamford hadn't required him to chase down a suspect in years—if you didn't count that errant goose at the Georgian Fair two years ago —and he was unpleasantly reminded just how out of shape he'd become. Especially now, when it might really count.

He straightened, looking around him. There was no sign of Felicia, but the house in front of him was quiet. That was reassuring, and he felt his heart rate drop slightly. Hopefully, it was all just a false alarm, and...

A crash from within the fabric of the house truncated that thought. Suddenly mindless of his screaming joints, Pettifer surged forwards, running faster than he ever had in his life.

———

"Get away from him, Evelina." Felicia stood in the doorway, facing the woman who'd sprung from the sofa with telling dexterity for someone supposedly hindered by an injured hip and advanced years.

"You're too late, my dear." Evelina said reasonably. "But don't worry, it was peaceful, no pain. I saw to that."

Felicia swallowed, trying to keep her head. Every sinew in her body strained to move towards Algernon, who lay prone on the sofa, eyes closed. But with Evelina hovering over him like that, she didn't dare make a move. The woman had already proven herself to be more than dangerous. Instinct screamed at her that if she wanted to save her son, her best chance was to be patient, not give in to panic…and choose her moment.

Even if it was the hardest thing she'd ever had to do.

"It was never me, was it?" She said, injecting a note of interested enquiry into her voice. Behind her, Pettifer came crashing through the front door into the hall, but she held out an arm, warning him to stay back. "Algernon was the real target all along."

Evelina nodded approvingly.

"A neat little trick of mine, I thought, to suggest that you might be in danger. You swallowed it nicely."

"I had no reason not to. I thought we were friends."

Evelina looked surprised.

"My dear, we *are* friends. This doesn't change any of that. It's just…" she gestured to Algernon, who lay utterly still and lifeless. "*Necessity*, that's all."

She was completely mad, Felicia realised, with a burst of terror.

"It's always been that way, though, hasn't it?" Pettifer said softly, stepping forwards. "Ever since you were a child. Anyone who got in the way of what you wanted had to be dealt with." He held up the photograph, and Evelina laughed brightly.

"Ah, she was such a tedious woman. I wasn't entirely lying, Felicia dear, when I said that Henry's family were against me mixing with him. They thought I was *common*." Her face dropped, the last word emerging as a hiss. Her hand twitched, fingers opening and closing like a claw at her side. "Not good enough for him to associate with."

"But you saw one another anyway?" Pettifer guessed.

"Henry loved me," she said simply. "It wasn't hard to persuade him. I knew my way around a man, even then."

"You were eleven years old," Felicia pointed out, trying not to look as shocked as she felt.

"But no innocent," Evelina snapped, her eyes a blue flame. "That had been taken from me long ago by my father, my uncle, their '*friends*' in business," her lips twisted in disgust. "That era… it wasn't quite as wholesome as everyone seems to imagine now. Not for a girl of my position in life." She shook her head savagely, as though trying to banish the memory. "I had plans, though. To get out, become something better. Be treated like a lady… literally, if possible. Henry Bunting was my ticket to that life." Then her face darkened. "Until that wretched woman went and ruined everything."

"She walked in on you doing something you… er… shouldn't have been?"

Evelina smiled thinly.

"How delicately put, Sergeant. But yes, she'd been watching me for a while, always snooping about. She never left us alone together if she could help it. One day, we managed to slip away to one of the unused bedrooms. But she found us, saw what we were doing. She was horrified; such a prim, virginal woman." The smile became malicious. "She would have sounded the alarm, so I hit her with the fire poker. It didn't feel wrong in the slightest; I was glad I'd killed her. But, Henry…" her lip curled disdainfully. "Well, he always was weak-natured. He would have gone completely to pieces if it weren't for me. He probably would have confessed it all! Can you imagine? But at least one of us was thinking properly. I helped him to put the body in the wardrobe for the time being. Then, later, he would take it out and drop it down the stairs." Her face took on a misty quality. "It worked like a dream. The police took it as writ that she'd tripped and fallen; amongst the other injuries, no one noticed the head wound. These days, with the new science, no doubt it would all be different, but, then… it was all just so *easy*. I couldn't *believe* how easy it was. And the problem gone, just like *that*." She snapped her fingers. The sound echoed around the high-ceilinged room.

"But Henry's parents weren't so convinced?" Felicia noticed that Pettifer's foot was inching forwards whilst he spoke.

"As I said, he was weak. He was cracking under the strain. I was just starting to think I'd have to deal with him, too, but then his parents came to the conclusion that he was the one who'd killed her. To my astonishment, he never contradicted them."

"And allowed himself to be shut away for a crime he never committed," Felicia finished quietly. He must have loved her intensely.

If Evelina had heard the slight note of censure, she didn't show it.

"Yes, that did rather put paid to my plans on that score," she sighed. "Such a shame. With him as a recluse, and the rumours going around town...well, he was just no use to me any more. I didn't only want the money, you see; I wanted to be *respectable*." Her chin quivered. "By the time we met again years later, I was already married to my late husband, Robert."

"And Henry...he still loved you." As she said it, Felicia realised that it was true.

Evelina nodded, looking satisfied.

"He proved surprisingly easy to control. Decades went by, and he still loyally kept my secret. It would have been cleaner, or course, to simply kill him and have done with it, but I don't know...I got rather fond of him, truth be told. There was something appealingly...*puppyish* about him."

"Until Barrington came along." It was a statement rather than a question from Pettifer. Out of the corner of her eye, Felicia could see him still inching infinitesimally forwards, even as his gaze remained firmly fixed on Evelina.

"Henry could be so naïve," Evelina sighed despairingly. "He was like a child, taking everything at face value. That shark Clay saw him coming; he managed to inveigle his way inside the house one day, on the pretext of valuing a few items for insurance. Of course, that's not what he was about at all. He wanted to see what Henry had in there, if there was anything worth his while."

"Then he saw the wardrobe."

"Oh, yes." Evelina's tone was dry. "He was *very* excited about that. Of all the pieces of furniture in the house, he *would* be interested in the one we'd used to hide a body in! The irony! Well, he wanted to come back, examine it properly with all the equipment...Henry might have been a recluse, but he was a voracious reader; there weren't many subjects he didn't know something about, and he knew how UV light could show up bloodstains, even if they've supposedly been cleaned off."

"So he...entered the cupboard into the sale?" Felicia was still confused about that part, and it must have shown in her voice, because Evelina frowned angrily.

"He should have consulted *me*! I would have worked something out. But the fool panicked; all he could think about was getting the thing out of the house. By the time he told me, it was done. I had to think on my feet. I knew we couldn't withdraw it from sale; Clay would still know where to find it, and I couldn't trust Henry to keep him at bay. He'd find his way back in somehow, and then..." she visibly shuddered. "If a man like Clay were to know our secret...well, it was simply unthinkable. But then I thought, what if an 'anonymous' bidder were to buy it?"

"So you engaged Mr Clancy to buy it back on your behalf?" Felicia turned to Pettifer, who nodded. "It seems he was telling the truth."

"But you still came along to the sale yourself," Pettifer challenged Evelina. "To...what? Oversee? Stage manage?"

"I've learned to rely on oneself in these matters," she replied crisply. "I wasn't intending to have to actually *do* anything, but nor was I about to leave it all to chance in my absence. As it was, my instinct turned out to be right. Clay turned up early to look over the cupboard. Well, I could tell by the nasty smug look on his face that he'd found something—he really was a *most* unpleasant man—and I knew then that I was going to have to improvise. The fates were obviously on my side, though, because I had a stroke of the most *marvellous* luck." She clapped her hands together. "He saw something which made him go as white as a sheet. Two girls, in flowery dresses. I have to say, I couldn't see what was so threatening about them myself…"

"The Belvedere sisters," Felicia managed. "Their mother was suing him."

"Is that who they were?" Evelina didn't seem particularly interested. "In any event, I'm grateful to them. They set things up for me very nicely. There he was, standing by the open door of the cupboard; they were coming towards him, and he quickly stepped inside. Hiding from them, I supposed. Anyway, the sale was about to start; I knew he'd be stuck in there for the duration. An absolute gift! All I had to do now was dispatch him without anyone seeing me. Not so hard," she added wryly. "When you're a little old lady. It's one of the great boons of age; no one thinks you're capable of anything."

Suddenly, Felicia wasn't entirely sure how, her walking stick was in her hand. It was only now that it registered that she'd been standing quite well without it.

"A classic case in point, Sergeant," Evelina tutted. "Did you really think that I haven't noticed you creeping forward while you tried to distract me?" She grasped the handle of the stick and pulled, the shaft sliding away to reveal a slim, shining blade beneath. "I'd advise you not to come any closer. I think we can all agree that I'm rather handy with this."

"I think we might just have found your mysterious murder weapon," Felicia said shakily to Pettifer, who was eyeing it in alarm.

"What the hell *is* that thing?"

"A swordstick," Evelina clarified, swishing it experimentally. "In common usage during the nineteenth century; useful for seeing off footpads in the great smog and whatnot. Now regularly found for sale at auction." She raised an eyebrow at Felicia, who groaned. Pettifer glanced across sharply.

"What?"

"The mix up with the lots. One was missing a swordstick; there was a standard walking stick there in its place."

"She swapped it." Pettifer looked at Evelina for confirmation.

"And then walked out with the murder weapon right under your nose!" She crowed. "I enjoyed that part, I can tell you." She raised the blade, pointing it straight at them. "Now, who's going to be first?"

"But…wait!" Felicia burst out, desperate to buy an extra moment. "What about Henry? After all of that time…"

"Henry was a liability!" She spat. "I was too sentimental about him for too long. When he found out what I'd done with Clay… well, he totally went to pieces. Said that an accidental death was one thing, but murder… that, he couldn't sanction. He was utterly hysterical, all ready to go to the police." She sniffed disdainfully. "I had to cut him loose."

"And Betsy?" Felicia gulped as Evelina advanced towards her, blade pointed at her throat. "Why *Betsy*? What did *she* know?"

"Nothing at all." Evelina looked faintly disappointed. "You know, I really thought she might catch on to the swapped sticks; she was in charge of the lots, after all. But she never did." She looked up at the ceiling. "It all worked out for me very well; she fairly fell into my lap that day. She came home in floods of tears; I was in the garden, tending to the tulips. Naturally, I helped her inside, asked her what the matter was. Well, it all came out. How she'd been working for Clay, how she was desperate to tell you but didn't know how she could face it. Immediately, I saw the possibilities, how I could wrap everything up neatly. So I told her to write it all down in a letter to you; that's what my mother always did when there was something difficult to be said. Then, while she did that, I made her some tea." Evelina smiled sweetly. "Ever the considerate neighbour." Then, just as swiftly, her face hardened, and she moved forwards with quick strides. Light glinted off the blade. "Now, I'm *very* sorry to do this to you, Felicia dear, but I'm afraid that I simply have no choice."

Suddenly, there was a brittle crash, followed by a dazzling shower of glass as the French doors exploded.

A blur of geranium pink tackled Evelina from the side, knocking her off balance. She stabbed out wildly with the swordstick as it slipped from her grasp, clattering to the floor.

Felicia lurched forwards with a cry. The tip of the blade was stained a glistening red. Dexter had sunk to his knees, palm pressed against his breastbone.

"I'm fine," he yelled hoarsely, waving her back. "Just get her!"

Felicia spun around, but Pettifer, for once, was faster. He had Evelina backed into a corner like a wild animal. Felicia watched as, quick as anything, she snatched at a potted palm from the side table, holding it aloft as she prepared to bring it right down on Pettifer's head.

"Watch out!" Felicia shrieked.

But the anticipated crash of terracotta on skull never came.

Evelina was staring at the bottom of the pot in stupefaction. Opaque white liquid was dripping from it, forming puddles on the floor.

"What on *earth*," she whispered. Then her gaze moved disbelievingly to the sofa, where Algernon had cracked one eye cautiously open.

"Is it over?" He sat up dazedly. "Did you get…"

His next words were smothered by his mother's fierce embrace. Struggling for air, he managed to surface over her shoulder. Then his eyes widened in horror.

"Dad!"

Scrambling across the floor, he flung himself at Dexter, who winced but said nothing, instead wrapping an arm around his son. The other was held out to Felicia with a shy, questioning smile.

Wordlessly, she sank to her knees, put her arms around them both, and held her family tightly.

Chapter Thirty-Eight

"I think you've more than earned this." Felicia deposited a gigantic slab of Victoria sponge in front of Algernon. She ruffled his hair, but briefly, knowing how much he objected to it. It was one of those things which seemed to be getting less acceptable the older he grew. "After all, you did miss the party."

They were in the kitchen of Peter's cottage, surrounded by leftovers. It was quite some time later; by the time Pettifer had taken Evelina away in the police car, and Dexter had point blank refused to go to hospital, requiring the paramedics to treat him at the scene—it had turned out to be only a shoulder wound, mercifully, and he'd got away with little more than bandages, surgical tape and a sling, although Felicia thought the strict advice for him to keep it on for at least a week was wishful thinking at best—the sun had begun to set, painting the sky with rosy strokes.

"I didn't mean to." Algernon spoke through a mouthful of sponge and buttercream. If she'd thought that after the ordeal he'd suffered there'd be nothing he'd want more than to crash out in bed, then she'd been woefully wrong. He was bright as a button, chattier than he'd been in days, and—as he'd earnestly declared the minute they'd got home—absolutely *famished*.

Apparently, that's what a near death experience did to you when you were twelve years old. For Felicia's part, she felt as if she could easily sleep for weeks. "I was actually just about to come back when Mrs Fielding called out to me. She invited me in, said she had some recipe which she'd told you she was going to give to me."

He looked askance at his mother for confirmation. Felicia nodded, feeling faintly nauseous at the memory.

"It's true, she did say that. When I told her how you'd used to bake with Betsy…"

She trailed off, a pall falling over them all at the reminder. Even Algernon stopped attacking the cake and rested his fork down momentarily. Felicia looked across at her father, who was sitting in the corner, being uncharacteristically quiet. They hadn't really spoken about Betsy since it happened; she suspected that he felt hurt, but also vaguely culpable.

The moment was broken by a rapping at the door.

"I'll get it." Peter wheeled his chair through into the hall, clapping Algernon on the back as he passed. "Eat up, lad. I need strong bones to help me out at the auction." He looked at Felicia and nodded curtly. No doubt he hoped she hadn't spotted the sheen in his eyes.

Algernon obediently resumed his demolition of the cake, although with less gusto than before.

"Evening all." Pettifer shambled in.

Felicia leapt half to her feet, alarmed.

"What is it? She's not…"

"Everything's fine," Pettifer held up his hands soothingly. "I just thought you'd like to know that she's safely charged and processed. After the time we had catching her, it was all surprisingly straightforward in the end." He flopped down in the chair next to Algernon and reached for a leftover scone, breaking it in two. "She was more than happy to recount it all again for the tape. In a way, I reckon she's been pretty desperate to tell someone just how clever she's been." He chewed ruefully. "The biggest problem actually turned out to be *stopping* her from talking."

"I suppose you'll have to tell her family," Dexter said. "God, what a phone call to get, telling you that your mother's a mass murderer."

"They've been informed. Although, I have to say, they didn't seem as astonished as one would have expected. I'm almost inclined to wonder if they knew something."

"They did," Felicia said suddenly. Then, at his querying look, she added, "the security camera on her house. I thought it was an odd precaution for a woman who didn't bother to lock her door. She told me her sons had it put in, made out it was because they were over-protective of her, but now I wonder. What if they weren't protecting her from the world... but the *world* from *her*?" Another thought struck her. "Just like their father did."

"You think that he knew all along?"

"I think he must have realised at some point that his wife wasn't entirely sane. What if all of that supposedly controlling behaviour was actually a sort of...guardianship?"

"It would certainly explain why he didn't want to take any cliff-top walks with her," Pettifer said dryly. "Not that it did the poor bugger much good."

Dexter pricked up.

"You think she did away with him? But he died of a long illness, didn't he?"

"A long, *mysterious* illness. When it comes to that lady, I'm not sure that anything can be written off as a coincidence."

Felicia shook her head.

"If that's true, then her sons have a lot to answer for; leaving an unstable woman on her own, allowed to roam about unhindered, when they knew full well that she was dangerous."

"She certainly is that." Pettifer turned to Algernon. "You're a lucky lad. Although, what I really want to know is how you knew that she was trying to poison you?"

"Well, I didn't really," Algernon looked sheepish. "While I was waiting inside, she brought me a glass of milk." He looked affronted at the mere memory. "*Milk!* I'm not a child; I don't drink milk any more. But I didn't want to seem rude, so I sort of… tipped it into the plant when she wasn't looking."

Felicia closed her eyes, not sure that she really wanted to know just how much of a role chance—and a healthy dose of teenage snobbery—had played in keeping her son alive today.

"Anyway, she finally went upstairs to look for the recipe, and I noticed that she'd left her stick behind. I thought that was odd, because she's always needed it lately. I took it and was about to call after her, when I realised…it wasn't the same stick I'd picked up for her at the auction. It was different. The one she'd had before was totally plain, whereas this one had decoration around the handle. Six little inlays…"

"And one was missing," Pettifer finished quietly.

"She must have overheard us talking about it in The George," Felicia realised. "I was telling Cassie how Algie had found this fabulous clue, and he wanted to show it to the police."

"Which is exactly what she feared most," Pettifer added. "That we'd realise there was a walking stick involved in the murder. It would have led us straight to her."

"I knew then that I was in trouble," Algernon said. "And then I remembered the milk, and how it was sleeping pills which Betsy had…" He swallowed. "Except, if she hadn't, and it was Mrs Fielding all along, then maybe she was using the same thing again."

Felicia moved towards him, but he shook his head.

"I'm fine, Mum, really. Anyway, I thought the best thing to do was pretend to fall asleep and wait for a good moment to escape."

"That was quick-thinking, lad," Pettifer said approvingly. Then his face became worried. "Look, there's something… I don't really know if I should give it to you, really, but I did promise." He handed Algernon a faded piece of paper. "It's her…er, family scone recipe. Apparently it was promised to you, and as she didn't manage to…well, you know, seeing as you're still here, she thought you ought to have it. She hopes there'll be no hard feelings."

There was a stunned silence, which Dexter, as usual, broke.

"Good God. The woman really is crackers, isn't she?"

"A total sociopath," Pettifer agreed. "I'm not even certain they'll consider her fit to plead. Straight to a psychiatric unit, I predict."

"Well, at least it really is all over now." Peter's sharp gaze caught Algernon in the process of attempting to stifle a yawn. "Right, that's it. Off to bed with you, boy. You're exhausted."

"I'll leave you all in peace." Pettifer rose to his feet, and Felicia automatically did the same, walking out into the evening with him.

"We found the car, by the way," he said, as they approached the bridge. "It was still in her garage."

"The one she made a big thing about not owning any more?"

"If it's any consolation, that was the one thing which really did seem to surprise her sons. They genuinely believed that she'd sold it. God knows why she was secretly keeping it for all of those years."

"I think she was a woman who liked to always have something up her sleeve. No doubt she thought it might come in useful one day."

They stopped on the bridge. The breeze was ruffling the surface of the water, whispering through the leaves.

"So, exactly how disappointed is Heavenly that it wasn't me?" Felicia made an attempt at levity.

"Crushed," Pettifer deadpanned. "He had you and Dexter down as South Lincolnshire's answer to Bonnie and Clyde." He shielded his eyes against the setting sun. "Of course, what makes it all the more galling for him is that it was *you* who solved the case."

Felicia almost laughed out loud.

"I did no such thing. It was a total fluke."

He shook his head slowly.

"You worked out it was her in the end."

"Only because Dexter found that photograph. That, and perhaps a little maternal intuition." She took a deep breath, then said what was prickling away at her. "But not before almost getting us all killed. And I can't help feeling that I'm probably partly responsible for Betsy's death, too."

"We've talked about this, Felicia," Pettifer said sternly.

"I know, but if I'd just let Algernon come to you with that inlay like he wanted to…"

"Then nothing might have changed. You don't know."

"No, I don't, and I never will." She gave him a tight smile. "And that will haunt me, I think. So you see, I won't be styling myself as a committed amateur sleuth anytime soon. I'll be sticking firmly to the day job."

"Which is?" He raised an enquiring brow.

So he'd worked it out, had he? Despite herself, Felicia's lips were curving upwards wryly.

"Auctioneer. Again." She pulled a face. "Talk about full circle."

"So you and the lad'll be staying, then?"

"I think we have to," she said honestly. "Algernon so rarely asks for anything. And he's right, I think this will be a good move… for both of us. Plus my Dad… well, he's just so thrilled that he's going to have Algie around on a permanent basis."

"That's what your dad looks like when he's thrilled?" Pettifer eyed her disbelievingly, and she laughed.

"It takes a connoisseur to spot the variation, I'll admit."

"Well, good luck. Perhaps I'll come up to the auction sometime. In a civilian capacity," he clarified. "You can trick me into bidding for all of your ropiest old tat." He rummaged in his breast pocket, his expression suddenly turning serious. "Before I go…there's something else Evelina wanted me to pass on. This time to you." He handed Felicia a scrap of lilac paper. "It's the rest of the letter from Betsy. The part she tore off to make it look like a suicide note."

Felicia stared at it for a moment, then reached out and took it, curling her fingers around it.

"Thank you, Sergeant. For everything." She summoned up a smile. "I hope you can finally get to that rugby match now."

"Oh, I think I've finally earned myself some time off." He inclined his head. "Goodnight, Felicia."

She watched him shuffle away across the bridge, shoelaces flapping, until he'd receded into the misty gold of the middle distance.

"Well, that was quite a day." Dexter had appeared beside her, leaning on the green-painted railings.

"That was quite a *week*," she corrected. "I certainly hope that things are a bit quieter around here going forwards."

They both gazed out over the water, to where the lights of town were just beginning to twinkle against the dusk.

"Your dad's over the moon that you're staying, you know. I can tell by the way he looks even grimmer than usual."

"He told me earlier that he's pleased that Algie and I didn't die," she said humorously. "Which of course, is his way of saying that he loves us both deeply and is desperately relieved that we're all right."

"Such intense expression of emotion. No wonder the chap's exhausted." Dexter grinned. "So, does this mean things are settled between you? He's happy that you're coming back to Grant's?"

"Not by a long chalk. It's going to be a rocky ride, I predict. We'll probably have all of the same arguments we did before." She paused. "But I'm older now. Not necessarily wiser, but certainly less hot-headed. I'm sure we'll muddle through one way or another." She nudged him with her elbow. "And what about you? What happened with those papers Pettifer gave you? Anything in there?"

"Not a sausage." His shoulders sagged. "The wardrobe isn't listed in any of the inventories. It's like…I don't know, like it never even existed."

"I'm sorry, Dexter," she said, really meaning it. "I know how disappointed you must be."

"To be honest, I'm not sure I have the right to be disappointed about anything ever again." He turned to her, looking uncharacteristically earnest. "We almost lost Algie today, Fliss, and it's probably all my fault for being so bloody selfish. If I hadn't been so self-obsessed…" He hung his head. "I can't blame you for not forgiving me."

For a moment, Felicia was too stunned to respond. She had never seen him so contrite. More than that, she'd never heard him come so close to saying sorry.

"Neither of us is perfect, Dexter," she said at last. "And to be honest, I'm not sure it would be all that good for Algie if we were. Besides," she continued, her voice softening. "You threw yourself in front of a sword-wielding maniac for the two of us tonight." She brushed his sling-covered arm with the tips of her fingers. "I think that more than makes up for past mistakes." She looked away, suddenly aware of how reluctant she was to ask this next question. She made an effort to keep her voice light. "When are you jetting off again?"

"I'm not."

Her eyes flickered back to his in astonishment.

"But… what about Treasure Seeker? Aren't you going to fight for it?"

"Not right now, no." His eyes in the fading light were the colour of ink. "I've been away for too long, Fliss. I don't want to miss out on any more."

"Of Algie's life, you mean," she prompted, when he didn't finish the sentence.

"Of course, yes," he said hastily, breaking his gaze away. "That's what I meant."

"So… what *will* you do?"

"What I did before. Articles, lectures, a book or two. Maybe I'll even try and get to the bottom of this blasted Charles I business; I'm convinced there's more to that."

Felicia hid a smile. Whatever he might say, Dexter would always be Dexter. She predicted he'd be back on the trail again within weeks.

"You won't be bored then?" She said archly. "In a little backwater like this? This week was a glaring anomaly, you know. It's terribly dull as a rule."

"Oh, I don't know about that," his mouth curved. "I've a feeling Stamford might be still holding plenty of secrets." He pushed away from the railings. "It's getting chilly. You coming in?"

"In a minute." As he walked back towards the warm glow of the cottage, she called after him, "so if Treasure Seeker's gone…is it curtains for the hat?"

"What do you think?" He doffed it with a grin, and she rolled her eyes.

But her smile didn't last. It slipped from her face as she unfurled her fingers to reveal the crumpled scrap of lilac paper.

It was now or never. Taking a moment to steady herself first, she unfolded it carefully, eyes moving along the continuation of the earlier note.

I never meant to get involved with Barrington Clay, really, I didn't. But I was feeling so unhappy. My daughter had just told me that she couldn't get away from work to fly over this summer; I haven't seen the children in almost three years now, and I was so desperately disappointed. I'd been looking forward to their visit for so long. I thought if I could just get together the money for a ticket, then maybe I could go and see them. But there didn't seem to be any way…until he came along.

I really didn't think there'd be any harm in it. It was only a client name he wanted; such a small thing. Of course, I only saw later what a fool I'd been; he'd never really wanted the name at all. The whole thing had been about making me beholden to him. Well, I felt so terribly ashamed of myself; I even tried to give him the money back, but he wouldn't take it.

I want you to know this, Felicia, because now he's dead, and I'm technically free. Except, I don't feel it, not at all. Now Hugo thinks that your father is losing his grip, and your father is starting to believe it, too, all because of what I did...and I just can't face that. I'd rather you all hated me, and you probably will once you've read this. But at least I'll finally have some peace in my heart.

I won't plead for your forgiveness, nor will I defend my actions any further. But one thing I do want you to know is that I never stole from Grant's. Everything else was me, but not that. It might seem like a small thing in the face of all I've done, but to me, it matters. It's the one thing I can hold my head high about.

You're probably waiting for me right now, wondering where I am. I'm sorry I can't meet you, but I think it's easier this way. I'll drop this letter through your door later on this evening. Obviously, you can consider this my resignation; I'll have cleared out my things by the time you get into work tomorrow morning.

Your dearest friend,

Betsy

A tear fell onto the curling signature as Felicia read it, blurring the violet-coloured ink. The breeze tugged at the paper in her fingers, and she let it go, watching as it spiralled down towards the water, carried away on the current towards the spires silhouetted against the pink and lilac sky.

Epilogue

Margaret Creaton paused on the landing, one ear pricked to the sounds downstairs. A whoosh of water, a tinny sound as the kettle was filled, the tuneless tumble of notes that Colin seemed to think passed for humming. Usually, it drove her to distraction, but today she was glad of it. It meant she knew exactly where he was in the house.

With shaking fingers, she inserted the key into the locked door, turning it with a loud click. She froze, listening intently again, but only the unbroken sound of humming met her ears, followed by the popping sound of the biscuit tin lid being prised off.

Furtively, silently, Margaret inched open the door and slipped into her inner sanctum.

The room was full, although not with cleaning products as she'd led Colin to believe. Instead, an Aladdin's cave of treasures stared back at her. They filled shelves, tables, and eventually, when she'd run of out space, the floor, where they sprawled in teetering piles. Tea bowls, dolls' heads, glass figurines, jewellery… all costume that, nothing remotely valuable. Nothing which would be missed, at least, certainly not enough to warrant a proper investigation. That was one criteria for the items she'd taken from numerous auction houses over the years; the other was that they be small. Small enough to fit in a pocket, or beneath a coat. This policy had served her well thus far; Margaret had never once been caught, although she did take the occasional risk, just to see if she might be. The Swedish coffee pot over there was an example, taken from an auction in Chichester, smuggled out within a rolled-up scarf. That had been tense, thrilling; she'd felt an almost acute sense of anti-climax when no one had noticed.

She wasn't quite sure why it had started, or even, these days, exactly how long ago. It wasn't a childhood foible, but one of advancing middle-to-old age. She'd been at another interminable viewing with Colin one day, waiting impatiently as he'd minutely examined every inch of a new carriage he was planning to bid upon, when suddenly, she'd *seen* it. A bag of toy cars, in bright, primary colours, and next to it, a red truck, lying on its side. It had obviously fallen out of the bag whilst someone had been looking through the lot, and no one had spotted it.

No one except her.

The next thing she knew, her arm was shooting out and closing over it, then drawing back into her pocket. At first, she was shocked by herself, having never stolen anything before (unless one counted those pens at the bank, which, really, they expected you to take).

Then the exhilaration had hit her in a Technicolor rush.

She'd walked around the rest of the viewing on a high, feeling the weight of the truck in her pocket, flushed with the secret that only she knew. She'd kept waiting for the guilt to hit her, but it never had. Instead, all she could think about was when she'd get to do it again.

A psychologist might have said that Margaret was fulfilling a need for danger and excitement that was otherwise lacking in her life. All Margaret herself knew was that it was like a drug, a moment of sheer aliveness she craved violently between doses.

Now, though, for the first time, as she looked around at her collection, she felt anything but her usual elation. Instead, she felt acutely nauseous.

That policeman had almost been in here, had almost uncovered it all. It was only by the sheerest of luck that they'd caught the murderer last night and thus wouldn't be coming back with a warrant. Suddenly, in the sobering light of that realisation, these things that she'd so gleefully acquired—and the method she'd acquired them by—seemed less like a game. These things, these beautiful things... she stroked a miniature bronze urn lovingly, then drew her hand back sharply as though it had been burned. They'd become her enemies. It *had* to stop. She *had* to find a way to...

There was a commotion outside on the landing, and the door swung open, splashing harsh daylight into the room.

"Sorry, Margaret," Colin's plaintive voice floated up the stairs. "She just barged in, I swear. I didn't..."

"It's all right, Colin." Margaret snapped, panic making her tone even more searing than usual. "I'll handle it. Who *are* you?" She demanded of the silhouetted figure who was filling the doorway. She took a faltering breath, summoning up a bravado she no longer felt. "And what are you doing in my house? You have *no* right, I tell you, *no* right at—"

"Apologies." A woman's voice. She stepped forwards, into the light. "You don't know me. My name is Magda Clay." She looked around the room, a slow, satisfied smile forming on her lips, then back at Margaret.

"It would appear, Mrs Creaton, that you and I have some business to discuss."

YOUR NUMBER ONE STOP

ONE MORE CHAPTER

FOR PAGETURNING BOOKS

One More Chapter is an
award-winning global
division of HarperCollins.

Sign up to our newsletter to get our
latest eBook deals and stay up to date
with our weekly Book Club!
<u>Subscribe here.</u>

Meet the team at
<u>www.onemorechapter.com</u>

Follow us!

 @OneMoreChapter_

 @OneMoreChapter

 @onemorechapterhc

Do you write unputdownable fiction?
We love to hear from new voices.
Find out how to submit your novel at
<u>www.onemorechapter.com/submissions</u>